A CORRUPTIBLE CROWN

John Hainsworth

Visit us online at www.authorsonline.co.uk

A Bright Pen Book

British Library Cataloguing Publication Data.
A catalogue record for this book is available from the British Library

ISBN 978-07552-1222-4

Authors OnLine Ltd
19 The Cinques
Gamlingay, Sandy
Bedfordshire SG19 3NU
England

This book is also available in e-book format, details of which are available at www.authorsonline.co.uk

My name isn't Windsor. My blood is the normal colour, and when my Auntie Annie paid a genealogist to research our family tree he got bogged down in Batley in 1883. But for all our humble origins our family have always been history buffs, and monarchists to a person. On our rare visits to London the first stop was always Buckingham Palace, and one of my earliest memories is an outing to the Tower, and a jolly yeoman warder in the Jewel Chamber lifting me up so that I could flatten my little nose against the glass. For a while I was spellbound by the glittering, magical objects behind it; then I threw a tantrum. Auntie Annie understood. 'Eee, the little love,' she said, 'He wants to try them on.'

Auntie would have been gratified to learn that, one day, her nephew would wear the Crown of England.

CHAPTER 1

The story starts with a man named Lord. Lord by surname, not by title, since Bob Lord made no claim to be anything but a commoner even though he could trace his own descent back to sixteenth century Chester. By the time I got to know him well he'd sold out his family estate agents' business to an insurance company at the right time and by 1989, when house prices crashed and the unsold properties piled up, he was living in enviable retirement on a glorious hillside in Wales and pursuing his oddly assorted hobbies full time. I'd first met him a year or two before when I was looking for a cheap cottage and he was running the office in Oswestry, and I'd been impressed by the service he gave and the amount he seemed to know about the properties he was handling. There was something about him that gave more confidence than his profession usually inspires, and it wasn't just the ruddy, cheerful face and the well-worn Harris tweed. He'd come up with what seemed the perfect solution to our problems. It wasn't his fault if it didn't solve them all.

When Bob rang it was seven in the evening and Sarah and I were sitting at opposite ends of our executive starter home. That meant that we were about twelve feet apart, which was as far as you could get unless someone was in the loo. That was half the problem; it's why battery hens pull each other's feathers out. I knew a certain amount about battery hens. At the time I was Regional Manager for a Midlands-based firm which marketed, among other things, poultry feed. Regional Manager actually means sales representative. It sounds better on the telephone and looks better on the calling card, but it doesn't fool the farmers. Or their dogs.

I picked up the phone and said, 'John Jones'. The alliteration still grated after thirty years, and my parents had compounded the offence by failing to give me a middle name. 'Just John?' people would say, pens poised. 'Just Johnny Jones' had pursued me round the playground more than once and produced the odd black eye, usually mine. However, it was a bit late to do anything about it now.

A soft, Shropshire voice said, 'Evening Mr Jones. Bob Lord here. Lord and Timpson. Something came in today which might suit you I think. A bit remote, but you said you didn't mind that. It's off our patch really, over towards Bala, but the owner says he doesn't want to go through the local firm. It's a quarryman's cottage, about 1860. I went out to look at it today. You'll need your wellies if you want to go and see it.'

I arranged to pick up a key on Saturday morning, and told Sarah. She sounded excited, and I really think she was. It was something we'd actually talked about. Both of us liked the country. We weren't exactly in the second home bracket, but my parents had died within a few months of each other; I'd been a late child and an only one, and the estate added up to the cost of a house. We could swap our starter home for a three bed detached in one of the leafier suburbs, or we could do something more imaginative with the money. Something that would get us out into the wide open spaces. Something to provide a fresh interest, a fresh topic of conversation in those long, boring evenings when we seemed increasingly to get on each other's nerves. Something to focus on, instead of the children Sarah didn't want. Maybe a cottage. Maybe in Wales.

The Regional Manager's job, like a lot of things in life, had come about more by accident than intent. My education hadn't taught me much about poultry feed. With characteristic indecision I'd opted for a joint degree, in history and something else. The something else was there because I'd listened to too much advice. The history was what I loved. Above all I was fascinated by history on the ground - and under it. I'd done a bit of caving; now I joined a mines exploration group which went off at weekends to explore a series of hair-raising shafts and tunnels in Derbyshire, and did my own burrowing in search of early maps and records of the mining companies. There were exhilarating days combing the high moors for spoil heaps and collapsed entrances. Then I sat down and produced a dissertation which I hoped might lead to another three years doing research. But there'd been a few distractions along the way and possibly I should have paid a little more attention to the something else. The examiners weren't sufficiently impressed, and in the end I was lucky to get picked up by an employer who had read somewhere that graduates were good communicators. I was quite attracted by the prospect of driving from farm to farm, listening to the birdsong through the sunroof and being welcomed with mugs of tea and slices of apple pie. But the company car didn't have a sunroof, and there wasn't much apple pie.

The weather that Saturday was a house agent's dream. The mud-spattered Escort took us up the M6, onto the M54 and the A5 and we were in Bob Lord's office before eleven. I glanced around it as he was looking out the key. The heavy oak furnishings and the antique maps seemed to match the man, though the framed engraving of the Ancient of Days, crouched above the earth with dividers poised to measure His creation, seemed over the top for a chartered surveyor. The key when he produced it was impressively ancient and heavy, and increased our sense of excitement.

Half an hour later we were crossing the border into Wales. Why Wales? Well, it was reasonably accessible from the West Midlands, and it was beautiful. Stomping over wild country was something both of us enjoyed, as long as the uphill bits weren't too prolonged. Also, though I hadn't stressed the fact to Sarah, Wales has been mined and quarried for just about every mineral men have ever wanted to extract, from granite to gold. And perhaps that surname did betoken some distant Celtic ancestry. Somehow I'd never really believed in myself as a Yorkshireman, let alone a Midlander. I wouldn't have been surprised if the genealogist had ended up in Bala instead of Batley. Whenever I crossed Offa's Dyke, it felt like coming home.

We found ourselves going further west than we'd envisaged when the idea first came up. We'd been thinking of the marches, a mixture of green pastures, oak woodland and steep, bracken-covered hillsides. The country we were heading into was altogether more austere. The Berwyn is as high as many more celebrated mountain ranges in Wales, even if its rounded outlines can be deceptively gentle. The road we were taking began gently enough, winding along beside the River Tanat through lush, pastoral country. But once we'd turned off the route to Bala the mountains began to close in. We passed through one last village, ignored the signposts to the highest waterfall in Wales, and found we were entering a narrow side valley that led deep into the hills.

Whoever laid out the roads in this part of Wales wasn't wasting land and money on verges. Tall hedges or dry stone walls flank some very single tracks, and picnickers could starve before finding a place to pull off. Our road had begun that way. But now we were descending through deep woodland where the ferns hung thickly from gnarled, moss-encrusted branches; crossing a narrow stone bridge with a glimpse of swirling water, then grinding up a short, steep hill flanked by little heaps of salt and grit until we reached a cattle grid where the road was wide enough to stop. In front were no more walls, just a narrow ribbon of potholed tarmac threading its way along a hillside with beetling crags above and steep, green pasture below. Across the brown, foaming waters of the stream at the valley bottom was a dense, dark plantation, broken by a great scar and the tell-tale scree of an abandoned slate quarry. Ahead the bulk of Cadair Berwyn rose against the sky.

Sarah was standing on the road trying to stop the Ordnance map from tearing itself to pieces in the breeze. 'The road goes as far as a farm. Blaen-y-Cwm it's called. If it's still there. Our house is on the other side of the valley.' We were both thinking of it as 'our house' even though we hadn't seen it.

Ahead the road dipped, and what looked like a forestry track led down from it into the valley bottom and up towards the trees. We got back into the car and set off towards the point where the track branched off. It proved to be bumpy but, as they say, negotiable with care. At the bottom of the slope it crossed the stream by a bridge surfaced with railway sleepers, rose sharply and rounded a spur. As we jolted up the hill Sarah said, 'There's a chimney!'

The cottage was below the track, about half way down towards the stream. The path leading down to it was definitely not negotiable, with or without care. Someone had built up a platform big enough to turn or leave a car, so we left ours, donned the wellies that we'd been warned to bring and slithered down towards the house. It was built close against the hillside so that from the back you couldn't see much except roof. When we rounded the end we found a narrow strip of slate paving, like a terrace, running along the front of the building. A dry stone wall separated it from the steep slope down to the stream.

The house itself was like something a child would paint. Downstairs were one small window and one green door. Upstairs were two tiny windows tucked under the slate roof. There was a lean-to at one end. The house was built of irregular, granite boulders, with crumbly looking mortar in between. Tumbled dry stone walls marked out a patch of bracken and bramble covered garden. About twenty yards away was a little stone hut like a sentry box, with a sloping roof.

Sarah was already struggling with the massive key. 'Mr Lord said you had to get it just right,' I reminded her. Eventually she got it just right. We stepped into a room which looked as if it hadn't been altered since the building of the house. There was a curious cast iron range with a flue going up behind the grate instead of over it; it had an oven on one side, a small water tank on the other and a sort of crane on top, presumably for a kettle. There was a plain and rather battered dresser in dark brown oak which almost filled the back wall, a pine table and one impressive chair with a high back and arms. A thick layer of dust covered everything, and the air smelt as if it needed breathing.

Sarah was climbing the cramped staircase in the corner between the fireplace and the cupboard. It led into a narrow space, half bedroom, half landing, lit by a tiny skylight. Beyond was another room which proved to contain a rusty iron double bedstead with a lumpy looking mattress. The windows were at floor level, and the ceiling sloped up like a tent. We each knelt down at a window, in a little pool of sunlight, and peered out. Beyond the stream sheep were grazing on the mountainside with half-grown lambs playing about them.

If it hadn't been Saturday afternoon we'd have driven straight back to Lord and Timpson's waving our cheque book. But in those days estate agents locked up for the weekend at lunchtime, so we spent a couple of hours pottering about. The lean-to, into which a door opened from the living room, contained a stone sink with one massive tap above it which could be persuaded to deliver a stream of brownish water. The little stone hut revealed an Elsan perched precariously on some rotting boards that concealed a hole of uncertain depth. In the overgrown garden were several unpruned damsons and some stunted currant or gooseberry bushes. The wall in front of the house had a coping of smooth slate slabs, and we sat on it and watched the sun go down behind the mountain. Then we scrambled up to the car. A couple of hours later the key was in the agents' letter box, and we were on the motorway.

On the Monday morning I rang Bob Lord, and within hours the deed was done. The price was more than we'd originally thought of spending and there wouldn't be much left for improvements, but I think Bob could tell that I was too smitten to haggle convincingly and we probably paid a thousand or two more than we need have. In a couple of months contracts were exchanged, and we were the owners of Tan-y-Coed.

Buying a house in Wales had raised a few eyebrows back in the Midlands. The Welsh, people declared, were clannish, unfriendly, unwelcoming, They spoke their own language, mainly in order to freeze you out. Or if they didn't freeze you out they would burn you out; witness the reports of English-owned holiday cottages destroyed in recent years by arsonists. I was asking for trouble, it was implied, and would probably get it.

I thought the allegations would turn out to be a calumny, and so they proved. In the villages, and in the countryside, most people were noticeably friendlier than in the suburban environment I'd been used to. Not only did they pass the time of day; they were genuinely interested in you and went out of their way to show it. They gave themselves time to talk, and to listen. My own halting attempts at Welsh were listened to with good humour, even if the answer was generally in English. There were a few, very few, who seemed to go out of their way to avoid contact - but then, unsociable people aren't confined to Wales.

Looking back, it's remarkable how closely the cottage brought us together. We spent our summer holiday camping out there, plastering over holes and papering over cracks. I did some basic plumbing and bottled gas gave us hot water, though we couldn't afford a septic tank and the Elsan was given a reprieve. We bought a trailer, and every weekend we towed endless loads of materials out to the valley and up the track before barrowing them down the path. But there was the constant distraction of the country around; hills to climb, streams to follow, paths to explore. Our part of Wales seemed completely undiscovered; you could ramble for days and never meet another walker. On a still day the peace could be felt. There was no point in hurrying the work on the house, and I didn't try.

If we had different priorities, it didn't show at first. But whilst I was always looking for excuses to drop my paintbrush and head for the hills, Sarah's interest centred on the house, and in particular on the changes we could make to it. There were times when she was as keen as I was to stride out over the mountains. But on other occasions, quite justifiably, she thought we should keep our noses a little nearer the grindstone. Going to bed amongst sacks of plaster and pots of paint tends to pall after a few months. Something needed doing about the water supply, piped from a stream further up the hillside, which was rather too popular with sheep. I made several attempts to patch up the roof, but the drips always seemed to reappear on Sarah's side of the bed. After several days' continuous rain - not an uncommon eventuality - a trickle of water would emerge from the back wall and make its way across the kitchen floor. The threshold was so worn that slugs used to wander in and out under the door. And as luck would have it, it was Sarah who was perched on the Elsan when it finally disappeared down the hole.

We seriously disagreed about the fireplace. There was a splendid beam over the top, and Sarah yearned to remove the range and expose the ingle-nook, complete with bread oven, which she was convinced must lie behind it. She was probably right, but I liked the range. I won the argument, largely because inertia and the status quo were on my side. But Sarah won the wrangle over the power supply. The absence of electricity had an indefinable, nostalgic appeal, and I loved the gentle hissing and the golden light of the Aladdin pressure lamp which we'd found at Tan-y-Coed. But there was no denying the inconvenience, and when I managed to set the curtains alight with a candle I felt at enough of a disadvantage to give way. The poles weren't too prominent but they were still an intrusion, and each appliance Sarah wanted to introduce for sensible, practical reasons provoked a resentment that was all the stronger for being irrational.

Tan-y-Coed postponed the inevitable, but not indefinitely. In the end it became one more source of conflict. I wanted to go there in winter, when we had to squelch down the hillside in the dark with sacks of coal: Sarah would point out the advantages of central heating. I was prepared to go to bed moderately dirty: she preferred to be clean. I pontificated on preserving the house's authenticity while Sarah was browsing through Laura Ashley Home. I wanted vegetables in the garden, she wanted flowers. I wanted to explore the slate quarries, she wanted to ramble in the woods. I wanted to read, she wanted to talk. She wanted a dog. I wanted children. Both of us were selfish. Both of us cared for other things more than for each other.

We had one of those 'clean break' divorces. They're not as painless as they sound, but at least we had no-one else to hurt. Sarah kept the executive starter home, I kept Tan-y-Coed. By one of those happy chances that really do sometimes happen, the Regional Manager who covered Shropshire and Mid Wales was discovered to have been fiddling his expenses just before I was to sign the lease on a scruffy bedsit in Redditch. I'd scored a few brownie points by initiating some much-needed computerisation, and when I asked for a transfer I got it.

The company even agreed with me that one of the little Asian 4 by 4 saloons would help me to get round the farms in bad weather, and the Escort went to auction. I'd wanted authenticity and the simple life; now I could experience it full time.

If anyone had asked me, I'd have said that I was blissfully happy. Certainly there was much about life at Tan-y-Coed that was good. The peace, the freshness were unbelievable. Not that conditions were always idyllic; the rainfall in the Berwyn is phenomenal, and the wind can be frightening. But the stronger the wind, the brighter burned the fire, and there was something comforting about the age and solidity of the cottage; it had defied the elements for several lifetimes, and would surely outlive me. If the trudge to the Ty Bach, as the little shed was properly called, was sometimes an encouragement to constipation, the view from the door, which it was now unnecessary to close, made up for it. The rows of vegetables grew longer, though I struggled to get through them. Fending for myself, despite the lack of amenities, was no problem, and I'd sometimes switch off the light and get the Aladdin out again. There was plenty of space now for my books - always a source of contention - and time to read them. And there were evenings of drowsy summer contentment, and mornings when the frost on the russet coloured bracken glittered in the winter sun. The one disappointment, though I was only dimly aware of it, was that there was no-one to tell how beautiful it was.

There was no trouble with neighbours. Most of them were sheep. There were only two other houses in the valley. One was Blaen-y-Cwm, the farm at the valley head. The Lewises owned or leased much of the Cwm, and it was their sheep that grazed around Tan-y-Coed. But the house was a mile away and out of sight, and we rarely seemed to meet. The other was Ty-Newydd, half-hiddden in the trees where the valley road climbed up towards the cattle grid; it belonged to a family called Mitchell who lived in London and only came up at holiday times. The vagaries of the county boundary were such that their house was in Clwyd, whilst the top of the valley was in Powys.

Not all my hours were spent in rural isolation. I was clocking up the miles in the Justy, as my home wasn't very centrally located in my Managerial Region and the Welsh border farmers liked to order more frequently and in smaller quantities. My boss had insisted that I installed a telephone, mobiles being unable to cope with the local topography, and the cost of taking the wires across the valley had made it all the more vital to keep the commission coming in. And there was the need for company. I found a friendly pub where incomers were made welcome, and dropped in for an evening or two each week. And I got in with a group of highly expert enthusiasts, male and female, called the Welsh Mines Exploration Group - WMEG, pronounced 'oomeg' - who provided me with some instructive and mildly hair-raising weekends.

It was through WMEG that I met Bob Lord again. In the winter they used to organise evening meetings in a pub near Wrexham which was reasonably central for their scattered membership. Often the speaker was one of the group's own members - one or two were mining engineers who seemed to enjoy a busman's holiday. What appealed to me most, apart from the actual exploration, was the historical side, and Bob had been invited to speak to the group about using old maps and estate documents to research the history of mines. The WMEG newsletter called him a well known local historian and a lively speaker, and though it was an hour's drive I resolved to go along.

A harmless, everyday decision. But one snowflake can release an avalanche. That trip to Wrexham would ultimately cost three lives, and change others for ever.

Spring was supposed to be on the way, but there were icy patches on the narrow valley road as I drove out that morning. A mile or so from Tan-y-Coed I met a battered Land Rover and pulled over to let it through. I recognised the narrow face and small, tight features of Glyn Lewis, the farmer up at Blaen-y-Cwm. He gave me the barest nod of acknowledgment, his eyes fixed on the road ahead. He'd always seemed to be one of the unsociable few; it was a pity my nearest neighbour wasn't a bit more forthcoming.

I went straight to the meeting that evening from my rounds of the farms, and had a couple of pies and a pint while the room slowly filled up. There were friendly nods, alternating with bursts of laughter and a lot of animated conversation about stopes and winzes. Beards and baggy sweaters were much in evidence. Val the Membership Secretary, an intimidating figure from any angle, pounced on me brandishing her receipt book and kept me pinned to the bar while she extorted a cheque she alleged was overdue.

Bob was ushered in by the Chairman, and sat patiently through the business: accounts of recent doings and diggings and an argument about whether to repair an antiquated winch or scrap it and buy another. At last he was announced, and when he stood up the big, quiet figure seemed to dominate the room without effort or self-consciousness.

Bob Lord might not have had a history degree, but as an amateur he'd have put a lot of professionals to shame. He knew his stuff, and his talk - 'Mining the Archives' - combined real scholarship with a lively turn of phrase which brought a seemingly dry subject to life. One or two pub-goers who had strayed into the wrong room even stopped to listen.

He'd recognised me, and in the bar afterwards I bought him a drink and we talked. He told me that he'd sold his business and retired, and was enjoying having the time to do the things he wanted to do. He asked how we liked Tan-y-Coed, and shook his head when he heard that there was only one of us now and that I was living there full time. 'I'm a countryman myself. But it would be a bit remote for me, on my own. Maybe if I was younger... It's a beautiful spot.'

I asked him how he'd come to handle the sale from Oswestry. He looked thoughtful. 'That fellow Wallis was a car dealer from Brum. Hadn't had it very long. He didn't seem to get on with the locals. Have you had any problems?' I said I hadn't. 'His dog was the trouble. Used to chase sheep. It doesn't do in farming country. And he used to go out taking potshots at things with a .22. Birds and rabbits. On other people's land. People made it clear he wasn't welcome. I think he got the message.'

I told Bob how impressed I'd been with his talk, and his knowledge of his subject. He said he'd been digging around in archives for years. 'As land agents we always did a lot of work for landowners and big estates. Some of them have preserved an amazing amount of stuff, though it's not always catalogued. There's plenty of interesting material on mines. Now I've got more time I've been doing a bit of work on trial mining for gold. People claimed to have found it in some pretty unlikely places.'

'Was any gold mined in the Berwyn?'

'There were a few scratchings, but nothing productive. Nothing on the scale of lead or slate. The gold came from further west. In the past a lot of the gold they used for jewellery and coinage came from West Wales. Everybody knows the Queen's wedding ring is made of Welsh gold, but the local tradition is that the metal for the crown jewels came from Meirionydd. I'd love to find some proper evidence.'

'I suppose you might. It's not all that long ago.'

'I'm not talking about the present regalia. Most of it's pretty recent, as you say. Even what they call St Edward's Crown was only made for Charles II. The Welsh tradition seems to be earlier. It must refer to the original jewels, the set that Parliament had destroyed after Charles I was executed. I want to find out more about them.'

Bob asked me about my own interest in mines. I told him of the research I'd done in my student days, and we talked till they started dimming the lights and piling chairs on the tables. He'd been invited to come out with WMEG on one of their underground trips, and we agreed to meet again then.

It was well after midnight when I started the car to drive home, and remembered I hadn't enough petrol to get back. The all night garage took some finding, and it was even later when I got on the road.

It was a dirty night, and driving conditions were bad. By Llanrhaeadr it was after two. I threaded my way through the maze of lanes, and turned up the valley road. Ahead was the steep bit where it dropped down through the trees to the bridge. It was pitch black, and my lights weren't as clean as they should have been. I drove across the bridge and started up the hill. Fortunately I was going slowly.

The road was barely wider than the car, but on one steep bend it widened out a bit. It was just as well. Somebody was coming down the other way like a bat out of hell. And without lights, not even sidelights. I had a brief vision of two white faces reflecting my own headlights before there was a splintering crash as the vehicle took off my front wing. It looked like a light van. It sheered down the offside of the Justy, slammed into the bank on the outside of the bend, bounced back to tear off the rear bumper and kept going. The whole thing took maybe two or three seconds and left me a quaking heap.

I tried to get out of the car. The driver's door was jammed, but I managed to shuffle across and get out on the passenger side. The Justy was slewed across the road with one headlight still glaring and the other smashed to fragments. The whole offside was a mess, and there were bits of car, mostly mine, scattered over the road. There was a long gouge in the earth by the roadside, but no sign of the van. My right knee felt bruised and was starting to stiffen up. Otherwise I seemed to be in one piece.

The car didn't look as if it would go. If it wouldn't there was the choice of walking up to Tan-y-Coed or back to Llanrhaeadr. I was examining the remains of the front wing when something caught my attention ahead. A red glow was coming through the trees. As I looked it flickered and grew brighter. I began walking up the hill towards it, limping a bit. Then I stopped, lurched back down to the Justy, reached in and grabbed the car phone.

It responded with a resentful buzz. Down here reception was nil. I hobbled back up the hill as fast as my knee would stand it.

A hundred yards or so further up was Ty-Newydd, the Mitchells' holiday cottage. It stood among the trees only a few yards back from the road, behind a hedge. Flames were already shooting from a downstairs window. A stream of sparks was flying overhead, and I could feel the heat on my face.

I scrambled over the gate, tried to head round to the side and ran straight into a dustbin. The glare of the fire seemed to dazzle more than it lit up the garden. Were the Mitchells there? It wasn't a weekend and there was no car, so the house was probably empty. I banged on the door in case: no response. I tried it and it was locked. I fumbled my way round to the back and found another locked door. Up above a window pane cracked like a gunshot. I got a sudden lungful of smoke, and my eyes started streaming.

You could hear the fire now, roaring and crackling inside. The glow was starting to light up the sky, and it showed an outside tap by the back door. There was an outhouse near it, and there might be a bucket or a hosepipe. I kicked open the door; inside it was pitch dark, and I was stumbling around blindly, groping among a heap of invisible, sharp-edged objects. Then my fingers were enmeshed in what felt like plastic tubing; I dragged it out and yes, it was a hose. It was in a horrendous tangle, and I struggled to find the end and jam it onto the tap. The fire was spreading all the time, and I imagined I could feel the heat through the back door. Eventually I got the hose on and turned the water on full. The end came off the tap.

When I got the hose back on the resulting jet of water would have taken minutes to fill a bucket. I might as well have tried to put out the fire by peeing on it. By now I was dancing with rage and frustration. The house was - had been - a charming place and the Mitchells' pride and joy. There was no way anybody was going to save it. The nearest phone was at Tan-y-Coed, the nearest fire engine ten miles away with the firemen tucked up at home in bed.

Smoke was starting to billow down into my eyes, and I couldn't see. I turned back towards the corner of the house to get away from it. There was a rumbling sound; something hit the ground behind me, and a split second later I felt a smashing blow on the top of the skull. The result was like pressing the off switch on the telly. The house, the garden, the glare of the fire shrank into a tiny point of light, far away. Then everything went black.

CHAPTER 2

The next thing that I remember was finding myself in bed. When I opened my eyes there was something wrong with them. My field of vision had shrunk to a sort of slit with fuzzy edges. In front of me was a wall with a notice on it. The only bit with letters big enough to read was at the top. I struggled to make it out. Every time I was half way through I'd forgotten the beginning. Finally, with intense concentration, I got to the end. It said: 'The Sir Robert Jones and Dame Agnes Hunt Orthopaedic and District Hospital National Health Service Trust.' No wonder my head was hurting.

The slit was suddenly filled by a delightful vision in a crisp white nurse's uniform. A cheerful voice said, 'You're awake now, are you? No, just lie still. Can you tell me how you're feeling?' I made some grunts to the effect that I was still alive, and she told me I was lucky. Then I drifted off again.

The next time I surfaced there was more activity round the bed. The slit had got wider, the notice had disappeared, and all around were white-clad figures against a background of peach coloured roses. I was wired up to various bits of technology, and somebody seemed to be poking around inside my skull. When I moved they stopped, and a friendly black face appeared and said, 'All right Mr Jones. We've just about finished patching you up.'

The roses were swept from view with a rattle of curtain rings, to reveal a hospital ward with several other beds and a lot of people coming and going. Another face appeared and asked if I could manage a cup of tea.

After that things improved considerably. A helpful sister came to talk, and said I'd had a nasty crack on the head. The fire brigade had got an ambulance to bring me in the day before; it was now afternoon, so I must have been unconscious quite a while. It wasn't until she said 'fire brigade' that the events of the previous evening started to come back. I could remember a fire, and trying to put it out, but still didn't know how it had happened.

There wasn't much the sister could tell me. 'The police want to see you. They told us to let them know when you were ready to talk to someone. But what about your family; is there anybody we ought to notify? They'll be wondering where you are.'

I felt suddenly upset, and somehow ashamed, that no-one would be wondering where I was. Sarah belonged to the past now, and whilst I had various aunts, uncles and cousins it hardly seemed worth letting them know I'd had a bump on the head.

'There isn't really. But I don't mind talking to the police. I'd like to find out a bit more about what happened. And could you let my boss know, if I give you the number?'

By the next morning the various drips, wires and flashing lights had been cleared away, and the hospital had clearly decided I was going to live. I began to take a bit more notice of my surroundings, and it was at that stage that I became aware of a man sitting just outside my section of the ward. Unlike most of the others around he wasn't wearing a white coat. He seemed to spend most of his time reading a newspaper. Presumably he was waiting for somebody.

The police took their time turning up. When they did it wasn't a constable in uniform, but two middle-aged men in raincoats. One of them introduced himself as Detective Inspector Humphreys. The other didn't introduce himself at all. Humphreys was a thin, round-shouldered man with sad eyes and mousy, thinning hair: he looked as if he wasn't far off retirement and wouldn't be sorry when it came. His companion was a bit younger, with a reddish moustache and a prim expression. They found themselves chairs and came and sat by the bed as if visiting a stricken relative, though with a less solicitous manner.

I started asking them what had happened, but Humphreys interrupted. 'We'd like to hear that from you, if you don't mind.' Unlike detectives on television, he didn't call me sir.

The night's events had more or less come back by that time, and I described them as clearly as I could while Humphreys prompted with questions that were sharp and to the point. When I mentioned the van he glanced at the other man, who was studying the wall. Humphreys wanted a description of the vehicle and its occupants, but there wasn't much to tell him: I'd only had a glimpse. He made a few notes in a little black book. The other just sat upright on his chair, holding a briefcase on his knee. Occasionally he dabbed at his moustache with a neatly folded white handkerchief which he kept up his sleeve.

By the time I'd finished Humphreys at least seemed to have relaxed a bit. 'You're not a local man, Mr Jones,' he said. It was a statement, not a question; my accent had made it obvious. 'With your name, it seemed you might be.' I explained about Batley, and he relaxed further. 'That would be your car on the road. The firemen saw it was damaged. They had to push it out of the way to get the fire engine up, though the house had pretty well gone by that time.' I asked where it was, and he said in a gateway opposite the Mitchells' cottage. I wondered what the firm would have to say.

'Are you treating it as arson?'

'What made you think it might be?' Humphreys asked casually.

'It occurred to me at the time. The van was going at such a speed, as if it was getting away. And there've been a few cases in North Wales in the last few years, though not locally. The Mitchells are English, it was a holiday cottage. They're the ones that go up in smoke. Maybe there was some resentment.'

'It seems quite likely arson was involved,' Humphreys said. 'They're still sifting through the debris, but there were signs of an inflammable substance. The fire certainly spread very fast. They saw the glow from Llanrhaeadr. Someone was out late and called the fire brigade. They found you by the corner of the house, half covered with fallen slates. You were lucky.'

People kept calling me lucky. Personally I felt distinctly unlucky, but it seemed unfriendly to say so.

'If it was arsonists, could somebody have come back, seen me and knocked me on the head?'

Humphreys looked sceptical. 'I don't see why they'd bother. Their main interest would be in getting away. It's more likely you were struck by slates coming off the roof.'

As he was being so forthcoming I tried another question. 'Did you think it was me? The arsonist, I mean.'

'Well sir, it could have been. You were there, after all. But we found the hose. It looked as if someone had been trying to put out the fire.' The sir was reassuring.

There wasn't much more to tell them, and eventually they went away. The man who had been sitting outside the ward got up and went with them. Humphreys had thanked me politely before they left; his companion had never opened his mouth. Maybe he was just a minion, but he had looked too authoritative somehow, and the quality of his raincoat was too good. I remembered reading that the Welsh arson cases were being treated as terrorism, and that the security services were working alongside the local constabulary. Perhaps I'd had MI5 by my bedside.

Later on the doctor came round, beaming cheerfully, and I asked how soon I'd be able to go home. When he heard I lived on my own he pulled a face. 'We'd better hold onto you for a day or two. You're on the mend, but there ought to be someone to keep an eye on you, just in case.'

Everyone was being very kind, but it was irritating having to stay. My head was pretty tender, but I'd been taught stoicism from an early age. At the age of ten or so I'd fallen off the shed roof and broken an arm. 'Now then Johnny, don't make a fuss,' they'd said as we waited for the ambulance. Making a fuss wasn't done in our family.

At visiting time the ward suddenly filled with other people's relatives, full of uneasy joviality and laden with Lucozade and Kleenex. I wasn't expecting visitors; the little pinboard over my bed, criss-crossed with pink tape, was the only one not stuffed with Get Well cards. So I was taken aback when the sturdy, tweed-clad figure of Bob Lord appeared at the door and headed in my direction.

He found a chair and perched himself on it. 'I read about you and the fire in the Shropshire Star,' he said, half apologetically. 'I realised it must have happened after we had our talk, on your way home. I was a bit concerned. Are you all right?'

'The fire wasn't at Tan-y-Coed.' He looked relieved. 'And yes thanks, I seem to be doing all right. They're letting me out in a couple of days. They'd let me go earlier, only I'm on my own at home. It was good of you to come.'

I told Bob about the fire, and the van, and the visit of the police. 'It's a while since we had an arson attack,' he said thoughtfully, 'Things had gone quiet. There were never that many, but they tended to make the headlines.' He changed the subject, asking me about life at Tan-y-Coed, and I began telling him about its ups and downs. He sat forward to listen, and there was something about his manner that encouraged you to keep talking. The steady grey eyes with little wrinkles at the corners didn't flicker around the ward as I spoke but stayed focused on mine, and the bushy grey eyebrows were constantly expressing a reaction: he could move them independently, and one or both of them would suddenly shoot up in surprise or wrinkle in concern. On one of my salesmanship courses I'd been taught about the importance of body language. 'Make sure the customers think you're listening to them,' they'd said. But you never doubted Bob was listening.

A bell jangled, and people started heading for the door with ill-concealed relief. Bob got up and then said a little hesitantly, 'Look. It's a pity to have to hang on here. There's plenty of room at my place. Why don't you let me put you up for a day or two?'

'I couldn't possibly. I'd be in the way.'

'You wouldn't be in the way at all. I'd be glad of the company. We can talk a bit of history. I've some mining stuff you might like to see. And there's something else I'd like an opinion on, something I've been working on.'

He obviously meant it, and I thought: Why not? It would be a bit bleak at Tan-y-Coed, and I wouldn't be able to drive for a day or two. 'It's very kind of you,' I said. 'I'd be very pleased to come for a couple of days.'

The hospital wouldn't let me out that night, but next morning the doctor, still beaming, agreed I could go if there was someone to hold my hand. They exchanged my bandage for sticking plaster, and I looked a bit less like someone from the trenches. I bought a few bits and pieces at the hospital shop, then rang the number Bob had left, and an hour later he turned up and I checked out. It was a long way to the car park, and I felt more unsteady that I'd expected. It was a relief to be able to climb into his Range Rover and let myself be driven.

Bob took the road for Wrexham and then turned towards Llangollen. I was happy to let him talk. 'I was hoping we'd heard the last of the arsonists. The campaign seemed to have petered out.' I asked him if he'd sold the house to the Mitchells and he said no, it, had been another firm. 'But we sold a lot of houses to English people. They tended to go for the remoter cottages. Some of the locals grumbled, but the youngsters want modern houses and most people were pleased to see the places occupied. This is border country, and people are used to mixing. The extremists mainly come from elsewhere. They had a go at our office, you know.' I said I didn't know.

'It was not long before I sold out. There'd been one or two attacks on estate agents on the English side of the border. Firms who'd sold

Welsh cottages as holiday homes. There was even one on an agency in London. Burned out the whole building. In our case there wasn't much damage done. Someone put a fire bomb through the letter box. It fizzled out, fortunately, so there wasn't much about it in the papers. But it could have been nasty, there was a tenant in the flat over the office. Looking back, I think it was one factor that influenced me to sell up. But then, they made me an offer I'd have been crazy to refuse.'

We had turned off the A5 after Llangollen, and after several miles of twists and turns were suddenly climbing through woodland where the leaves were just beginning to appear. The sunlight was slanting through them, sparkling with silver and green. Occasionally there was a glimpse of the fields below. Then the narrow road widened, and we swung back in a hair-pin turn between two stone gateposts and up a steep drive through a tunnel of trees. Suddenly we emerged onto a broad terrace cut out of the hill, brilliantly sunlit.

I got out of the Range Rover, walked across a narrow strip of lawn to a stone balustrade, and looked out over the Vale. Its clusters of grey cottages were sharply defined against the fresh spring green, the woodlands still dark patches on the steep hillsides. Castell Dinas Bran was a jagged shape against the sky, and in the distance the limestone scars above World's End gleamed a brilliant white.

Bob had come up behind me. 'It still takes my breath away. I sold this place for a client once, nearly thirty years ago. I loved it then, but I never thought I'd be able to live here. Then it came back on the market just at the right time, and thanks to General Accident I bought it.'

The house was long and low, painted white like many on the valley side, with generous windows and a big, welcoming porch. I followed Bob into a panelled hallway, and then into a sitting room, long and low like the house and full of sunlight. There was a fireplace with a big woodburning stove. Most of the back and end walls were lined with books.

Bob sat me down in one of two large armchairs by one of the windows, then went out through another door. He was gone a few minutes, and I got up to look at the spines of some of the books. I can never resist a library. I'd expected to see works on history, or on Wales, but instead there was a lot of sociology, volumes on crime and delinquency, and a long row of Famous British Trials. Another bookcase was full of poetry, some in collections I had myself, but others by people I'd never heard of. There were religious titles too and a whole series of publications with the imprint of the Society of Friends. I'd sat down again before Bob reappeared with two mugs of coffee.

In the window was a low table with a little group of photographs. One showed a smiling woman, grey-haired against a background of flowers. Bob followed my eyes. 'Doris. My wife. She died three years ago. She loved it here. I wish she'd had longer.' Later I learned he'd nursed her through cancer. 'That's my son Ian. He's in Canada. And my daughter Helen. She's teaching in London'. Helen's was a graduation photograph, in hood and gown, on a lawn with old stone-buildings behind.

'You've got quite a library here. I could do with more space for books.'

'I've always been a reader.' He ran his hand affectionately along the spines on the shelf beside him. 'I had some good teachers. I'd have liked the chance to go on studying. But in those days, when there was a family business you were expected to go into it. And I've done pretty well out of it, I can't grumble.'

Bob took me up to the room he'd given me, which looked out over the valley. I lay down for a while, still feeling below par. When I came downstairs Bob had provided a cold lunch, and with some food inside me I started to feel better.

There were more books in the dining room, this time mostly history and topography, and between the bookcases were several big framed maps. I walked over to have a look. They were clearly originals, mainly seventeenth century by the look of them, hand coloured and beautifully engraved. They showed Shropshire and several of the Welsh counties. One looked a bit later; it seemed to be an estate map and had an elaborate crest in one corner.

'It's part of the Berwyn Estate,' Bob said.

'That belonged to the Morgans, didn't it?'

'That's right. The family still have the big house of course, and the park, but a lot of the agricultural land was sold off over the years. In fact, I handled some of the more recent sales. But the area on the map is nowhere near the main portion of the estate. It's up in the mountains, over towards Bala. The valley's called Cwm Llwyd. It's where the Morgans struck it rich.'

I knew something about the Morgans of Berwyn. They had been - perhaps still were - one of the great Welsh families. Madog Morgan had been a friend of Henry Tudor, and when Tudor came to the throne as

22

Henry VII he'd been rewarded with lands and influence. His grandson had built the great house of Berwyn on the site of one of the old border castles; it's one of the few historic seats still in the hands of the family that built it, and despite its name it's some way from the Berwyn Mountains themselves. The Morgans had nearly bankrupted themselves building the house, and the family fortunes were saved when lead was discovered on land they owned high up in the hills.

'The map's pretty inaccurate,' Bob said. 'At least, it doesn't bear much resemblance to modern maps of the valley. But it shows the general area where they drove the first adit.' He pointed to a few dots on the map. 'It was an incredibly rich vein, one of the richest in Europe at the time. This was one of the first deep lead mines; we're talking about the reign of James I. It didn't last, though. There was just the one vein, and it was soon worked out.'

'Is there much to be seen on the ground?'

'It's all rather confused. Later a lot of slate was quarried in the same area. Some of the lead workings were probably destroyed in the process, or covered with waste slate. Above ground you wouldn't expect to see much at all, after so many years. I've been wondering if some of the levels could still be there, underground. It would be very interesting to see.'

Something in his voice made me take notice. 'Old metal mines can be pretty unsafe. They're not like the underground slate quarries, where there's usually a solid roof. Still, there are some places where the cavity's quite stable and then the passages can remain for years. The copper mines on the Great Orme have survived since the Bronze Age.'

'What about artefacts? For example, if something had been, say, concealed down there. Could it have survived?'

'People have found tools. There was a wooden shovel over at Alderley Edge, dating right back to the Bronze Age. And Roman coins were discovered in some of the old levels at Llanymynech. It would depend on the materials. Wood generally rots and iron rusts. Pottery will last for ever if the roof doesn't fall in on it.'

'But gold would survive,' said Bob quietly.

I wondered if I'd heard him properly. 'The gold mines were worked out, weren't they? Or were you thinking of something else?'

He hesitated, then seemed to come to a decision. 'I'll show you something.'

He took me through into another room at the back of the house, a small study or office with still more books, a couple of filing cabinets and a big desk with an obsolescent computer on it. From under the desk he lifted a rather bulky metal box, and carried it, grunting a little, through the hall and back into the big sitting room. When he opened the box, which was full of papers, I noticed the sides were unusually thick.

'It's supposed to be a fireproof deed box. I kept it when I sold the firm. I don't know how effective it would be in a fire, it's pretty old fashioned, but I thought it might be useful.'

We sat down again by the window with the box between us. 'Before we look at these,' Bob said, 'You need to know a bit more about the Morgans. The lead made them wealthy, and they invested the money mainly in land. But then came Charles I, and the Civil War. Like many families, the Morgans were split down the middle. The eldest son was Owain Morgan, and he'd inherited the estate. By the time of the Civil War he was in his fifties. He stuck by the King; he was with Charles at the Battle of Chester, and afterwards he went back to Berwyn and lay low. But one of his brothers had been elected to parliament, and several of his relatives took the parliamentary side.'

'What happened to Owain?'

Bob grinned. 'Owain was quite a character. He was a big man in every sense of the word. In his youth he seems to have been better known as a drinker than a fighter. It was said he used to drink a gallon of ale for breakfast. They still keep a barrel at Berwyn that he's supposed to have been able to drain at one draught. But one of the accounts of the Battle of Chester includes quite a well known allusion to him. It says that, once he saw the battle was lost, 'Owain Morgan did lower his britches, and turning did bare his posterior parts at the enemie and did make lewde and unseemlie noises.'

'Tactless, in the circumstances.'

'He wasn't a tactful man. Later, after Charles lost his head, it was lucky for him that he had friends in the other camp. He was allowed to keep his estate, when many Royalist gentry lost everything. But he never made any attempt to hide his sympathies; he even had Berwyn adorned with Royalist symbols and slogans. It's a wonder he wasn't charged with treason. But the house was pretty remote in those days - it still is - and he stayed there and kept out of the way. He died in 1660.'

'That would be around the time of the Restoration.'

'Just before. Owain must have known it was coming. But he never saw Charles II on the throne.'

'Do those papers relate to Owain Morgan?' The documents in the box looked about the right age.

'I came across the papers over twenty years ago.' Bob was enjoying telling his story, and he wasn't going to be hurried. 'My firm were auctioneers as well as land and estate agents. At one time we had a saleroom, we sold house contents and had a quarterly antique auction. That wasn't really my side of the business; another of the partners looked after it. But I always kept an eye on what was coming in, and used to put in bids for anything interesting. All above board, the lot went to the highest bidder and that wasn't always me. But a lot of my books came that way, and some nice bits of furniture. One day we got in a box of papers. Some of them were deeds on vellum; people used to buy documents like that to make lampshades, believe it or not. I managed to outbid the lampshade makers.'

'Where did the papers come from?'

'From a house called Bryn Teg, up the Cain valley. At the time I didn't know it had once belonged to the Berwyn estate. The Morgans sold it in the 1800's. The documents had been hidden away in part of the roof space that had been sealed off for years. The valley's not far from the lead mining area, you know. Some of the papers obviously referred to the mines. But there were some others written in Welsh, and I didn't have time to look at them properly.

After I retired I started to take more of an interest. I've always had a bit of Welsh; one of my grandmothers came from Caernarfonshire, and a lot of our customers on this side of the border are Welsh speaking. Over the last couple of years I've been teaching myself more, from books mainly. I can read most things now. And I've been having another look at these.'

He took a bulky document from the box between our chairs. It was tightly rolled, and he winced as he unrolled it. 'I'm always afraid of damaging old papers. I had photocopies made to work from, but I want you to see the originals. These are just as I found them.'

The bundle contained several documents, not just one. The outer sheet was large, much discoloured and closely covered in neat, rather laborious writing. The initial words and letters were in a larger, more florid script. At the bottom were several signatures and a couple of scrawled crosses, marks of the illiterate. The language was English.

Bob perched a pair of half-moon glasses on the end of his nose. 'This is an agreement between Owain Morgan's father, Gruffydd, and a team of miners. It describes an existing gallery which they are to extend, and lays down the conditions on which they're to work. Pretty stingy they seem today. It doesn't say precisely where the mine is, but I assume it's in Cwm Llwyd. The date is forty years or so before the Civil War. These other papers were rolled up inside it.'

There were two batches. One looked like a set of accounts, with neat columns of figures. The other papers were a series of loose sheets, smaller and apparently torn from a binding. They were in a different hand: less regular but more self-assured, with lots of vigorous curlicues wherever there was space to fit them in. They were written in Welsh.

'The accounts seem to refer to sales of lead,' Bob said. 'And silver too; a lot of the Welsh mines had a little silver mixed with the lead.'

'Why should the accounts have been hidden?'

'I've been asking myself that. Apparently Charles received silver from the Welsh mines during the Civil War, so that he could mint coinage. Perhaps Owain had been supplying the King, and had to keep it dark later on. But it's these papers in Welsh that are really fascinating.'

He laid the smaller pages carefully on a low table and placed a pile of typed sheets beside them, evidently an English translation.

'They look like pages from some sort of journal.' I picked up a couple of the fragile, yellowed pages, handling them gingerly. Every now and then what looked like a date appeared.

'That's exactly what they are. The question is, whose? There's no name. But there are several references to Berwyn. And there's no doubt about the period. The dates just give a month, not a year, but there's one clear indication in the text.' He pointed to a sentence on the first of the sheets, separated from the others by blank space, and written in larger, blacker characters that seemed to leap out of the page. 'Translated as well as I can, that means: "On this day news came to Berwyn that the King's Majesty is most foully murdered. God save the King his Son!" The date is February 4. King Charles I was beheaded on January 30, 1649.'

'So this could be Owain Morgan writing. But would he have used Welsh? Surely at that time a man in his position would have written in English.'

'Up to Queen Elizabeth's time the Welsh gentry mostly spoke their native language, at any rate at home. This was less than a hundred years later. The Morgans were a conservative lot, and Gruffydd Morgan was something of a Celtic scholar. I've no doubt Owain knew Welsh and probably spoke it to his retainers, if not to his family. I think this was his Journal, and he had his own reasons for writing it in Welsh.'

I thought about it. 'I don't suppose many of Cromwell's men spoke Welsh. The text wouldn't have meant much to them if they came across it. But what might he have been trying to conceal?'

'Some of the language seems deliberately obscure. But take this entry, on the next page. I've translated it here. "Great evil has been done by vile and unworthy men, who have dared to lay foul hands on the head which God anointed. Yet his greatest treasure has not yet been destroyed." Then here.' He was riffling eagerly through the sheets, and his glasses fell off his nose. He crammed them back impatiently. 'Look. "The treasure was refused them, but they will return. How is it to be saved?" Then on the next page: "The treasure shall be saved for the King, when he shall come again."'

The idea of a royal treasure struck me as improbable. They hadn't let me spend all my time at university on mining history: I'd done a bit on the Stuarts, and enjoyed it.

'What does he mean by treasure? Charles was pretty well bankrupt by the end. The whole Civil War was sparked off by his need for money. He'd already sold a lot of the royal jewels in the 1620's. He can't have had much stashed away.'

'Owain - if it is Owain - is never specific. He just keeps using the Welsh word "trysor gwerth fawr", which means a precious thing, a treasure of great price. He seems obsessed by it; he mentions it again and again without giving any further clue about what it is. But here, in the summer, he's written: "Thomas shall take the treasure, and it shall be preserved. King Harry's shall serve."'

'Who was Thomas?'

Bob spread his hands. 'That's something I need to find out. I haven't come across a Thomas in the family of that period, but he may not have been a Morgan. I don't understand the reference to King Harry, either. But Thomas crops up again. Here, in September 1649, Owain has written: "Today Thomas shall take it, and make it safe. God preserve him in his brave endeavour."'

'Thomas, whoever he was, was taking a risk. The parliamentarians were pretty ruthless about getting their hands on the royal assets. They kept accounts of every last penny. Detailed inventories were made. After Charles's execution they sold off most of the royal palaces and auctioned the contents. Any gold was melted down for coin. They'd have dealt harshly with anyone who tried to spirit money or valuables away.'

'But Thomas seems to have succeeded. This is the crucial bit. It's the last entry.' Bob picked up the final sheet, and a corner crumbled as he did so. 'It's rotten paper. We'd better use these.' He lifted a wad of photocopies out of the box and passed me a sheet from the bottom. 'You can keep that. It's a duplicate. Now look; here's the wording in English.'

He'd underlined three sentences heavily on the photocopy. I tried to follow the Welsh as he read out his translation. '"Thomas has brought the treasure to Berwyn. That which is most sacred is under my roof. But soon it shall be hidden under the rock, in a high place, till the King shall come again."'

'What does it mean: "hidden under the rock"?'

Bob hesitated. 'He's written: "gorchuddiwyd y tresor â charreg". It actually means "covered or buried by rock". The word "carreg" means "rock" or "stone". And then there's "in a high place - mewn uchelfan". So it's underground, but high up. Remember where the pages were found, and the other documents they were wrapped in. He must be referring to a mine. Probably one of the lead mines the Morgans had been digging since the beginning of the century, high up in the Berwyn. What better place to hide a treasure?'

'Charles II came back to England in 1660,' I said slowly. 'But Owain Morgan died just before. Maybe the new king never received his treasure.'

Bob looked at me solemnly over his glasses. 'If he did, no-one has ever heard of it. So perhaps he didn't. Which means that, whatever it is, it's probably still there.'

By the time evening came, the dining room looked like a cartographer's workshop. Bob had a fine collection of maps, old and new, on every conceivable scale, many stamped with the name of his old firm. 'GA would have thrown them out,' he said defensively, 'And I can't bear to throw a map away. They tell you more about the history of an area than any book, if you know how to read them.' The geological maps with their brilliant reds and blues and yellows made pools of colour on the carpet, whilst the dining table was spread with various editions of the Ordnance Survey as well as the framed estate map which Bob had taken off the wall. That should have been the most helpful, but whilst highly decorative it was frustratingly short on detail and didn't bear much resemblance to the country the modern maps depicted.

'I've looked through all these, of course,' Bob said, 'But you might notice something I missed. The documents from Bryn Teg tell us plenty about the miners and the ore they mined, but they don't actually give the location of the workings.'

The later maps were fascinating but confusing. 'There are mine workings marked everywhere, but it's hard to tell what's lead and what's slate. And we really need to know where the Morgans were mining in the 1600's. Are there any records?'

Bob pulled a face. 'There's still an archive at Berwyn. In fact, there's masses of stuff. The trouble is, it's in a bit of a state. The contents have never really been listed, though various people have had a go. Research there might well turn something up, but it could be a long job.'

My head was starting to buzz, and after a few minutes spent rolling and folding we left the dining room looking tidier and Bob drove me down to a pleasant, old-fashioned Llangollen hotel for dinner. 'I won't inflict my cooking on you,' he said. I was glad to find my appetite was unimpaired. We regaled ourselves on roast pheasant and then treacle pudding, and I risked a glass of the house red, even though my hair still concealed a row of stitches. Then we headed back to the house on the hillside, and I excused myself for an early night.

I lay there for a while, thinking about Owain Morgan and his mysterious treasure. What was it that he'd risked so much to save? Could it really still be buried beneath a Welsh hillside, awaiting discovery? Had Owain known, when death overtook him, that his efforts to secure it for the future king had come to nothing? Had he tried to pass on the secret before he died? And who was Thomas, and how had he spirited it away? But no answers came before I fell asleep.

The next morning I felt as right as rain, and said so. 'Look, I ought to get back to Tan-y-Coed. I've no idea what's happened to my car. And I can't impose on you indefinitely. You've been very kind.'

'You've been very welcome,' Bob said. 'I've been glad to have someone to talk to about Owain and his "treasure". If there really is something there, I'd need help to find it. I was wondering whether to go public. But I wanted to know whether I'd be laughed at.'

'I'm not laughing. And I don't think many other people would. But going public might not be the best thing to do. The place would be overrun with treasure hunters. Idiots would start poking around in old mine workings and getting themselves killed. Why don't you let me

give you a hand? If you need a bit of help, I'd love to be involved.'
'I don't know.' He sounded doubtful. 'Not that I don't think you'd
be the right person. But I think we'd need some sort of official backing.'

I didn't press him further, and Bob agreed to run me back home in
the Range Rover. 'If you're sure you're OK,' he said. 'I'm supposed
to be in Liverpool this afternoon. I could take you back this morning,
and then if everything is all right I'll drive up after lunch. But you're
welcome to stay on here.'

I insisted I was feeling fine, and after breakfast we set off. Bob
took the steep and tortuous road that leads over to the Ceiriog valley
and then south towards the Tanat. The sun was shining again, and the
lambs were gambolling like scraps of white paper blowing across the
fields. I remarked to Bob it was a pity to have to spend the afternoon on
Merseyside, and asked what took him there.

He chuckled. 'I'm due at Walton Gaol.'

'Why Walton Gaol?' I couldn't think of anything to take a retired
estate agent with historical leanings into one of Britain's more notorious
prisons.

'Prison visiting. I've been visiting prisoners for years. Anyone can
do it, though you have to be vetted. A lot of the cons are sent miles
away from their families, and some don't get visited at all. A bit of
human contact helps. I sit and listen to them, and chat if they want to
listen to me. Some of them are extraordinarily interesting men. I've
learned a lot from them. I often think: there but for the grace of God...'

I was sceptical. 'Surely most of them are there because they deserve
to be there.'

'In the sense that they're guilty as charged, that's generally true. But
it's how they came to be guilty that interests me; all the combinations
of circumstances that led to them going to gaol. There are some quite
gifted people in there, you know. A few of them are taking Open
University courses. Take the chap I'm seeing now; he has a pretty
appalling record, but he's as fascinated by history as I am. I talk to him
every week. We've got a lot in common.'

That was as far as our conversation got; we were approaching
Llanrhaeadr, and I was having to direct Bob through the maze of lanes.
Soon the blackened walls of Ty-Newydd came in sight. There was no
sign of the Justy, but the Mitchells' Volvo was parked in the gateway.
We stopped and I got out. Colin Mitchell, bald and bespectacled, was
poking about dejectedly in the ruins. Charred timbers lay at drunken

angles between the walls; a bath had fallen through the upstairs floor and was standing on its end in one corner. You could see up into the bedrooms, the teddy-bear wallpaper scorched and blackened.

'I'm desperately sorry,' I said. 'What a waste.'

'We were insured, thank God. But you feel so sickened. The kids are heartbroken. We've come here every holiday. What was the point? The place had been empty ten years when we bought it. I gather you were trying to put the fire out and got hurt. Are you all right?'

I told him I was fine, and he thanked me for trying to save the house. I said I'd been pretty ineffective and mentioned the hose.

'The water supply has always been dodgy. We have - had - to pump the water up to the tank in the roof.' I asked if they were going to rebuild, and he said they didn't know.

Bob had got out of the Range Rover and was making sympathetic noises. I wondered if Colin knew anything about my car.

'That would be the Justy. I think Glyn Lewis towed it up to your place with his Land Rover.'

That was unexpected; I'd had so little contact with the people at Blaen-y-Cwm, and was pleased Glyn had put himself out to be helpful.

'Thanks. We'll go and see if it's there.'

We left Colin standing in the wreckage of his family's dream, and soon came to the end of the familiar track to Tan-y-Coed. The Justy was neatly parked just opposite. In daylight the damage didn't look as bad as I'd feared, though it obviously wasn't driveable. Bob drove me down over the bridge and up to the turning point above the cottage, and refused the offer of coffee or lunch.

'I'd better be on my way. Visiting hours at Walton are fixed, and we have to conform.'

As he was about to drive off I stepped up to the car window. 'Thank you very much for putting me up. It was very good of you. And about Owain's journal: seriously, I'd very much like to be involved. I know a bit about mines, and I've worked with archives. And I'd keep it confidential.'

'Thanks for the offer, John. I'll keep in touch and let you know if anything comes up. To start with I want to look at the papers at Berwyn, if they'll let me in. Then maybe we could do a bit of prospecting. But I'm not hung up about secrecy. If there really is something to find I think I ought to publish, and let other people in on the act.' With a wave of his hand he was bumping off down the track.

CHAPTER 3

I made my way down to Tan-y-Coed. Some early daffodils were blowing among the damson trees; little ragged doubles that had been naturalised there long ago, and more sophisticated varieties that Sarah had planted. The ground at the back sloped so steeply that the bedroom window, on the first floor, was only a few feet above the ground; I'd left it slightly open, and the blue check curtain was flapping. Round at the front, the little house had a closed up look. I felt I'd been away a long time. The key squeaked a little in the lock. It still seemed wrong not to call out 'I'm home'.

Everything was in its place, just as I'd left it. As usual, I lit the range; not that I was proposing to sit by it, but it brought the kitchen to life, and the house never looked right without smoke coming from the chimney. Once banked up, the fire would burn for hours and keep the place warm and welcoming. I found myself a hunk of cheese, a bag of crisps and a stick of celery and went and sat on the terrace wall to eat them.

I couldn't get Owain Morgan and his 'treasure' out of my mind. It wasn't the urge to get rich quick. I must be one of a tiny minority who've never bothered to buy a lottery ticket. But this treasure, if it still existed, was of royal provenance. It had been lost for three hundred and fifty years. It was somewhere within a few miles of where I sat, perhaps in a tunnel like the ones I'd explored. Whatever the treasure was, it surely wasn't just a hoard of money. It had meant more than that to Owain. So many wonderful things had been lost or wantonly destroyed in that terrible period when the puritans had smashed and burned and looted. Now it looked as if something really precious might have survived. The more I thought, the more convinced I was that Bob and I, working together, had a real chance of rediscovering something of national significance.

I'd finished the cheese, and was poking the last fragments of crisp around the bottom of the bag. The next priority was to do something about the car. As Glyn Lewis had retrieved it for me, the keys were presumably at Blaen-y-Cwm. I'd better go and get them.

I set off down the track and along the road; the farm at the valley's end was about half an hour's brisk walk. The road led along the hillside where the blackthorn was crammed with blossom and the hedges exploding into leaf. The wind was chasing the cloud shadows across the pastures and blowing my hair into my eyes. Blaen-y-Cwm was visible ahead, flanked by a clump of sycamores: squat, grey-rendered and pebbledashed, its back to a wall of rock, it had defied everything the Welsh weather could throw at it for a couple of centuries or so. The threat to its survival now was not from natural forces, but from economic ones; even the level ground on the valley floor was reedy and poor in quality, and there was little enough of that. Life here must be a struggle in more senses that one.

A child's shaggy pony stuck its head over the wall beside the gate. There was no sign of Glyn Lewis's battered Land Rover in the farm yard, but the kitchen door was open and I knocked on it. A voice came from behind me and Glyn's wife, Gwen, came round the corner of the house carrying a lamb tucked under her arm. An anxious looking ewe was trotting after them. It was surprising to see a lamb so early in the spring; lambing is usually later in the hill country.

'How are you, Mrs Lewis?' I'd soon learned that that was the universal greeting in this part of the country, spoken with the stress on the 'you': the equivalent of the Welsh greeting 'Sut 'dych chi?'. When people said it to me it always sounded warm and personal, as if they cared.

'I'm fine, but how are you, Mr Jones? I heard you'd had a nasty bang on the head.' She was eyeing my plaster with motherly concern.

'I did. But it's mending fast. I understand you rescued my car.'

'Glyn gave it a tow. He'll be back any minute. Will you have a cup of tea?'

I knew better than to refuse. 'Yes please, just a quick one.'

'I'll just put this little chap in the barn and I'll have the kettle on', and she was off across the yard with the ewe in pursuit.

The tea was served in a quantity, and at a temperature, which made quickness out of the question. I sat in the kitchen clasping a china mug that must have held nearly a pint of scalding liquid. The room was full of bright colours, cheerful, practical and comfortable like Gwen Lewis herself. She sat looking at me with the quizzical, half amused expression that I'd seen in the eyes of other local people when confronted by an incomer.

'How are you finding it now, over at Tan-y-Coed? It must be a bit different from where you come from.'

'It is. That's why I moved. But I wasn't trying to get away from anything. I just wanted to be here.'

She nodded. 'We wouldn't be anywhere else. I was born on your side of the valley, you know, at the Waen. We left when I was ten, that's over thirty years ago. It's a ruin now.'

I'd walked past the remains of the house, a roofless shell two or three hundred feet above Tan-y-Coed. 'It's not lasted long.'

'A house won't last up here if it's not looked after. Once the wind gets under the slates you can lose the roof in a winter. But it was hard up there, even for us. No proper road, and there were problems with the water in the summer.'

'How did you get to school?'

'Two miles' walk,' she said with a laugh, 'But they've closed the old school now. Eiluned has to travel six miles, but the minibus comes right up to Blaen-y-Cwm. And Gareth's away at agricultural college. He runs a car, when he can make it go.'

There was a clatter from the yard, the sound of Glyn Lewis's Land Rover. Then he was in the kitchen, a small, dark, wary-looking man, quick in his movements. He seemed a little younger than his wife, but there were shadows in his face. He looked momentarily taken aback to see me, then gave me a nod and spoke to her in Welsh. She answered and then said, 'Mr Jones has come for his keys.'

'It was very kind of you to move the car. I'd been wondering what had happened to it.'

'We just gave it a pull up the road. It was blocking the gateway. The keys were in the ignition.' He went to a drawer, took them out and laid them on the table in front of me.

There was a pause. The mug was still half full and I was trying to blow on the tea surreptitiously whilst taking quick and painful sips. My efforts led to an attack of hiccups. Gwen Lewis looked amused.

'I never got the chance to park it properly. I was trying to put the fire out, but it had too much of a hold. It's a pity about Ty Newydd. I was talking to Mr Mitchell this morning. They're very upset.'

'Maybe they'd have done better to stay in London,' Glyn Lewis said. I felt a flush of anger at his response and was going to answer him, but a hiccup intervened. Controversy was best avoided anyway. 'Well, thank you for the tea. And for looking after the car.' I took the keys from the table and went out into the sunshine.

Gwen Lewis followed me to the door. 'Don't mind Glyn,' she said quietly. 'He's fine when he gets to know people. We don't get enough visitors up here.'

Still hiccupping I retraced my steps to the end of the Tan-y Coed track where the Justy was parked. I managed to get the door to open, started the engine and was relieved to find it ran normally, but the car didn't look fit to drive so I walked back to the house and did some telephoning. The eventual result was a recovery vehicle, and it turned out that the firm's insurance included the provision of a courtesy car. I'd soon be back on the road.

Over the next few weeks there wasn't much chance to think about Bob Lord and the mystery he'd told me of. My Sales Director, as always a disembodied voice on the end of the phone, clearly expected me to make up for lost time and wasn't looking for a protracted convalescence. Moreover, the appetite of the local livestock seemed to have suddenly increased, and all the farmers wanted their orders attending to yesterday, or preferably the day before. The answering machine ran out of tape. The weekend disappeared along with the evenings, and the courtesy car's mileage had increased dramatically by the time I exchanged it for the renovated Justy.

When the phone rang late one evening I'd already got my work diary in my hand when I picked up the receiver. But it was Bob Lord's voice. 'Evening John. Business must be good. Your line's permanently engaged.'

'Everyone in the county ran out of concentrates while I was out of action. It's nice to talk about something else. How's the treasure hunt going? Any news?'

'Well now, things have moved a bit. I think I've tracked down the mysterious Thomas. Were you planning to be over this way in the next day or two? I could fill you in on what I've found.'

'I have to go to Llanarmon tomorrow. I could pinch a couple of hours.' We agreed I'd call the following afternoon.

I speculated enjoyably while driving along the Ceiriog Valley. Identifying the unknown Thomas might not help to locate the treasure now, but it could shed light on where it had come from and what it might consist of. It would be marvellous to make an actual discovery, but at present just the quest seemed enthralling enough. I was pleased and gratified that Bob had got back in touch; it meant he wanted me to work with him, and that I could be useful. At Llanarmon I actually refused a cup of tea. My chest was tingling a little as I drove up to the house on the hillside.

Bob offered me an almost colourless malt whisky from a prestigious looking bottle. Whisky wasn't really my drink but I accepted a small one, deciding I wouldn't be driving back for a while. Bob's ruddy face bore a broad grin; his eyes were sparkling and his eyebrows were all a-twitch.

'After you were here I wrote to Lord Berwyn. Asked if I could consult the archives at the house. He wrote straight back and more or less told me to help myself. I was a bit surprised, to be honest. But it's not easy working at Berwyn. There are shelves full of stuff, and an awful lot of boxes. It's in no sort of order, and it was pure luck I found anything at all. Practically everything's in English, thank God; Owain must have had a reason for keeping his journal in Welsh.

There's quite a bit of correspondence from Owain's time. Not on the mines, at least none that I've found so far. But he was in touch with a lot of people. There's a good deal on religious subjects. Owain seems to have been a died-in-the-wool traditionalist. You know, there's a story about him that once, during a particularly contentious sermon, he threw his prayer book at a puritan minister and knocked him clean out of the pulpit. He obviously had no time at all for the changes they were trying to make to the Church. And that's where Thomas Davies comes in.'

'So your Thomas wasn't a Morgan.'

'Not a blood relative, as far as I can see. More of a protégé. He seems to have been a clever lad, from a family that didn't have much money. There's a whole series of letters from him, thanking Owain for what he's done for him and responding to his advice. Owain evidently helped to pay for Thomas's education. He sent him to Oxford, to Jesus College, and he went into the Church. He evidently shared Owain's views on Church matters. Comes across as an out and out Laudian.'

Charles I's Archbishop of Canterbury, William Laud, had antagonised members of the puritan tendency by his love of ceremonial and supposedly popish practices, and had helped to provoke the unrest that led to the King's overthrow. It wasn't surprising that Owain and Thomas had been among Laud's supporters.

'So where was Thomas in 1649, when they took the treasure? Are there any letters that tell us?'

'There are indeed.' Bob was watching my face, taking his time. 'Back in 1641, when Laud was still in control, Thomas Davies went to London. Quite a desirable appointment. He was made a minor canon. Guess where.'

'Tell me.'

'Westminster Abbey.'

He was waiting for a reaction, and grinned broadly when it finally came.

After the reformation and the dissolution of the monasteries, Westminster Abbey had been pillaged like all the others. The glittering reliquaries and shrines were smashed and plundered, the gold and jewels that the faithful had contributed over centuries were carried off, the metal melted down, the sculptures broken and defaced, the relics ridiculed and thrown away. At Westminster the great shrine of St Edward the Confessor, last but one of the Saxon Kings of England, had suffered the fate of all the others.

But the Abbey held one treasure, one collection of ancient and precious things, that Henry VIII and his protestant successors would never destroy, because it was the source of their legitimacy, and ultimately their power. It was still there when Charles Stuart went to the block. But its symbolic force was too great for his murderers to allow it to remain.

'Westminster Abbey. Could they have tried to make off with the regalia - the crown jewels?'

Bob's eyes twinkled between the shaggy eyebrows and the half-moon spectacles. 'There were two sets of jewels, you know. One was kept in the Jewel House, at the Tower of London. That included the State Crown, the one the King wore on state occasions, and most of the more intrinsically valuable items, at least those that Charles hadn't already sold. But another set of regalia, much older, was kept at the Abbey. And those were the objects that were used for the coronation ceremony, all through the middle ages. I've been doing some reading. There was the original Crown of St Edward, which was used to crown the King. There were a couple of other crowns, several sceptres, a staff, a cup, a mantle and tunic, and various bits and pieces - things that had accumulated over the centuries.'

'But everything at the Abbey was seized by order of Parliament, and destroyed. There are detailed inventories made at the time. It would have been impossible for Thomas to make off with the regalia.'

'I've been having another look at the Journal.' Bob was speaking very deliberately, one finger raised for emphasis. 'That phrase 'trysor gwerth fawr'. I don't think it means a treasure in the sense of a collection of valuables. It means one precious item, one thing of great price. What was the single most precious thing kept at the Abbey? What would Owain have regarded as the object most worth saving, to hide away 'until the King shall come again'?'

'There's only one thing it could be.'

'Only one thing. Thomas Davies stole St Edward's Crown.'

For a while, neither of us spoke. 'It would fit in with Owain's description,' I said slowly, 'He obviously thought his 'treasure' was something of enormous significance. But how could he possibly have taken the Crown, of all things? Thomas could never have got away with it. Too many people would have known. And the parliamentarians would hardly have failed to notice it had gone.'

'Removing the Crown in the first place might not have been too difficult.' Bob was still holding his whisky glass, its contents untouched. 'It seems it was kept in a wooden box in the Abbey undercroft. I've been reading about how the regalia were seized. The Abbey had plenty of warning. In fact, the first time Parliament ordered the Dean to give them up he refused to hand them over, and the authorities at the Tower did the same. In the end the Parliamentary Commissioners actually broke in and took them by force. But that was several weeks later. There'd have been plenty of time to get them away to a safe place, and there must have been people willing to help Thomas if he needed it.'

'But the Commissioners would have found the box empty. That's not what the record says. The Crown was on the list of the things they seized. There's a published description: I remember reading it somewhere.'

'That's something of a problem. But couldn't they have been fooled in some way? The people who were sent to remove the regalia had almost certainly never seen them before. They wouldn't know what they were looking for. And the process of seizure was pretty chaotic, by all accounts. The chap in charge was a notorious republican called Henry Marten. He took along a mad poet by the name of George Wither, and when the box was opened they dressed him up in the mantle and the tunic, stuck the crown on his head, and sat and cheered while he pranced round the room.'

'So they did get their hands on a crown of some sort. If Thomas took St Edward's Crown and brought it to Owain, what was it that the Commissioners found?'

'Thomas and the people at the Abbey had several weeks to plan. Maybe they arranged some kind of substitution. There could have been a cover-up. There are more letters to look through at Berwyn. Maybe I can find a clue. But I can't believe that Owain would have regarded anything but the Crown as so important. And whatever they took, John, where did they put it? And where is it now?'

'Down a lead mine somewhere, if your theory's right,' I said. 'I'd like to get a look at the area. Just to get a general idea of the country. I've been part way up Cwm Llwyd, but I've never been up to the site of the old Morgan mines.'

'Why don't we go out there now?' Bob put his glass down; he hadn't touched a drop. 'We've time for a quick look. We can get fairly close in the Range Rover. I can show you what there is to see. It isn't much, apart from the slate.'

Bob took one of the steep roads back towards the Ceiriog, his big, capable hands guiding the bulky vehicle smoothly round the many blind bends along the way. I'm normally a reluctant passenger, but his driving inspired confidence and the high seat gave the opportunity to take my eyes off the road and see beyond the hedges. The weather was still clear, though the sun had gone and the sky was clouding over.

'Did you make it to Walton?' It was still hard to picture this tweed-jacketed figure, with his antiquarian interests, parking his Range Rover at the prison gate and socialising with the criminal classes.

'Oh yes. It's a good road these days, and I know the way well enough. I never miss a week. I think I mentioned, the chap I'm talking to at the moment is a pretty good historian. He got his degree last year, in History of Art. He's very interested in Owain Morgan.'

'Who is he?' This was disquieting. 'You haven't talked to him about the Crown?'

'Have you heard of Carl Quinn?'

The name sounded vaguely familiar, but I couldn't place it.

'He's been out of circulation for a while, but his name was in the papers back in the eighties. Quite a gangster in his time. Violent too. Master-minded a few robberies. But he's an intelligent man. I find him impressive. He seems genuinely penitent now about his past and the crimes he's committed.'

'He's probably just trying to get parole.'

'I've met quite a few criminals,' Bob said. 'I've been visiting getting on for twenty years. When they talk to you, a lot of them of them are wanting sympathy, or out to impress. Others just fantasise. I've heard plenty of sob stories, some of them true and others probably embroidered a bit. But when you get down to it most of them have had a rotten life, with no sort of stability and a lot of neglect and abuse. You have to feel sorry for them. And I don't believe anybody's wholly bad. You know what Shakespeare said:

"There is some soul of goodness in things evil,
Would men observingly distil it out.'"

I was taken aback by the quotation. 'If Quinn's so intelligent, he must have known he was doing wrong.'

'Carl doesn't make excuses for himself. He won't even tell me about his childhood. He says he accepts responsibility for what he did, and he's planning a different life when he comes out. I think he's sincere and so does the Governor, believe it or not. I've been seeing him for eighteen months. These days we mostly talk history. I've got him a lot of books. He's very knowledgeable. He's fascinated by the way that great works of art reflect the history of their time. I've told him all about Owain's journal, and when I was there yesterday I told him about Thomas's letters. He knows what I think.'

Mentioning the existence of buried treasure to a convicted criminal, however penitent, sounded like lunacy and I was tempted to say so. But I didn't know Bob that well, and it was his secret, not mine. I had to respect his sincerity. I remembered the books in his sitting room, published by the Society of Friends. If Bob was a Quaker, it wasn't for me to question his beliefs.

We were driving up a rather bleak valley now, with none of the lushness of the Vale of Llangollen or the hanging woodlands of the Ceiriog. The cliffs below Cadair Berwyn were visible ahead. I knew this bit of road: there was no habitation now at the head of the valley, but I'd often visited what was presumably the last farm, the property of a jovial old bachelor by the name of Cadwaladr Pugh. He used to order his feed a bag or two at a time and it was a long way to go for a tiny order, but he generally had the kettle on and I enjoyed his banter.

Bob drove through the gate of Cadwaladr's farm and switched off the engine. Cadwaladr was splitting logs, swinging the heavy axe over his head and bringing it down with unerring accuracy. He carried on until he'd finished the log he was working on, then leant on his axe and greeted us with a jerk of the head. His shape always fascinated me; he was almost completely square. Bob got out and they passed the time of day in Welsh.

The public road ended just past the farm, and Bob was asking permission to drive further up. A lot of people would have carried on without, but Bob was clearly punctilious about that sort of thing. I got out and said hello, and Cadwaladr's sharp blue eyes twinkled at me beneath shaggy white eyebrows. Instead of the flat tweed headgear preferred by most of his neighbours he was wearing a brightly coloured baseball cap with the insignia of the New York Yankees. 'I've plenty of chicken feed,' he said, 'You're not due for another month.'

'He's not here on business,' Bob said, 'It's his day off.'

'Every day's a day off for some people. He only comes out here for a cup of tea, you know.'

'He has a teabag with my name on it,' I told Bob, 'He uses it every time.'

Time was short if we were to reach the site of the mines, and we turned down Cadwaladr's offer to recycle the teabag. He gave us a cheery wave as we backed out of the gate. A quarter of a mile further on we drove across a cattle grid and were on an unfenced road, out in open country. The hillside ahead was split by a great cleft, with a long scree slope of slate waste fanning out below it. Higher up were other spoil heaps, some partly grass-covered but most still bare; it's a century or more before anything will grow on this shifting, sterile terrain. There were ruined buildings, and one gaunt stump of a chimney.

To many people the scars and remains left by the miners and the quarrymen are simply ugly, a despoliation of the landscape, but to me there's a romance, a poignancy about them. Many of the Welsh slate quarries aren't quarries at all but deep mines, extending far underground and often unbelievably vast in size and extent, and every yard was hewn out of the mountain by the pick, the drill and the hammer, and by charges of old-fashioned black powder. Generations of men had laboured there; a whole culture, with its music, its religion, its language, had flourished. Now the men were gone, but their legacy remained.

The road had a gravel surface, maintained no doubt to give access to the dark plantation of Sitka spruce that cloaked the higher hillside on our side of the valley. Presently it forked; the forest road climbed to the right, and the roughest of tracks descended steeply to the left and crossed the river by a ford. Bob pulled off the road.

'We'll walk from here. I don't want to plaster the car with mud.'

Evening was coming on, and a damp, chilly wind was blowing as we descended the track. I was trying to make sense of the mass of old workings opposite. 'A lot of what you can see is the result of the slate quarrying,' Bob said. 'It started here in the eighteen-seventies, and lasted well into this century. There's a big quarry opposite us, and another further up towards the head of the valley. They went pretty deep; you can see from the size of the heaps. But further down the valley they quarried the granite for roadstone, and on the tops there were potash mines. And before all that there was the lead.'

I remembered the geological map, with its confusion of colours. 'The geology must be incredibly complex. It reminds me of the hills above Llangynog, over in the Tanat Valley. There you've got slate and lead workings all mixed up together, and roadstone too. One of the inclines they built to take the slate down the mountain actually crosses the stope where they dug out the lead. And the old lead spoil heaps were mostly obliterated by the granite quarry.'

There were enough stones exposed in the river bed for us to cross the ford dry-shod; it was little more than a stream today, though it was clear from the rocks in its bed that it could turn into a torrent after rain. It seemed unlikely that anything of the seventeenth century lead mines could have survived the cataclysms of more recent times. Bob had brought a photocopy of part of the Morgan estate map that hung on his dining room wall, and was peering at it. 'This is hopeless,' he said, 'Whoever drew it probably never got off his horse. The lead mines seem to have been on this side of the valley, but that's about all it tells us. We should have brought the six inch.'

'I'm not sure it'd be much help. All this slate quarrying must have happened since it was made. The waste heaps have smothered everything, changed the contours. There can't be that much left.'

Beyond the river we hit an older track, long disused, which had clearly served the quarries. It took us to the foot of what had been an incline, where wagon loads of slates had once been lowered from the workings high above. We started to climb, our feet slithering and sliding in the loose slate which made a squeaky, metallic sound. Fortunately

I'd brought my boots. Bob climbed slowly, but he was no more out of breath than I was.

At the head of the incline was a broad shelf cut in the mountainside; in front of us was the stone housing which had once held the massive winch drum around which the steel cables had been wound. The long, rusting metal strip that had been the brake still lay there on the ground. Behind us the incline descended steeply, with great heaps of slate waste to left and right. Further along the shelf another incline climbed towards more slate workings, but above the point where we stood was natural hillside, covered in heather and last year's bracken.

'Those humps could be earlier spoil heaps,' said Bob dubiously, pointing to some ill-defined mounds higher up to the left. 'Or they could be natural.' We scrambled through the heather until we were standing on them. They were largely overgrown, but where erosion had taken place the ground was partly composed of a greyish-white, crystalline material. I kicked at it with the heel of my boot, and hacked out a few lumps.

'This isn't slate waste. There's a lot of quartz here. Of course you find veins of quartz among the slate, but there doesn't seem to be any slate at all in this heap. I don't think it's natural. It could well be spoil from a lead mine.'

Poking at the heap, I was doubtful whether it could be as old as Owain Morgan's time. Had there been any later attempts to find lead? It was hardly likely that no-one had tried, after the successes of the seventeenth century. We moved further across the mounds. The afternoon was becoming murky, and it was becoming hard to distinguish artificial features from natural ones. Ahead was another hump, and I climbed to the top of it. Beyond was a shallow hollow, with gently sloping sides and a sheer rock face rising at the back. Brambles and rushes were growing in the bottom, and there was a coil of rusty barbed wire.

Bob had joined me, and was walking down into the hollow. I didn't follow; there was something about the place that was ringing warning bells. He'd just reached the bottom when I realised what it was.

'Bob! Stand still. Stay where you are.'

He stopped, perplexed, looking back over his shoulder.

'Don't move.'

I walked carefully down the slope. Under his foot was a piece of rotten timber.

'Just take a step back.'

He did as he was told, and then said, 'My God. It's a shaft.'

The timber looked like the remains of boarding. Grass was growing on it, and the tangle of wire had probably been dumped there years ago to keep the sheep away. There were several dark holes among the grass and rushes. I knelt down cautiously, picked up a small stone and dropped it through one of the holes. There was silence for several seconds, and then a dull, echoing plop.

Bob looked thoughtful. 'I'd have made a bigger splash than that. Good thing you stopped me. This place is bloody dangerous.' It was the first time I'd heard him swear.

'This shaft couldn't possibly be seventeenth century. It would have fallen in long ago. But it's not like a slate quarry. Someone must have been looking for lead more recently, maybe in Victorian times. The shaft is pretty deep, but there's not much spoil around it. They can't have got very far tunnelling from the bottom.'

'Trial diggings, probably. But they must have thought this was the right place. Maybe there was more to be seen of the older mines in those days.'

It felt cold down in the hollow, and the gloom was gathering fast. As we walked back up to the top of the mound the wind was suddenly driving rain into our faces, ice-cold and stinging. It was hard to see our way down the steep hillside, and the grass was treacherous and slippery. We came to the incline and picked our way down sideways, the wet slate sliding away under our feet. The rain was coming down in sheets, blowing under my hood and trickling down my neck. Bob's Gore-Tex looked a lot more effective at keeping out the elements than my cheapo version from Welshpool Market; by the time we got to the bottom I was drenched to the skin.

It was growing dark when we reached the ford, but I saw something glinting in the water and picked it up. It was a small piece of rock, and I could make out little square crystals of a metallic colour. 'Galena,' I said, 'Lead ore. Probably washed down quite recently. Maybe we're not so far away.'

It was a relief to climb into the Range Rover and get the heater going. We drove back to Bob's with the wipers on double speed and the country just a blur through the streaming windows. Bob offered me a meal, but I said I'd better get back, find some dry clothes and see what was on the answerphone. He was going back to Berwyn next day to look at some more letters, and I promised to find out more about the mines in Cwm Llwyd, and see whether they'd ever been researched or explored. Then I drove back to Tan-y-Coed in the Justy, had a shower and listened to a series of resentful Welsh and Shropshire voices, talking reluctantly to a machine and implying that I should have been there in person.

But I couldn't stop thinking about the Crown. When I was little I'd spent hours with Auntie Annie's Pauline, regal at six and a half, dressing up as kings and queens. We'd only had one crown between us, cardboard covered with gold paper. Auntie had made us another one, but it was silver. I always wanted to wear the gold one. The memory kept coming back.

CHAPTER 4

Saturday morning came, and I felt I owed myself a weekend. WMEG were planning a descent into some particularly interesting workings out near Minera, and I'd rung the Potters, who were organising the trip, and got myself a place in the party. I was planning to pick a few brains; the Group had its own collection of mining journals and records, and there were several people who might know something about Cwm Llwyd. In any case, a day underground was an inviting prospect and I wouldn't be able to hear the phone.

I packed a duffel bag with a disreputable boiler suit, a belay belt, an old pair of boots, my battered helmet and lighting gear, locked the door and made my way up to the car. It was a blustery morning; the spring had been notably windy. As the Justy bumped across the bridge and up to the road I felt a pleasant thrill of anticipation. This was going to be a good day.

At the road I looked right, then left, and saw a horse. It was pelting along the lane towards me, reins flying, with no sign of a rider. It was still fifty yards or so away, and I had the sense to pull forward across the narrow lane till the front of the car was touching the hedge, blocking the road completely. The horse slowed, then slithered to a halt: bits of gravel spattered against the passenger door. I waited for a moment as the horse plunged about in the lane, then got out of the car, keeping the bonnet between myself and the animal, and stood there for a while trying to make soothing noises.

It was a pony, dark brown and shaggy. It looked familiar, and I remembered the Lewises' pony at Blaen-y-Cwm. It was starting backwards and forwards across the road, ears back, eyes rolling, its sides heaving. On its back was an empty saddle.

I edged warily round the front of the car. I've never had a lot to do with horses, but Sarah liked to ride and we sometimes used to go out for half a day from the stables at Glyn Ceiriog. They normally gave me one of their more geriatric animals; on one occasion it had actually lain down in the road, leaving me standing astride it in the stirrups. Sarah had commented on my ability to send anything to sleep.

The pony gradually calmed down a little and I moved closer, reached out and touched it tentatively and then hooked a finger round the reins. The first thing to do, if possible, was to get it off the road while I went to look for the rider. There was a field gate a little way down the lane, and I led the pony towards it; it had suddenly become quite docile. I unhooked the gate, tucked the reins over the saddle and persuaded the pony into the field. Confident now, I patted it reassuringly on the neck and it bit me in the arm.

I managed to get the gate shut and started walking along the lane, then thought the better of it and went back for the car. There was no knowing how far the pony had come. In the event I didn't have to drive far. I rounded the bend just before the blackened shell of Ty-Newydd, and saw an ominous little heap in the road. My heart came into my mouth.

As I braked there was a movement; a child's head was raised from the road, and I recognised Eiluned Lewis. When I reached her she was trying to sit up. Her plump little face was grazed and smeared with dirt, but she was wearing a hard hat which looked as if it had done its job. I knelt down, said 'Hallo' and asked her where it hurt. She said something in Welsh and then recognising a stranger, switched automatically to English and asked, 'Where's Seren?'

'I've put him in a field. He's all right.'

'It was that sheet.' Flapping in the hedge was a blue plastic tarpaulin. One like it had been tied over a surviving section of roof at one end of the Mitchells' cottage. The wind must have blown it off. 'It blew right over his head. He couldn't see.'

There was no sign of any major injury, but she was holding one wrist with the other hand and it looked as if it might be broken.

'Can you stand up?' She tried, wincing, and I helped her slowly to her feet. She was dazed, and a little tearful now.

I wondered what to do. The child obviously needed medical attention, but her home wasn't far away and it seemed best to let her parents see to things. 'You live at Blaen-y-Cwm, don't you?' I said, 'I think we'd better go and see your Mam.' I reversed into the Mitchells' gateway, helped her into the car and strapped her in. Then we set off back up the valley for the Lewises' farm. On the way we passed the field where I'd put the pony, and she seemed reassured to see him peacefully munching the grass.

Gwen Lewis was pegging out washing when we drove into the yard and came hurrying over, full of concern. Soon she had Eiluned sitting in the kitchen and was gently bathing her grazes and talking to her soothingly in Welsh. The little girl was obviously in pain, though she was being very brave about it.

Gwen switched languages. 'We need to get you to the hospital, and let a doctor have a look at that wrist.' She looked at me. 'I think I'll have to phone for an ambulance. Glyn's gone to Bala. He won't be back till teatime, and I've only got the tractor here. We can't take you on that, can we love?'

'I'll take you to the Orthopaedic,' I said, 'There's a casualty department. We can be there before an ambulance finds its way out here.' Gwen Lewis protested that they couldn't possibly let me, but I persisted and she gave way, clearly relieved. I asked if I could give Val Potter a quick ring and explain I wouldn't be turning up that day. Then we wrapped up Eiluned in a couple of blankets, put her in the back of the Justy with some chocolate to nibble, and set off for Oswestry.

Casualty at the Orthopaedic was cunningly concealed round the back, but we found it eventually. It wasn't long since I'd been back to the hospital to have my stitches out, and a plump, cheerful nurse on duty recognised me.

'Now then Mr Jones, have you had another roof fall on your head?'

'I'm just the ambulance driver.'

'He ought to have a blue light and a siren,' Eiluned said, evidently feeling better.

Eiluned trotted off obediently after the nurse, and Gwen Lewis and I were left sitting side by side. 'It's ever so kind of you,' she said. 'First bringing her home, and then driving us here. I'm afraid we've spoilt your day.'

'I wasn't doing anything vital. I'm just glad I was able to help. She's been very brave. It was quite a nasty fall, on the road.'

'She's a good rider. And she loves that pony. She doesn't get a lot of chance to play with other youngsters, living where we do. We're the only family with children now, in the valley. And it's difficult in emergencies.'

'But it's a wonderful place for children to grow up. She looks the picture of health.'

'And she's happy. We wouldn't have it any different. Glyn's family has farmed at Blaen-y-Cwm for four generations, you know. And Gareth wants to carry on, he's very keen. He can really handle sheep, and he's wonderful with a dog. He's won quite a few trials. Glyn doesn't say much, that's not his way, but he's really proud of him.'

The wait in casualty wasn't a long one - the football matches hadn't yet got under way - and Eiluned was soon back with a gleaming new plaster cast and a sling. The staff had made a fuss of her and given her pain killers, and on the way home she chattered excitedly for a while and then fell asleep. As we passed the field where I'd left the pony we stopped and removed the saddle and bridle; he didn't seem to be coming to any harm. Glyn would collect him when he got back.

It was mid-afternoon before we reached the huddle of buildings at the head of the valley. I refused Gwen Lewis's offer of a cup of tea, and drove back to Tan-y-Coed for a belated lunch. The day hadn't turned out as planned, but I wasn't really disappointed. At least I'd been useful to someone.

That evening I sat reading one of my collection of history books: I'd never been able to bring myself to sell the books I'd used at university, and instead kept adding to them. I wanted to get a feel of the Civil War period, of that time of boundless confusion when the King was in the Tower and the arguments raged about his fate; of the bitter January morning when he was led out onto the scaffold in Whitehall; of his last words, when he spoke of exchanging a corruptible crown for one that was incorruptible; of the chaotic time that followed, when new ideas were championed and old scores were settled. Lives were risked, and lives were lost; often it was largely a matter of chance which families were ruined, which houses burnt, which men of substance exiled or condemned. Owain Morgan had played a dangerous game.

I read a chapter or two, but I couldn't get engrossed as I usually did. There was something unsatisfying, irritating even, about the cool, academic prose. Something that day had unsettled me. I made myself a coffee, but it didn't help. There was a hollow feeling inside me, and it wasn't going to be filled by a mug of Maxwell House.

That warm, natural relationship between Gwen Lewis and Eiluned, the sense of domesticity and mutual affection that seemed to pervade the house at Blaen-y-Cwm, had hinted at a void in my own life. Or perhaps the void was somehow in me. I'd been happy to bury myself in this remote and delectable place. Its beauty and peace had been food enough for the spirit, my books and the firelight had given me companionship. But today I'd been reminded that it wasn't quite normal.

The parting from Sarah had been a bruising experience. Not that we'd had more rows; there'd been a weary acceptance that we'd come to the end of the road. You invest so much of yourself in a marriage. Picking it apart is a bleak business, a dreary round of dusty offices, of tense meetings where a life together is reduced to inventories and accounts. There's an overwhelming sense of failure and waste. And yet somehow the long term effects of the divorce had been less that they should have been. In a way I'd even welcomed being on my own. Maybe I was just too self-contained. Could it be that I wasn't really capable of a proper relationship? I knew Sarah had another partner now, but I wasn't exactly consumed with jealousy. Perhaps I should have been. Even my interest in caving might be unhealthy; crawling into holes in the ground, hiding myself away in the dark. Maybe it wasn't just my lifestyle that wasn't normal, but me.

A knock at the door interrupted this depressing train of thought. An unexpected visit was a rare event at the cottage; in fact I don't recall any caller finding his way to Tan-y-Coed without a sketch map and detailed route instructions. I opened the door to find Glyn Lewis standing a little awkwardly outside.

'Come in Mr Lewis,' I said, and he sat down by the fire, his eyes taking in the books on the table, the rocking chair and Sarah's patchwork cushions.

'I wanted to thank you. For helping Eiluned and Gwen today. The girl could have been there a long time before anyone found her. There's not much traffic on the road. And Gwen was on her own.'

'I just happened to be passing. How is she now?'

'Eiluned's tucked up in bed. She'll soon mend. She got treated promptly, thanks to you. And Seren's back home, none the worse. He's very steady, normally. But a sheet like that, blowing over his head, would make any horse take off. It was lucky Eiluned wasn't hurt worse.'

I offered him a drink, and he accepted a can of Wrexham Lager. 'You've made the place comfortable. I haven't been here for a long time. Not since old Edward Ellis owned it. He was born here and died here. That fellow Wallis bought it afterwards.'

'Didn't Edward Ellis have anyone to inherit?'

Glyn Lewis shook his head. 'Only cousins. He was a bachelor. We've had too many bachelors, round here. The work was too hard for them to think of anything else, I reckon.'

'It was lucky for me. I think it's a privilege to live here. It's a wonderful spot. And it's a good thing for the house to be permanently lived in, and looked after.'

Glyn's quick eyes focused on me, a little sceptically. I suddenly thought how at home he looked, sitting by the range, the firelight flickering over his dark, narrow face, the weathered hands folded on the knee of his old cord trousers. A man just like him had built this house, had sat where he sat now after a day on the mountain or a journey to a distant market, had perhaps fretted over an injured child.

He didn't reply, and the lack of response made me flounder on. 'At least the houses don't fall into ruin, when people move into the area. And it brings more customers to the shops, and the pubs. Even the holiday cottages bring business.' I was thinking of what he'd said about the Mitchells. It was something I'd have been happy to take up with him, but I felt guilty at raising it now, when he'd come to thank me.

'I won't quarrel with you,' Glyn Lewis said. 'It's a waste when houses are left to decay. And it's better to have a good neighbour than none. We don't dislike the English, how could we? My sister married an Englishman. But a lot of people like them better when they're in England.'

'That's absurd. They're the same people, wherever they are.'

He had tensed now, and there was an edge to his voice. 'It's not something you could ever understand.'

'Try me. It's something I've wanted to talk about. What gets into the people who try to burn the English out?'

'I won't answer for them,' Glyn said. 'There's only a handful, and they don't know what they're doing. They'll kill somebody before long. But I know why they do it. It's desperation.'

'What is there to be desperate about? The English who come here come because they love Wales. What harm do they do?'

'Some people destroy the things they love.' He was leaning forward, the dark eyes not leaving my face. 'Wales isn't just the scenery. Wales is the people, it's the culture, it's the language. Welsh is the oldest language in Europe, so they say, and the purest. It used to be spoken all over Britain, before the Saxons came. It's been spoken here for two thousand years, maybe three. Twenty years ago you would have heard it everywhere in these valleys. We still use it every day, Gwen and Eiluned and Gareth and me. When the children go to school the teachers use it, or try to. But every year we get more English families. We've had two more since September. When I pass the playground now, it's English I hear. We're losing the language, slowly but surely. And when a nation loses its language, it loses its soul.'

I was taken aback by the bitterness in his voice. 'But it's not just the incomers. People are more mobile. And there's television. A country can't cut itself off from the world.'

'Do you think I don't know that?' he said savagely. 'That's why the arson campaign's so bloody pointless. The young people, or the brightest of them, move away. There's little enough work here. Or they go away to study, and marry English girls or boys, like my sister did. Who'd want to stop them, even if they could? Then even if they move back, the language of the home is English. When the English miners came to South Wales, the language was lost in a generation. And now it's happening here.'

'A lot of English incomers are learning Welsh. There are evening classes everywhere.'

Glyn pulled a face. 'They can all say "Bore da." And some of them get further. They're intelligent people, graduates most of then, looking for the simple life. There's a fellow over at Llanarmon, a doctor of philosophy, who's set up as a chimney sweep. And as soon as they've settled in they all have to start doing good, setting up playgroups and civic societies and committees to preserve the Welsh countryside from the farmers.'

His tone had changed now; the tension had gone from his voice, and had been replaced by a sort of irony, self-parody even, as if he were mocking his own attitudes as well as those he was describing. Half of me felt offended by what he'd said, but I knew what he meant. Full of good intentions and untapped creativity, the English immigrants were apt to take over, antagonising the very people they thought they were helping whilst the native Welsh crept into their shell, hiding their resentment at their neighbours' tactlessness until, perhaps, it erupted to the surprise and distress of both sides. It wasn't just escapism that had made me come to Wales: I was happy to endure the winter as well as the summer, to work here as well as to relax. And I liked and admired the people, their warmth and spirit of community. But I would always be a guest here, and it behoved me to behave as one.

Glyn Lewis had put down his empty glass. 'We're a contrary lot. Here I am drinking your beer after you've taken my daughter to hospital, and I'm still complaining about the English. After today you're an honorary Welshman as far as I'm concerned. Just do me a favour, will you, and forget the 'Bore da', your accent's bloody awful.'

Glyn thanked me again warmly before he left, and suggested we drop the 'Mr'. What he'd said about the language stayed in my mind. I've always had a gut feeling that continuity and tradition are somehow important. I suppose it explains why I've always had a love of history, and why I've always hated the smooth-talking vandals who advocate bulldozing old buildings or desecrating ancient landscapes in the name of some sort of progress. Sarah once told me I was the sort of person who's irresistibly attracted to lost causes. I thought afterwards, all causes are lost if nobody's prepared to fight for them. Glyn's grief at the slow death of his language was something I could share.

That line of thought brought me back to the Crown. Whilst I'd set out that day to enjoy myself, I'd been intending to make a few inquiries about Cwm Llwyd. I suddenly felt frustrated at the day's lack of progress, at my failure so far to contribute anything to Bob's researches. It was time to show some initiative. The WMEG party should have got home by now, and I picked up the phone and rang Val Potter. When her cheery voice answered I apologised for my failure to show up that morning, and asked if I could come over to consult the WMEG library - if possible tomorrow. Yes, she said, after the day's exertions they were planning a quiet Sunday at home. So I arranged to turn up next morning and went to bed feeling more comfortable, and with my sense of anticipation restored.

CHAPTER 5

Val Potter and her husband Derek lived in Wrexham, in a big Victorian semi that extended almost as far upwards as it did backwards. It always seemed to be full of dogs, cats and teenagers; they never appeared quite sure which ones belonged to them. Val and Derek virtually were WMEG, at least as far as the admin was concerned, running off the group's magazine on a rickety duplicator and chivvying people like me for unpaid subs. One of their back bedrooms was the WMEG library: an impressive collection of largely nineteenth century books, maps and periodicals which members were allowed to consult on request.

When I rang the bell at 9.30 on Sunday morning there was a long delay. Val finally appeared after I'd thumped several times on the door. 'Sorry,' she said, 'I didn't hear you ring.' The reason was apparent, as the whole house was throbbing to the beat of heavy metal from somewhere on the top floor. 'That's Ben. He's into Megadeth.'

Val was cheerful and roly-poly, her shape emphasised by a predilection for horizontal stripes in primary colours. Surprisingly, it didn't stop her from squeezing through some tight spots underground. Derek came out of the kitchen, holding a piece of toast: he was wearing a frayed grey sweater which went with his beard. 'You missed a good day yesterday,' he said, 'It got a bit tricky, though. Too unstable. We had to bring them out in the end.'

'I don't know why we have some of those people,' Val said. 'There are always one or two who want to push on when it isn't safe. What can we do for you, John?'

'I want to find out about lead mining in Cwm Llwyd. I know it started very early, around 1600 I think, but I'm interested in finding out whether there were any later workings.'

'I think you'll find there were,' Derek said. 'Have a look through the Mining Journal volumes for the 1860's. There was a lot of activity in the Berwyn around then. I'd be surprised if they didn't have a go in Cwm Llwyd.'

Megadeth's exertions redoubled as Val led the way up several flights of stairs. She showed me into a room where rickety shelves groaned under the weight of rows of impressive Victorian tomes. Other volumes were piled up on the floor. 'We really ought to extend next door,' she said, 'But Ben likes it up here. He can make more noise.'

She left me to it, and I made a start on the Mining Journal. The heavy volumes were handsomely bound in dark blue buckram, close-printed and packed with detail. There was no effective index, and I found myself turning pages, trying to scan the headings for Welsh place names. All through the century mines were constantly being abandoned and reopened, and there was a period when the most shameless scams were perpetrated on gullible investors and tempting prospectuses gave glowing accounts of veins that had long since been worked out. I thought I was in for a lengthy hunt, but Derek as usual proved to know what he was talking about. In November, 1861 a prominent notice had been printed in the Journal:

'Reopening of the Cwm Llwyd Mine. Captain Charles Taylor, Engineer, has recently completed a Survey of land in the valley known as Cwm Llwyd, in the Berwyn Mountains. This land was formerly a part of the Berwyn Estate, owned by the celebrated family of Morgan, and lead ore, with an admixture of silver, was first discovered there in the reign of King James I. The mines were prosecuted successfully for upwards of thirty years, but were suspended in consequence of the exigencies of the time. Capt. Taylor has caused a trial level to be dug, and reports the existence of a vein of excellent lead ore some 30 inches in width.'

The notice went on to announce the formation of a company to exploit the find, and the issue of 2000 shares.

Turning the pages of this and subsequent volumes, I was able to build up a picture of the fortunes of the new Cwm Llwyd mine. At first things seemed promising. There was an enthusiastic report:

'Capt. Taylor is greatly pleased at the appearance of the lode lately discovered. A fine pile of ore has been taken out and is spread out at the surface for inspection. The lode promises to be highly argentiferous, and the silver content alone is likely to defray the cost of exploration.'

The optimism continued for several months, though actual figures for output were scarce. Then the miners struck a snag.

'At a meeting of the Committee of the Cwm Llwyd Mine the Engineer, Capt. Taylor, reported that a fault has been encountered and that the vein on this level has ceased. There are however strong indications that the vein continues at a lower level, and Capt. Taylor recommended that a winze be driven to a depth where the vein may be again encountered.'

The Engineer's recommendation was evidently accepted, and a substantial pocket of ore was found, yielding over 300 tons. But problems began again, the vein branching and fragmenting, and now consisting mainly of quartz. I could imagine the tension and frustration of the miners, hacking and chiselling by the light of a guttering candle, knowing that untold wealth might be concealed behind one last inch of rock. The lead miners were as much gamblers as the gold miners of the Klondyke, especially when mines might yield a significant content of silver as well as lead. There was always the temptation to push on a little further, to risk one more stake, to sink more good money in what might well prove to be a bottomless pit.

I'd become sufficiently absorbed to ignore what sounded like a pneumatic drill in the process of tunnelling its way through from the next room, and was startled when the door opened to reveal a gangling youth in a black tee shirt which bore a grinning death's head in fluorescent purple.

'Hallo,' he said politely. 'Is my music too loud?'

I said perhaps it was, a bit.

'Sorry. I'll turn it down.' He vanished, and the volume was reduced by a couple of decibels. I carried on turning the pages.

I was now on my fourth volume, and scanning a number of short reports I nearly missed the most significant entry: a brief note on the further progress of the Cwm Llwyd mine. One sentence leapt at me out of the page.

'The miners have now met the old people's workings.'

When Victorian miners spoke of 'the old people' or 'the old man', they were referring to their distant predecessors, often long forgotten. Coming across the old man could be a bitter disappointment, for it probably meant that the vein they were seeking had been exhausted centuries before. To the miner, the feeling must have been not unlike that felt by Scott and his men, struggling on to the Pole only to find the flag of Norway flapping in the breeze.

But for me the old people had a more exciting connotation. They could only be the miners who first explored Cwm Llwyd early in the seventeenth century on the Morgan family's behalf, who excavated the passages where Owain Morgan, if Bob Lord's theory held good, had concealed the Crown of England. Two hundred years later it seemed that some at least of those passages had still been in existence, and the Victorian miners had broken into them.

Leafing on through the next volume, the later history of the mine made depressing reading. The lead vein evidently proved elusive; there was more faulting, and it sounded as if they'd run into an area of solid slate. Statements by the company continued to be optimistic, and more money was raised to sink a shaft to try to locate the vein further along the hillside. The shaft was duly dug, but it must have been their final throw, for shortly afterwards both finance and optimism were exhausted. In 1868 a liquidator was appointed and the Journal contained an advertisement for the sale of the mine, along with all the moveable plant and machinery. Soon afterwards it was knocked down for a fraction of what had been spent on it. Whilst there wasn't time to do more than flip through the later volumes, there was no evidence that any significant work had been done after that date.

The research had been dusty and thirsty work, and I'd been grateful when Val had arrived with a mug of coffee and a sandwich. 'All part of the service,' she said. 'When people get up here they forget the time.' I'd had a worthwhile day, but one thing my researches hadn't shed light on was the actual location of the original Morgan mine. The most practicable way of entering the seventeenth century workings would probably be via the tunnels the Victorians had dug. The entrance to the later workings should surely be easier to find, and they ought to be better documented.

I tried to picture the slopes of Cwm Llwyd, scarred by centuries of mining. It was a reasonable assumption that the shaft I'd read about was the one Bob had nearly fallen into, but it had apparently been sunk some distance away and as the mine had closed soon afterwards it might never have linked up with the nineteenth century galleries, let alone the older ones. We needed to find the entrance to the Victorian mine. As long as it wasn't buried under mountains of waste slate.

I turned back to the earlier volumes, but there were no plans or geographical details. One other thing however caught my eye. It was a list of subscribers who had contributed towards the initial trials in 1861. Among them was one 'Wm Morgan, Gent.' As far as I knew the Morgans had sold the land earlier in the century, but clearly they'd retained an interest in its development. If William Morgan had been a subscriber, he would have received more detailed reports than appeared in the Mining Journal. Maybe some of them were preserved in the Berwyn archives.

I told Val and Derek what I'd found, though not why I'd been looking. Derek was quietly smug. 'I thought you'd find something in the Journal,' he said, sucking a bit of beard. 'I know my way around the Welsh references pretty well.' I asked whether WMEG might consider taking a look at the workings, but both of them were non-committal. The group had its schedule worked out months ahead, and there were more exciting places to explore than Cwm Llwyd. Still, they didn't say no, and I thought at some stage Bob and I were likely to need some help.

Back at Tan-y-Coed I rang Bob and told him what I'd discovered. He sounded excited at the news and pleased to be getting some assistance. He picked up my suggestion about the archives at once.

'If William Morgan was a shareholder in the mine, there could well be some reports at Berwyn. There's loads of stuff there from William's time, from the 1840's right through to the 1890's. He was the first Lord Berwyn of course, raised to the peerage in 1874. He had a finger in a lot of pies, and made a lot of money. I suppose he could have invested in Cwm Llwyd, though I doubt whether he'd have sunk a lot of cash in a dud mine. I'll see what I can find. By the way, have you ever heard of the Royalist Fellowship?'

I said I hadn't, and they sounded like a bunch of cranks. Bob chuckled down the phone. 'Maybe they are. They're some sort of splinter group from the Monarchist League. But their Secretary is apparently a leading expert on the crown jewels of Europe. I've written to him. I'd like to find out more about what we're looking for.'

We agreed to meet later in the week to compare notes and plan the next stage of the quest. And all that evening I thought pleasurable thoughts and dreamed pleasurable dreams. Somewhere beneath the mountains, in a dark tunnel, lay an artefact of glittering gold, ancient and beautiful, untarnished by time. I imagined the moment of discovery: saw myself reaching out at last to take it in my hands. But the next day disaster struck, and treasure hunting had to take a back seat.

CHAPTER 6

During the 1980s and into the 90s the livestock industry had been increasingly troubled by a mysterious affliction known as BSE, or mad cow disease, which had infected a large proportion of the national herd. For years the government, the feedstuffs manufacturers and the farmers had maintained that there was no evidence of any link between this and a related condition called CJD which affected humans and was invariably fatal. I'd listened to the experts, and seen no reason to disbelieve them.

That morning, when I arrived at a farm near Llanfair Caereinion which produced first class Welsh beef, I was confronted by a furious farmer who asked if I'd heard the news. I hadn't so he marched me into his kitchen, where the radio was just giving the ten o'clock summary. A government spokesman was saying that it was now considered 'most probable' that a link existed, and that the new strain of CJD derived in some way from eating meat infected with BSE. As it was almost certain that BSE had in its turn been communicated to cattle by feedstuffs containing animal offal, and that that offal had been contaminated with a similar disease affecting sheep, the feedstuffs manufacturers were in big trouble. I was their local representative.

The farmer, normally the soul of good humour, was almost incoherent with anger and anxiety, directed inevitably at me. His herd was not just his livelihood but his pride and joy, the product of a lifetime's labour and good husbandry. It was mainly grass fed, but he'd bought our products from time to time to supplement the grazing and I remembered him pressing me to tell him precisely what they contained. That of course was a commercial secret; I didn't even know myself. The farmer was an intelligent man; he could foresee a potential disaster.

Such reassurance as I could offer sounded pretty thin, and I got away as soon as I could and tried to ring head office. The line was permanently engaged. No doubt every Area Manager in the country, and a fair proportion of their clients, were trying to get through at once. When I finally got a reply towards evening my boss wasn't available, and a harassed secretary said they'd ring me back.

Back home the answering machine relayed a succession of angry messages. Quite a few of my customers had had BSE in their herds at some time, especially the dairy farmers. They all had questions I couldn't answer. I turned on the radio and listened to a succession of shifty politicians saying it was nobody's fault, or if it was it wasn't theirs. The fact that the government had relaxed the regulations a few years before and ended the requirement for high-temperature treatment of the feed was glossed over or ignored.

My firm never did get back to me that evening, probably because my own line was busy with farmers ringing me. When I finally got through next day they said that the company had decided to come clean; our feed had contained not just sheep products but meal derived from cattle bone and offal, much of it quite possibly infected with BSE. We had been turning vegetarian animals into carnivores, even cannibals, in the name of efficiency, productivity or whatever. In fact the use of the more questionable ingredients had been discontinued some time ago, and it was emphasised that we should stress the total purity of our current product range. The damage, however, had been done.

I had to ring Bob Lord and put our meeting off until further notice. There wasn't time to think about the quest we were engaged in, let alone talk about it. After a couple of days all the A.M.'s were summoned to an urgent meeting at head office; the message from the Sales Director was upbeat, but the mood in the coffee breaks was despondent. Some of our competitors were already laying off staff.

We were each given a pile of newly printed, glossy brochures full of impressive statements from ministers, scientists and vets and illustrated by reassuring looking graphs and charts. It was our job to visit our customers in person and distribute them. The task proved a thankless one. At the first farm on my list I was met by a youth of about eleven, perched on an enormous tractor. When I introduced myself as the Area Manager the lad turned his head and yelled, 'Dad! It's the feed rep.'

A voice came from a nearby shed. 'Tell him to bugger off.'

'Dad says you can bugger off,' the child repeated happily.

I was already on my way.

The temperature of my reception on other calls over the next few days varied from cool to sub-glacial. I persevered, assuring sceptical farmers of the firm's determination, which was almost certainly genuine, to clean up its act. Most of them heard me out, though I doubt if the glossy brochure got more than a glance. After the days' visits I spent whole evenings on the phone. But orders had slowed to a trickle. Even if our customers had been disposed to buy their cash flow didn't permit it. Cattle sales had slumped and prices were ruinously low. Even the dairy farmers, who had to go on buying something, seemed to be switching to other sources of supply.

It was three weeks before the next summons to head office. I'd expected it earlier. Ominously, they asked me to bring all my files with me. When I arrived, the Sales Director's secretary gave me a sympathetic smile. The Sales Director was sympathetic too, up to a point. The firm had to retrench, he said, to restructure, to downsize in order to face the leaner times ahead. Sadly, it could no longer afford so many Area Managers. I'd done quite well, very well in fact, but my Area with its many small farms had always produced too many small orders to be viable in the current climate. They appreciated my help with computerisation, but that would have to be shelved, of course. They wanted to make the changes with the minimum delay. He was sure that I would understand.

They were more generous than they might have been and offered two months salary in lieu of notice. I hadn't been with them long enough to qualify for a lot of redundancy pay, but they gave me the option of taking the Justy instead. I did a quick calculation and accepted it. I didn't know how long I'd be able to afford to run it, but life at Tan-y-Coed without transport would have been impossible.

I should have felt gutted. I'd made a decent fist of the job, and now I'd been blown away by forces way beyond my control. But driving back along the M54 I felt an odd kind of freedom. The future was an unknown quantity, but the present suddenly looked more attractive. I'd managed to save a little, and wouldn't be on the bread line for a while. I wasn't a bad salesman - maybe it was because I didn't push too hard - and I was reasonably confident of my own ability to find another job. Meanwhile my time was my own, and I didn't have to go on hawking my brochures round increasingly hostile farmers.

There was only one message on the answering machine when I got back to Tan-y-Coed that evening. Later it dawned on me that my customers must have had a letter that morning from the firm telling them of the new arrangements. The farmers had learned of my departure before I did. But it was good to hear the voice of Bob Lord on the tape. 'Hallo John. Hope the dust has started to settle. If you've got time, there are a few things I'd like to talk through with you. I found something at Berwyn. And I wanted you to know I've decided it's time for us to go public on the Crown. Can you ring me when you get back? Don't worry if it's late.'

It was late, but I rang Bob straight away, and told him about the sudden increase in my free time. His sympathy was warm and genuine, but I said I was looking on the bright side. He would be out the following afternoon, so we arranged I'd drive over to see him in the evening. I went to bed, and slept till lunchtime.

I got to Llangollen a little early, and stopped in the town to buy a few essentials. The place was full of posters in Welsh, advertising some kind of rally. Llangollen's a sleepy sort of place for much of the year, though it awakes from its torpor for a week or two in the summer when the International Musical Eisteddfod brings exotic visitors from all around the globe. It's one of the biggest gatherings of choirs and folk dance groups in the world, and thousands come to watch and listen as well as to compete. The presence of the Eisteddfod Pavilion means that the town hosts a variety of gatherings at other times, and they're trying to build up the conference trade.

The streets in Llangollen are a mixture of down to earth butchers and ironmongers for the locals and twee little giftie shops for the visitors. Ignoring the latter I soon had what I needed, and wandered down the main street to the bridge over the Dee. The bridge has deep cutwaters projecting into the river, and it's a pleasant place to stand and watch the canoeists tackling the rapids below. I was surprised to see Glyn Lewis there, leaning over the parapet in conversation with a bearded man I didn't know. As I drew level he turned and saw me and gave me a grin.

'Do you feel safe here today, then, with the whole town full of savage Celts.'

'Are you here for the rally?'

'What else would I be doing in Llangollen? We're all here trying to save the language. We've certainly generated plenty of it this afternoon.' He leaned forward conspiratorially and put a finger to his lips. 'Trouble is, the main speaker's from Swansea. We can hardly understand a word he says.'

We chatted for a few minutes, inevitably about BSE among other things. Fortunately Glyn had never been one of my customers: in fact I don't think he ever bought concentrates, though he had a few cattle and would be affected by the disaster like everybody else. The other chap listened but didn't say much, and Glyn didn't introduce us. Eventually they set off back towards the Pavilion, and I headed for my car and drove up to Bob's house above the town.

I lost a wing mirror on the way up. It wasn't my fault, though the lady who lost hers when the two of them made contact on a particularly narrow bit of lane evidently thought it was. Not a local from her accent, and certainly not used to local roads. It didn't seem politic to tell her she could have been a yard further in, and that I'd been driving at a perfectly reasonable speed. Hers was a rather expensive wing mirror, attached to a rather expensive car, and she might have been less affronted if it had come into contact with a better class of vehicle. We exchanged the usual details and I drove on, thinking that a sense of proportion is a useful thing to have.

It was good to sit and talk at leisure after the frantic and futile activity of the last few weeks. Bob's slow, borderland voice was reassuring; his big, freckled hands poured bottled beer into a well polished silver tankard with the same assurance and precision with which they handled the wheel of the Range Rover. He made me tell him about the implications of the crisis, for the farmers and for me, and it was good to talk to someone who wasn't immediately affected. The way he listened encouraged you to keep talking. Maybe that was the way some of the prison inmates felt. I drank deeply from the tankard, and felt myself unwind.

At last we got down to the topic we'd planned to discuss. 'Your suggestion about the mine reports was very useful,' Bob said. 'It gave me something to look for. I'd spent days at Berwyn, mainly looking through earlier stuff. A lot of it was fascinating, but it wasn't getting me anywhere.

I started on the nineteenth century documents, at least they were easier to decipher. The problem is the quantity: old William Morgan was involved in virtually every project, public and private, in Montgomeryshire for half a century. He was an MP for fifteen years, he was Chairman of the County Council, and he was also overly fond of going to law. As a result he accumulated vast amounts of paper which he never threw away. After days of wading through it I finally located some mining reports in a box along with a stack of railway company prospectuses. And I think I struck gold - or rather lead.'

Bob fetched the big deed box in which he kept everything related to the Crown, and dug out a sheet onto which he'd transcribed several sentences in his neat, old-fashioned handwriting. Then he settled his glasses on his nose. 'I found a printed report from Charles Taylor, the mining engineer, to the Committee and shareholders of the Cwm Llwyd Mine in 1867. Obviously it came to William Morgan, as a subscriber.'

'Just what we wanted,' I said. 'Is there a plan?'

'There's no plan. But he's arguing for the construction of a shaft, presumably the one we found. The interesting bit's here. He says: "I respectfully submit to the Committee that consideration be given to the sinking of a shaft, which I am confident will intersect the Great Lode at a lower level, and that the Lode will again prove to be highly productive of good quality ore."'

'Was there any indication of where the shaft was to be sunk, relative to the other workings? Working back, it could give us an idea of where the main entrance was. And it would be useful to know whether the shaft ever linked up with the rest of the mine.'

'Taylor doesn't say anything here about the position of the shaft. And so far there's nothing to pin-point the entrance to the mine. But having found one report, I'd expect to find more in the other boxes. It's a start. I'm still less than half way through.'

I'd hoped for more, but as he said it was a start. 'Look, if we can get a rough guide to the position of the entrance it shouldn't be difficult to locate it. There'd be spoil heaps. With a day or two's digging we could well find the level. Alternatively we could try the shaft. I could probably get a few people to help, WMEG members who've done this sort of thing before. We don't have to tell them just what it is we're looking for. Why don't we give it a try?'

He gave me a friendly but sceptical smile. 'We'll have to get a team together eventually. And your WMEG people could be very useful. But first we have to put the whole project on a proper footing. We need to get a reputable organisation involved, with some academic experts and maybe some official funding. I'd like some advice on interpreting the documents, especially the ones in Welsh. It's time to go public. I'd always intended to publish something in writing, but I think we should speed things up a bit. Tomorrow afternoon there's a Members' Meeting of the Powysland Club. I'm going to report on our discoveries and see if we can set up a committee to oversee the project. I'd like to propose you as a member.'

My heart sank. The Powysland Club, for all its quaint title, is one of the oldest and most prestigious of antiquarian societies and has been charting the history of Montgomeryshire for well over a century. It would certainly have some very expert people in its ranks. But the idea of handing the search over to a committee was profoundly unappealing, and once the press got hold of the story, which it inevitably would, every treasure hunter in Britain would be making a beeline for Cwm Llwyd.

'Bob,' I said, 'Committees are a hopeless way of getting things done. The story will be all over the papers, and while we're arguing about who's going to take the minutes the whole valley will be swarming with cowboys waving metal detectors.'

'If we start poking about down there on our own we'll be no better than cowboys ourselves,' Bob said stubbornly. 'We have to have proper backing. I think we should inform the County Archaeological Service too, and maybe the Welsh Office.'

'I think the first need is for security. The fewer people who know the Crown could be hidden in the Cwm Llwyd mine, the better. We're not ready to publish: we need to do more research, in the records and on the ground. So far all we have is a theory, there's no real evidence. And if the Crown is found, you should be the one to find it.'

'That's just what Carl said,' Bob said with a grin. 'He got quite heated about it. Said I should keep it quiet and go and look for it myself, and then get the credit. Ridiculous idea: I wouldn't have a clue what to do down a mine, and I'm not bothered about the credit.'

'You mean you're still telling Carl Quinn what's going on?' I wanted to shake him.

'I keep him in the picture. I see him every week, as you know. I was at Walton on Tuesday, and told him I was going to spill the beans tomorrow. He kept saying I'd regret it. But I told him my mind was made up. There are right ways and wrong ways of going about things. I'm doing this the right way.'

I opened my mouth to protest further, and then closed it again. Bob's calm assurance was impervious to argument, and there was no point in trying to dissuade him. His serenity, his total conviction that he was doing the right thing, were quite unshakeable. And after all, it was his discovery. So instead we talked about how Bob's committee might proceed. I argued strongly against referring to Cwm Llwyd by name in an open meeting and he saw the sense of that, though obviously other people would soon have to know. We discussed the techniques, and the dangers, of underground exploration, and I stressed the need to involve experienced people. And later, talk turned to Owain Morgan, to his courage and his loyalty. All these were things we could agree on.

Bob provided supper, with cold roast pork and a hunk of Stilton cheese. As we crossed the hall on our way back from the dining room he opened the front door and we stepped outside for a moment into the darkness. It was a cold, clear night and the lights of Llangollen twinkled far below. 'I always like to come out for a bit in the evenings, when it's clear,' Bob said, 'I like to see the stars.' The Plough was unmistakable, arching far across the sky over the dark outline of the crags above Eglwyseg and the hills around the Horseshoe Pass. 'They always make me think that Creation's an incredibly wonderful thing. On a night like this you can marvel at it and still feel part of it. Do you know Meredith?' And he quoted:

"Not frosty lamps illumining dead space,
Not distant aliens, not senseless powers.
The fire is in them whereof we are born."'

We stood there for a while until the chill began to penetrate, and then went back into the warmth of the sitting room. The doors of the woodburner were open, and there was a comforting glow.

'Bob,' I said, 'Could I ask you a personal question?'

He smiled at me. 'Go ahead.'

'Are you a Quaker? I was looking at your books. Some of the titles...'

'I go to Meeting most weeks. But I don't know if that makes me a Quaker. The Friends are a pretty flexible lot, theologically speaking. Actually, if I'm anything I'm a Unitarian. They're a bit like Quakers with hymns. I like a good sing, the Welsh hymns especially, and the Friends' Meetings are a bit too subdued for me. But there aren't many Unitarians around these days. I go over to Shrewsbury sometimes, to chapel: we're trying to keep the witness alive, but we're a bit thin on the ground.'

'I know the Quakers have always been involved with penal reform. Was that how you got into prison visiting?'

'I suppose it was. I know other Friends who do it, though of course we're not the only ones. But a lot of us believe that it's wrong to write people off, whatever they've done. It's not a question of being soft, or sentimental. You just have to acknowledge that human beings can change. All that stuff about original sin is pernicious nonsense. There's always got to be the possibility of redemption.'

'Do you really think you can redeem Carl Quinn?'

He laughed. 'I can't redeem anybody. That's up to Carl, and his Maker. I'm sure he's capable of being redeemed; he has to be. But I'm not going to Walton to convert people. It's enough to offer some human contact, with people who aren't other cons. It's good that they know other people are still prepared to accept them if they'll make the effort. And at the same time I'm interested in listening to them, trying to make out how they came to be where they are. It's like history: you try to reconcile cause and effect, even if you don't always succeed. You want to know why, and how. And so often, when you talk to prisoners, you find their present is largely a result of their past.'

'What was it in Quinn's past that made him turn criminal? You said he's a highly intelligent man. What turned him into a gangster? Why is he in Walton?'

Bob spread his hands in a gesture of frustration. 'Carl's past is buried very deep. Like Owain's treasure. It's one of the things he won't talk about. He says he's done with it. He'll delve into other people's history, but not his own. That's something I've had to accept. But it just makes me all the more convinced that there's a secret there somewhere, maybe some experience he's suppressing, something that made him want to take his revenge on society. We had a minister once, at chapel, who always used to quote AE:

"In the lost boyhood of Judas
Christ was betrayed.""

'Couldn't Judas have been born that way?'

'I don't know. Perhaps there really are a few people who are born wicked, just as some people are born blind. We can't rule it out. But I don't think it applies to most of the criminals I've known. Many of them had the most appalling lives as children. And if people can be influenced for evil, then it ought to be possible to influence them for good.'

I was impressed by Bob's sincerity. But it has occurred to me since that, even if Judas's childhood experiences really had been the source of his wickedness, the personal influence of Christ Himself had not been enough to cure it.

Before I left the talk came back to the Crown, and I asked Bob if he'd got anything useful out of the Royalist Fellowship. 'Good Lord, I forgot to tell you' he said, 'I met their Hon. Sec. - Hon. everything else too, I shouldn't wonder. Strange fellow. Calls himself Charles Angevin Greene. He certainly knows all there is to know about crowns. He was pretty sceptical to start with, but I think I convinced him there might be something in my ideas. I had a letter from him yesterday. He's been doing some research of his own, and wants to come up and see me. You can come and meet him if you like.'

I said I would, and Bob promised to ring me after the Powysland meeting to let me know what had transpired. It was well after midnight when I finally left. He shook my hand warmly on the threshold, and wished me luck with my hunt for a new job. Most of the lights in Llangollen had been extinguished, and the houses down in the Vale were in darkness. Bob stood in a pool of light on the steps in front of the long, black shape of the house, one hand raised, as I set off down the drive between the silent trees.

CHAPTER 7

I slept in again next morning, and reflected that I was getting into a pattern of late nights and late mornings. You need something, or someone, to get up for. Washing up after a sort of brunch I switched on the radio and got the news. There was still plenty about the BSE crisis, which had suddenly become less relevant. Then an item made me take notice. There had been another suspected arson attack in North Wales, the newsreader said. It was feared there had been at least one fatality. The house had been in the hills above Llangollen.

There were plenty of houses around Llangollen, but I suddenly wanted to be sure. I went to the phone and rang Bob's number. A continuous note came down the line. The number was unobtainable.

I could have done more telephoning, but I didn't know who to ring. After a moment of indecision I went out to the car and set straight off for Llangollen. I took the shorter but tortuous route over the mountains, driving it at a speed Bob would have strongly disapproved of. Even so, it seemed to take forever.

I knew well before I reached the house. Driving up the road I passed a fire engine coming down the other way. There was a thin haze of smoke hanging above the trees where the house stood. Swinging into the drive I noticed marks of heavy wheels in the gravel: something had caught one of the gateposts and pushed the stones out of alignment, and on the other post somebody had sprayed a symbol, a sort of loop with an arrow on the end. There was more scrawl on the gate.

The house was a pitiful sight. Most of the roof had gone, and charred timbers pointed to the sky. There were great black stains on the walls above the windows. The fire was out, but the stench of burning still filled the air.

A police car was parked on the terrace, but there was no sign of its occupants. I went up to the front door, the remains of which were hanging open, and looked inside. The staircase and ceiling were partly burned away, and water was dripping from the blackened woodwork onto the sodden remnants of the carpet.

I stepped through the doorway, picked my way between the puddles and bits of charred debris, and walked through into the big sitting room where Bob and I had sat the evening before drinking brown ale and talking the night away. All was devastation.

Somebody must be around, somebody who would know what had happened to Bob. I was drawing breath to shout when a face appeared in the gaping hole where the window had been and said: 'What do you think you're doing? Come out of there at once!' I stepped out through the vanished window and recognised Detective Inspector Humphreys. At the same moment he recognised me.

'What the hell are you doing here?'

'Where's Bob Lord? What happened to him?'

'How did you get in?' He turned and shouted 'Edwards!' A uniformed constable appeared out of the shrubbery, doing up his trousers.

'Sorry sir. Call of nature.'

'What's happened to Bob Lord?'

'How did you know Mr Lord?'

'Just answer!' I blazed at him, suddenly furious.

Humphreys looked taken aback. 'The firemen got him out. But he was dead on arrival at hospital. Effects of smoke. Nothing they could do.'

I felt utterly sickened. How could a good man's life be wasted like this, his home and work destroyed? I wanted to ask more, but at that moment another car came bumping up the drive and disgorged one man with a camera and another with a notebook. 'More bloody reporters,' said Humphreys. 'We've had two film crews already.' Another policeman in plain clothes had materialised, and was sent to deal with the press. Then a van marked 'Police' arrived with various technicians in overalls. 'Don't go away,' Humphreys said and went off to speak to them.

I wandered over to the balustrade overlooking the valley and sat on it. My mind was starting to clear. The radio news had said that arson was suspected. The assumption would be that extremists were behind it. Maybe they were. Or possibly there was another explanation. Connected with the Crown. And somebody in Walton Gaol.

Thinking of the Crown brought something to mind. I stood up and walked back across to the window. The technicians were still unloading their van, and Constable Edwards was being engaged in conversation by one of the reporters. What had happened to the documents Bob had collected relating to the Crown? They'd been in a fireproof deed box. It was large and bulky, and shouldn't be hard to find.

I stepped back into the gutted sitting room. Last night the box had been between the chairs where we had sat. Today it wasn't there.

Bob had kept the box in the study, and would probably have put it back there. I'd reached the door when I was stopped by the exasperated voice of Detective Inspector Humphreys. 'Will you come out of there? You've been told once. If you touch any evidence you'll find yourself arrested for obstructing the police.'

He marched me out of the house and along the terrace into a sort of summerhouse where he seemed to have set up shop. There he made me sit down in a garden chair, and planted himself between me and the door.

'Right Mr Jones. You seem to make a habit of turning up at the scene of the crime. Just what is your connection with this?'

'Bob Lord was a friend of mine. I heard on the news there'd been a fire, I came over to see if it was here.'

'Lots of houses round Llangollen. Why should you think it was your friend's?'

'There was no reply on the phone. I thought he might be at risk.'

There was a pause. 'I think we'd better ask you to make a proper statement', Humphreys said finally. 'I'll get Sergeant Pritchard to look after you for a while, if you don't mind. Just in case you feel like wandering about.'

He called the other detective over and gave him some muttered instructions, and Sergeant Pritchard and I spent the best part of half an hour sitting in the summerhouse. He was a heavily built man with an extra chin and a surly expression, and when I tried to get him to tell me more about what had happened he deliberately ignored my questions. He spent a lot of the time with his back turned so I couldn't see he was picking his nose; presumably he didn't realise he was reflected in the window. I hadn't yet mentioned my visit to Bob's house the night before, and decided I'd save it for Humphreys. Meanwhile activity continued outside, with vehicles coming and going and making deep gouges in the once immaculate lawn. The house with its garden, that had fitted so perfectly into its natural surroundings and yet had been so orderly and tranquil, had seemed a perfect reflection of its owner. Now it was desecrated and defiled.

I sat there, waiting. Humphreys and the overalls were inside the house. Across the terrace a radio was crackling in a police car. Constable Edwards was sitting in it, talking into a microphone. Eventually he got out, holding a piece of paper. He was looking at it as he sauntered towards the house, and almost walked into the Justy which was still parked rather untidily where I'd left it. He did a sort of double take and hurried on inside.

Shortly afterwards Humphreys emerged and came over to the summerhouse.

'Would you like that statement now?'

He didn't respond to the question. 'Have you had another accident recently, by any chance?'

I gaped at him. 'What accident?'

'You were reported last night. Careless driving, allegedly. A lady came in with a car number. Your number. I see you've lost a mirror.'

'That's ridiculous. She was on the wrong side of the road.'

'So you don't deny that you were there.'

'Of course not. But I certainly wasn't driving carelessly.'

'It's not your driving we're concerned about,' Humphreys said. 'The accident took place last evening, just down the road. Would you mind telling us what you were doing?'

'I was coming here. To see Bob.'

'And did you see him?'

'Yes. I was here all evening.'

'Were you? What time did you leave?'

'After midnight. Half past, maybe.'

'Was anyone else present?'

'No.'

'Why didn't you say this before?'

'I was going to,' I said, exasperated. 'I haven't had the opportunity yet.'

'You had the last half hour didn't you?' Pritchard asked, aggressively.

'Look, I want to help. Just give me the chance, all right? I'll tell you everything I know.'

'I think we'll take your statement at the station,' Humphreys said.

He and Pritchard accompanied me to a police car. I pointed to my own, and was told I could collect it later. Pritchard opened the car door, pushing my head none too gently below the door frame as I got in. 'We wouldn't want you to bump it now, would we?' he said when I objected.

They took me to an interview room at Llangollen Police Station, a grim little hole with three chairs and a stained and battered table, and Pritchard switched an a tape recorder and announced the date, the time and the names of the persons present. He pronounced mine like something insanitary. Then Humphreys asked a long catalogue of questions: how I'd come to know Bob, how often I'd visited him, and what we talked about. There was nothing to be gained by being secretive with the police and I told them about Bob's theories and our belief that the Crown of England lay buried somewhere beneath a Welsh hillside. Humphreys cocked an eyebrow, and Pritchard didn't bother to hide a grin.

I soldiered on, describing our discussions and Bob's intention to reveal the secret. During the interview the door opened and another man came in. I recognised him as Humphreys' companion at the hospital: the one with the moustache who had sat there and said nothing. They didn't announce his presence on the tape.

When the questioning got as far as the previous day, Humphreys wanted to know precisely where I'd been before visiting Bob. I told him I'd been in bed most of the morning, and mentioned my stop in Llangollen. Then he took me through my conversation with Bob in detail. He asked me again what time I'd left, and whether I'd met anyone on the road and if anyone had seen me arriving home. I said no to both questions; the countryside was pretty deserted by that time, and I lived alone. He wanted to know how I'd spent that morning, and I said I'd got up late. 'You spend a lot of time in bed, Mr Jones,' Humphreys observed.

The interview took a long time, and they'd had to change the tape once before they finally turned it off. 'Look,' I said. 'I've answered all your questions, which no doubt you have to ask. If you think I burned Bob's house down, I'm afraid you're mistaken. Somebody murdered him, and maybe you should be trying to find out who.'

'That's what we're doing,' Pritchard said. 'Funny coincidence isn't it, you turning up at two arson incidents in succession.'

Humphreys took up the theme, his Welsh lilt particularly strong. 'When I was a young detective, I was always taught to be suspicious about coincidences. Look for the link, they said. At the moment, the link seems to be you.'

'This is getting us nowhere. Why should I want to burn Bob's house down? As far as I can see there are two parties who might conceivably have had a reason for setting fire to the house, apart from some passing drunk. One's more likely than the other. Neither of them includes me.'

'Two parties?' Humphreys' eyebrow went up again. 'I'd have thought one alternative suspect was enough. Who are the two?'

'Presumably you're looking for some sort of terrorist group. There was a symbol sprayed on the gatepost, and something written on the gate.'

'Observant, aren't you?' Pritchard said.

'I've seen the symbol before. Though not round here.'

'Meibion Llewelyn,' Humphreys said, 'Sons of Llewelyn the Last. We haven't heard from them in a long while. Maybe they've got some new blood.'

'I don't believe a Welsh separatist group would have attacked Bob's house,' I said. 'The spraying could have been a blind. It wasn't a holiday cottage. Bob was well known around Llangollen. And up to now, the terrorists have only attacked empty properties.'

'Sometimes they get careless. It wouldn't be the first time they burned down the wrong house. Mr Lord's office was fire-bombed a few years ago. Estate agents have been targeted before. Who are your other suspects, Mr Jones?'

'One suspect,' I said. 'Carl Quinn.'

Humphreys opened his mouth. Pritchard sniggered. 'Carl Quinn has an alibi, Mr Jones,' Humphreys said. 'He happens to be in prison.'

'No doubt he has associates who aren't. I gather he was a gangland boss in his time. Perhaps he still has influence.'

'And why should Carl Quinn want to burn Mr Lord's house down?' Humphreys asked.

'Because,' I said, 'I believe he's after St Edward's Crown.'

I told them of Bob's conversations with Carl Quinn at Walton. They listened without comment, but the atmosphere of scepticism was palpable. When I'd finished there was a pause. 'So you're telling us Quinn is planning to steal the crown jewels while he's in Walton Gaol,' Sergeant Pritchard said eventually. 'Quite a feat, that would be.' He smirked at Humphreys.

'Quinn tried to stop Bob from making his ideas public. He told him he'd regret it if he did. I believe he was planning to find the Crown himself, maybe when he came out.'

'You told us that you tried to stop Mr Lord from publicising his ideas yourself,' Pritchard pointed out. 'So you had a motive too, didn't you? In fact, you had the same motive you're telling us Carl Quinn had.'

'But I didn't do it,' I said desperately.

'Have you any evidence that this Crown of yours actually exists?' Humphreys asked.

'There's historical evidence, but it's not conclusive. At present it's just a theory. But Bob believed in it, and I think Quinn did too.' There was another silence.

For the first time, the third man suddenly spoke. His voice was high pitched and a little affected.

'Just what are your Welsh connections, Mr Jones?'

'I haven't got any,' I said, 'I just live here.'

'But your name is Welsh.'

I stared at him. 'I'm one of the Batley Joneses. And we're not exactly a rare breed, even in England. When I lived in Birmingham there were fifteen pages of us in the phone book.'

'You have chosen to live in Wales,' the man said, precisely. 'In a rather isolated locality, I understand. A long way from your place of work.'

'I don't have a place of work any more. But when I did it was all over the border country. Tan-y-Coed was as central as anywhere.'

He pursed his lips. 'Would you say that you were on good terms with people in the locality?'

'I get on well with my neighbours, if that's what you mean.'

He never seemed to react to my answers, either by his expression or the inflection of his voice.

'What is your attitude to - er - local aspirations?'

He wasn't the type to be lost for words. the 'er' was part of his act. It took me a moment to work out the implications of his question. 'My politics are my affair, and their politics are theirs,' I said eventually. 'Could I please know who I'm talking to? At least these gentlemen have introduced themselves.'

He extracted a card in a leather holder from his pocket, held it out, and put it away before I got a proper look. 'My name is Fenshaw.' At the time I thought he was a Fanshawe with a plummy accent; it was only later that I discovered he spelt it with an 'e'.

'I'm English,' I repeated. 'Batley is in Yorkshire.' He'd probably never ventured so far north.

'In the case of the Irish republicans,' Fenshaw said, 'It's remarkable how many of the most fanatical of them were actually born in England.' It was like wading through treacle.

Humphreys asked a few more questions, then they adjourned to somewhere else, presumably to discuss what to do with me. Somebody kindly brought me a cup of tea. It was a long time before Pritchard came back and informed me, grudgingly, that I was free to go. They would be obliged if I would let them know if I was proposing to leave the locality, as they would want to talk to me again. His manner implied that it wouldn't be long.

My car was still up at Bob's house, and Pritchard reluctantly arranged for me to be driven up to get it. They sent me up in a panda car with a civilian driver, an elderly man who shook his head when he saw the gutted house. 'Why should anyone have done that? Everyone knew Mr Lord, and liked him. Wicked, it is.'

Dusk was falling, the van had gone and there was a single police car in the drive with a bored looking officer sitting in it, obviously ready to go home. I started the Justy and headed back over the mountains for home. It was getting dark, and I hadn't eaten for what seemed a very long time. The chip shop was open in Glyn Ceiriog, and I stopped, bought haddock and chips and sat in the car eating them out of the paper. When I'd finished I sat there a while longer; then I turned the car round and drove back over the tops towards Llangollen.

Would the police leave a guard on Bob's house all night? It seemed unlikely with their current manpower problems, but it would be wise to check. I didn't want to find myself in a cell.

It was quite dark when I reached the entrance to the drive. I drove the last hundred yards on sidelights, and they picked out a tape across the gateway and a sign that said 'Police. Keep Out'. I parked on the road, took a flashlight out of the glove compartment and, without switching it on, walked quietly up the drive.

The police car was gone, and the ruined house seemed deserted. The white of the walls reflected what light there was, and the black fire stains looked like huge, gaping holes in the stonework. I was surprised no-one had boarded up the windows. There was another tape across the front doorway, and I ducked under it and stepped inside.

I stood in the darkness of the burned out hall, listening, for a full minute. There wasn't a sound. I risked switching on the torch and picked my way across the littered floor between pools of black water.

The door to Bob's study hung open, and I walked through it and played the light around.

The study was less damaged than the other rooms; the furniture was scorched but more or less intact; the books, their spines charred, were still on the shelves. The plastic casing of the computer was partly melted, the screen cracked. Everything was blackened by smoke. The smell of burning stung my nostrils and the back of my throat.

There was no sign that anything had been moved. I shone the torch into the corner where Bob had kept the deed box. It wasn't there. I searched the room systematically, taking my time, following the little pool of light. The box was too big to be easily concealed. It was nowhere in the study.

I risked going back into the sitting room for a second look, and found nothing. The silence of the house oppressed me; somewhere water was dripping, but there was no evidence of life. I stepped back into the hall and walked over to where the dining room had been. The ceiling had gone, its charred remains lay on the blackened dining table where Bob and I had spread out the maps. Here too, there was no sign of the fireproof box. It was possible the police had moved it, but why should they? Everything that wasn't actually burned seemed to be still there.

I switched off the torch, waited a moment, and stepped cautiously out through the doorway onto the terrace. The night was still. A watery moon had begun to glimmer through the thin cloud overhead, and by its light I made my way quietly down the drive to the car. It wasn't until I was driving away that I started to shake.

When I finally got to bed the ideas raced through my mind. Carl Quinn had had Bob murdered. It was obvious. Bob had told him of the treasure he was seeking, had told him what it was, had told him all we knew of where it was hidden. No doubt he'd also mentioned the deed box and its contents. And then he'd told him that he was going public, that he intended to announce his findings and theories to the world. Quinn had tried to warn him off. When he wouldn't be persuaded, Quinn had sent somebody to kill him, and to recover the evidence that might help him find the Crown. He was unlikely to be suspected; as Humphreys had pointed out, being in prison was a fairly convincing alibi. The fire, and the symbol on the gatepost, were just a device to divert suspicion. And Bob was dead, killed by a man he had set out to help and to befriend. Dawn was breaking before I fell asleep.

CHAPTER 8

Next morning the sense of anger and loss was as strong as ever. I wanted somehow to convince the police that Bob's death wasn't the result of some sort of crazy nationalist conspiracy, and that it had nothing to do with me. I wanted them to believe it had been planned, deliberately, out of greed and treachery. And I wanted to do something, somehow, to carry on the work that Bob had begun. But to start treasure hunting at this juncture seemed indecent, and the police were in no mood to listen to me. So I went and got a spade, and took out my frustrations on the neglected garden.

As I chopped the blade down into the hard ground, kicking it in deeper with the heel of my boot and flinging the sods and stones in front of me, some of the anger started to drain away. I worked all day, digging deep and trenching the ground, pulling up the nettles and docks that had begun to invade the plot where I'd dug last year's final crop of potatoes, ignoring the drizzle which set in during the afternoon. And for the next two days I carried on, till the air of neglect had gone and the soil was clean and brown, raked and ready for the seed. I didn't know who would share the crop with me, but at least some kind of wholesome order was restored.

The work was interrupted at one point by Sergeant Pritchard, who had come to ask me all the questions I'd been asked before in the hope I might have forgotten some of the answers. I hadn't, and his manner needled me enough to deter me from volunteering any further information, even if I'd had any. His wheels spun contemptuously as he drove off down the track.

On the morning of the third day I was hacking away at a wild carrot root when I heard noises from above the house. Presently a face appeared around the wall end.

'Would you be John Jones?' A youngish man in a smart new car coat scrambled down the slope. At the bottom he looked down in distaste at the mud on his leather shoes and trouser bottoms. 'Hell of a place to live. You must like to keep out of the way. Wayne Drew.' He stuck out a hand and named a middlebrow tabloid.

I'd hardly seen a face for three days, so I gave him coffee and tried to answer his questions. The amount he seemed to know took me by surprise. Somebody had told him that I'd visited Bob Lord on the night of the fire, and that somebody could only have been in the police. That was irritating, and slightly disconcerting. He asked what my connection with Bob had been, and I said we shared an interest in local history. Then he wanted to know about my feelings on Welsh terrorists, and I told him I didn't think terrorism was primarily a Welsh problem and that in this case I didn't believe it was relevant anyway. He picked that up straight away, and asked who I thought had started the fire. I found myself back-pedalling: the last thing I wanted was to see my own thoughts about Bob's death in the papers. He could see I was prevaricating, and as an interrogator he was every bit as effective as Humphreys. I began to wish I hadn't opened my mouth. It took the best part of an hour to get rid of him.

The next morning I went shopping, and picked up the local weekly and a copy of Mr Drew's paper. There I was, prominently featured. The assumption that there was a terrorist aspect to Bob's death had made it big news; fatalities in fires might be commonplace, but in this context the media clearly scented a major story. As I read the item I was appalled. Without saying so in so many words, Wayne Drew or whoever wrote his stories for him had made it sound as if I were a suspect, who probably had something to hide. The article made it clear that I had been the last person to see Bob alive.

Back at Tan-y-Coed I went and placed Mr Drew's publication in the Ty Bach for future use. Then I looked through the weekly until I found the notice of Bob's death, and of the funeral arrangements. The length and warmth of the obituary surprised me, and the tributes occupied nearly half a page. Bob had been well known and widely respected. The funeral was in a couple of days, and I made up my mind to go.

I started to think about the next move. If it was true that Carl Quinn had been behind the fire and responsible for the disappearance of the deed box, then he or his henchmen must be looking for the Crown. He would now know of the documents in the box, though he probably wouldn't be able to make much of them. Anyway I knew more than he did. The thought that he might succeed stuck in my gullet. Surely I owed it to Bob to see that the quest ended as he would have wished.

There were two possible ways ahead. One was to do more exploring on the ground, or rather under it. The shaft was worth a look, though it would probably turn out to be isolated from the rest of the workings. And I'd need to get someone to join me; exploring shafts on your own isn't recommended. Finding the mine entrance and digging it out would be a more hopeful way of getting in. But there was a lot of ground to cover, and Bob's collection of maps had been burned. And again, if I was going to start digging on spec, I was going to need help. Maybe I was obsessed with the idea of secrecy, but I wanted to delay involving other people as long as possible.

The second avenue was to carry on Bob's hunt through the archives at Berwyn. He'd planned to go back the day after we'd spoken. He'd said there would probably be more mining reports, and they might well contain a plan of the mine or a map of the location. That could save a lot of fruitless digging.

I decided that to start with I'd give Berwyn a try. That would be carrying on where Bob had left off, and I could keep any discoveries to myself. And I'd always wanted to see the house, which had never been open to the public and was buried in a vast park that made it invisible from any road. It was notorious among architecture buffs because Lord Berwyn had been one of the handful of owners of great houses who had refused to admit the learned editor of The Buildings of Wales, among other luminaries, when they'd wanted to publish details of the house. That made me a little uncertain of my welcome, but Bob had apparently been let in and allowed to work there more or less at will. If only I'd been able to take him up on his offer to go there with him; at least I'd have had an introduction.

Not knowing how else to get in touch, I looked in the phone book and found Lord Berwyn listed like anybody else. I picked up the phone, put it down again, picked it up and rang the number. The ringing tone continued for a very long time; I had visions of someone striding down long passages, across echoing halls and down endless flights of stairs to answer it. Then there was a click and an abrupt voice said, 'Berwyn'.

The response took me off guard; I didn't know whether I was speaking to the peer or the butler. 'Er - I'd like to speak to Lord Berwyn,' I said, feeling as if I was selling double glazing, 'My name's Jones.'

'Speaking.'

'Oh. Good morning. I'm - I was - a friend of Bob Lord. He was working on the archives at Berwyn. Had you heard that - that he had died?'

There was a fractional pause. 'I had indeed. We were very sorry to hear about it.'

'I was working with Bob on some of his research. I'd very much like to be able to continue what he was doing. I wondered if I could possibly consult some of your papers, some of the mining records, for instance.'

'When?'

I was suddenly bold. 'Could I come tomorrow?'

'No reason why not. Just come to the house. Someone will be here.' The receiver was replaced. I couldn't believe it had been that easy.

The house known as Berwyn lies ten or twelve miles from the Berwyn Mountains, in deepest Montgomeryshire. It's farming country, green and prosperous-looking, with small fields where sheep and cattle graze contentedly. The route, as so often starting from Tan-y-Coed, was roundabout. I took along the Ordnance map which marked the house and the park, but didn't make clear which was the way in. The obvious approach led to an elegant pair of Georgian lodges, like miniature temples, with splendid wrought iron gates between them. Evidently they were never opened; long grass was growing through them, and there wasn't even a track beyond, just a field. I drove off along a narrow road parallel to the park wall, and after half a mile or so came to a less imposing entrance from which a pot-holed drive led into the park. The only sign was one which said 'Private Property'. I decided to try it.

The road led through rolling parkland: smooth green turf dotted with venerable trees. There were young ones too, with little fences round them; there might not be money to repair the drive, but the park was being cared for. I crossed a couple of cattle grids; cows were grazing, but there was still no sign of a building. Presently the drive forked; one way presumably led to the house, the other perhaps to a farm or stables. But there were trees ahead, and no obvious indication which one to take. I pulled up to consider.

A figure on horseback was cantering gently towards me on the grass beside the right hand road. The horse was sturdy and powerful, a dark chestnut with shaggy black hooves. The rider was perched high like a jockey, standing in the stirrups, a slight figure on the big horse, but perfectly balanced and very much in control. I watched in admiration;

for all the poverty of my horsemanship I'd always dreamt of being able to canter out across my own parkland on a fine spring morning.

The girl eased her horse to a walk and came up alongside the car. She had a snub nose and freckles, and wonderful dark red hair that flowed out from under a battered riding hat. She was wearing a checked shirt and jeans. She looked about sixteen.

'Hallo,' I said. 'I'm looking for the House.'

She looked amused. 'Try that way,' she said, pointing the way she had come.

'Er - is there any particular entrance?' I thought perhaps I should go somewhere round the back, where the tradesmen went.

'Just go the front door and ring the bell. You can't really miss it.' Then she was off, cantering delicately across the park.

I drove on through the trees, and unexpectedly came upon the house. It lay in a hollow, so that from my viewpoint on the drive I was about level with the roof. And it was the roofline of the house that made me gasp. Owain Morgan or his forbears had topped the walls with a balustrade that was punctuated by a weird and wonderful array of finials, miniature obelisks, stone balls and heraldic beasts. Behind it rose a splendid row of chimneys, joined together by stone arches like an abbreviated aqueduct. Below roof level the house was relatively plain; tall grey walls relieved by broad mullioned windows like grids of stone. As if all that wasn't enough some Victorian Morgan, no doubt the first Lord Berwyn, had added another range at the back with an incongruous tower, complete with clock, that would have been more at home attached to a town hall.

As the drive descended it brought me round to the front of the house. The old part was more or less E-shaped, with two projecting wings flanking a gravel forecourt and a sort of porch in the centre. The drive ended at the forecourt, and I parked the Justy as unobtrusively as I could in one corner, got out, and looked up.

The central part of the house was four storeys high. It would have been stern and forbidding but for its fantastic skyline and the even more fantastic porch. The porch projected twenty feet or so from the front of the building. At its foot was an imposing stone staircase. It led up to a tall arched doorway flanked by two inadequately draped female figures whose noble proportions would have qualified them for filming on a Californian beach. Above was a profusion of carving in the same dark grey stone: fancy strapwork, pot-bellied columns, grotesque masks grinning through swags of vine leaves, curls, scrolls and lozenges of all shapes and sizes and, in the centre, an immense achievement of the Stuart royal arms complete with mantling and supporters. All this must surely be Owain Morgan's work; the crazy exuberance of the design reflected his personality every bit as much as the arms proclaimed his politics. The porch was a storey lower than the rest of the building, but it was topped by an obelisk at each corner and a little stone helmet in the middle, supported by a rather portly lion on either side. Above and behind, on the roofline of the house itself, a stone dragon pranced along the balustrade.

Just go to the front door and ring the bell, the girl had said. Apparently this was the usual way in; beside it was a tall metal contraption with what looked like a pair of pedals at the top, connected by a loop of bicycle chain to a large round brush at the bottom. The pedals were handles, and the device was designed to clean your boots. It looked as if it was in regular use. I fought off the temptation to try it out.

I looked around for the traditional bell pull, dangling on a length of rusty chain. In fact there was a neat electric bell push tucked in beside one of the stone ladies, around nipple level. It was helpfully labelled 'Bell'. I pressed it, half expecting to hear a set of electronic Westminster chimes.

I was about to press it again when the door swung open. A tall, rather gaunt lady with wispy greying hair, in a faded print dress, stood there. She was holding a feather duster tied to the end of a billiard queue.

'Good morning. My name's Jones. Lord Berwyn is expecting me.'

'Good morning,' she said with a nice smile, 'Come in. My husband said you would be calling.' Somehow I'd known it was Lady Berwyn, in spite of the feather duster.

The inside of the porch was half filled with logs neatly piled against the wall. We passed through another door into a dark passage, and then turned into a quite stupendous hall, two stories high, its plaster ceiling embellished with a riot of strapwork from which little pendants descended at intervals. There was a cavernous fireplace with the remains of a vast log fire, no doubt fuelled by the store in the porch. The room smelled sweetly of wood smoke. High on the walls was a row of slightly moth-eaten stags' heads.

'I was just dusting the stags,' Lady Berwyn said, propping her long-handled duster against the wall, 'This thing's handier than a ladder.'

We crossed the hall into another room, lower but almost as

large. The scent of wood smoke was stronger here, for the fire was smouldering gently beneath an overmantel resplendent with the Morgan arms in which dragons featured prominently. The walls were rather severely panelled in oak, but topped by a richly ornamented frieze - more dragons - and then by another of those extravagant ceilings. The Morgans evidently liked their decoration high up. The whole room was a mixture of grandeur and domestic clutter. A superb refectory table was piled with well thumbed gardening books. The fireplace was flanked by a pair of richly carved chests, one carrying a television set and the other a music centre, neither top of the range. Facing each other in front of them were two settees about twenty feet long, covered in faded chintz and scattered with books, newspapers and knitting. On the hearthrug, which had several large holes burnt in it, three scruffy border terriers were lying in a heap.

'Francis is in the garden,' Lady Berwyn said. She strode over to a window and opened it. On the sill was a large, brass bell like the one they used to summon us in from the school playground. She seized the bell, brandished it out of the window and rang it vigorously.

In a surprisingly short time the door opposite flew open and an electric wheelchair came trundling into the room, leaving tyre marks on the carpet. Francis, Fifth Lord Berwyn, was a little, bird-like man, sitting very erect, with a white moustache, a pink, well scrubbed face and soil on his finger tips. 'Mr Jones,' he said, 'You've come to see the archives. Haven't wasted much time.'

Bob hadn't told me that Lord Berwyn was in a wheelchair. 'Yes. I was helping Bob Lord. I was hoping to carry on where he left off.'

'Bad business. Good man, Bob Lord. His father did a lot of work for us. Grandfather too. Old firm, you know.' I wondered if he'd read the reports of my alleged involvement in the fire. If so he didn't mention it.

'Bob was doing some research on mining in Cwm Llwyd. In the seventeenth century and in the nineteenth. I'd been working with him. He'd got a long way. I'd like to carry on.'

Lord Berwyn nodded. 'We often get historians here. They're welcome as long as they behave themselves. But I'll have no papers taken away from the house. Fellow came last year, tried to persuade me to give everything to the National Library of Wales. Told him to mind his own business. I'll show you the Muniment Room, and you can see what there is. Hope you've got a week or two to spare.'

I followed the wheelchair down a long corridor with an endless row of bells suspended high up by the ceiling, through two more doors and along a flagged passage to a third door. On the straights I nearly had to run to keep up. Lord Berwyn opened the doors expertly, even though they opened towards him, flicking the chair into reverse and back into forward drive. From the last door a wooden ramp led down into a courtyard. As the chair bumped over the cobbles there was a clatter of hooves, and the girl I'd met in the park came leading her horse under an archway.

'My daughter,' Lord Berwyn said. 'Paeony, this is Mr Jones. He's come to see the archives. Would you mind showing him the way?'

'We've met.' She gave me a faint smile, 'Yes, I'll take him up.' Lord Berwyn executed a neat turn and shot off up the ramp.

'You can come this way if you like. I'm afraid you'll have to wait till I've rubbed him down.' I followed her and the horse across the courtyard and into a stable which had been turned into a big loose box, with a generous layer of straw. She indicated an old chair without a back, and I sat on it while she loosened the horse's girth and removed the saddle.

'What's your interest in the family papers?' she asked. I was still trying to get used to the name, which seemed decidedly exotic for what was clearly a home-grown product, though a very attractive one. Perhaps I'd underestimated her age; her manner was a little too direct, too assured for a teenager. I explained about the mines.

She was rubbing the horse down now with an old towel, working quickly, her movements vigorous but gentle. The beast looked as if it could have crushed her with one kick, but there was no doubt who was in charge. She'd taken off the riding hat, and kept tossing the dark red hair back as she worked. She had rolled up the sleeves of the checked shirt, and there were little freckles on the smooth skin of her forearms that gave it the texture of a speckled egg. 'Why don't you just go and look for the mines?' she asked. 'Couldn't you explore them? That's something I've always wanted to do.'

'I need to locate the entrance. It collapsed long ago. I'm hoping to find a plan. But once it's dug out I could probably take you down, if your parents don't mind.'

'They could hardly object,' she said with a grin, 'I'm twenty-four.'

I was embarrassed. 'I'm sorry. You looked - I thought...'

'I'm used to it. I still have problems getting into pubs. But I'll take you up on your offer. I could even come and dig.'

'I'll find you a shovel.'

She gave the horse a smack on the rump and said, 'Move over, Arnie.' It snorted and did as it was told, nuzzling her shoulder affectionately.

'Why Arnie?'

'Use your imagination.' She flashed me a quick grin.

She'd finished rubbing down the horse and was hanging up the tack, stretching to reach the hooks high on the wall. 'Right', she said, 'I'll show you the dreaded archives.' She gave the horse a pat on the rump and led the way out of the stable and across the yard to a doorway in the foot of the tower. Just inside she reached up and took a large key from a hole in the stonework. Then we climbed the stone spiral staircase till she stopped at a door leading off it and unlocked it.

It was clear what Bob Lord had meant about the problems of working at Berwyn. The room was big, high and poorly lit, and the walls were lined right up to roof level with wooden shelves or racks holding row upon row of black metal boxes. There were more free-standing shelves in the middle of the room, and other boxes stacked on the floor. There must have been a couple of hundred of them, and whilst some were numbered none had labels. All of them were covered with dust. There was a rickety wooden ladder, but trying to negotiate it whilst carrying a heavy box wouldn't be easy. Heaven knew how they'd got the boxes up there in the first place. As for the ladder, it must have been pieced together in the room: they could hardly have carried it up the spiral staircase.

'Everyone complains about the shelves,' Paeony said. 'A lot of them take one look and don't come back. Historians don't seem to be very good on ladders. But Mr Lord kept going. I think he'd got to there.' She pointed to where a trestle table had been placed close to the shelving. On the table was one of the boxes, and there was a gap on the fourth shelf up. Approaching, I noticed a neat little tick in chalk on every box to the left of the gap. It was typical of Bob's meticulous approach.

'What are you doing for lunch?' she asked. I said I'd got a sandwich in the car. 'Eat it in the garden if you like. You'll be glad to get out of here.'

She left me to it, and I opened the box on the table. On the top, where Bob must have left it, was a folded document, printed on blue paper, entitled: 'Report to the Shareholders of the Cwm Llwyd Mine'. The year was 1867. Opening it out I soon found the section Bob had copied down. The reference to the new shaft was frustratingly brief. Captain Taylor had appended it to a lengthy account of the troubles the miners had had in following the lode beyond the fault which seemed to have halted his predecessors two hundred years before. There was no reference to the location of the shaft or the mine, and looking through the rest of the box there was nothing else of interest.

Perched rather precariously on the table I managed to lift the box back onto the shelf and took down the next one. All the papers it contained were from the same year as the last, 1867. Whoever filed away William Morgan's papers did so purely by date, certainly not by topic, as these covered every conceivable aspect of his life and business ventures. Everything, that is, except mining. I humped the box back and got down the next: the shelf above was too low for me to be able to lift the lid with it in situ. I was briefly excited to see that its contents almost all related to mining, but they mostly concerned slate quarrying in Caernarfonshire and there was no mention of Cwm Llwyd. As the box was full to the top and most of the papers had to be unfolded, sifting through them was a slow business.

The next box on the shelf proved to contain material from the 1880's: the boxes were in no sort of order. After three or four more I was starting to think of sandwiches. There was just one box left on the row: this would be the last before lunch. I heaved it down, blew off the dust, lifted the lid, and found a Cwm Llwyd report almost at once, on the same blue paper.

The first impression was disappointing; it seemed to be concerned largely with the purchase of pumping equipment. But the pump was to be installed in a new shaft, and reading on I came to the sentence I'd been looking for:

'I have personally surveyed the direction and inclination of the Lode, and have no doubt that a shaft of no more than 30 or 40 yards in depth, sunk 400 yards in a south easterly direction of the entrance to the adit level, will enable us to rediscover the vein and restore the productivity of the Mine.'

Carefully copying down the wording, I reflected that I'd been extraordinarily lucky. The search for that piece of information could have taken weeks. I'd found it in a morning. Anyone who measured 400 yards north west from the shaft wouldn't be far away from where the mine entrance had been. No doubt there were still more clues to discover, but for the moment I had enough to get back into the field.

I put the box back on the shelf and went out down the spiral staircase and into the sunlight of the courtyard. It was a fine, warm late spring day. It would be more tactful to walk to the car round the house than through it, and I set off through the arch and turned left. It was a long walk, but eventually I came to the forecourt and retrieved my sandwiches. There had been no sign of the garden so far, so I started to walk round the other way. Passing through a hedge, I came to a broad expanse of lawn flanked by curving borders where the plants, not yet in flower, were growing lushly. An area in the middle was marked out with pegs and hoops, and Paeony and her father were playing croquet.

The game was nearly over and I watched as Lord Berwyn, sitting in his wheelchair, leant forward and with deadly precision drove his ball into hers so that it flew across the grass and into the herbaceous border. Then he rolled forward a few yards and tapped his own ball so that it struck the peg with a gentle thunk. 'My game I think, Molly,' he said cheerfully, and went humming off across the lawn towards the house.

Paeony was collecting her ball from a clump of delphiniums She saw me on her way back, and pointed to a green painted metal seat. I sat down and she came over. 'My first game of the season,' she said, 'Daddy's been practising secretly all week. Have you found anything yet?'

'I have, actually. I was trying to locate the entrance to a particular mine in Cwm Llwyd. I think I've probably got the information I needed.'

'I know Cwm Llwyd quite well. I used to go climbing there. There's a rock face that's quite challenging, and people go abseiling in one of the open quarries.'

I moved up the seat, and she sat down. Out of politeness I offered her a rather limp cheese and pickle sandwich, which she understandably refused.

'Have you done a lot of climbing?'

'I used to. But I haven't been for a couple of years, not since - someone was killed.'

'What happened?'

'He was up in Scotland, with some other students. A belay gave way. It had been used hundreds of times before. Just his bad luck.'

'Was he a friend?'

'We didn't realise - I didn't realise how close we were, till it was too late to tell him.' Her eyes were suddenly brimming, and I was kicking myself for asking such an insensitive question in a casual conversation.

'I'm sorry. I shouldn't have asked.'

'Are you going to go down your mine?'

'It depends whether we can dig out the entrance. That's usually the first part to collapse. There's generally loose subsoil before you get to more solid rock, and the miners used timber to shore it up. It soon rots if it's not renewed, the entrance falls in, vegetation grows over it and in a few years you wouldn't know there'd been a hole. The passages behind it can last for years, centuries sometimes. At Cwm Llwyd there's another possible access, via a shaft, but that would mean rope work of course.'

'Why is this particular mine so interesting?'

'It's not exceptional in itself. But according to the documents, it may link up with mines your family dug just after the death of Queen Elizabeth. They'd be some of the oldest in Wales. Bob and I were hoping to find them.'

'I meant what I said about going down,' Paeony said, 'And there's the family interest too. I'd like to see what our ancestors got up to. If you need any help, let me know.'

'I can let you know now. Your offer's gratefully accepted. At present I'm on my own. I'm John, by the way.'

'You heard my name.' She pulled a face.

'Actually I heard two. Your father called you Molly.'

'That's just his pet name. He lumbered me with Paeony in the first place. He's a fanatical gardener. The paeony's his favourite flower. He breeds them, he's won medals for it. But his favourite's a yellow one called Paeonia Mlosekosewitchii. I'm named after it. It's otherwise known as Molly the Witch, hence the Molly. I don't mind being named after a flower, but he could have chosen something more ordinary, like Daisy.'

I was trying to think of a reply that wouldn't sound like an empty compliment, but couldn't. 'If you want to come to Cwm Llwyd, I could go up the day after tomorrow. Bob Lord's funeral is tomorrow, and I ought to go to it. But I'm free after that. No work, no ties. My time's my own.'

'No ties at all?'

'I'm divorced.' I found myself telling her about Sarah. She looked me in the eye as we talked. Her eyes were big and grey, with long dark red lashes. Her skin with its delicate powdering of freckles on the cheekbones had an extraordinary freshness and translucency; it was that, along with the small, slightly upturned nose that had made me think of her as a child.

We arranged to meet at Cwm Llwyd at ten in the morning in two days' time. 'Do you know Cadwaladr Pugh's farm'? she asked. 'We always used to park there when we went climbing.'

'I used to sell him poultry feed. I'll see you there at ten.'

I went back up to the Muniment Room, largely because it didn't seem politic to depart without putting in a full day's work, and looked through a few more boxes without finding anything of interest. Then I locked the door myself, put the key back in the hole at the bottom of the staircase, and went in to thank the Berwyns for their kindness before driving home. Paeony wasn't there, and I felt a pang of disappointment.

CHAPTER 9

Shrewsbury wrecked its beautiful Square and High Street in the sixties, when it tore down Robert Smirke's coolly elegant Shire Hall to make way for commercial mediocrity. They've already had to paint over the concrete. But the Unitarian Church is still there: a handsome brick building in classical style. It was pretty full for Bob Lord's funeral – probably fuller than it had been for a long time – with an odd mix of mourners. There were many farmers in tight, shiny suits, and Welsh was being being spoken in the pew behind. And there were other, more dubious looking characters too, whose ravaged faces spoke of desperate lives. The traditional hymns were sung in fine style, though I don't know what the chapel-goers made of some of the readings from Walt Whitman and Rabindranath Tagore. The minister gave a simple, moving address in which he talked about Bob's love of the past, paid tribute to the help he gave people in the present and praised his faith in every human being's natural tendency to good.

I recognised Bob's son and daughter, sitting with other relatives in the front pew, from the photographs I'd seen in his house. Ian had flown over from Canada. After the service there was a little queue of people waiting to shake hands with them, and I joined it. When it was my turn I said, 'I'm John Jones. I was working with your father on some of his local history. I think I was probably the last person to talk to him.'

Helen gave me a smile. 'He mentioned you when he wrote. He said you were onto something quite exciting.'

'We were. I'm hoping I can carry on where he left off.'

'Dad's history meant a lot to him. I hope you find what you were looking for.' We quickly exchanged telephone numbers, and agreed we'd keep in touch.

Leaving the church I noticed Detective Inspector Humphreys and Sergeant Pritchard, sitting at the back. I gave them a nod, and

Humphreys nodded back. They hadn't come to pay tribute to the deceased; no doubt they were interested in who would turn up.

Driving back I could hardly wait for the next day. It wasn't the mine - it was Paeony. She had been constantly coming back into my thoughts; at night, getting a meal, doing the washing up, even during the funeral service. Those eyes had been like deep, unruffled pools; I'd felt myself swimming, floating, drifting as I looked into them. I could picture the softness of her cheek in the sunlight, the neat firmness of the chin that belied any thought of immaturity. I thought of her rubbing down the horse, the slight body in the tight-fitting jeans, the open-necked shirt that revealed a few more freckles on the skin. I found myself wondering how far down they went, then recoiled guiltily. The attraction wasn't just physical; there was a toughness and directness in her that I could respect, but I'd seen a vulnerability too. Both of us had been bruised, in different ways, both of us had a gap to fill. We seemed to like - and dislike - the same things. I told myself this was ridiculous, we'd only met once.

It had been late shopping night in Shrewsbury, and I'd stopped to make some much needed purchases. My wardrobe was starting to show signs of neglect; socks and underpants had holes in them, sweaters were beginning to unravel. I'd dawdled over the shopping and then stopped for a pizza; basically I didn't want another long evening at home. So it was dark when I turned onto the track for Tan-y-Coed. The headlights lit up the sleeper bridge along the alders in the valley bottom, and disturbed a couple of sheep lying at the side of the track; they lumbered off indignantly into the darkness. I parked the Justy in its place by the wall and took the house key from the dash; I never bothered to lock the car at home.

I stood by the car for a moment as I often did, listening to the silence. The night was clear and cloudless. Before Tan-y-Coed I'd never known a sky unpolluted by light; here there were no street lamps, and the stars had been a revelation. Tonight there was no moon, and the Milky Way swept in a great arch above me; a billion points of light that seemed to wheel around my head as I cast it back and gazed upwards into the sky. The lines Bob had quoted came back to me: 'The fire is in them whereof we are born.'

I knew the way down to the cottage well enough not to need a torch, and the stars gave enough light to see by. I made my way slowly down the steep path at the side of the cottage, and turned onto the terrace at the front. Then I froze.

On the terrace in front of me was a great, dark shape that blotted out the stars. It didn't move. It didn't make a sound. It looked too big to be human, but it was. I saw the outline of shoulders, and a massive head that seemed to grow straight out of them. At first I couldn't make out features. Then I realised why. The face was black.

A voice that seemed to rumble out of the earth said, 'Mr Jones, I think.'

'Yes,' I said, my chest thumping, 'Who are you?'

'We can talk inside.'

I was trying to fit the key into the door with trembling hands, knees turned to jelly. I didn't want to be inside with whoever it was, but there was no possibility of running away.

I got the door open, and switched on the light. I was propelled across the threshold, and the door was closed firmly behind me. I turned and looked at my uninvited visitor.

He must have stood six and a half feet tall, or would have done had there been room under the beams. He wore dreadlocks, and his skin was as dark as skin can be. He was wearing a black sweatshirt and black jeans. His arms looked longer and stronger than my legs.

'Shall we sit down?' I felt a gentle push in the chest and was seated on the sofa. He took a chair, which creaked in protest, and leaned forward till his face was almost touching mine. 'Tell me about Bob Lord.'

'Who sent you?'

'I am asking the questions, my friend. You are providing the answers.'

'Carl Quinn sent you didn't he?' There could be no other explanation for the presence of this apparition in my sitting room. I should have realised that Quinn, or one of his associates, would come looking for me. Bob had quite possibly mentioned my name to him; he'd told him everything else.

The face moved back a few inches. 'What do you know about Carl Quinn?'

'Quinn wants something. He thought Bob knew where it was.'

'Carl Quinn is in Walton Gaol.'

'But you're not.'

There was a pause. 'Mr Jones,' the black man said, 'I have no connection with Carl Quinn. You can be sure of that. But I am interested in your connection with Bob Lord. What is it?'

'Bob was a good friend. We'd been working together, doing historical research. I'd been with Bob the night he died. He'd told Carl Quinn what we were looking for. I think Quinn wanted it too. When Bob insisted on going public about his researches, his house was torched the night before he was going to tell the tale. Somebody made sure he didn't.'

'Carl Quinn is interested in one thing only. It's not historical research.'

'What's your interest? Why are you concerned about Bob?'

He sat back a little in his chair. 'Bob Lord helped a lot of people. He helped me. I would probably be serving life by now, if it hadn't been for him. I'd been in and out of detention since I was ten. He broke the cycle. He had a way of making people believe in themselves again.'

'Bob thought he could help Carl Quinn.'

'Carl Quinn is beyond help.'

Suddenly he seemed to reach a decision. 'I think I believe you. My name is Joseph.' He stuck out a massive hand, and I took it tentatively. 'I read about you in the newspapers. They gave the impression that the police suspected you of causing the fire. I came here to find out if that was true.' I thought it was lucky for me that it wasn't.

Joseph leaned forward again. 'What is it that you and Bob were looking for? And does Carl Quinn know enough to find it?'

'Something old, and very valuable. And I doubt if Quinn has enough information to find it at present. He doesn't know what I know.'

'That could be dangerous for you. You will need to be very careful. Quinn reads the papers, just as I do. He'll know you were associated with Bob Lord. He has a long arm. And he won't be in Walton for ever.'

'The police didn't think Quinn could have arranged the murder from Walton. Obviously you disagree.'

'Two years after Quinn was locked up, the principal witness against him fell down a lift shaft. Death by misadventure, the inquest said. No evidence of foul play. A fault in the door mechanism. The manufacturers even admitted liability. But all the villains knew. Carl still pulls the strings, even from inside.'

I told Joseph more about Bob's conversations with Quinn, and he listened without comment. Then he shook his head. 'Bob Lord could see into people's hearts. He made them look inside themselves, and see the good they didn't know was there. But some people's hearts are so black that no-one can see into them. Or perhaps there's nothing there to see. Bob couldn't accept that. He could be pig-headed, you know. So sometimes he was wrong. But maybe he was right to be wrong.'

Joseph eased himself out of the chair, keeping his head cautiously lowered. He wrote a number on a slip of paper and gave it to me. 'If you have trouble, you can get a message to me,' he said. 'I run a sports club now, in Birmingham, boxing and athletics, mostly for kids whose dads are inside. And I'm involved with a hostel for ex-cons. Ring me from a public phone if you can, not from here. I can't promise I can do anything about Quinn, he's bigger time that I ever was. But if he had Bob Lord killed, there will be others besides me who would want to see him dealt with.'

He walked out into the darkness, refusing my offer of a torch to light the way. A few minutes later a motor cycle engine rumbled in the distance and faded into the night.

I was up early the next morning, sorting out some equipment: a compass for bearings, some canes to use as markers, a pick and a shovel. Optimistically I added my lamp and helmet, and then as an afterthought took the bag that I kept my harness in and unhooked a couple of coils of rope from the wardrobe where, to Sarah's disgust, I'd always hung it among the clothes. By a quarter to ten I was pulling into Cadwaladr's unglamorous farmyard to find his chickens scratching around two unexpectedly shiny vehicles. One was a smart new Land Rover, evidently Paeony's, the other a gleaming quad bike painted bright yellow. Paeony and Cadwaladr were looking at it. Today he had his baseball cap on back to front.

'Good God,' I said, 'I never thought I'd see you riding one of those. Has the Fergie popped its pistons?' Cadwaladr's one and only means of transport was, or had been, a grey Ferguson tractor so old that it qualified as a vintage vehicle and was exempt from road tax.

'I won the damn thing in the raffle at the West Midlands Show,' Cadwaladr said. 'Second prize was a load of silage, but they wouldn't let me take that instead. Insisted on delivering it, they did. Can you imagine me bouncing around on one of those?'

'Half the farmers in Wales have got them. They save a lot of leg work.'

'There's nothing wrong with my legs.'

'You can always sell it, Mr Pugh,' Paeony said, 'But I think you ought to try it out. I'll show you if you like. We've got one at Berwyn. They're a lot handier on rough ground than a tractor.'

The idea of a girl demonstrating the bike clearly didn't appeal, and Cadwaladr changed the subject. 'Miss Paeony says you want to go messing around in the old mine. Are you sure you know what you're doing? If you get stuck I won't be coming to get you out. I'm the wrong shape for tunnels.'

'I've had a bit of experience. But we may not be going underground.'

Cadwaladr's keen eyes squinted at me under the snowy eyebrows. 'Last time you were here you were with Bob Lord. You were at his funeral in Shrewsbury.' I hadn't seen him there, but that wasn't surprising in the crowd.

'Bob's death was a tragedy. He was a good man, and a good historian too. I'm trying to carry on where he left off.'

'It was a terrible thing. Lunatics they are, some of them.' He took off the baseball cap and scratched his head. 'And now you're a gentleman of leisure, I hear. So it's archaeology instead of chicken feed.'

'For the time being.'

Paeony and Cadwaladr chatted for a while like old friends. Then we transferred my gear from the Justy to the Land Rover and Paeony drove over the cattle grid and up towards the mine.

We reached the top of the rough track that led down to the bottom of the valley, and she sized it up and selected four wheel drive. 'We can get down as far as the stream,' she said decisively, 'After that we'll have to walk.' She handled the vehicle expertly, guiding it gently over the bumps with the same intuitive sense of balance that she had shown on the horse.

We left the Land Rover near the bottom of the track with most of the gear still in it; there was no point in carting it up the hill till we knew what we were going to do. 'We'll head for the shaft to start with,' I said, 'And get a bearing on where the entrance ought to be.'

We picked our way across the stream and struck off up the hillside, ignoring the old incline and climbing diagonally towards the shaft. The circle of spoil around it was clearly visible about half way up. I was reasonably fit but Paeony was fitter, and I had to exert myself to keep up. She was wearing a pair of fawn-coloured jeans that fitted her precisely, and a thin, cream-coloured sweater that had obviously shrunk a bit. They suited her colouring to perfection. I tried to stop myself admiring the effect as she forged ahead.

We reached the spoil heap, and Paeony walked down towards the bottom of the depression.

'Take care. Don't get too close.'

She stopped well short of the shaft and walked around it, looking at the steep rock face behind.

'There's a good belay here, if we need it.'

'Let's get the bearing.' I took out my compass and, standing above the shaft of top of the spoil heap, sighted along a line to the north west. There was a prominent rock on the skyline in more or less the right direction that could be used as a marker, and I pointed it out. 'That's the direction. Four hundred yards, the report said. We'll measure it properly; it's hopeless trying pace it out on this sort of terrain.'

I'd brought a hundred foot tape, old enough not to be metric, and we took it in turns to hold one end whilst the other walked off in the direction of the rock. The day had dawned cloudy, but now the sky was blue and even the grim landscape of Cwm Llwyd had begun to sparkle in the spring sunshine. There was only the gentlest of breezes. Twelve times we walked away from each other. I watched Paeony stepping out through the fresh, green shoots of the young bracken, the tape trailing behind her, moving lightly and easily, then turning as the tape tautened and standing, smiling back at me as I walked towards her, reeling in. We began to make a game of the handover, exchanging the reel for the little ring on the end of tape with a mocking bow. I felt a growing reluctance to turn my back on her and walk away, but I was sure I could feel her eyes following me as I went. I looked over my shoulder once to see, and fell over a boulder. I was in danger of losing count.

The going was easier than expected, and it turned out that we were actually following the remains of a track. The line was still visible as a long indentation in the bracken and heather. It curved a little following the contour and at one point the bearing took us away from it, but soon we were back on it again. It was logical that a road, perhaps even a tramway, might have linked the shaft with the main entrance to the mine. There was a vast heap of slate waste from one of the later quarries not far ahead and I'd been afraid the mine entrance might have been buried beneath it, but it looked as though the tip hadn't extended that far.

The next time we met Paeony said, 'Eleven.'

'Er - I made it ten.'

She looked at me sympathetically. 'I held the reel the first time. We took turns. I've just held it again. That makes an odd number. We've measured 1100 feet. There should be 100 feet to go.'

'You just could be right.'

I held the reel, and she walked off towards a series of grassy humps. She disappeared over the top of one, and the tape ran out. I followed, winding in, and found her standing between two parallel banks which seemed to run into the hillside, with a narrow flat area between them. Below there were some biggish mounds.

'You know, this could well be it,' I said, 'It looks right. I wasn't expecting either the distance or the direction to be this accurate. But this was almost certainly the entrance to a mine. Look at the rushes growing in the bottom; there's probably seepage from the adit.'

'There's no sign of an entrance now.'

'There usually isn't. If the entrance is timbered it falls in pretty quickly. This probably collapsed seventy or eighty years ago. But the passage could well be quite intact behind it. The trouble is, it'd take a fair while for the two of us to dig it out, and it would probably need fresh timbering. It would be easier with some help.'

'What about the shaft? At least that's open. Why don't we go down and take a look, while we're here?'

I hesitated. 'There's no indication that it ever linked up with the rest of the mine. It was sunk to open up a fresh area, and the company went bust soon afterwards. It's probably just a hole in the ground.'

'Why not find out?'

'We'd need proper equipment. And the shaft could be unsafe.'

'I've brought my climbing gear. Let's go and get it.'

I'd been trying to head Paeony off the idea of attempting a descent of the shaft. No doubt she was a competent climber, but climbing and caving techniques are very different and exploring a mine is very like descending a cave system. I didn't know her capabilities, but I was pretty sure they wouldn't extend to the sort of rope work that would be needed. While I was trying to marshal my arguments she had already set off downhill, and I found myself following her down towards the Land Rover.

We collected our rucksacks and my rope bag and began to climb back up towards the shaft. She was ahead again. 'Look,' I said, trying to get my breath, 'We can make a preliminary inspection. If it looks OK I could probably go down a little way. But I'd rather you stayed at the top. You're not trained for this sort of thing.'

'How do you know?'

'Well… I mean, you're a climber. It's a different technique. I'm sure you could abseil down all right. But you'd need to come back up a vertical rope. It takes practice.'

'I thought you people climbed up and down ladders all the time,' she said condescendingly.

'Not nowadays. We've moved on a bit. We use SRT.'

SRT, or Single Rope Technique, has more or less replaced the traditional electron ladders for exploring shafts and potholes. It's far less exhausting, and a lot easier providing you're properly trained. I'd spent a long time practising it in a gym before they let me try it out underground. Going down involves abseiling, which most climbers can do as a matter of routine, but going up is a bit more complicated. When you're a long way down a hole in the ground, it's the going up you need to worry about.

'I can prusik,' Paeony said.

We'd reached the hollow surrounding the shaft, and she dumped her rucksack on the grass.

'We're not just talking about a short climb. Have you used jammers before?'

'Once or twice,' she said sweetly, and produced a pair from a pocket of the rucksack, one ready attached to a loop of rope. 'You said there was a shaft, so I brought them along in case.'

'Look,' I said again, 'I don't want to cast aspersions. It's just that I'm responsible for you...'

'Like hell you are.'

She had planted her hands on her hips and stuck out her chest, and I was discomfited. 'I - I don't mean like that,' I said desperately, 'It's just that - I don't know how good you are. It's the same with climbing, you need to know the other person's sufficiently experienced.'

'Fair enough.' Paeony pulled a climbing rope out of her rucksack, and without a word set off along the hillside. The rock face behind the shaft was about thirty feet high at its tallest point, but further along it became lower until it merged into a steep slope of grass and bilberry. She stomped up the slope, and I heard her coming back along somewhere above my head. There was a brief delay, and I was suddenly smothered in coils of rope falling from overhead. 'Below!' she called, belatedly.

A moment later she was back, looking up at the rope which she had belayed somewhere out of sight. Then she quickly got a climbing harness out of her rucksack, held it out in front of her, stepped into it and pulled it up. I watched her tightening the thigh straps, stretching the webbing belt across her midriff and buckling it tightly round the slender waist. A belay belt came next, a little higher up. She'd used canvas tapes to improvise a chest harness too, and began strapping them in place. I looked away.

Prusiking is the technique of climbing a single rope using a pair of metal jammers which resist a downward pull but can be slid upwards. One of them is attached to your harness at chest level, the other to a rope footloop that you can stand up in. Having stood up you let your weight come onto your chest jammer, slide the footloop jammer further up and stand up again. Then you slide the chest jammer up, and so on until you get to the top. Climbers tend to look down on this sort of thing, because after all the skill of climbing involves getting up rock faces using nothing but fingers and toes. Cavers aren't fussy, and in any case coming back up is the boring bit. Miners are only too happy to be winched up and down in cages.

Paeony was clipping various attachments to her harness with quick, emphatic movements. She attached the footrope jammer to the rope, clipped the other jammer to her chest, and was suddenly on her way. She moved upwards a little jerkily, raising herself with one foot in the loop while she kicked against the rock wall with the other, her slim body alternately flexing and straightening like a caterpillar on a twig. She was climbing a little faster than was strictly necessary, making a point. In a minute or so she was pulling herself over the top. She must have detached the jammers in seconds, because a moment afterwards she was abseiling smoothly down again to stand beside me.

'All right,' I sighed, 'You win. But you've got me confused. I thought climbers were only supposed to use ropes for emergencies. They're always going on about climbing ethics.'

'I'm a very unethical climber.'

The mouth of the shaft was only a few yards behind us, and we approached it cautiously. 'The edge could easily crumble away,' I said, 'And we don't know what this grass is growing on.' I'd brought one of the canes and was probing with it; the ground seemed pretty solid.

What had looked like the remains of planking was in fact an old gate, which was supporting the roll of wire. It had been placed across the mouth of the shaft, which seemed to be only about eight feet wide. I walked round to the other side, and we each got hold of one end. Grass and rushes had grown through it and it had become embedded in the turf, but eventually it moved and we managed to drag it sideways.

'Wait a minute.' The rock face that Paeony had climbed was jagged and had several promising-looking lumps and spikes. I selected one, got out a length of lifeline and belayed the end securely round it. Then I buckled on my body belt and clipped the rope to it at a length that wouldn't allow me to fall too far if the edge of the shaft gave way. When I looked back, she was belaying a lifeline as I had done. Thus secured, we proceeded to inspect the shaft.

Around the lip the rock was close to the surface, and much of the edge seemed quite firm. The danger of a descent of this kind isn't just from the ground giving way under your feet, but also from chunks of it following you down. I removed a few lumps of turf and loose rocks, and then peered into the shaft. A foot or so down the walls looked as good as the day it had been sunk.

'I think we could risk a look down there. But I'd rather have a double belay.' I was proposing to entrust my life to a rope, and liked to think that the end was adequately attached. The spiky rock wall behind was fine for one belay point, and there was a large boulder on the opposite side of the shaft to provide another. I spent some time rigging loops of rope from each of them at the right angle, with a big karabiner to join them above the shaft.

Paeony was looking on with interest. 'This is the first time I've ever started a climb from the top.'

'It won't really be climbing at all. You climbers just use ropes to stop you falling off. Cavers use them to go up and down on. That's why I'm taking so much trouble over this one. If a shaft's vertical and the rope's properly rigged, you shouldn't need to touch the rock at all.'

We agreed I'd go down first to see if it was possible to stand at the bottom of the shaft. From the plop I'd heard on my first visit it was clear there was water down there; if it was deep - and some shafts are flooded for hundreds of feet - she wouldn't be able to descend with me still hanging on the rope. If it was safe and practicable, she would follow me down.

I kept my lifeline rigged while I knotted my long rope to the karabiner and then fed it down the shaft. I'd tied a stop knot in the end: I didn't know just how deep the shaft was, and abseiling off the end of a rope isn't a good idea. Then I went to sort out the rest of the equipment.

Paeony was buckling on a climbing helmet; a hi-tech model which made my builder's version look distinctly proletarian. It didn't have a light attachment, but I had a spare electric helmet lamp with straps to attach it. She watched fascinated as I got out my scuffed and dented carbide lamp, unscrewed the cap and poured water into the reservoir from a plastic bottle.

'What's wrong with electricity?'

'This gives a better all-round light.' That was true up to a point, but the attraction of the carbide was partly its old-fashionedness, just like the Aladdin lamp at Tan-y-Coed. The old miners used candles, after all. I twisted the valve to let the water drip onto the carbide powder, and heard the hiss of the acetylene gas that it produced. There was a small flint attached to the lamp like an old-style cigarette lighter, and when I clicked it there was a little pop and a stab of flame, pale in the bright sunshine. A lot of mining enthusiasts won't use carbide: it's lethal down old coal mines where a naked flame will ignite pockets of methane gas, but that wasn't likely to be a problem here.

I pulled on my caving harness, clipped on its various attachments, and risked a look at Paeony's.

Everything was in place: all the complexity of webbing loops, cows' tails, karabiners of different shapes and sizes and assorted ironmongery which make up a modern SRT rig. She looked confident and relaxed, and I decided I could stop fretting about taking her down.

There was a ledge a few feet below the rim of the shaft that provided a handy foothold while attaching myself to the rope. I checked my various bits and pieces, threaded on a stop descender, unclipped my lifeline and began to abseil gently downwards into the darkness of the shaft.

The walls moved slowly upwards on each side of me. I paused about ten feet down, letting my eyes become accustomed to the soft, yellow light from the carbide lamp on my helmet. It revealed rough, irregular rock, dark grey streaked with black where water had trickled down. At this depth there was still a little moss on the damp stone. Looking up I could see Paeony's head against the brightness of the sky. Looking down there was nothing but blackness: one disadvantage of carbide is that you don't get the narrow, focused beam of an electric lamp. I squeezed the handle on the descender and glided smoothly down the rope.

I was turning slowly, my lamplight sweeping the jagged walls, looking for a passage opening off the shaft. There was the odd depression, but none went in more than a few feet. I was surprised at the almost complete absence of white quartz or other obvious mineralisation: there was nothing that would have encouraged the miners to think they were approaching a vein.

'What's it like?' Her voice came echoing down the shaft.

'Nothing to see. No passages yet.' I kept going, maintaining the same slow pace of descent. Then I released the handle and braked to a stop as a dark opening appeared to one side. It was a few feet away from me, and I pushed out a boot against the rock wall on the other side to swing myself nearer to it. The only effective light now was that coming from my helmet. I managed to revolve a little and shone my lamp into the hole. It went in all of six feet. On the back wall was a tiny band of quartz, just a few inches across. 'There's one dead end,' I called, and heard the hollow reverberations of my voice coming back from above and below.

I was around sixty feet down, and there should be about the same length of rope below me. I peered downwards to check, and saw a glint. It was a reflection of the bright daylight far above. Not far to go.

I was creeping down now, and suddenly made out the rope below me disappearing beneath a murky brown surface. I let myself slide down until my toe touched the water and poked my boot into it. Almost at once I felt soft, clinging mud. Cautiously I let myself down another foot or so, and was standing on a hard surface. The water was gently flowing over the tops of my boots. 'I'm at the bottom.'

I stood holding the rope and turned my head, lighting up the walls on either side. At this point the shaft was maybe ten feet across, though the walls were so irregular that the diameter varied greatly. Here, at the bottom, was the place where I might have been most likely to find galleries leading off. But there was nothing, nothing at all. I looked carefully down at water level, in case a low passage might have been almost blocked by debris, but there was no sign of an opening. I shifted my boots around in the mud; there were rocks buried in it, and bits of indefinable detritus. People throw some nasty things down shafts. This one didn't smell too bad though, relatively speaking. I picked one foot up and edged over towards the side. What appears to be the bottom of a shaft sometimes proves to be nothing but a blockage, wedged precariously above a continuation of the drop, but the water down here made that seem unlikely. This was evidently as far as it went. I released myself from the rope.

'You can come down now. Rope's free.'

High above movement was visible against the bright circle of light. Then Paeony's voice rang out: 'Coming down.'

The dark blob on the rope grew quickly bigger, and I could see the beam of her lamp flickering over the walls of rock. She was descending faster than I had but smoothly, fully in control. I was standing under a slight overhang, protected to some extent from any loose rocks that might accompany her down. When her boots had almost reached the water she glided gently to a halt, then slid a little further till she was standing beside me. 'Yuk!' she said, 'What a hole. Is there anything to see?'

'Not a thing. Look at the rock. No mineralisation, no lead vein, nothing. There's no sign of any galleries even having been begun. Either the money ran out, or they just gave up in disgust.'

'What a waste of effort. They must have been fed up. I don't suppose we could have missed anything on the way down.'

'I doubt it. But we'll keep an eye open on the way back.'

'All this way down just to go back up again.' She was looking round the dark, dank hole we were standing in with disgust. 'This mud's foul. Why isn't the water deeper? You said it would probably be flooded.'

'I expect there are fissures in the rock. We're still well above the floor of the valley, and the geology's pretty chaotic.'

'It pongs.'

'You're probably standing on a dead sheep.'

'Let's go,' she said hastily, 'I'll prusik up.'

Paeony fumbled a little as she attached her chest jammer to the rope. Cavers are used to doing these things in the dark. I watched unobtrusively to make sure she got it right. Her improvised harness was functional enough, though probably less comfortable than mine. She attached her footloop so that the end just trailed into the water, got both feet into it and pushed herself upwards. Then she was on her way, saving her energy now, grunting each time she straightened up. I held the rope, pulling it downwards so that it slid more easily through the jammers. She ascended slowly in the soft light from my lamp, a supple, ever-changing shape highlighted against the dark wall of the shaft. Old Dr Prusik would have been impressed.

It took her about a quarter of an hour to make the climb. Several times she paused for a rest, letting her harness take the strain, and I saw her light moving around the walls of the shaft. I guessed she hadn't climbed that far before on a rope, though she'd obviously practised the technique. Her footrope was a fraction too long, which slowed her down. At last her figure was outlined against the sky, and she disappeared from sight. I attached my own jammers and followed her up.

I checked the walls again on my way to the surface, but I hadn't missed anything on the way down. It was a straightforward ascent, and I was soon standing on the ledge, clipping on my lifeline. A quick scramble, and I was out in the daylight. Paeony was sitting on the grass, looking puffed but pleased with herself, her harness already unclipped, her gear stowed away. 'I don't quite know why, but I enjoyed that,' she said, 'I still prefer mountains though. The views aren't as good down there.'

I pulled the rope up hand over hand, and tried to clean some of the mud off the end; I'd rinse it properly later. Both of us were pretty grubby, and she was emptying muddy water out of her boots. We each had a tide mark where the water had come to just below our knees. It felt good having accomplished the descent, even though it hadn't led anywhere.

'At least we've ruled out the shaft. It doesn't look as if it ever connected with the main part of the mine. The only way we're going to get in is by the original entrance.'

'Never mind. We've had a good day.'

We dragged the old gate back over the shaft, and threw the wire back on top. A lot of the grass was actually growing on the rotten wood and the dirt that had built up on it, and when the gate was back in place the opening was quite effectively camouflaged. It would be sensible to have a word with Cadwaladr about getting it fenced. Paeony went up to unfasten her rope from the rock face, and we spent a few minutes coiling down.

'There's no point in doing anything else here today', I said. 'The next job is to get the tools up to the entrance and start digging. That could take a day if we're lucky, or a week if we're not.'

'I'm starving.'

'We could get a meal at the Hand Inn in Llangwm. If they'll let us in.'

'I've got a change of clothes in the Land Rover. I just need a sink.'

We humped the rucksacks down to her vehicle and drove back to Cadwaladr's farm. He put his head out of the back door. 'One, two', he counted, 'So you're both back in one piece.'

'Paeony's pretty good on a rope.'

'It's not her I'm worried about.'

We drove the two cars down in tandem to Llangwm, and headed for the Ladies and the Gents. Ten minutes later and smelling rather sweeter than before, we were enjoying the warmth and comfort of the lounge bar. Paeony looked fresh and scrubbed, wearing an oversize check shirt outside a clean pair of jeans. The pub wasn't crowded, and we bagged a table near the fire. She opted for draught cider and there was a doubtful look in the barman's eyes as he passed it over; she'd said she still had problems getting served in pubs. We both ordered gammon, double egg and chips. When they arrived the gammon steaks were grilled to perfection, tender and succulent with a little fringe of crispy fat. They were big enough to hang off the plate at both ends, and there was a separate basket for the chips. She tucked into her portion with gusto. Her slender figure wasn't the result of dieting.

After the plates were cleared away I felt a deep sense of contentment. Paeony sat opposite me, her skin glowing, the warm light glinting in her hair, her hands clasped around a glass in which the golden cider reflected the brightly burning fire. Neither of us had spoken for several minutes. It wasn't awkwardness, more the reverse; both of us seemed to feel sufficiently relaxed in each other's company not to need to make conversation. It was a companionable silence.

'It was good to go climbing again,' she said at last. 'I haven't been since Gerry was killed. I've enjoyed today.'

'So have I. When can we go back?'

'Not tomorrow.' She looked regretful. 'I've got to see some tenants. What about the day after?'

'We won't be climbing. Just tunnelling.'

'I'm quite good with a shovel as well as a rope.'

Then she said, 'John, just what is it exactly that we're looking for? Why are you so keen on the Cwm Llwyd mine?'

I was taken a little off guard. 'Bob was researching into it.'

'But why was Bob so interested?'

I hesitated. But I realised that nobody knew about the Crown and the mine but me, and possibly Carl Quinn. As a descendant of Owain Morgan Paeony had more right to the secret than I had, and anyway, I wanted to tell her. I didn't want to dissemble, or tell her less that the truth. And there was nobody within earshot. So I told her everything that Bob Lord had told me: about Owain Morgan's journal, about the link with Thomas Davies and the Abbey of Westminster, and about the Crown of England and where it might be hidden. I told her about the fire at Bob's house, about his death and the disappearance of his box of papers, and my subsequent run-in with the police. And I told her about Bob's visits to Carl Quinn in Walton Gaol.

She listened closely, putting in the odd question, nodding thoughtfully and raising an occasional eyebrow. She didn't jib at our conclusion that Owain and Thomas had spirited away the Crown and concealed it beneath the hillside of Cwm Llwyd. 'That would be just like Owain,' she said. 'There are all kinds of family stories about him. He would take the craziest risks. As a boy he's supposed to have climbed up the wall of the house at Berwyn, using the windows like a ladder, crossed the roof and climbed down the other side. I always fancied trying that myself, but I never had the nerve. And he was a passionate royalist. He added that porch, with the royal coat of arms, only two or three years after they cut King Charles's head off. It's a wonder they didn't cut his off too.'

It was when I was talking about Quinn that I felt a stirring of unease. Joseph's visit had reminded me, if I needed reminding, of Quinn's ruthlessness. I was already in some danger myself. Involving Paeony would put her at risk too.

'Swine like Quinn shouldn't be let out at all,' she said. 'Surely the police must have him down as a suspect. He'd been in contact with Bob Lord, and he had an obvious motive.'

'So had I, according to them. And I wasn't in gaol. Moreover, my name's Jones. MI5 think that's highly suspicious. Whatever I say, the police won't take much notice and I can't see them providing much protection either. Just knowing about the Crown is dangerous. I'm not sure I should have told you.'

'I'd have been pretty fed up if you hadn't. The Morgans started the job of rescuing the Crown, and it's about time they got it finished. We'll just have to be careful, that's all.'

I noticed the 'we'. 'If I'm right, this man's killed once already for the Crown. He's quite capable of doing so again. You'd be safer not getting involved.'

'Try and stop me,' said Paeony.

I didn't try very hard. I knew I should have done, but with shameful selfishness I couldn't resist the prospect of pursuing the hunt with her beside me. And sitting there in the warmth and comfort of the bar, it was easy to underestimate the dangers ahead.

'If anyone's in danger at the moment it's you.' She was resting her elbows on the table, holding the cider glass in both hands, tilting it slightly, caressing the rim with her lips and letting the amber liquid sparkle on her tongue. 'You live on your own, in a pretty remote spot.

Carl Quinn could easily arrange another fire. Did Bob Lord tell him that you were working with him?'

'I don't know. He may have done. Bob didn't try to keep secrets. But the newspaper report made it clear we were working together. Quinn might think I had information that could help him. I suppose he might send someone to pay me a visit. I'll take some precautions.'

I changed the subject. 'I've been thinking about the digging. It might be sensible to try to get some of the WMEG people to help us. It's hard to tell from the surface how deeply the entrance is buried, and how much has collapsed. The work could take days.'

'Why don't we give it a try ourselves for a day or so?' she suggested. 'We can always call them in if we find we need to. There isn't really room for more than two to work in that gully anyway.' I suspected she might find we'd bitten off more than we could chew, but I was happy to agree to another day on our own.

'Okay. We'll give it a day anyway.'

'If we do get into the mine, what then?'

'The search is going to take a long time. The nineteenth century miners didn't find anything hidden underground as far as we know, and they spent years down there. The inside of a lead mine is a pretty complicated place, and a dangerous one too. Imagine Hampton Court Maze in three dimensions, much bigger, with a lot of the passages choked with mud or fallen rock, others on the point of collapse, and all in pitch darkness. You never quite know when the ground is going to disappear under your feet. The lowest sections are certain to be flooded. Moreover, they used the worked out passages and chambers to store the waste rock, so there's every chance the older workings will be blocked off or filled in. Even if we knew for certain where the Crown was, we might never be able to recover it.' She didn't seem deterred.

We arranged that I'd pick her up at Berwyn in two days' time at nine in the morning. She thought somebody else might need the Land Rover that day. Outside the warm brightness of the bar the night air was cool and still. On the car park we lingered for a while. 'Thanks for today,' Paeony said, and gave me a peck on the cheek. My head swam, and I found myself trying to poke my key into the door of someone else's car. By the time I'd located my own, she was gone.

Driving home, I sang a selection of operatic arias, interspersed with bits of 'The Messiah'. I'd never appreciated quite how good my voice was. It was a pity there was nobody else to hear it.

CHAPTER 10

All the way back to Tan-y-Coed I remained in a state of euphoria. I hadn't felt like that since...: in fact, I hadn't felt like that at all. I'd thought I'd been in love with Sarah, and for a time we'd been happy together, or what I thought was happy. But this was different. The time until Saturday seemed an infinity. I kept picturing Paeony: the sparkle in her eyes as we'd planned our campaign, the incisive gestures, the flash of anger when she thought I was being patronising, the flow of her hair framing the curve of her cheek and neck, the hands gently stroking the long glass. There was a tightness in my chest that wouldn't go away. Even so, when I reached my dark, deserted house below the wood I'd collected myself sufficiently to approach it cautiously, and to lock the door before I went to bed.

Alone in the little room under the roof, doubts started to creep into my mind. I was starting to feel frightened by the strength of my own feelings, and painfully aware of my own shortcomings. There was an age difference. Six years isn't much, I told myself, three or four is quite normal, so what does it matter? But I had a nasty feeling that the life I'd settled into at Tan-y-Coed was more appropriate to one of the old bachelors Glyn had talked about than to the average thirty-year old. I'd taken to going around in an anorak, and maybe it was symptomatic. To someone as youthful as Paeony I must seem like a relic. Even if the unbelievable happened and she found me a halfway acceptable partner, her family was hardly likely to be impressed by my ex-Regional Managership. Heiress marries unemployed Travelling Salesman. My life was turning into something out of Mills and Boon.

I hadn't bothered to check the answerphone when I got back, but I played the tape the next morning and heard an unfamiliar voice. It was high-pitched and affected, like a ham actor playing an absent-minded professor. 'Ah - good evening,' it said. 'I hope I am speaking to Mr

John Jones. My name is Dr Charles Angevin Greene - Greene with an -e. I had been in touch with the late Mr Robert Lord regarding - ah - a certain matter which was of interest to him. He mentioned to me that you had been assisting him. We had planned to meet again before his sad - ah - decease. I hope that I have been successful in ascertaining your telephone number - your name is a rather - ah - frequent one in these parts. I am staying in Llangollen at present, in the Royal Hotel. I wonder if I could ask you to telephone me when you return -ah -.' He gave the number and his voice tailed off awkwardly, uncomfortable with the technology.

Bob had talked about Charles Angevin Greene and his Fellowship of Royalists. He'd said that Greene knew all there was to know about crowns, and suggested I might like to meet him. I didn't really know much about the Crown, only what Bob had told me. I ought to be better informed about the thing I was looking for.

I rang the Royal Hotel, and a comfortable Welsh voice said that Dr Greene was expecting a call. A moment later the voice from the answerphone said, 'Angevin Greene speaking. Ah - Mr Jones. How good of you to ring.'

'How can I help you?'

'Ah - Mr Lord had been telling me something of his most interesting researches. I had hoped to be able to offer him some assistance. I was greatly distressed to hear that he had - ah - passed away so suddenly. I was most anxious to know how he had progressed, and took the liberty of travelling to Wales in the hope of meeting you. If you - ah - happen to be free I could take a taxi and come to visit you.'

I couldn't imagine Dr Angevin Greene bumping down the track to Tan-y-Coed in a taxi.

'That's all right. I'm free today. I can come to Llangollen.'

'That is really most kind. Extremely kind. I am really most grateful. Very grateful indeed.'

'Not at all. I'm sure we can help each other.'

Greene invited me to lunch - 'The very least I can do...' - and I was happy to accept.

I made the cottage as secure as I could before leaving and resolved to buy some window bolts in Llangollen. Driving along the valley road I met Glyn Lewis's Land Rover. He stopped in a gateway to let me past, and I pulled up level with him and wound the window down. He gave me a friendly 'How are you?'

'Glyn,' I said when we'd passed the time of day, 'Have you seen any strangers up the valley lately, or any strange vehicles?'

He looked at me quizzically. 'There were a few tourists at the weekend. Was it anyone in particular you were thinking of?'

'There could be someone looking for me, people I'd rather avoid. I don't think they'd look like tourists. If you do see anything odd, could you let me know?'

'I'll keep an eye open. We're the only ones living up here, so we generally notice if anyone comes up.'

'Thanks,' I said, and we drove our separate ways.

When I walked into the lounge of the Royal Hotel one figure stood out from among the tweeds and twin sets. Charles Angevin Greene was younger that I had expected: his hair was fair rather than white, though there wasn't a lot of it. He wore a sort of Norfolk jacket of green loden, complete with piping and horn buttons. There was a badge like a gilt crown in his button hole. As he got to his feet he revealed plus fours with long green knitted stockings.

'Dr Greene?' I held out a hand.

'Angevin Greene. It was most kind of you to come. Most kind. I really am extremely....'

'Delighted to help.'

Greene headed for the restaurant rather than the bar, and insisted that I ordered a more substantial lunch than I was used to, whilst he requested the waitress to bring him an omelette which wasn't on the menu. His volubility gradually wore down her resistance, and he was still thanking her triumphantly as she disappeared through the swing doors for what was probably going to be a confrontation with the cook. Then he transferred his attention back to me.

'I understood from Mr Lord that he had confided in you regarding his - ah - theories. He came up to London to see me, you know. I must admit that I was sceptical. Your friend was not the first person to postulate that St Edward's Crown had survived and been concealed.' I must have looked surprised, because he went on, 'Mr Lord was quite open with me, Mr Jones. He was acting purely in the interests of scholarship.'

'Who else thought the Crown might still exist?'

'For one, Sir Arthur Conan Doyle,' Greene replied with a faint smile. 'He made it the subject of one of his tales. You are following in the footsteps of Sherlock Holmes.'

'I gather you're now more inclined to take the idea seriously. What made you change your mind?'

'You may know that the circumstances in which the Crown was seized from the Abbey were more than a little confused.' Now that Greene was on his favourite subject the hesitancy was gone. 'I have been investigating them more closely. The creatures who took it, along with other sacred relics of the Confessor, had no idea what they were looking for. The Crown of St Edward had rarely been seen in public, other than at the coronation ceremony. On other occasions the King wore the Crown of State, which was kept at the Tower. What they found at the Abbey was a wooden box with the inscription: "Haec est principalior corona cum qua coronabantur Aelfredus, Edwardus et ceteri..." They naturally assumed that that was what it contained. And so the wretched fellow Wither, in the words of Anthony a'Wood: "Being crowned and royally arrayed, first marched about the room with a stately garb, and afterwards with a thousand apish and ridiculous actions exposed these sacred ornaments to contempt and laughter."'

Greene's ability to quote from memory was impressive. 'But if the crown they found in the box was the wrong one, why wasn't the deception discovered?'

'The regalia taken from the Abbey were originally listed by a military officer, a Colonel Dove. In addition to the Crown itself there were two lesser crowns, two sceptres, two staffs, an orb, a ring, a mantle and other items. They were all removed to the Jewel House at the Tower, and it was some time before they were properly examined. When they were, it was discovered that many of them were not made of gold, as had been anticipated, but of silver gilt, or in the case of the staffs of iron or wood with a thin sheathing of gold. I imagine there was considerable disappointment. The one exception is described as: "King Alfred's Crowne of gould wyerworke sett with slight stones and 2 little bells poz 79 Ounces one half."'

'Why King Alfred's Crown? Surely the Crown wasn't as old as that.'

Greene smiled thinly. 'No indeed. Until the Reformation it was always known as the Crown of St Edward. The Confessor had been canonised in 1161. But after the Reformation it was not politically correct, so to speak, to refer to St. Edward. The veneration of saints was frowned upon. So they officially adopted a legend that the Crown had been worn by Alfred the Great, a patriotic figure who was suitably

112

uncontroversial. That was nonsense of course, but it demonstrates that the Crown was regarded as being of great antiquity.'

Greene was interrupted by the waitress who deposited an omelette firmly in front of him, placed an appetising plate of roast beef more gently in front of me and surrounded it with little dishes of vegetables. I helped myself to a generous portion. Greene began to dissect the omelette with archaeological precision, as if something fragile and precious might be concealed within.

'The Confessor's crown was made for him in the year 1052,' he went on. 'The craftsman responsible was a celebrated monastic goldsmith, Spearhavoc by name. He was Abbot of Abingdon, a man of some substance, though of dubious character. On Edward's death in 1066 the Crown was buried with him, in the abbey church of Westminster which he had built. It was subsequently removed when the tomb was opened, either in 1102 when the Abbey was seeking to promote the cult of the Confessor, or by Henry III in 1269. Henry greatly venerated St Edward, and built a magnificent shrine for him in the Abbey to which his remains were removed. We know that St Edward's Crown was used for the coronation of Henry's son, Edward I, so it must have been available by then. It was subsequently used for every coronation up to that of Charles I – the martyred King.'

I was happy to let Greene talk; my mouth was full of Yorkshire pudding with a nice crisp exterior and a soft centre that soaked up the gravy.

'When the Crown was seized in 1649,' Greene said, 'Parliament's instructions were that it should be broken up, and the metal melted down and sent to the Mint to be turned into coinage. It has always been assumed that that was indeed done. However, some years ago a very curious anomaly came to light. In the nineteen-thirties the Constable of the Tower and Keeper of the present-day Crown Jewels, a Major-General Sitwell, carried out an investigation into the fate of the original regalia. He examined the records of the Royal Mint, which are preserved in their entirety for the period which concerns us. The Mint were always most meticulous in recording every ounce, or fraction of an ounce, of gold which passed through their hands. The General found no trace of the seventy-nine and a half ounces of gold allegedly contained in St Edward's Crown; indeed, there was no entry of any kind, in that or later years, that could have been identified with it. We are speaking of a very substantial sum, which could not possibly have been overlooked. Evidently the gold was never received.'

'Did Sitwell suggest any explanation?'

'He did indeed.' Greene detached a sliver from the slowly congealing omelette, 'He noted that the modern St Edward's Crown, made for the coronation of Charles II in 1661, was of a similar weight to the old Crown; he therefore concluded that the gold had probably been kept back and reused. There is however no evidence that this was the case, and the discrepancy has never been satisfactorily explained. If the gold was indeed preserved in some way, it was in direct contravention of the orders of Parliament which were, as I said, that it should be turned into coin. It seems to me more likely that the gold never came into the government's possession.'

'So there must have been some sort of cover-up. When they found they hadn't got the Crown at all, they didn't want it to be known.'

'That seems highly probable. Quite apart from its intrinsic value, the Crown was greatly revered. It possessed a symbolic importance, as Owain Morgan clearly recognised. To announce that the government had been deceived, that the Crown had been spirited away and that its whereabouts was unknown, would have been embarrassing to say the least. No doubt discretion was considered to be in the public interest.'

'No doubt it was in the interest of certain people,' I said. 'But how was the original deception managed? How could Thomas Davies find a substitute that was even remotely convincing?'

'When Mr Lord showed me the translation which he had made of Owain Morgan's journal, one sentence at first appeared to be obscure. If you remember, he had written: 'King Harry's shall serve.' It is not clear which King Harry is meant, or what attribute of King Harry he is referring to. Now there is one noun which Morgan consistently refrains from using. That noun is 'Crown'. You may not be aware that many of the Kings of England were buried wearing a crown. The later funeral crowns were replicas, made of silver gilt or often of base metal: gilded iron or tin. A gold crown was far too valuable to bury. Henry III himself is known to have been buried wearing a crown of this kind. As I said, King Henry greatly venerated Edward the Confessor. What could be more likely than that he should have been interred wearing a replica of the Crown which he himself had taken from the grave?'

'The clergy at the Abbey would have known of the existence of the funeral crowns,' I said. 'I've read about them myself. Attempts were made at different times to steal them from the tombs. Thomas Davies could have taken the funeral crown from the tomb of Henry III, put it in the box and spirited the original away. The replica would have fooled George Marten and his gang; maybe it passed an initial inspection afterwards.'

'You have followed my train of thought precisely,' Greene said with a condescending air.

Angevin Greene's fascinating but lengthy exposition had allowed me to finish an excellent lunch, whilst the remains of his omelette still languished reproachfully upon his plate. The waitress whisked it away without a word. I declined the offer of rhubarb crumble with custard but accepted coffee, and we moved through to the lounge to drink it.

Greene leaned forward in the chintz armchair, his watery blue eyes gleaming behind thick rimless glasses. 'So, Mr Jones. I believe I have been able to demonstrate the - ah - authenticity of Mr Lord's suppositions. Now I was hoping that you would be able to assist with the next and most vital stage of the inquiry: the location of the Crown itself. It appears that it was concealed beneath the ground, in some kind of mine.'

'That may have been the case,' I said cautiously. For all his expertise I wasn't sure how much I wanted to confide in Charles Angevin Greene, and I couldn't see him being much help in the actual search. 'Even if that were true, it would be very difficult to find it.'

'But you have some knowledge of the mines in question,' Greene persisted. There were little glistening beads on his domed, pink forehead. 'And Mr Lord informed me that you have much experience of both historical and - ah - subterranean research. It is our clear duty to pursue this quest to its conclusion. Think of the prize to be gained. It is no less than the rediscovery of the rightful Crown of England.'

'I've knocked about a bit underground. Of course I'd like to find the Crown. It's a unique object. I'm sure the House of Windsor would like to get it back.'

'No doubt they would, Mr Jones,' Greene hissed, 'No doubt they would. But the Crown must go to the man who is truly entitled to wear it, and not to Elizabeth of Windsor.'

I gaped at him. 'Who's entitled to wear the Crown, if not the Queen?'

'Your ignorance, if I may say so, is all too typical,' Greene said venomously, blinking furiously behind his spectacles, 'I have devoted my life to upholding the cause of the true sovereign of this kingdom. The House of Hannover and its descendants gained the throne through the machinations of the English Whigs, who would stop at nothing to assure a protestant succession. The true catholic line of the House of Stuart lives on, though few are aware of it. I have travelled to Rome, I have stood in the crypt of St Peter's beside the tomb of King Charles Edward of glorious memory, and of his brother King Henry the Ninth, and I have sworn that their kin shall one day be restored to the thrones of England and of Scotland.'

'But the Stuarts died out. Bonnie Prince Charlie was too drunk most of the time to sleep with his wife, and his brother Henry became a Cardinal at 22. Neither of them did a lot towards maintaining the succession.'

'That was a great misfortune,' Greene said bitterly, 'But they were not the last of their royal House. Though their line was extinguished, today the Head of the House of Stuart is His Royal Highness Prince Francis of Bavaria. His title has been established by numerous genealogical studies, including my own. He and none other is the rightful occupant of the English throne.'

'Does he know?' I asked, faintly.

'His Royal Highness has graciously acknowledged my findings. And many other scholars have supported my conclusions. Prince Francis is not only a Wittelsbach, and thus a scion of one of the most ancient ruling houses of Europe: he is also directly descended from Princess Henrietta, youngest daughter of our martyred King Charles I. Mr Jones, we are seeking the true Crown of England, the Crown of St Edward, with which our greatest monarchs - Edward I, Henry V, Elizabeth, and Charles himself - were duly crowned. If that Crown can be found and restored to Prince Francis, then I believe that he will come forward and claim what is his by right.'

'If by any chance I do find the crown I'm not going to hand it over to some Prince of Bavaria. The Queen we've got is good enough for me.'

Greene's eyes popped; he half rose from his chair, and for a moment I thought he was going to strike me, but then he suddenly subsided. He gulped and cleared his throat several times, his adam's apple bobbing up and down. At last he said in a strained voice, 'I am greatly dismayed to find you so - ah - ill-informed on a matter of such significance, Mr Jones. Perhaps we must agree to differ in this respect for the present. Clearly it will be necessary to locate the Crown before we - ah - determine its disposition. I trust that I can count on your co-operation in this, at least.'

I made co-operative noises, and he proceeded to question me eagerly about the mine. Whilst he'd been generous with the information he had given me, I was reluctant to reciprocate fully. The eccentricity of his ideas was disturbing, and I wasn't sure how reliable an ally he would be. So I told him a lot about lead mines in general, and rather less about Cwm Llwyd in particular - though from his questions I inferred that Bob had probably given him the mine's general location. I gave a particularly hair-raising account of the hazards and exertions of mine exploration, and hoped I'd deterred him from trying to pursue the investigation underground in person.

The empty coffee cups had been whisked away, but I didn't want to leave Greene without getting him to tell me a little more about the thing I'd been seeking. 'What would the Crown have been like? How much is actually known about it?'

He responded eagerly. 'Alas, there are no written records. But we may postulate a good deal. We are looking for a closed or imperial crown: not merely a circlet, but a crown with arches over the head. The type originated in the East, possibly in Byzantium. It derives of course from a military headdress; the arches would give protection against blows from a sword. Such a crown was worn by the Emperor Constantine along with the state armour which he originated. The design had reached the West by the ninth century. It was subsequently modified...'

I risked an interruption. 'Are there any illustrations of St Edward's Crown itself?'

'There are indeed. There are representations of the Crown to be seen to this day in the Abbey of Westminster. Where the Confessor is depicted in carvings he is normally shown to be wearing it, and it appears in the coronation scene carved upon the chantry of King Henry V. The archaic, flattened shape is unmistakeable, and as the Crown was kept in the Abbey it is reasonable to assume that it is accurately represented. But the best illustration is undoubtedly in the Armada portrait of Elizabeth I, at Woburn Abbey, where the Crown is shown placed upon a table. The shape is the same, and the circlet is seen to be set about with large rounded stones, balas rubies no doubt, or garnets. The vulgar diamond was a later innovation. So Mr Jones, you will appreciate the historical significance of the object we are seeking. It was from this Crown that England's sovereigns derived their legitimacy, until the usurpers sought to overthrow the House of Stuart.'

It seemed that another diatribe was about to begin. So I hinted at a reason for needing to cut short our discussion, thanked Charles Angevin Greene warmly for my lunch, and took my leave. I promised to keep in touch without actually making a further appointment for us to meet, and assured him that I'd let him know if there were any really exciting developments. His disappointment was evident, but he seemed to accept that I wasn't going to take him below ground to discover the thing he'd set his heart on. I left him standing rather disconsolately, an exotic and incongruous figure, in the reception hall of the hotel.

Before leaving Llangollen I went into a pleasantly old-fashioned ironmongers and invested in a few basic security devices for Tan-y-Coed. The halogen lighting system on display was too incongruously modern, and I didn't fancy having it constantly activated by passing sheep. But I bought a good door bolt to supplement the antique lock, as well as a chain, and some proper window fasteners. I'd never been security-conscious and had rarely bothered to lock the door at night; now it seemed a good idea. Then I stocked up with food, and drove back home. It took most of the evening to fit everything, and I resented having to do it: part of the freedom and innocence of life at Tan-y-Coed had been lost.

CHAPTER 11

The next morning I was up early, loading assorted tools into the Justy, and just managed to manoeuvre a wheelbarrow into the back seat. Then I took the road for Berwyn.

It was a sparkling blue morning as I drove through the park where I'd first seen Paeony cantering across the grass. I parked on the broad forecourt and stood for a moment looking up at the great house and the white clouds scudding past behind the chimneys, the finials and pinnacles. Just as I was about to head for the door a voice behind me said, 'I still can't believe I live in it.'

'I saw you driving round this way,' Paeony said, 'I've got some stuff to pick up in the stable yard.' She came and stood beside me. 'That was Owain's work.' She was pointing to the great porch with its riot of carving. 'Have you noticed the date?' High up above the Stuart arms, was the royal cipher CR, and the date 1653.

I worked it out. 'Charles I had been dead for four years when that was carved. Charles II didn't return to England until 1660. But Owain was proclaiming his allegiance to the second Charles seven years earlier, in the middle of the Commonwealth. He was taking quite a risk.'

'Risks never worried him.'

We took the car round to the back of the house where she produced an impressive looking mattock and a stainless steel spade; an improvement on my own rather battered implement. As usual, the stable yard was empty.

'Does nobody else live here?'

'Daddy won't have living-in servants. Anyway, we can't really afford them. A lady comes in from the village in the mornings. The estate workers live over the far side of the park. And I've no brothers or sisters.'

'Neither have I.'

As we set off Paeony suddenly asked, 'Would you like to see where Owain's buried?'

It hadn't occurred to me to look for Owain Morgan's grave, and I didn't even know where it was.

'Yes, I would, very much. Is it far?'

'He's buried in Llaneifion Church, with the rest of the family. It's just down the road.'

The church was long and low and grey, set in a round churchyard filled with slate headstones and guarded by ancient yews. Paeony pushed open the heavy door, and we took a step down: the church floor was lower than the ground outside. The nave was dark and narrow, with humble, roughly joinered pews, but on the far side there was a broad aisle with larger windows, crowded with monuments and defined by a wooden screen.

'The Morgan Chapel.'

In front of us was a large tomb chest of black granite, Victorian by the look of it, with a cold white marble effigy stretched out upon it.

'Great great grandfather.'

William, first Lord Berwyn gazed unblinkingly at the ceiling.

Paeony pointed to another monument on the wall of the chapel. It was an imposing confection, with the figure of a stout, bearded man wearing old fashioned armour supporting himself at an uncomfortable angle on one arm and pointing with the other at a pair of cherubs overhead, carrying a sort of garland. It was surmounted by the Morgan arms, surrounded by fancy strapwork and crowned by miniature obelisks and little marble balls. Two cheerful looking dragons were perched on either side. Its exuberance immediately recalled Owain Morgan's work at Berwyn.

'The man who did "The Buildings of Wales" thinks it's by the same architect as the porch', Paeony said. 'He's rather rude about it. Says something about "retrograde in style and provincial in execution", but perhaps that's because Father wouldn't let him in. He always says Berwyn's a private house, not a tourist attraction.'

'This has character. Like Owain.'

I walked across to read the inscriptions. There were two. One in Latin recorded Owain Morgan's death on the twenty-first day of April, 1660. The other, in English, was in rhyme:

'Here lyes an honest gentleman,
The juste his praises synge,
He laboured long to serve his God,
And long to serve his Kynge.
Now enemyes of God and Kynge
Are utterlye caste downe,
He drynkes the draughte that hath no end,
And weares th' eternall Crowne.'

'I'd rumbled the bit about drink,' she said, 'But not the reference to a crown.'

'The old blighter must have written it himself, in anticipation. We know we're on the right track now.'

I was working out the dates. 'So Owain died as late as April, 1660. That was the same month that the Convention met and invited Charles II back to take the throne. He arrived in May. Owain must have known the Restoration was about to happen. Had he lived a few weeks longer, he could have retrieved the Crown and handed it over. What a shame. How did he die?'

'He's supposed to have caught the plague. Though I thought the Great Plague in London was later than that.'

'It was in 1665. But there were other minor outbreaks all through the 1660's. They were mainly in London though.'

'Owain died at Berwyn.'

I walked along the chapel looking at the other monuments, some of them older than Owain's, some more recent. Most were a good deal more restrained. Then, beyond the end of the chapel on the wall of the chancel, a tablet caught my eye.

'Paeony! Look at this.'

It was a simple slab of black slate, with plain lettering and no other decoration. The inscription read:

'Thos Davies, D.D. Canon of Westminster. D. 15 Apr 1660.'

She stared at the tablet, wide-eyed. 'I'd never noticed it. That was only a week before Owain died. And why was Thomas Davies here, and not in London?'

My mind was racing. 'Thomas must have known the Restoration was imminent. Maybe he came down from London to consult with

Owain, to talk about returning the Crown to the Abbey, or handing it over to the King. And brought the plague with him.'

Paeony's eyes suddenly filled with tears. 'That would have been so unfair. They'd risked so much, and waited so long. And they'd succeeded, the Crown was safe, all they had to do was give it back. They must have been so happy.'

'And no-one knew,' I said, 'No-one but them.'

We walked silently out of the church and back to the car.

Forty minutes later we were driving into Cadwaladr's farmyard. He came stumping out of one of his sheds, a broad grin splitting his stubbled face. 'So you're back again already, are you?' he called. 'It's a pity you've nothing better to do.'

'We're working today.' Paeony indicated the tools in the back.

'You've come to dig, have you? I've a dead ewe you could bury, if you want to start here. I expect it's his feed finished her off.'

'She probably starved. You never did buy more than a bag at a time.'

'High pressure salesmanship I had to put up with. Once he got his foot in the door I couldn't get rid of him.'

We explained what we wanted to do, and he shrugged and let us get on with it. We drove as far as we could, and then loaded the tools into the wheelbarrow and set off for the mine. We ended up carrying the barrow between us as we struggled up the hillside; the going wasn't fit for wheels of any kind.

We parked the barrow in the gully that we'd identified as the entrance and surveyed the tussocky bank at the end. It was quite smooth and sloped gently into the bottom of the gully. 'It sometimes pays to dig a bit higher up, just above where the tunnel entrance would have been,' I said. 'There's often less depth of earth at that point. We can dig down to the entrance.'

I took the mattock and swung it tentatively; it was sharp, and dug deeply into the turf. Soon I'd stripped a couple of square yards, revealing the peaty soil full of stones and bracken roots. I exchanged the mattock for a pick.

When enough soil was loosened we worked together, using the spades to fill the barrow. It was hard work in the stony ground. It's advisable not to deposit the dug out soil too close to the excavation; you always end up having to shift it again. Fortunately the bottom of the gully was reasonably smooth, and Paeony wheeled the barrow to the end and tipped it while I went back to work with the pick.

It was soon evident that the bedrock wasn't far below the surface, and we found it necessary to dig a little lower down the bank where the ground was looser. We worked away steadily, changing places periodically, and the hollow we were excavating gradually deepened and widened. Eventually we decided it was lunch time. We'd each packed a picnic, mine being rather basic, and we sat at the end of the gully and munched. The sky had clouded over, but it was reasonably warm.

'Where do you think the first entrance to the mine would have been?' she asked, 'I mean, the one Owain would have used when he came to hide the Crown.'

I shrugged. 'Possibly further uphill. The old miners tended to stope down: that is, when they reached the vein they dug into the floor of the tunnel they'd made and kept going downwards. The later miners preferred to stope up: that's to say they tried to start as far down as possible and hacked away at the roof. That way they didn't have to dig the ore out; it simply fell down. Of course, they had to take care it didn't fall on them.'

'I keep thinking of Owain and Thomas, dying just before the King returned. Couldn't Owain have told someone where the Crown was, or left some sort of message?'

'The plague could strike very quickly. People became unconscious, or delirious, before they knew what was happening. Perhaps they never had the chance.'

The grass was damp, and we were sharing a flat stone which was a bit on the small side. As we talked my thigh came into contact with hers: I was aware of its warmth and softness through two layers of tightly stretched denim. Neither of us tried to move apart.

At last we went back to work, and Paeony took the pick. She swung it high above her head and brought it down as forcefully as she could. The head buried itself completely in the soil, catching her off balance so that she half fell into little pit we had dug above the head of the gully. She pulled the pick out and knelt down, thrusting her hand where it had landed.

'Look John! It's a hole.'

I knelt down beside her, and peered into a dark cavity that seemed to extend downwards. I found a sizeable pebble and poked it through the hole. There was a clatter and a plop. 'That's it. There's bound to be a bit of water in the mouth of the adit.'

We proceeded to dig and lever away to enlarge the cavity. Stones and clods of earth kept falling through it; others we threw down into the gully where the barrow stood, forgotten. It wasn't long before the hole was a couple of feet or so across. I'd brought a torch, and I dug it out of my rucksack and shone it down the hole. It revealed a muddy bank sloping down into what was clearly a level. There was water in the bottom. I stuck my head down and trained the lamp along the tunnel walls. They looked rocky and fairly solid.

'I think we're in luck. It looks reasonably sound.'

We dug more carefully now, and reverted to barrowing the spoil away. I was anxious to clear away any loose material above and around the entrance, to avoid any possibility of a fall that might seal it again. That meant a good deal of extra digging and carting, and with only two of us it was hard work. Some of the rocks were too big to lift, but we contrived to roll them along the gully floor. We came across the remains of some timbering, rotting and splintered, and managed to dig them out and drag them clear. There wasn't much timber though, and I began to hope that we were going to find a clean, rock-cut tunnel right from the start. The presence of bedrock just above had been a hopeful sign.

I dug a narrow trench in one corner of the entrance, and water started running out through it. It would help to reduce the depth behind the earth dam that still blocked the lower half of the adit. Soon there was quite a stream running along the floor of the gully.

At last I threw my spade down and said, 'That'll do.' We hadn't dug the entrance out completely; the opening was only about three feet high. But there was a solid rock lintel over it, and we'd stripped the turf and soil above.

'It looks reasonably safe,' Paeony said tentatively.

'It's pretty good. At some stage we could dig for a bit more headroom, and some timber and metal sheeting would help to stabilise the ground in the longer term. And we could get it dryer. But for the moment it's O.K. I think we could risk a look inside.'

'It's only four o'clock. Let's fetch the gear.' So we pushed the barrowload of tools down the hill and up to the car, and exchanged it for helmets, rubber boots and a rope in case. Paeony flinched as I donned my torn and filthy boiler suit, which I'd given up trying to wash. 'I suppose I'd better get one of those,' she said doubtfully.

'You can get them in white. But they don't stay white for long.'

By the time we got back up to the mine it was spitting with rain. 'At least it can't rain underground,' Paeony said.

'Don't you believe it.'

The time was now nearer five than four, and we decided that this had better be a quick preliminary inspection. We fixed the lamps, and I ducked under the rock and slithered down the slope to the floor of the level. There was a foot or so of water, not quite enough to come over the tops of my boots. We had about five feet of headroom. The roof looked solid enough. 'It's okay,' I said, and she followed.

We splashed cautiously along. My carbide lamp illuminated the walls and roof, whilst her electric light with its more efficient reflector cast a longer but narrower beam which danced over the dark, jagged rock ahead of us as she walked. It was a relatively easy walk-in; the height wasn't too uncomfortable, and the level rose gently so that the floor soon became fairly dry. There were the remains of wooden sleepers at regular intervals, where a tramway had run, and we stumbled over them. The walls and roof were rough and irregular, just as the blasting had left them. I pointed out the long, smooth cylindrical hollows made by the drills, where the explosive had been packed. Each represented hours of work, swinging a sledgehammer by candlelight in the confined space of the level.

Paeony kept looking anxiously up at the roof. 'You should be looking at the floor,' I said, 'If there's rubble lying there it shows there's loose stuff above. Also, there can be shafts. They might be covered over with rotten timber, and the timber could be concealed by stones and mud. It's best to look down.' She looked down, and then banged her helmet on a protruding lump of rock.

After a hundred yards or so we were beginning to feel the stabbing ache in the small of the back that comes from walking in a stooped position. 'Ouch,' she said, 'I'm surprised the miners were ever able to straighten up.' Just then the beam of her light showed a dark opening on the right hand side of the tunnel. We stopped and directed our lights into it. It only went a few yards and ended in a rock wall. She was about to take a step forward when I put out an arm to stop her.

'Look down!'

As she looked down, the beam from her helmet was directed into a circular pit with rocky walls that descended sheer into the darkness. From below there came a hollow, echoing sound of dripping water.

'It's a winze. An underground shaft. Probably used to bring up ore from a lower level. Look, those are the remains of the winding gear.' Hanging at a drunken angle in the mouth of the shaft were a few rotten beams supporting some ironwork, bright orange with rust, and the remains of a wooden windlass barrel. Everything was covered with a slimy black and green encrustation that glistened in the light of the lamps. Paeony shuddered.

'It's odd.' I was peering down. 'You'd expect this to be full of water. The level we're in looks as though it should be the main drainage adit, but there isn't enough water flowing along it. And everything below it ought to be flooded, but it obviously isn't.'

'That shaft we went down wasn't flooded either.'

'There's no sign of pumping gear here. I suppose it could be natural drainage again, letting the water get away. Or maybe there's another adit somewhere lower down.'

Beyond the winze the roof was lower and we had to walk with our necks thrust awkwardly forward. One of my vertebrae received a nasty graze from a sharp projection in the roof. The floor was covered with several inches of greasy, yellow mud which tried to swallow our boots and then released them reluctantly with a disgusting, sucking sound. The passage remained completely straight, but looking back we could no longer see the faint grey light from the entrance; without the lamps we would now be totally blind. We plodded along for another hundred yards or so, our squelching footsteps echoing from the rock around us. Then, quite suddenly, the roof disappeared.

We were looking into a narrow chamber, its walls only four or five feet apart, which soared high into the darkness above. As we peered upwards our lights played on baulks of timber, roughly trimmed branches or sections of tree trunk, jammed and wedged across between the rock walls, some of them horizontal, others at crazy angles. The highest must have been fifty feet or more above our heads. At our feet was a chaotic heap of rubble and slabs of rock.

'We're in the stope.'

'What exactly is a stope?'

'It started as a natural fissure in the rock. Formed anything up to 400 million years ago. There was intense volcanic activity going on. The cracks were filled with liquid material from way down below the earth's crust. When it cooled down it solidified and crystallised. A lot of it is metal-rich; it formed lodes of lead, or copper, or other metals, all mixed up with different minerals like quartz or calcite. Some of the fissures are thousands of feet deep. Most of them are vertical, or nearly. They usually outcrop on the surface and that's where the mining generally starts, but then the miners will try to get at the lode lower down with shafts and tunnels. The stope's basically the productive part of the mine. All this space was full of rock, some of it ore, some of it rubbish. The miners have dug it out, and left a big empty space.'

I directed my light straight ahead, and saw that our level continued straight on beyond the stope, partly blocked with rubble. 'This is where we need to be careful. Stopes can be nasty places. This one could well go down as far as it goes up.'

'But the floor looks pretty solid.'

I pointed to the rubble in front of us. 'We don't know what's holding all that up. Almost certainly there's a wooden platform under there. The stope will carry on down underneath it. There'll be a similar space to this down below, and probably another below that. It's amazing how long the platforms can last, and often the fallen rock will jam together and stay in place after the timber's rotted. There'll be another platform somewhere overhead.'

Paeony beamed her light up into the dark spaces above. 'I think there is a sort of roof. What are those other timbers for? They look as if they're holding the walls apart.'

'They're not, really. They're called stemples. They're basically there for the miners to stand on. Remember they generally worked upwards in the stope, so as they cut away more and more rock they got higher and higher. The stemples formed a sort of ladder as well as a working platform. The men would stand up there for hours balanced on a stemple, forty feet up above the floor, drilling and hammering. Imagine it all by candlelight, with the rock crashing down and the air full of dust.'

'It must have been incredibly dangerous,' she said thoughtfully, 'No safety harness presumably, and no helmets. Life was incredibly hard.'

'It was short. And cheap.'

I looked at my watch. 'It's late. We'd better not explore any further today.'

'I was hoping you'd say that.' Whereupon Paeony took a step backwards, caught her heel on something and sat down with a squelch in several inches of liquid mud. 'Damn!' she said furiously, as I helped her up. 'I'm soaked through. Yuk! It's freezing.' Muddy water was dripping from the seat of her jeans. She'd put her hands down to try to save herself and now she held them up in disgust. She might have been wearing shiny yellow gloves.

'You'll be crawling through that before we're done,' I told her unsympathetically.

We made our way back along the level and past the winze. The return journey always seems quicker, and it wasn't long before we saw the pale shape of the entrance ahead, reflected in the water.

When we reached it, rivulets were coursing down the muddy slope into the pool at the level mouth, and looking out of the opening we saw that the rain was beating down, driven by a wind that hadn't been blowing an hour before. 'Blast,' I said, 'My waterproofs are in the car'.

'So are mine.'

We waited for a while in the shelter of the entrance, watching the water-laden gusts flattening the bracken. 'We're going to have to get wet,' Paeony said eventually, 'Let's make a dash for it.'

As we emerged from the gully great curtains of rain were sweeping down the valley. At times it was hard to see where we were going as we slithered down the hillside; the wind was blowing the water in our faces and into our eyes. I could feel the wet soaking through my boiler suit and the shirt under it. This was the second time I'd retreated from that hillside in a downpour, though today's was worse. At the valley bottom the stream had already begun to run deeper, the water coffee-coloured and foaming over the stones. We splashed through it and squelched up the slope towards the car. When we reached it we were as wet as if we'd swum.

We loaded the barrow, the tools and a fair quantity of mud into the Justy and set off down the track, the windscreen wipers struggling to cope.

'Now what?'

Paeony was trying to get her dripping hair out of her eyes. 'I think we're a bit wet for the Hand Inn. I'm soaked to the skin.'

'If you don't mind taking pot luck, it's not so far to Tan-y-Coed. We can get the fire going.'

'All right. I'd like to see where you live.'

It was still pouring when I parked the car by the wall above Tan-y-Coed, and water was dripping down the steps to the cottage. 'I'm afraid it's a bit primitive. There isn't a proper bathroom. The Ty Bach's along there.'

'I'd better go before I get dry.' Paeony splashed off along the terrace.

I unlocked the house and set a match to the fire I'd laid that morning; with a combination of dry wood and firelighters it was soon crackling.

I grabbed some dry clothes from the bedroom along with a pile of towels. When I came down she was standing dripping by the fire, looking round appreciatively. 'This is nice,' she said, 'You're tidy. My place is a tip.'

'There's plenty of hot water. I use bottled gas.'

I spread out some dry things on the sofa, and she selected a Tattersall shirt and a pair of cords. 'They'll be a bit big,' I warned her, 'I can't offer you anything else, I'm afraid.' Sarah had taken all her feminine garments with her, and I didn't think I could proffer any of my tatty and garish collection of boxer shorts.

'I'll manage.' She disappeared upstairs with a couple of towels.

It was getting murky and I lit the Aladdin oil lamp, put the kettle on the gas cooker, had a quick wash at the sink and then changed by the fire. I'd bought some steak in Llangollen and I got it out of the fridge, peppered it quickly and shoved it in a frying pan with some butter and a clove of garlic. I was quickly washing some salad when Paeony came downstairs.

She'd rolled my trousers up round her ankles, and put on a pair of my woolly socks as slippers. She'd rolled the shirt sleeves up too, though it still hung around her like a tent. She'd dried her hair on a towel, and obviously hadn't found a comb. She looked ravishing. She wrinkled her nose appreciatively at the aroma from the pan. 'And you can cook, too,' she said.

'My range is a bit limited. Do you mind crisps with this? I've used the last of the potatoes from the garden.'

'I like crisps.'

I laid the table, and found a bottle of red wine that we'd brought back from Provence a couple of years before. Sitting opposite her, I saw the firelight playing in her hair, just as it had when we'd eaten in the pub together. Her eyes twinkled as she looked at me, and a smile kept dimpling the corners of her mouth. Her skin had a wonderful bloom and smoothness, a depth of subtle colour which seemed to have been enhanced by its exposure to the wind and rain. We ate slowly, savouring the food and sipping the wine which was filled with sunshine. We talked about nothing in particular, but we were sparring playfully, teasing and provoking each other, laughing easily. I think we knew what was going to happen, but we didn't want to hurry it.

The meal was over, and our talk suddenly dried up. There was a moment of uncertainty, of tension. I stood up and cleared the table, taking the dishes to the sink. I waited there for a second, and felt Paeony behind me. I turned and she was standing there, smiling uncertainly, her hands by her sides, their palms turned a little outwards. I took a step towards her so that our bodies touched. My lips brushed against her hair, and I felt her cheek against my neck. Then she turned her face up to mine, and her eyes sparkled. I kissed her very gently, again and again. I was stroking her back, lifting the loose shirt and letting my hands slide under and upwards, caressing the skin, feeling the little corrugations of her spine between the shoulder blades. Then I let them slide downwards, to the waist, where the gentle rounding began. I felt her tremble under my fingers, and press herself against me.

It seemed strange to undo the familiar fastenings on another body. As I slipped my shirt from her shoulders the soft golden lamplight played on the smooth, translucent skin. At last I knew how far down the freckles went. The zip stuck a little, as it always did. She was naked under my clothes. I felt her fingers fumbling. Soon, I was naked too.

It had been a long time for both of us. We were passionate, but gentle with each other. We wanted to explore, to be intimate, to find what the other wanted and needed, to let every inch of skin make contact. We didn't want it to be over too soon. At last all my being was sucked into hers, and we went spinning away together into oblivion.

CHAPTER 12

I took Paeony back to Berwyn the next morning. At one stage we'd adjourned from the hearthrug to the bed, and eventually slept. I wondered whether anyone would be concerned about her absence, but she made it very clear that her life there was her own. 'I came home on condition that I had my own flat, and came and went as I wanted,' she said.

The flat wasn't in the old part of the house but at the back, on the first floor, and had its own entrance to the stable yard. She invited me up and I found it comfortably untidy, but not as much of a tip as she'd alleged. There were big windows, cheerful colours, a lot of pictures and shelves of cassettes and CDs. Books were lying about where she'd happened to put them down. On a bookcase was a snapshot of Paeony with a young man; each had a rope looped over one shoulder.

Paeony went off for a shower and a change, and then we drank coffee and discussed a plan of campaign. 'I've got to see to Arnie,' she said, 'And then I'd better show my face in the estate office. I'm supposed to be running it.'

'I could always spend another day in the archive. Now that I've seen more of the mine, I might be able to make more sense of what turns up. There ought to be more engineers' reports, if I can only find them.'

'I'll take you over.'

When we went down the stairs, Lord Berwyn was trundling up and down the courtyard in his wheelchair. He had a plastic tank strapped to one side of it, and was holding a nozzle with which he was spraying weed killer on the cobbles. If he was surprised to see me emerging from his daughter's flat, he didn't show it. 'Morning, Jones,' he said affably, skidding to halt, 'Back on the trail? Making progress?'

'I did very well last time.' I was trying to dodge the spray which was settling on my shoes. 'The first Lord Berwyn was a shareholder in the Cwm Llwyd mine, and the reports they sent him are in the archives. But I'd still like to find a plan, if I could.'

He stroked his moustache thoughtfully. 'If we were shareholders, I dare say you'll find one. When the company went bust, they'd have tried to sell off the mine as a whole. There'd have been a sale catalogue. Should have included a map. We'd get a copy of it. If we did, it's there somewhere; God knows where.'

The jet from the nozzle gradually drooped and died away to a trickle. Lord Berwyn glared at it. 'Damn stuff's run out again.' He jolted off across the cobbles towards the archway.

'That wheelchair does a fair turn of speed,' I commented as it lurched round the corner.

'Daddy had it specially souped up. He's a bit of a menace. He nearly ran over the vicar last week.'

'How did he come to be disabled? Was it a riding accident?'

'No, he can't stand horses. He came off a motor bike. That was years ago. He can walk a bit, but not far, and he can drive a car. Just before Christmas they got him for doing a ton on the M6.'

Paeony let me into the Muniment Room, and I spent a frustrating morning going through more boxes. I did have a brief moment of excitement when I discovered a mine sale catalogue with a plan in it. Unfortunately it proved to be a different mine. Then I struck a lot of boxes of purely agricultural interest. The second Lord Berwyn had evidently been an enthusiast for root vegetables, and there were copious records of the relative yields of turnips, mangolds and swedes.

There was one interesting distraction when I came across a larger box containing old plans of the park and gardens around Berwyn. I was looking at these when Paeony came back.

'Oh yes, we've got copies of these in the house,' she said. 'They're fascinating. There was a big formal garden here once, with parterres and avenues, but it was all cleared away when Capability Brown laid out the park. And there was a romantic garden over the other side of the lake, with a grotto and a petrifying well and a hermit's cave complete with hermit. It was quite a tourist attraction in the eighteenth century, but there's nothing left of it now.'

We went up to her flat for a snack lunch. While she was getting it I spotted a newish looking book on the window sill. It was partially concealed by others, but some of the wording on the front was visible and I tweaked it out. On the cover was a dramatic photo of someone prusiking in a vast underground chamber, and the title in big, bold letters: 'An Introduction to Single Rope Technique'. I was looking at it when she came back.

She had the grace to blush. 'I'd just been brushing up on it.'

'I suppose you were practising up the tower.'

'How did you guess?'

After lunch Paeony went off to see somebody about land drains. I went back to the tower and did some more boxes. Most of the papers were done up in bundles tied with faded red tape that some Victorian clerk had carefully knotted. Once the knot was undone every document had to be unfolded to see what it was. Then I had to bundle everything up again, and somehow get the box back onto the shelf. I went through ten boxes, and found precisely nothing.

That evening Paeony dissuaded me from going back home. She cooked me a meal in the little kitchen of her flat, and put on a disc of Lotte Lenya singing songs by Weill and Brecht. The bittersweet lyrics, the jangling rhythms and the haunting voice stayed with me long afterwards. Then we made unhurried love in her single bed, until sleep came.

Next day we agreed I'd go back to Tan-y-Coed, and that we'd meet again in the afternoon at Cwm Llwyd. I drove happily home, feeling unbelievably lucky. The rain had freshened up the countryside, and everything was a lush and brilliant green. The hedges were full of campion and bluebells. I turned onto the Tan-y-Coed track without a care in the world, parked the car with a flourish and almost skipped down the path, fondly admiring my little house.

The small window at the back was slightly open.

A day or two ago that wouldn't have been unusual. I rarely bothered closing windows. But having recently become security-conscious, I knew I'd fastened it. I made my way down the rest of the path with considerably greater caution, stopped on the terrace and listened. There was no sound from inside the house, and it didn't seem likely that anyone would still be there. Even so, I waited several minutes before inserting the key in the front door. It was locked as normal. I turned the key and pushed it open. Everything looked as it usually did. The damp clothes I'd left to dry by the fireplace were still there.

Nothing seemed to be missing, but on closer inspection it was evident that things had been moved. Some papers were now on the other side of my desk; one of the drawers was slightly open, its contents disarranged. A gap in the books on one of the shelves was now further along. Somebody had been looking for something; somebody who wasn't out to make a deliberate mess, but wouldn't be too worried if I realised the place had been searched. At first I couldn't see how the window had been opened; but of course the glass had been loose, held in not by putty but by narrow strips of wood tacked to the frame. Someone had neatly removed the glass to undo the window fasteners, which worked with a simple screw key. The glass had been replaced and the wood tacked back again, but the layer of paint all round the frame was broken.

It could only have been one of Carl Quinn's associates. No-one else had any reason to search the house. There were things that a casual burglar would have taken, not of great value, but convertible into cash. Perhaps Quinn thought I'd have notes, or a map of some kind, that could lead him to the Crown. In fact, there was nothing on paper that would have made much sense to him, and they must have drawn a blank. The break-in had almost certainly happened last night, when I was at Berwyn. Maybe it was as well I hadn't been at home.

I went round moving things back into their proper positions, fuming at the way my privacy had been invaded. I thought about calling the police. There'd been no theft, and the only damage was some cracked paint. They wouldn't treat it as a high priority, and I didn't fancy trying to explain my theories about Carl Quinn to another sceptical policeman. So I sorted out some food and clothes, refastened the window and locked the house up again. When I got to the end of the track I turned right instead of left, and drove up to Blaen-y-Cwm.

Glyn Lewis was in the kitchen with Gwen, having his lunch. Gwen asked if I'd had mine, and when I admitted I hadn't she cut me a large slice of ham and added a big spoonful of pickle from a stoneware jar. 'It's my own', she said, 'It won first prize at the W.I.'

'I'm not surprised.' I tucked in appreciatively.

'You were asking me about strangers the other day,' Glyn said.

'That's what I've come about,' I said through a mouthful of pickle, 'I wondered if you'd seen anyone.'

'There were two fellows up here yesterday in one of those Land Cruisers. I was going to give you a ring about them. Not the usual midweek tourists. They're generally pensioners. They came right up to the farm, and had a bit of a job turning round.'

'I went out to see if they needed any help,' Gwen said, 'But they just drove off.'

'What did they look like?'

'A bit younger than Glyn. Both dark. The driver was quite a big man, heavy you know. His hair was down on his collar. Quite smartly dressed, he was. I didn't really see the other, I think he was smaller.'

'I think someone broke into Tan-y-Coed last night, while I was away. But nothing was stolen. I wonder whether there was any connection.'

Gwen looked concerned. 'There've been quite a few break-ins round Llanrhaeadr. People from the Midlands, so they say, looking for antiques. They caught one fellow with a van full of furniture.'

'I'll let you know if I see those two again,' Glyn said, 'And I'll ask around. Strangers get noticed round here, especially when there've been burglaries.'

I finished my lunch, thanked Glyn and Gwen warmly, and left. Then I headed for Cwm Llwyd. I kept an eye open on the road, but there was no sign of a vehicle like the one they'd described, or anything else suspicious.

Cadwaladr was in his farmyard, clearing the accumulated bedding out of a byre he used for lambing. He leaned on his pitchfork, removed his cap and mopped his brow. 'Terrible weather. Hot, I mean.' I thought it was pleasantly mild.

'There was someone else up here yesterday, looking for your mine.'

'Who was it? Not two men in a Land Cruiser, by any chance?'

'No, it was not. It was one man in a taxi. He'd come all the way from Llangollen. It must have cost him a pretty penny. Funny little fellow in trousers that stopped half way down his legs.'

'Charles Angevin Greene,' I said disgustedly.

'He didn't give his name. But he tried to persuade the taxi driver to take him up the valley. The man said it was too bumpy so he walked. Left the driver here with his meter going. He must have more money than sense.'

'How far did he get?'

'I don't know, but he was gone a fair time.' Cadwaladr chuckled. 'And he looked a bit the worse for wear when he got back. I don't fancy he does a lot of walking.'

Paeony arrived in the pick-up. She was wearing a sparkling white boiler suit that fitted like a glove and set off her colouring and her figure to perfection. 'Sorry I'm late. How are you, Mr Pugh?'

'Champion.' Cadwaladr was grinning appreciatively. He squinted at me. 'You're a lucky fellow, you are. Mind you take good care of her, now.'

'Have you been out on your quad bike yet?' Paeony asked him.

'Bah! Why don't you take the thing, if you're going up to that mine of yours? It's just sitting in the barn doing nothing. It could do with an airing. I can't make up my mind whether to ride it or sell it.'

Paeony looked taken aback. 'That's very kind of you.'

'I can ride a motor bike,' I said quickly, 'I expect it's much the same.'

'It has twice as many wheels, you know,' Cadwaladr said. He opened the door of the barn to reveal the gleaming machine standing among rolls of rusty chicken wire. 'They gave me a full tank of petrol with it. And an instruction book'. The book was still in a plastic bag tied to the handlebars, and with its assistance we soon had the engine purring away. It started with a key like a car. There was a twist grip throttle, and a pedal on the left that worked the gears, like the bike I'd bought years ago, to my mother's horror, with the money I'd saved from stacking supermarket shelves. I got astride and guided it a little jerkily out of the barn and round the farmyard.

'Where am I supposed to sit?' Paeony inquired. She looked a little needled that I'd volunteered to drive.

'There's a luggage rack on the back.' Cadwaladr pointed it out. 'Just mind you hold on tight.'

I told Cadwaladr where we were going, and he suggested that, instead of using the forestry track, we took an alternative route which crossed the stream just below the farm and then headed diagonally up the opposite hillside towards the shaft. It avoided the slate tips, and the quad bike ought to manage it without much trouble. So, a few minutes later, he was opening the gate which led to it, grinning from ear to ear as Paeony hung on grimly. 'Don't break your necks, now,' he called after us.

'I'd like to break his,' she said between her teeth, 'Next time we're at Berwyn I'll get you on a horse. I've got just the one.'

I took it gently, and the bike coped easily with the pasture. There was one gate to open and beyond it the ground was a little rougher, but we made good progress. Our gear was strapped to the back of the luggage carrier, and there was room to spare. The main problem from Paeony's point of view was that, riding along the hillside, one wheel was higher than the other, which produced a tendency to slide off. After what seemed to me to be a minor jolt there was a squawk. I looked back to see two white-clad legs waving from a clump of bracken. 'That does it,' she spluttered, 'I'll walk.'

Progress was slower after that, but eventually we reached the mine and I parked the bike in the gully. She arrived a moment later looking pink. The contrast with the brilliant white suit was enchanting. I thought of what Cadwaladr had said; I was starting to realise how lucky I was.

'I love you in that outfit,' I said suddenly, 'Even more than usual, I mean.'

There was a pause. 'You mean you do usually? You never mentioned it.'

'Didn't I? I meant to. I sort of thought you knew.'

'You have a funny way of showing it,' Paeony said. 'But - it might be mutual.' She looked at me a little defensively, and then I lifted her off her feet and we kissed and kissed till we were both out of breath. 'Come on,' she said at last, 'We've got a mine to explore.'

We'd both brought a fair amount of gear, and at least we hadn't had to carry it up. I had a careful look at the mine entrance. No loose soil had descended, and it was just as we'd left it. The trench had reduced the depth of water a little, and I resolved to bring a spade again and dig it deeper. Paeony was checking the contents of a substantial rucksack, and had brought a bundle of climbing rope. My own bag was pretty heavy too. Preparations complete, we fixed our lamps and squeezed down into the level.

Knowing our way we made quick progress, and in ten minutes or so we were at the stope. I looked carefully at the rubble-strewn floor in front of me, and poked at it with a stick I'd brought for the purpose. 'It seems solid,' I said, and stepped out of the level. I dug a big hand lamp out of my rucksack. It was an old motor cycle headlamp, and connected with a heavy power pack that could be strapped to my belt. I switched on, and it beamed up into the blackness of the void above like a searchlight.

The stope was a chaos of rock and timber; everywhere rotting stemples were jammed at crazy angles between the walls with huge slabs of rock wedged precariously above our heads. Everything was covered with rubble and dust. Paeony looked at it dubiously.

'It's not a pretty sight,' I said. 'But maybe we ought to get up there and have a look.' I tapped one of the lower stemples with the stick. 'This one sounds firm. But it's often the wedges that rot.'

The stemples were fixed in place by wooden wedges driven between their ends and the face of the rock. I poked at the wedges, then reached up and pulled gently at the baulk of timber. It seemed solid, and I tugged harder. Finally I got hold of it with both hands and swung myself off the ground.

'You'd be a lunatic to trust those things.' She was sitting down, pulling off her wellingtons and producing a pair of climbing boots from her rucksack. As she laced them up she was scanning the rock face in front of her and noting the dangers above. A moment later she had a loop of rope over her shoulder and had begun to scale the side of the stope like a fly going up a wall.

The stope wasn't vertical: the angle was maybe twenty degrees from the perpendicular, but it was an impressive performance just the same. She moved cautiously, testing each hold and brushing away the grit and loose material that covered every protuberance before transferring her weight to it. I held the lamp as she climbed up into the darkness, and a great, black shadow climbed before her, looming above my head. She seemed instinctively to find the best route, rarely pausing for more than a second or two and supporting herself on almost invisible projections. When she was about twenty feet up she stopped and made a belay over a knob of rock.

'There's a ledge here. You can come up.'

My rock climbing skills didn't begin to equal hers, and I needed assistance from the rope and a stemple or two to get myself up beside her. The ledge wasn't very wide but it gave a good view up, down and along the stope. At this level the fissure was ten or twelve feet across, and seemed to extend lengthways for twenty yards or more.

'What's that?' Paeony pointed to the opposite wall.

I aimed the lamp across. A few yards further along the rock wall gave way to rough timber boards, blackened, bulging and splintering, and wedged in place by baulks of timber jammed against the rock face on which we were perched.

'There are deads behind the timber. That's the name they gave to waste rock that didn't contain ore. The miners used any convenient cavities to dispose of the stuff. There are probably hundreds of tons of rubble behind those boards. One day they'll give way. It's best not to be underneath when they do.'

The ledge extended a good way along the stope, and edging along it we were able to direct the lamp into many of its dark recesses.

When I shone it upwards it showed clearly the bottom of the wooden platform marking the next level: there were crude sections of tree trunk supporting it, still with the mouldering bark attached, about thirty feet above us. In places we were able to climb higher, but it was a nerve-wracking business. Reaching up we had to take infinite care not to disturb loose material above, and when seeking footholds neither the rock nor the wood could be trusted. Repeatedly our boots would send loose stones crashing down to the floor below, followed by miniature landslides of rubble. At one point the stope narrowed to under three feet in width, and it was almost choked by boulders and loose rock.

'This is getting silly,' Paeony said at last.

'You're right. It's too dangerous. There's no way we can explore it all. There are no obvious passages, though. We've seen quite a lot. Let's go down.'

Normally descending is worse than ascending as you're forced to look down, but in this case it was probably less frightening than looking up. All the dangers were above us. Nevertheless we climbed down very carefully.

'Let's not do that again for a while.'

'We'll try the continuation of the level.'

The level by which we had entered the stope continued straight ahead. As we'd seen on our first visit, the start was partly choked with material that had fallen down from above. I set to work to shift a few boulders, and it was clear that the blockage didn't extend more than a yard or two. It wasn't long before we were able to pass. Our helmet lights showed a tunnel similar to the one we had come along, though this one was even muddier. The mud was shin deep, slimy and glutinous, snatching at our boots as we tried to pick them up. 'Damn,' said Paeony, 'I left my wellies in the stope.'

I took it slowly, examining the rock with care: it all seemed sound. It wasn't long before our lights picked out a mound of stones and clay on the floor of the level. There were bits of rotten timber half buried in it.

'There must be a shaft coming down from above.'

Sure enough, when we got there we were standing at the bottom of a shaft. This one didn't go straight up, but sloped at about the same angle as the stope had done. I switched on the headlight. The angle wasn't quite constant, so I couldn't see how far up it went. 'It's an inclined shaft. And a pretty old one. The later ones are mainly vertical, like the one we went down last week. Originally they used to drive them more or less parallel to the stope. It must have caused all sorts of problems with winding. Up's the direction we want to go, but starting from the bottom is a lot harder than starting from the top.'

'It's just basic rock-climbing technique,' Paeony said, 'If the shaft were vertical it would be trickier, but this one slopes and the walls are quite rough. The one problem is that there isn't much choice of route; you can't traverse along to find an easier bit. I'll probably need to be unethical again.'

She was already unstrapping her rucksack, and getting out her climbing harness. Then she took out a bundle of short lengths of steel wire or webbing tape, attached to oddly shaped bits of metal. 'These are nuts,' she said, 'You just shove them in a crack and clip onto them. For emergencies only, of course; they're only supposed to be there in case you fall off. But if I use them to concoct a few holds, no-one's going to see.'

'I thought climbers banged pitons into cracks.'

'We've moved on a bit.'

She stepped back, peering up the wall of the shaft planning a route. 'Give me a leg up.'

I stood on the mound and lifted her so that she could get a grip, marvelling how light she was. She started to climb with a steady rhythm, spread-eagled against the rock wall which was jagged and irregular. I envied her sense of balance. I tried to avoid shining the light directly at her, so that she wasn't dazzled. After a while she wedged herself in a corner, took one of the nuts from her belt and jammed it into a crack. She clipped a karabiner into the wire loop, passed her rope through it, and carried on climbing. If she fell, the belay would protect her. She was repeating the process at regular intervals. All her movements were economical, neat and incisive.

Two or three times she came to a point where the holds seemed to give out. Then she simply jammed in a nut, tied a tape loop to it, and put her foot in the loop. Unethical no doubt, but effective. In this way she had climbed a considerable distance, perhaps fifty feet, and the light from her helmet lamp seemed a long way up. Then her voice echoed down the shaft. 'There's another tunnel.'

'Which way does it go?'

'Back towards the stope, I think. Come on up. I've belayed the rope. You can prusik. Get the nuts out as you pass them. We can abseil down.'

I'd brought the gear with me, and made my way slowly up the rope to join her. The incline made it more awkward than if I'd been hanging free, but it still felt safer than climbing in the stope. The rock was firm, and there wasn't the constant stream of stones and pebbles pouring down as I climbed. Most of the nuts came out surprisingly easily, though the last one was awkward and Paeony passed down a bit of metal she called a nut spanner. With its help, I managed to tease it out.

I came to where she was crouching in the mouth of a gallery that opened off the shaft. It seemed to lead in the direction we'd come from, at a higher level.

'It almost certainly leads back to the stope, higher up.' I led the way along it, my helmet banging on the roof. This passage was low, but dry. Sure enough, in only half a minute or so the level opened out and we found ourselves back at the stope. I let my light illuminate the floor. 'We'd better not go any further. This looks rather weak. Look, there's a hole'.

I directed the big lamp downwards through an opening about a foot across, and suddenly we could see down into the section of the stope we'd explored from below. The ledge was clearly visible.

'There are those beams that were holding up the deads,' Paeony said. The baulks of timber were right below us.

This part of the stope was much narrower, and partially choked with debris; it must have been difficult to work in such a confined space. 'There's not much room here to swing a pick,' I said, 'It doesn't look as if it goes much higher.' We couldn't see any sign of other galleries, and decided to go back to the shaft and climb further up.

I was now automatically allowing Paeony to lead when climbing, though I went first in the levels where I was more aware of the dangers above and below. 'Do you think it goes right up to the surface?' she asked, looking up the shaft.

'I don't know. If it does, the top's almost certainly blocked. But it may be a winze: it probably ends in another level.'

So it proved. She'd only climbed twenty feet or so when she called, 'I'm in a tunnel. It goes both ways.' I climbed up to join her, and pulled myself up into a broad gallery. The mouth of the shaft took up most of the passage floor, but there was room to edge around at one side.

'Which way?'

I shone the lamp one way and said, 'Not up there.' A few yards ahead the level was completely blocked with rubble. 'It doesn't look like a collapse. It's been filled up with deads. They'd take a lot of shifting, and there's nowhere to put them without blocking the shaft. We'll try the other way.'

'Could this be part of Owain's mine?'

'No. The passage is too big. Also it's been drilled for blasting.' I pointed out the grooves the drills had left in the wall of the level. 'They wouldn't have used explosives so early. The older miners hacked everything out by hand. That's why their levels were smaller.'

We made our way carefully round the mouth of the shaft and started down the level, keeping a look out for further openings in the floor. This one wasn't parallel to the levels below. I was increasingly aware of the scale of the task we'd taken on. The mine was complex, and access to the older workings could well have been blocked off. Clearing the passages would be a massive task and well beyond our resources. I kept a careful look out for side passages; I didn't want us to lose our way on our return.

This passage was fairly dry and there was more headroom, which made progress easier. As the light from my lamp flickered over the tunnel wall it fell on what looked like a little knob of rock. I stopped. 'What do you think that is?'

Paeony examined it.

'Don't break it off,' I said, 'It's something the miners left.'

'It's a candle,' she said suddenly.

'That's right. It's been stuck to the wall with a lump of clay. There's just the stump left. It's covered with calcite.' There was the thinnest coating of shiny mineral overlying the little lump of wax and the clay that some unknown miner had used to secure it a century or more ago.

We reached a higher section, actually a miniature stope where the miners seemed to have found a pocket of mineralisation. The passage continued beyond it, still quite broad, and we kept going.

'This could be an adit. Perhaps it leads to the surface, or did at one time. It has that feel about it. Look, there are sleepers here. And it's been dug from the direction we're heading in. You can tell from the drill marks.'

But whether or not the level had once led out onto the hillside, it didn't now. Ahead I saw several massive lumps of yellow rock heaped on the floor, and put out a warning arm. 'The roof's bad here.' I shone the big lamp further ahead: the passage was completely choked with clay and boulders. 'The entrance could have been through there. But I wouldn't attempt to dig it from this side. The rock's far too fragmented. Some of this fall's quite recent.'

Rather dispirited, we retraced our steps to the section where the roof rose and we could stand upright.

'I'm hungry,' Paeony said, 'Let's break out the rations.' We sat down on a heap of rubble, and the rucksack disgorged some savoury pasties and a couple of Mars bars. They tasted good, and energy began to flow again.

As we were chewing away, she said, 'Is that a tunnel?' Seven or eight feet up there was a shadowy recess. Our helmet lamps didn't show us much, and I got the big lamp out again and turned it on.

'It does seem to go some way back. But it's not very big. It could be just a trial boring, or a place where they extracted a parcel of ore.'

I crammed the rest of my Mars bar into my mouth and scrambled a little way up the rock. Then I wriggled into the recess. It did seem like a rough passage, if hardly wider than the average culvert. I squirmed further into it and found it widened out a little, though it was still barely three feet in height.

The beam from Paeony's lamp lit up the rock around me; she was squeezing into the passage behind. 'There aren't any drill marks.'

I peered at the rock around me. It was pitted with little indentations. 'I think these are pick or chisel marks. You know, these could be earlier workings. I've never been in a mine older than the eighteenth century, when they'd started to use gunpowder, but this is like the ones I've read about. This could be part of the first Morgan mine.'

We crawled further, and felt my hands sinking into mud. 'We're going to get dirty,' I said. The mud wasn't very deep, but it was the usual soft, greasy stuff that always seems to accumulate underground. I was used to crawling through it, but there were muffled squeaks from behind.

'It's revolting.'

'This is nothing. I went down a mine in Shropshire where the farmer had been tipping pig manure down the shaft for fifty years.'

We came to a place where the passage divided, and soon after it divided again. I got out my knife and scraped a small mark on the tunnel wall. 'We'll have to be careful we don't get lost. It's a bit of a warren down here.' Everything was on a smaller scale than in the later mine, and more irregular; the passage twisted, rose and dipped. The dips tended to be full of mud and water.

At one point I noticed a rock face that was reddened and cracked.

'They could have used fire here. Before they invented blasting the miners sometimes built a fire against the rock and then dashed water against it to cool it quickly and make it crack. I'm certain these are the "old people's workings". We need to try to chart them if we going to explore them systematically. They're probably less extensive than they seem; the old mines weren't usually very big.'

'I'm getting cold.' Paeony shuddered. 'We've had a good day. We can't do much more now. Let's come back in the morning.' We'd set out fairly late, and I was starting to feel tired myself. So we reversed along the tunnel until it was wide enough to turn round, and crawled back through the mud.

The return trip didn't take long, now that we knew the way. We switched ropes at the shaft, substituting my static caving rope which was more suitable for SRT than the more elastic variety that Paeony used for climbing, and abseiled down. We left the rope fixed for next time, and in a few minutes we were crossing the stope and starting back down the entrance level. We were out of the mine in little more than half an hour. Even so, it was a relief to see daylight again, and to straighten up properly and stand outside in the fresh air. The sun was still shining, and I poured a hot drink from a flask.

Paeony's once white overalls were now various shades of dirty yellowish-brown; her face was filthy, and she was trying to clean her hands on the grass. I knew I didn't look much better. We sat close together on the hillside above the gully sipping coffee that tasted of plastic, but was welcome nonetheless. 'I can't believe I did that,' she said, 'We must be crazy. It's weird, but I think I actually enjoyed it. Or perhaps I just enjoyed getting out.'

'It's addictive. And the great thing is, we've found Owain's mine. It's been much easier than we had any right to expect.'

'It was quite hard enough for me.'

Then, looking across the valley, I said, 'What's that car?' Parked on the forestry track on the opposite side of the valley, more or less where Bob Lord had left his Range Rover when we first came to look at the mine, was a bulky looking vehicle.

Paeony was following my eyes. 'It's one of those big four-wheel drive estates. A Shogun or something.'

'It could be a Land Cruiser.' It was too far away to see who was in it. As we watched it set off, lumbering slowly down the track towards Cadwaladr's farm and the mouth of the valley.

'There were two men in a Land Cruiser up near Tan-y-Coed the other day. Glyn Lewis saw them.'

She looked sceptical. 'There are plenty of those cars about. It's probably just tourists. Or maybe your Mr Angevin Greene has hired one to save his feet.'

'Whoever was in it could have seen us. We're quite visible up here. But as you say, there's probably no connection.'

We packed up and took the gear down to the quad bike. Paeony pointed to a warning notice stencilled on the mudguard. 'This thing isn't supposed to carry passengers. It's my turn to drive it anyway.' So we loaded it up and she started the engine, twisting the rubber throttle grip mischievously with her right hand to produce a satisfying roar. 'I like the feel of this. Sensitive, isn't it? See you at the farm.' She set off considerably faster than I'd taken it, and I trudged along behind.

When I caught up Paeony was still sitting astride the bike, chatting to Cadwaladr. 'Oh, there you are,' she said, and steered it neatly into the barn.

'She knows how to handle that contraption, doesn't she?' Cadwaladr said admiringly.

We thanked him warmly for the loan of the bike, and offered to pay for the petrol. 'You can fill this up for me,' he said, and gave me a battered can. I asked him if he'd noticed the vehicle I'd seen on the track, but he said he hadn't. 'I was watching the rugby all afternoon. Though I think they've forgotten how to play. Should be ashamed of themselves, losing to Argentina. Maybe you two should be playing, you look as if you'd been in the scrum yourselves. Plastered you are.'

Paeony said she had to go back to Berwyn, and I reluctantly let her go. We arranged to meet again the following morning. I made my way back to Tan-y-Coed, where everything was as it should be. There was a letter from Charles Angevin Greene, reiterating his anxiety to help 'in your momentous quest' and enclosing a genealogical table illustrating the ancestry of Prinz Franz von Bayern and his descent from Charles I. 'I remain convinced that Owain Morgan, in his devotion to the Stuart cause, would have wished the rightful King to bear the Crown which he had rescued for posterity', he wrote. I stuck the letter behind the clock.

After a little thought and ignoring my own telephone I drove down the valley to the call box and rang the Birmingham number which Joseph had left with me on the occasion of his nocturnal visit. It already seemed a long time ago. A woman's voice answered, and in the background I could hear the thunder of feet on a wooden floor, high-pitched voices and the squeals of a whistle. I gave my name and asked for Joseph. A moment later the deep voice came on the line. 'I've blown early for half time. How can I help you?'

I told him about the two men who had been seen in the Land Cruiser, and asked if he knew anything of them.

'I had been thinking of telephoning you, Mr Jones. There have been rumours that Carl Quinn has been hiring himself a little help. I have heard not two names, but three. Two could possibly be the men you mentioned. One is a big man who wears his hair long. His name is Frank Inman. He works with a man called Lou Martin, who is smaller. The third man is black, though not as black as me. His name is Ogomo. Two of them have convictions for wounding, and Martin has one for indecent assault. None of them are people you would want to know.'

'Could they have been involved in Bob's murder?'

'That is possible. But I am not sure how long they have been working for Quinn. No doubt he has other associates. There is little I can do about Quinn, as you know. But I have friends who might be able to put a little pressure on people like Inman and the others. If they become troublesome, let me know.'

'Thanks. I'll do that.'

'There is something else you should know, Mr Jones. Carl Quinn has applied for parole. He has been a good boy in prison. He may not be in Walton much longer.'

I thanked Joseph again, and put the phone down feeling a mixture of emotions. The news that Quinn might soon be released was disturbing, but there was some comfort in hearing Joseph's deep, reassuring voice and knowing he was on my side.

CHAPTER 13

Paeony and I spent the next two days at the mine. I took a clipboard and a compass, and using the measuring tape we made a rough survey of the old people's passages. Luckily the rock was stable, and there was no sign of any recent falls. The tunnels were so confusing that it would have been easy to search the same place twice, and there were loops which left the main passage and rejoined it further on. A couple seemed to have been blocked off, and we spent some time trying to clear them with the help of a garden trowel - a useful implement that fits into a pocket and is handy in a confined space. Both proved to be dead ends. Trying to draw a plan, even a rough one, taxed my powers of spatial reasoning to the limit; the paper was in two dimensions but the passages were in three.

We weren't sure what we were looking for. Owain was hardly likely to have left the Crown down there unprotected. It might have been wrapped in something, or more probably placed in some kind of box or chest. On the other hand, the box might have rotted away. He could have walled it up in a crevice, and we studied the rock walls carefully for any sign of masonry. One thing was certain: gold never corrodes, and if we did find the Crown it would gleam as brightly as the day it had been hidden centuries ago.

Half buried in the mud Paeony found a curious hammer, thick with rust, with one pointed end and the remains of a broken shaft. Why had it been left there? Four hundred years ago even a hammer head was a valuable object, and the shaft could surely have been replaced. In a small chamber we came across beautiful calcite crystals that would have sent a mineral collector into raptures. We left the hammer and the crystals as we'd found them, reluctant to damage the integrity of this place which had stayed untouched for so long.

Despite the tortuous course of the passages, the compass suggested we were heading consistently towards the head of the valley; at the same time, the trend was upwards. At last, towards evening on the second day, we reached a point where the passage was almost choked by boulders, and it looked as if several hours' labour would be needed to clear it.

There had been no sign of the Crown, but we weren't discouraged. The exploration process was exciting, and we were enjoying each other's company. I was quite sure we were looking in the right place. Our search had been thorough and I was fairly certain we hadn't missed anything, but we knew there was still more to explore. And even at the boulder choke I thought I could detect a draught of air, which implied that the passage continued beyond and perhaps connected somehow with the surface.

Paeony had brought along two little paraffin lamps of the kind that farmers use in their outbuildings. We left one in the stope, and the other at the top of the inclined shaft. We lit them when we went in and left them burning; they weren't really necessary, but it was comforting to see them twinkling in the darkness on our way back, and we dowsed each one as we passed it and left them ready for our next visit.

We kept an eye open for strangers on our way to and from the mine. I told her what Joseph had said about Carl Quinn, and the help he had hired, and gave her Joseph's number as a precaution. But we saw no-one, and there was no sign of the Land Cruiser.

On the second evening I went back to Berwyn with Paeony. She cooked a Chinese dish with cashew nuts and crisp vegetables stir-fried to perfection. We sipped a fragrant white wine, and listened to Monteverdi. She'd changed into a clean white boiler suit, brand new and zipped up tightly to the neck. I told her how gorgeous she looked in it.

'I bought two. You said you liked the other one.'

Something about her look made my heart jump.

'Er - just what are you wearing underneath?'

'If you're good, you can unzip it and find out.'

I was late leaving for Tan-y-Coed that night. On the road I marvelled again at how fortunate I was. Why someone so incomparably lovely and alive should show the remotest interest in me remained an unfathomable mystery. And with that thought came a twinge of fear, that it might not be for ever.

Next morning the phone rang early. It was Paeony. 'I can't get out this morning. There's been a pollution incident on the home farm. Some diesel's leaked into a stream. The Council are there, and it means trouble. Someone has to clear up the mess, in both senses.'

She said she'd ring again at lunchtime, and I spent the morning drawing out the rough plans we'd made and comparing them with the map. Plotting the bearings and distances it was clear that, as I'd thought, the passages were taking us further up the valley; a ravine broke into the hillside around that point, and whilst I couldn't be sure how deep we had been when we reached the boulder choke we were probably nearing the surface. But the ground beyond was broken up by the slate quarries, and the contours were confused.

At midday Paeony rang again and said she could make it by two. I met her as usual at the farm, gave her a kiss and saw Cadwaladr grinning through his kitchen window. On the last two days we'd walked to the mine from the track, but this time he offered us the quad bike again and Paeony gleefully accepted it. 'I'll ride,' she said. I refused her offer of the luggage rack, and plodded along behind.

We went straight into the mine, trying to make up for lost time. It was starting to feel like routine. With practice Paeony was finding it easier to walk with a stoop, and we were getting to know where the low bits were. When we reached the stope I knelt down and struck a match to light the hurricane lamp which we'd left on the floor between the tunnels. As the wick flared she said, 'What was that?'

Both of us had heard it: a faint noise, as if two stones had clicked together. It seemed to come from along the passage behind us. The tunnel magnified the sound.

We stood and listened for a moment. There was no further noise.

'Probably a pebble falling from the roof,' I said at last, and we pressed on to the inclined shaft.

We left our rucksacks at the bottom, went up the ropes in what had become a routine manoeuvre, and along to the start of what we now called Owain's Mine. We crawled as far as the boulder choke that had thwarted us the previous day. I started pulling out boulders and passing them back along my body to Paeony, who was just behind. It was hard work in a prone position. She stacked the stones carefully in a wider section of the passage just behind us; we didn't want to wall ourselves in. The cool draught from ahead was still playing gently on my face.

Eventually the hole was big enough, and I started to wriggle through. I got jammed on an apple in my pocket, and had to reverse out again.

I ate the apple, moved a few more stones, and tried again. This time I was through. She followed with considerably greater ease.

The passage here was higher, and it was a relief to be able to sit upright. There were more chisel marks on the walls and you could tell we were still in Owain's Mine, though the level didn't seem to branch as it had done earlier. There were occasional hollows where pockets of ore seemed to have been chiselled out. We crawled onwards on all fours for maybe thirty or forty yards, and came to a sudden halt.

The floor of the passage dipped, and so did the roof. The dip was full of water, which seemed to come right up to the top. I bent my head down almost to water level. There didn't seem to be any space between the rock and the water surface, but I could still feel a cool draught on my cheek. Maybe they didn't quite meet. It was impossible to see how far on the low section extended. The water looked quite deep; it was still, and inky black.

'Damn,' I said, 'We need wet suits to get further, maybe even diving gear. Or a pump to lower the level.' We gazed despondently at the water. So far we'd not had much water trouble; many mines are very wet even where they're not completely flooded, but here we were well above the level of the valley bottom and natural drainage seemed to have kept the passages relatively dry.

'It's not a major problem. The passage is still there under the water, and the air's getting through. But it's too risky to push on without proper equipment. We can't get any farther today.'

We'd been in the mine for barely an hour, but it looked as if it was time to retreat. We wriggled back through the choke, and before long were at the top of the shaft. We were feeling rather glum, and not saying anything. In retrospect, that was fortunate.

I went down first, and being rather downcast I didn't kick out with my boots against the rock as I usually did, but abseiled down more sedately and therefore quietly. I'd descended twenty feet or so, as far as the gallery leading to the upper level of the stope, when I heard a cough. It was quite distinct. It came from somewhere below.

I halted my descent and froze for a moment. Then I whipped off my helmet and held it so that the lamp shone into my face. I laid the finger of the other hand to my lips and looked up. Paeony was just putting out the oil lamp at the top of the shaft. She glanced down and saw me. I mouthed frantically at her. She opened her mouth, then closed it again.

As silently as possible I pushed myself into the mouth of the gallery, sat on the edge with my legs dangling, and unclipped myself from the rope. Then I gestured to her to come down quietly. She began to let herself down very gently until she was hanging on the rope level with me. I put my mouth close to her ear and whispered very softly, 'There's someone down there.' Her eyes widened.

I thought for a moment; the cough had been muffled, it hadn't come directly from the bottom of the shaft. It might have come from the direction of the stope. I started to crawl into the gallery, trying to mask my light with my hand, and burned myself in the process. When I got to the stope I turned it off completely. A faint glimmer came up through the hole in the floor from the hurricane lamp we'd left burning fifty feet below. Taking infinite care not to dislodge anything, I peered down through the hole into the lower level of the stope.

It took a moment to realise what I was looking at. There was a man directly below me. I could see the top of his head and his shoulders, and also his knees because he was seated on something. He seemed to be perched somewhere between me and the ground. At first I thought he was sitting on a stemple, and then I realised he was on the upper of the two timber baulks that the miners had wedged across the shaft to hold back the boards behind which the deads were stacked. His feet were resting on the lower one. He was sitting close to one wall, quite still. He might have been ten or twelve feet above the floor.

The light from the lantern was fairly dim, but I could see from the man's shape that he was bulky, even fat. Once or twice he looked down, and there was something odd about his hair. It was tied in a pony tail. He was holding something across his knees, something thick and heavy, about three feet long. After a while he raised it and inspected it. It looked like some kind of gun.

Paeony's lamp glimmered behind me. I motioned her back a few yards down the tunnel, and crept after her. 'He's down there, in the stope. A big man with long hair. It could be Frank Inman. I think he might have a gun.'

She stared at me. 'Take a look. But better put your lamp out'. She switched it off, and I heard her inching her way forward to the hole. She stayed a long time, looking down. Then she crept back.

'I think it is a gun,' she whispered. 'A shotgun. I've got my own, at home. The end's been sawn off.'

'We'll get back towards the shaft. He's less likely to hear us. Switch on but keep it masked.' I didn't want to relight the carbide lamp; the flint would click, and the gas would light with a pop.

We crawled a few yards and I tried to think. 'It must have been him we heard before, in the level. He must have followed us in. Now he's waiting for us.'

'What the hell does he think he's doing?' Paeony's voice was trembling, but with anger, not fright.

'We've led them to the mine. Now they know where the Crown is supposed to be hidden, that's all they need. They could eliminate us down here, and no-one would ever know. They could get both of us at once, and drop the bodies down the winze. He can blast us as soon as we come out into the stope.'

She didn't answer. It was hard to make out her expression against the glare from her lamp, but what I could see looked grim. 'I suppose he might just want to hold us up, to make us give him information,' I said, without really believing it.

'They could have got to us outside, if that was what they wanted. He hasn't come in here to talk.'

'The only way out is right under where he's sitting. And he's bound to hear us coming.'

I was thinking furiously. We hadn't any kind of weapon. Our only advantage was that we knew he was there, and he didn't know we knew. And for what it was worth, we knew the mine.

Paeony was suddenly moving back along the passage. 'Where are you going?' I hissed after her. She didn't reply, and I scrambled along after her on hands and knees.

I caught up with her back at the stope. She had got hold of a hefty boulder. At first I couldn't make out what she was doing; then I saw she was propelling it towards the hole. I grabbed her wrist and mouthed at her. She mouthed back. In the end I got her to move a little way back towards the shaft.

'What do you think you're doing?'

'I'm going to knock the bastard off his perch. I'm going to drop a rock on his head.'

'You can't do that,' I hissed frantically, 'He hasn't got a helmet. You'll kill him.'

'He's waiting there to kill us.'

'We don't know that for certain.'

'Would you like to ask him?'

We were conducting our argument in whispers, but I was afraid the man would hear. He quite probably wasn't alone. 'Look, we might be able to scare him away. We could drop a few stones near him, start a small fall. He's pretty exposed down there.'

'He'd probably wait for us further down the tunnel.'

'Even a minor fall sounds pretty frightening underground. I don't believe he'd hang about.'

'I suppose it might work,' she said, grudgingly. 'He can't be used to mines.'

'If he were he wouldn't be sitting on those timbers.'

I borrowed Paeony's lamp and crawled back to the hole. Inman, if it was Inman, was still there, in the same place. I located a few suitable stones, and turned off the lamp before I picked them up. It was as well because he heard the rattle and glanced up momentarily.

I selected a rock about the size of half a brick and held it over the hole. I was aiming to miss, but not by much. Several times I almost released it, but my hand was trembling and I was afraid it would affect my aim. Then at last I let it go.

The stone hurtled down, glanced off the rock wall and flew past his shoulder. There was a curse, and I saw a face peering up towards me. I was in total darkness and knew he wouldn't be able to see that I was there. I grabbed a fistful of smaller stones and shoved them blindly over the edge, so that they went crashing and rattling down to the floor of the stope. The noise was magnified in the confined space and made the rocks sound much bigger than they were. I sent a few more after them, and then looked down again.

The man was scrambling along the beam to get away from the shower of stones. His body was silhouetted against the lamplight below. I aimed another largish rock, and it clattered past him and hit the bottom with an echoing crash. He looked up again and scrabbled desperately further on.

There was sharp crack. I saw him freeze, then reach back towards the rock wall. As he did so the beam he was sitting on sagged momentarily, then snapped in the centre. The timber and the man went crashing down into the bottom of the stope. The distance wasn't more than ten feet or so, but he fell heavily and landed spread-eagled on the stones, close beside the lamp. For a moment he didn't move. Then he raised his head, supported himself on one arm, and started to scramble to his feet.

There was a loud creak from below me, followed by a groaning, splitting sound. Looking down I saw the wall of timber boards which the beams had supported suddenly bulge and buckle. A stream of dust and rubble was pouring out from between them. The man's face was turned upwards. His mouth opened. At that instant the dam burst. I glimpsed a torrent of rocks and boulders hurtling down. There was a thunderous roar. The lamplight was instantly blotted out.

I pulled back from the hole and collided with Paeony in the dark. We clung to each other blindly. The echoes were still reverberating. Then there came a sudden crack, and a great, deafening rumble that seemed to go right down to the bowels of the earth. The rock shivered around us. I thought the noise would never end. Not just my eardrums but my whole body was vibrating to the sound. At last the roar began to resolve itself into individual crashes, then to a sound like hail, then to a rattling of pebbles, and finally to a pattering of dust. And the mine was silent.

Paeony was trembling violently, and I was shaking like a leaf. 'My God. The deads came down. The whole wall collapsed.' I tried to ignite my lamp, but my fingers were so unsteady that it took me nearly half a minute. When it was burning I looked into Paeony's eyes, wide and staring. Mine must have been the same. I crawled back to the hole and tried to look down, but the air was full of dust.

'We'd better go down and see what happened.' We crawled back to the rope and lowered ourselves slowly down to the bottom of the shaft. I led the way along to where the passage crossed the stope. The dust was slowly settling, but it threw back the light from our lamps like fog at night.

Suddenly I stopped, and grabbed her arm as she came up behind. 'Don't go any further.'

'The floor,' she said incredulously, 'It's gone'.

We were standing on the edge of a yawning chasm. The whole floor of the stope had collapsed into the level below, and probably into the level below that. Paeony's lamp couldn't penetrate the darkness beneath us. She was staring down in horror, holding on to the wall of the tunnel.

'Don't move.' I went back to the bottom of the shaft where we'd left the rucksacks, got out the headlamp, brought it back and shone it downwards. The rock walls descended like some great gorge into the depths. Dust still swirled between them, and it was some time before the light could reach the bottom. At last we could make out a huge mass of boulders and rubble, with jagged pieces of timber projecting from it, fully a hundred feet below.

'He was buried alive,' Paeony said, unbelievingly.

'He's buried dead.'

'John!' She pointed across the stope. 'Look at the tunnel!'

Opposite us, where the mouth of the entrance level had been, were two immense slabs of rock, wedged together. The rock had cracked at the join of the walls and the roof, and the roof itself had collapsed. The whole face above was fractured and bulging. The level was now less than a foot high, and separated from us by a six foot gap and a hundred foot drop.

We sat down on the edge of the abyss and held each other tightly. For a while neither of us could think straight. I was struggling to suppress a growing sense of panic. The passage was clearly impassable, even if we could reach it. Clearing it would require explosives, and some means of shoring the roof. Our only hope was to sit and wait to be rescued - if rescuers could find us and get to us in time.

She was the first to recover. 'We have to get out. This way's blocked. We have to find another.'

I pulled myself together. 'We've got the rucksacks.' I thanked my lucky stars we hadn't left them on the floor of the stope. 'We've got spare batteries, and a bit of food. Plenty of carbide.' I was starting to think more clearly. 'Cadwaladr will know something's wrong when we don't show up with the bike. With luck he'll raise the alarm. The rescue teams could be here by morning. They'll find the bike outside the mine. Maybe they'll be able to blast a way through.'

I knew I should have left a proper message to say where we were going, and when we expected to be back. It's an elementary precaution, and I hadn't taken it. By failing to do so, I'd compounded the danger we were in.

'It could take weeks,' Paeony said. 'They'll have to shift hundreds of tons. Look how fractured that rock is. And what if those men have moved the bike? How much food have you got?'

I had a look. 'A bar of mint cake and a bag of crisps. What about you?'

'An apple and a banana. We'll probably starve to death. It's pointless sitting here waiting. If there's any other way of getting out, we ought to look for it.'

I tried to think straight. We'd explored the levels pretty thoroughly, without finding a way out. 'The only possible way would be through Owain's mine. There was that draught of air. It ought to mean some sort of connection with the surface. Maybe we can get through the water. But it's a long shot.'

'It's better than doing nothing,' Paeony insisted, 'If we're going to get out we have to do it now, when we've still got the energy and the light. If we can't get through, we can always come back here and wait.'

'You're right.'

Once we'd decided what we were going to do we didn't waste time. Neither of us looked into the stope again. We went back to the shaft, collected her rucksack and went up the rope. At her suggestion we pulled it up and took it with us. Her lamp would soon be getting dim, and we agreed to use it as little as possible. We scrambled through the passages of Owain's Mine, wormed our way through the choke and crawled on to where the water filled the passage. Its surface was black and forbidding.

Lowering my head till my cheek touched the water, I could still feel the air current. The water couldn't make a perfect seal with the roof, or maybe there was a crack just above water level that it was blowing through. But there was no room for my head between the surface and the rock above; no room to breathe.

Doubt gnawed at me. If we failed to get through, and got soaking wet in the attempt, our survival chances would be reduced. And going underwater without proper equipment and backup was against all established safety principles. There was a risk of becoming trapped, or losing our way beneath the surface. But the thought of sitting in the darkness, slowly starving, waiting for rescuers who might never come, was even worse. And there was the feeling that I'd got us into this situation, and that it was up to me to get us out of it.

'I'll see what it's like.'

I managed to turn round, and inched my way into the water feet first. I was gasping; it was every bit as cold as I'd expected, and I felt the chill creep up my legs. After a yard or two it was waist deep. I reached the point where the roof almost met the water. 'Pass me the headlamp.' I shone it along the water surface, half submerging my face. The low section seemed to extend a long way.

'A lot of people go diving in caves,' I said, 'But this isn't the way to do it. The experts have a wet suit, and an air supply, and a safety reel, and an underwater lamp.'

I was hating the thought of what I'd got to do. It might be just a matter of ducking under for a yard or two, but I'd no idea how far I'd have to go before there was enough headroom to breathe and I'd be completely blind. The electric lamps weren't designed to function under water.

I turned off the carbide valve, hung on to the roof with one hand, ducked my head under the water and pushed it as far along as I could. Then I turned my mouth up towards the roof and opened it. It immediately filled with water. I struggled back again, spluttering.

'Give me the end of that rope.' I clipped it onto my belt. 'If I get trapped you can pull me back again. If I give one tug it means I'm OK. Two means pull me out.'

'Be careful,' Paeony said, 'Please. Be careful.'

'I intend to.' Then I took several deep breaths, ducked my head under and struggled forward along the flooded passage.

What I was doing was foolhardy, and born of desperation. I was half crawling, half swimming, moving totally blind and aware I hadn't much time. Twice I tried to straighten up, and felt my helmet crash against the roof while my mouth and nostrils were still submerged. My shins and knees were striking against invisible boulders, and my shoulder banged painfully against a sharp projection. It was difficult to keep a sense of direction. My chest was bursting, and I was rapidly beginning to tire.

I straightened up again, thinking this would have to be the last attempt, and my head broke the surface. I stood there in total darkness, gasping and retching, trying to wipe the water out of my face. Then I remembered to give a tug on the line. I felt a comforting tug back.

I turned on the carbide valve and heard it hiss, then flicked the lighter. It was wet, and it was some time before I could get a spark. At last there was a pop, and the light shone out. The roof was a couple of feet above my head. For a moment I couldn't work out where I'd come from, then the rope helped me to orientate myself. Ahead of me it dipped again to within six inches or so of the water; then it seemed to rise.

I refilled my lungs, ducked back under water and fought my way back along the rope. It didn't seem nearly so far this time. Suddenly I broke the surface and saw her lamp shining at me, only inches away.

'You were a long time,' she said.

'It's all right. We can get through. It's only a few yards.'

We had to get not just ourselves through, but the ropes and the rucksacks. Both of us knew that there was still only a slender chance of finding a way out, but if we were to do so we'd need all the help we could get. Paeony was already edging down into the water, her teeth chattering.

'I'll go first. I'll give a tug when I get to the higher bit. You can use the rope as a guide, and I'll pull it in. Just keep your head down until you bump into me. It really isn't far.'

'Get on with it,' she said gruffly.

I stuffed the spare rope into my rucksack with the big lamp, which I tied up as tightly as I could in a plastic bag. There might not be much chance of it working afterwards, but it was the best I could do. My hands were torn and bleeding from scrabbling at the rock: I hadn't been aware of the pain.

Holding the rucksack in front of me I struggled back under water and through the flooded passage. It seemed much shorter this time. Back in the higher section I got my lamp going, planted my feet firmly, and braced my shoulders against the roof. Then I gave a tug.

She must have set off at once because immediately I was taking in more rope, trying to maintain the tension so that she would know which way to go. She would drown if she lost her way.

The rope went tight. She must be stuck. Waves of panic washed over me. Should I pull harder, and risk a jam? Or dive back and try to find her in the dark?

The rope was suddenly slack again, and a second later her helmet crashed against my ribs. Then she was gasping and spluttering beside me. I cursed myself for letting her take such a crazy risk.

'Are you all right?' We were still sitting neck deep in the icy water.

She didn't reply for a moment. Then she said, 'Where do we go from here?'

'Hang on.' I crawled forward. The next low bit proved to be just a short duck, and we didn't even need to put our faces under water. After that there was a full three feet of headroom. To our relief Paeony's lamp was still working, a tribute to the manufacturers who didn't claim it was proof against immersion. We dragged our soaking bodies on through the mud, pushing the sodden rucksacks ahead of us; the tunnel remained wet for some distance, but the depth of water never exceeded a few inches and eventually we were back on dry rock.

We crawled on and on, silent now, saving our breath for the physical effort of moving forward. Surely the passage couldn't continue much longer. Owain's Mine had already proved far more extensive than I'd anticipated. I'd begun to suspect that its origins must be even older than his day; so much excavation with the methods then available must surely have taken centuries. Soon we must come to an end of some kind and I hoped to God it wouldn't be a dead one. I was placing my faith in the draught of air which was still perceptible, though it seemed fainter than before. The thought that we might have to go back through the water was more than I could bear, and I shut it out of my mind.

As we crawled I became aware that the rock had changed; it was darker, and the planes were smoother. There were prominent white threads in it: we seemed to be following a vein of quartz that showed up in the passage roof. But I was too tired to think of the implications.

I'd let Paeony lead the way for a while, and was a few feet behind when I heard her say, 'My God!'

'What is it?'

'Come and see.'

The passage here was low but fairly wide, and I was able to crawl up beside her. 'Don't go too far,' she said.

In front of us was an enormous void: an immensity of blackness which the feeble rays from our lamps were quite incapable of crossing. Paeony turned her head this way and that, but the light from her helmet simply shone out into space.

I found the headlamp in my rucksack and turned it on. It too still worked. The powerful beam flickered over the walls and roof of a vast cavern, the height of a cathedral. The rock was smooth and almost black: great, flat slabs littered the steeply sloping floor. The mouth of the passage where we lay opened into the gulf like a window, so that there was a sheer, vertiginous drop below us.

Paeony was awestruck. 'Where are we?'

'It's a slate quarry. An underground quarry. Owain's Mine has been quarried away.' I shone the lamp across the chamber to the opposite wall. Directly in line with us was a small opening. 'Look, the passage continues on the other side.'

I was trying to direct the beam into the opening opposite. 'It doesn't go in very far. Only a few feet. Either it's walled up, or it was the end of the mine.' Then I said, 'Look. There's something there.'

Across the chamber, at the back of the opening, there seemed to be something of a regular shape, with square corners. It was quite small, and a long way off. 'Look over there! It can't be natural, surely? It's perfectly square. Do you think it could be a box?'

'For God's sake!' she said with sudden vehemence. 'We've still got to get out of here. It's probably a lump of slate. You can come back and look another day.'

She had pulled the rope out of the rucksack and was overhauling it as she spoke. 'I hope it's long enough. It's quite a drop.'

'There's nothing here to belay to.'

'We'll use a nut.' Paeony was back on her own ground now, with a rock face to negotiate. She wedged a big nut in a crack back in the tunnel wall, and I pointed out another.

'Use a double. It's a long way down.'

We rigged a sling to each nut, and she gave them a tug. 'That'll hold.'

'Thank God we brought the gear with us. We'd never get down there without it.'

I'd turned the headlamp off, and as my eyes re-accustomed themselves to the gloom I thought I could detect a slight variation in the blackness of the cavern. 'Look. Up towards the roof. At that end, where it gets higher. Is it light?'

We shielded our lamps. It took a moment to convince myself that it wasn't wishful thinking. But high up to our right there was the faintest greyness. 'It's daylight!' said Paeony. 'It must be.'

I took her hand and squeezed it. 'We're going to get out.'

She let the end of the rope fall down the face of the rock. It didn't quite reach the floor of the chamber, but there were slabs of slate piled against the wall and the rope was brushing against them. 'We can do it,' she said.

She was rigging a descender, carefully and methodically. She had to turn round in the confined space of the tunnel and I crawled back to give her space. She wormed her way backwards till her legs were dangling in the void, and lowered herself over the edge. I wriggled back to the brink and watched her lead the way down the pitch, descending rapidly, pushing off with her feet against the wall of slate. Her helmet lamp was swinging to and fro in the blackness. At the bottom she scrambled onto the slabs and called, 'Come on down.' Her voice echoed in the gloom.

I followed rather more steadily till my feet struck solid ground. 'We'll have to leave the rope.'

Once on the floor of the chamber we could clearly see daylight filtering down at the far end. It was pale blue in colour, as though we were under water. The cavern sloped steeply upwards, and the floor was a chaos of slabs and loose flakes which slithered away under our feet.

'There might be another way out. We may not have to climb up there.' This part of the quarry seemed dry: it must have its own drainage and there was probably an adit leading out directly onto the mountain side. But Paeony's face, smudged and drawn in the light of my lamp, convinced me that it would be better to head for the daylight we could see.

The climb was gruelling, but we were spurred on by the knowledge that the surface was within sight. At the upper end of the chamber, where the floor almost met the roof, huge boulders towered above us, but there were gaps and we scrambled up between them.

Slate caverns are dug in a series of huge underground steps. We had climbed up into another cavern, equally vast, at a higher level, and here the light was stronger. We could see each other by it now, tiny figures dwarfed by the great space around us. We toiled on up the slope and came to a third chamber, where huge pillars of rock supported a roof that had partially collapsed. The evening sunlight streamed in, its rays slanting across the blackness of the rock. I turned off my lamp. One final scree of shattered slate led us out into a great open gouge in the mountain side.

Paeony sat down and buried her head in her hands. Her shoulders were shaking. I sat down beside her, put my arm around her and held her close. 'I'm sorry. I'm sorry I let you into this. You were superb. We'd never have got out without your climbing. Thank God we're safe.' I was ready to sob myself.

We gradually recovered, and I found the rather soggy mint cake in my rucksack. It made both of us feel better. We'd been trapped underground for several hours, and had gone through trauma. We needed to get home quickly. I could see a passable-looking track leading from the slate quarry towards the forest road on the other side of the valley, and pointed it out. 'Look. Stay here, and I'll go and get the quad bike. We should be able to ride it down there together.' She looked all in, and I wasn't sure she'd be capable of walking.

'OK,' she said, 'But look out. There might be more of them about.'

I left her sitting there and set off briskly. It couldn't be far to the mine entrance, but the hillside was a chaos of boulders and slate heaps and it was hard to get my bearings. At last I realised it must be lower down the hill, and then I spotted the spoil heap below the gully. We'd come a long way underground.

Paeony had warned me to be cautious. Inman, if it had been Inman, might well have had someone waiting for him. I took a line that kept me behind humps and boulders; that way I was out of sight, but it was hard to get a view. On a slight brow a couple of rocks offered a vantage point with cover, and I crawled up to them and peeped through. It felt ridiculous; this was like a kids' game. Any minute someone was going to jump out and shout, 'Bang! You're dead!'

There was no sign of anyone, and I kept going till I was just above where the mine entrance ought to be. Thick bracken grew at the head of the gully, and I snaked through it until I could look down. There was nobody below, and the quad bike was still there. Everything was quiet. I felt for the key in my wet pocket, and found it. Keeping it in my hand I climbed slowly down until I was level with the opening that led into the mine. Someone could be in there. I waited, listening. Then I stepped forward and looked inside. Just blackness.

The bike was only a few yards away. I walked towards it. Still nothing. I got astride, inserted the key and twisted it. The engine started with a startling roar. Quickly I turned the bike round and headed down to the end of the gully.

I almost collided head-on with a Toyota Land Cruiser, with two men in it. They must have been parked out of sight, below the spoil heap, and heard me start up the bike. I wrenched the handlebars over and careered up the side of the gully. The Land Cruiser's transmission screamed. I went skidding up the slope and onto the hillside, and looking back saw it lumbering over the crest in pursuit.

The last thing I wanted was lead them back to Paeony. I peered desperately around for the best line of escape. Uphill looked smoothest, and I steered that way.

I was revving the engine furiously. In low gear the bike was agonisingly slow, but as soon as I tried a higher one it couldn't cope with the gradient and the bracken. It just wasn't powerful enough. The bike was bucking violently under me, the wheels were bouncing over the tussocks and I struggled to stay in control. I looked back to see the Land Cruiser lurching and rolling as the driver gunned the engine. It seemed to be gaining.

The wheels hit a boggy bit and started to spin. They were chewing into the wet, mossy turf, throwing up clods and lumps of mud as the engine screeched. I was down to walking pace now, the bike slewing from side to side. With bigger tyres and four wheel drive, the Toyota would catch me in seconds.

Heading uphill was a mistake; I had to change course. I jammed a foot down, heaved the bike round bodily and shot off to one side. Now I'd oversteered and was tearing back down the mountain. I glimpsed the Toyota coming to cut me off, but there were rocks in between and he had to steer round them. I'd gained a few more yards.

I needed to find some better going. I was almost level with the mine entrance again, close to the line of the old track which led across to the shaft where we'd first gone underground. If I could find the track I might manage to stay ahead, but the bracken was taller now.

There were rocks beneath the vegetation: when I hit one the handlebars would jerk round without warning and threaten to throw me off. There was no chance to take my eyes of the ground ahead, to look around or look back. I thought I glimpsed a flatter stretch to the right, headed for it and found I was on the track.

I changed up and twisted the throttle, plunging through the bracken, and risked a look over my shoulder. The Land Cruiser was on the track too now: it was tearing along behind, leaping in the air and crashing down again. It was getting closer.

I heard a clang, and saw a dent had appeared in the engine casing of the bike. It might have been a stone, or it might not. I crouched as low as I could, and screwed the throttle grip a bit wider.

Ahead was the ring of spoil around the shaft. It would screen me for a moment. I rode up onto it, and something flicked past my ear. I accelerated down the slope, slithered round between the shaft and the rock face and crashed the gears to get up the far side. Jolting over the crest I looked back and saw the Land Cruiser pitching wildly on its springs as it plunged down the slope behind.

Beyond the shaft the track ended, and I was steering between boulders. From behind came a screeching and grinding of metal. I looked back again, and that was my undoing. A front wheel of the bike hit a rock and it stopped dead. I flew straight over the handlebars and landed in a patch of gorse.

The gorse was painful, but it saved me from more serious injury. I struggled out of it, scratched and bleeding, and grabbed the bike. Amazingly it seemed relatively undamaged. The Land Cruiser should have come up out of the dip, but it hadn't. Then it dawned on me that it wasn't going to. I restarted the bike and shoved it into gear. It moved, and I steered it up the hill, looking for somewhere to hide.

I hadn't intended to lure my pursuers towards the shaft. No doubt it would have occurred to James Bond, but it hadn't occurred to me. But we'd replaced the wire netting over the mouth, and the rushes and brambles had concealed it fairly effectively. They might deter a sheep, but they wouldn't do much to keep out a Land Cruiser if the driver didn't see the hazard in time.

I stopped the bike behind a rock and switched off the engine. My chest was pounding so hard I almost expected them to hear it. I listened, but couldn't detect any sounds of pursuit. After a while I plucked up courage to scramble up the rock, and peered over the top.

I'd expected to see nothing but a hole. In fact the rear end of the Land Cruiser was sticking up at a steep angle out of the brambles. It looked to be wedged by the top of its windscreen against one side of the opening, with the back wheels still on the other side.

A man was scrambling around on top of the vehicle, reaching inside. As I watched an arm appeared; the first man was trying to pull the other out. At last he succeeded in dragging him clear, and the two of them staggered away from the shaft and sat down on the grass. One was holding his head. They stayed like that for quite a while.

Eventually one got to his feet: the other stayed sitting down. There was a lot of gesticulating; they looked to be arguing, and the fitter one kept looking round. I thought he was black, though it was hard to be sure. I kept my head well down; he was armed, and he could still come after me on foot. But in the end he pulled the other upright and they started walking away from me, the casualty limping heavily and leaning on the other. They were picking their way down painfully through the loose slate towards the stream and the road beyond. Evidently the vehicle was being abandoned.

A sense of hatred overcame me, and for a moment I wished they'd plunged to the bottom of the shaft. But it was quickly replaced by relief, even triumph. I didn't beat my chest, but I came pretty close.

They'd almost reached the stream when a screeching noise came from the shaft. There was the crash of shattered glass, and the rending of metal. The Land Cruiser was sagging, slipping further down. It only took a few seconds; there was a sudden crunch, the roof tilted sharply and the vehicle abruptly disappeared from view. I heard a grinding, then a muffled crump from deep within the mountain. One of them looked back. The other kept on hobbling.

I let them get well out of sight and hearing before I set off back to the quarry. When I got there the light was fading fast, and Paeony was standing waiting for me.

'Where have you been? I was worried stiff.'

'I ran into some friends of our friend. It's all right. They've just written off their Land Cruiser.'

'You're bleeding. What have you done to your ear?'

I felt it; there was a distinct nick in the lobe, and blood on my finger. 'Let's go home. I'll tell you later.'

There was no sign of the two men as we rode together down the track to Cadwaladr's. He came out to meet us, looking concerned. 'You're mighty late,' he said, 'I was ready to send for the search parties.'

'Sorry. We got held up. I'm afraid your bike had a bit of a bump. I think it's OK, but if you find there's any damage I'll pay for it.'

'As long as nothing else is damaged.' Cadwaladr was looking at our wet and filthy clothing and my bloodstains and scratches, 'You'll have to take better care of that girl, you know.'

'I know.'

Paeony insisted she was all right to drive, and we both went back to Berwyn. We were exhausted, and after a hot bath she collapsed into bed while I took myself off to the sofa. Sleeping seemed to be the most sensible thing to do.

CHAPTER 14

The next morning we were still pretty shell-shocked. We'd barely surfaced when Paeony's phone rang. 'Yes....yes.....yes...,' she kept saying sleepily, 'Yes, all right.....I'll be in this morning.'

'You can't possibly go into work. Not after yesterday.'

'I've had too many days off. The jobs are piling up.' She disappeared into the shower.

Reluctantly I rooted in the kitchen and dug out something for breakfast. We sat opposite each other, eating it in silence. After a while I said, 'I'd better do something about that man.'

'There's not much you can do about him, is there? You saw the rock fall. He's buried under tons of it.' There was an edge to her voice.

'We'll have to report what happened.'

'I don't suppose anyone will miss him,' she said brutally, 'It served him right.'

'I'd better ring Humphreys at Llangollen.'

I didn't look forward to telling a sceptical Inspector Humphreys that, if he cared to clear the level and shift several hundred tons of underground rubble, he would find the remains of a gangster dispatched by Carl Quinn to murder me. Nor did I fancy explaining that he'd died as a result of me dropping rocks on his head.

'Look,' I said again, 'You had a hell of a day yesterday. Perhaps you ought to see a doctor, get checked over or something. And then get some rest.'

She was shovelling muesli into her mouth, not listening. 'Damn this stuff. You can't chew it quickly. I've got an estate to run. Some of us have work to do, you know.'

I was disconcerted by the sharpness of her tone, and changed tack. 'I've been thinking about that thing up in the cavern wall. I'm sure it was a box. I'd like to get another look.'

166

'If you think I'm going back down that bloody mine you've got another think coming.' She banged her dish into the sink. At that moment the phone rang again. 'Yes. I'm on my way.'

I said I'd go back to Tan-y-Coed and wash the mud out of my boiler suit. It looked as if work was going to be Paeony's way of coping with the after-effects of yesterday's events, and it would be best to make myself scarce for a while. Last night I'd played down the chase across the mountain side, feeling she'd had enough to worry about already, and hadn't mentioned gunshots. I couldn't quite believe myself that I'd come under fire; there was just a little scab forming on my ear to remind me. But I was constantly under-estimating her toughness. The way she'd handled an appalling experience had been deeply impressive. I hadn't exactly covered myself in glory yesterday. If she was angry with me, I had only myself to blame.

Before I left Berwyn I made myself ring the police at Llangollen and ask for Humphreys. 'He's away just now,' someone said, 'But I'll put you through to Sergeant Pritchard.'

'It's all right,' I said hastily, 'I'll call back later.'

I meant to. But I put it off.

Back at Tan-y-Coed I did my washing. The weeds were sprouting in the vegetable plot, and I spent the day hoeing them out and drilling the ground for seed. The activity was therapeutic, just like Paeony's estate work; there was a need to get back into some sort of comforting routine. But when I thought of my recklessness the day before, I felt consumed with guilt and shame. If she'd had any respect for me, she would surely have lost it now.

In the afternoon the phone rang, and I managed to get into the house before it stopped. A voice with a mid-Atlantic accent said, 'Wayne Drew, from the World. Remember me, Mr Jones? Out in that garden of yours again, were you?'

'I was, as it happens.'

'All that rustic tranquillity. Nothing to do but sit and watch the cabbages grow. It'd bore me to death. Still, every man to his own, as they say.'

'What can I do for you?'

'Someone's been in touch with our News Editor. Bloke with a funny name. Charles Something Greene. Do you know him?'

'I've met him.'

'He mentioned you. I'd been to see you once, so they put me on the job. Small world isn't it?'

'What did he want?'

'He said he's looking for the Crown Jewels. Or a crown anyway. Wants to give it to the Prince of Bavaria. He seems to think you know where it is.'

'He's a nutcase,' I said angrily, 'And he'd no right to go to the press.'

'Everyone has the right to go to the press. It's one of our great democratic freedoms. You and Bob Lord were looking for something, weren't you? It couldn't have been a crown by any chance?'

'Look,' I said, 'It was an academic enquiry. A piece of historical research. The chances of it ever leading anywhere are pretty remote. Your readers aren't that interested in history. Greene's a crank. If you let him lead you up the garden path, you'll end up with egg all over your face.' I was mixing metaphors, but it seemed to have some effect. He pushed a bit more, but I was determined not to give anything else away. In the end he said he'd be in touch again, and rang off. I went back to my cabbages. But my mind dwelt on Paeony, and what she thought of me.

Trying to think positive thoughts while marking out the rows I let my mind dwell on the object I'd seen in the cavern wall. Paeony had said it was probably a lump of slate. Certainly slate did split neatly into slabs, but they'd be regular in one direction, not both. What I'd seen had been almost square in shape. It was hard to get a sense of scale in the vast chamber: it could well have been a couple of hundred feet across. If the bit of passage where I'd seen it was three feet high then the box, if it was a box, would be about a foot square. It wouldn't be visible from below, but it was surprising the quarrymen hadn't seen it when they were cutting higher up. On the other hand, they would have blasted that section away and then cut it up where it fell, so they wouldn't necessarily have looked into the passage. The opening wasn't far from the lower end of the cavern, and maybe they hadn't drilled at that level again.

I forced myself to wait till six before telephoning Paeony. She was a little cool, and said she was going to have an early night. But I sensed I'd been forgiven, which was more than I deserved. We arranged I'd go over to Berwyn the following evening. I went round to check my security arrangements, such as they were, and had an early night too. But I woke up sweating, drowning in the dark.

The next morning I went out to buy some seed and picked up a copy of Drew's paper. There was a prominent item about Charles Angevin

Greene, with a photo of him standing outside the Tower of London. It made it sound as though Greene knew more than he did. The tone of the article was half sensational, half facetious, as if the paper was hedging its bets and uncertain whether to treat him as a crank or a man with a mission. The silly season wasn't far away, and it looked as if they were going to run the story of the Quest for the Crown on the same lines as UFO sightings or the hunt for Nessie. Slightly to my surprise my name wasn't mentioned, though apparently 'another historian' was believed to have 'confidential information'. The article said that the Crown was thought to be hidden underground, but didn't actually mention a mine. There was a strong element of 'Watch This Space'.

In the evening I drove over to Berwyn, and found Paeony much more cheerful. She gave me a kiss and challenged me to a game of croquet on the lawn where she'd played with her father. People don't appreciate what a vicious game croquet can be. She delighted in knocking my ball into the shrubbery every time I was in line for a hoop, and even when she was several hoops ahead she came back to blast me off the lawn. Having thrashed me once she offered me the chance of getting my revenge and slaughtered me again. Finally honour was satisfied, and we adjourned to her flat where she cooked savoury pancakes with a mouth-watering filling. I felt deliriously, undeservingly happy.

I showed her the article about Angevin Greene. 'He's got a nerve,' she said. In the end I risked mentioning the box, and this time she didn't bite my head off.

'I can visualise it. The shape looked too artificial to be a rock, or a piece of slate. That bit of passage could well have been the end of the mine. They'd found nothing but slate, and decided it wasn't worth going any further. If it is a box, it's the right size to hold the Crown.'

Paeony frowned. 'I didn't look at it properly. I was more concerned with getting out. You might be right, it was shaped like a box. But it was very high up. It wouldn't be easy to get to it.'

'You could do it with those nuts.'

'I've had enough of mines', she said firmly, 'And I'm damned if I'm going back down there with a lot of gangsters waiting for me. Anyway, you're talking about a major climb. That face is sheer and it's all big slate slabs with hardly any holds. There'll be precious few cracks to take a nut. You'd need expansion bolts, and a proper team. It's too risky for the two of us, from all points of view.'

'I agree. We need a team. There'd be safety in numbers. Quinn's lot wouldn't try anything if we had a full scale party. I'm going to get on to WMEG. They've got a few climbers, as well as crawlers. A lead mine that links up with a slate mine is a real find. There's only one other in Wales, and that's inaccessible now. The mine enthusiasts would be out like a shot.'

'Now that's more sensible. If you get a party together, I might even come with you. But we're not going down alone any more. And don't even think of going out there on your own, either; even if you survived the villains, you wouldn't survive me afterwards.'

'It's nice to know you care.'

Later we showed each other how much we cared. Our love-making was becoming bolder, more confident, more relaxed. We were always tender to each other, but her incisiveness gave an extra dimension to our relationship. 'Just lie back and enjoy it,' she said. Paeony was the sort of girl who likes to be on top.

I stayed over, and next morning, which was Saturday, I rang the Potters in Wrexham. Derek was sceptical, but as I described the attractions of the mine in more detail his excitement grew. 'That sounds very interesting,' he said. 'The only mine I know where they worked slate as well as lead was Cyfannedd, over near Fairbourne, but that collapsed years ago. There were a few copper mines in the Lakes where they quarried slate, but nothing else in Wales. And if it's a seventeenth century mine it's well worth exploring anyway. There's a party of members going to Caernarfonshire next weekend, but they might be prepared to switch to Cwm Llwyd. Huw Griffiths is down from university just now, he could climb up to your tunnel, no problem.'

'I think there could be some interesting artefacts down there. One place looked particularly promising.'

'All the better,' Derek said. He promised to ring round and let me know.

That weekend Paeony and I walked the hills together above Dinas Mawddwy, and I showed her some of my favourite places. We kept ourselves and our minds well above ground. There was a blustery wind which helped to blow away the memories of our confinement; heavy showers alternated with brilliant sunshine, and you could see for miles in the sparkling air. We walked hand in hand, bracing each other against the gale, and returned exhilarated and refreshed. On the Sunday night Val Potter rang to say that an WMEG party, fully equipped for climbing, would turn out for an expedition to Cwm Llwyd next weekend.

170

I'd begun to feel a little guilty at my lack of any gainful occupation. My money wouldn't last for ever, and I was going have to do something about it. My pride was at stake, and Lord Berwyn would hardly think me a suitable match for his daughter if I stayed on the dole. I told Paeony I was going to do some job hunting, and she didn't demur. So I went back to Tan-y-Coed and got on the phone.

The week provided a few leads, though nothing definite. My old company had promised good references, and whilst the feedstuffs sector remained depressed I had marketing skills that could be put to use in other areas. I still had hopes for my computer programme too. One fertiliser company was expanding its sales force, and I should be in with a chance. I sifted through the newspapers, national and local, and wrote fifty-odd letters. Finding a job shouldn't be too difficult: the problem was the location. I didn't want it to be too far away.

As the weekend approached my excitement grew more intense. I kept picturing the box high up on the rock wall. I imagined it as it would have been three hundred and fifty years ago, newly made, an oak chest perhaps, with iron bands. I thought of Owain Morgan placing his Treasure reverently within it, closing the lid, handing it to a trusted servant or perhaps carrying it himself into the deepest recesses of the mine, where the miners had finally abandoned their search for metal in the barren slate. Maybe the last few yards of the passage had been walled off, only for the blasting two centuries later to destroy the barrier but leave the box and its precious contents intact. And I imagined the moment when I would open it, and hold the Crown of England in my hands.

Two disturbing things happened that week. The first was on the Thursday, when I was driving back from posting another batch of letters. I met Glyn Lewis's old Land Rover coming down the road. But it was Gwen driving it, not Glyn. That was a bit unusual; she didn't drive much. When I pulled over to let her by she stopped alongside me, and I thought she looked worried. 'How are you?' I asked her. 'Where's Glyn?'

'He's had to go with the police to Llangollen. They're still asking questions about those fires. Really nasty, they were. A fat sergeant called Pritchard, and another one with a posh accent, from England. Glyn's been gone all day.'

'That's ridiculous. I thought they'd given up. Why should they think Glyn had anything to do with it?'

'Sometimes he gets a bit heated, you know how he is. He feels very deeply, you know, about the language. Sometimes he says things he doesn't mean. I was only just thinking... You remember, when you came to see us after Mr Mitchell's house burned down. He said something then. I hope you didn't think...'

'I didn't think anything, Mrs Lewis. And I'm not thinking anything now. And I certainly wouldn't mention it to the police, if they ever came asking.' She started to thank me, but I wouldn't let her. 'They should have more sense. The real criminals must be laughing at them'. I gave her a ring that evening and she said Glyn had come home; she sounded relieved, but still worried.

The next day, Friday, an envelope arrived with a Birmingham postmark. There was no letter in it, but I knew it came from Joseph. It contained a press clipping dated the previous day. It was quite brief. It said 'Carl Anthony Quinn, who has served nine years for a series of armed robberies, was due to be released on parole from Walton Prison, Liverpool, today.' That night I locked my door with extra care.

The Saturday dawned wet, but that wouldn't deter the WMEG members. We'd agreed to meet at Cwm Llwyd at ten. Val had insisted that we got Cadwaladr's permission, and I'd spoken to him on the phone. I went over to see him in good time. It was time I told him about the shaft, and I wasn't sure how much to say.

We'd hardly passed the time of day when a car arrived. I expected it to be some of the members, but it was a taxi bearing the name of a Llangollen firm. Out stepped Charles Angevin Greene, attired in Barbours and green wellies. 'Ah - good morning, Mr Jones,' he whinnied. 'I was up here the other day speaking to Mr Pugh.' Cadwaladr was looking guilty. 'He said that you would be - ah - undertaking an exploration this morning. I was hoping that you might be kind enough to allow me to join you.'

'Why did you tell the newspapers about the Crown?'

'Ah. Yes. I hope you were not displeased. I have always found it beneficial to avail myself of the assistance of the press. We have a duty, do we not, to ensure that the public is kept informed of such - ah - momentous developments.'

'You had no business to give them my name. And the last thing we want out here is a crowd of reporters.'

'Ah - no. No indeed,' Greene said hastily, 'You will have noticed that I have said nothing regarding the mine. I am sorry if I have caused

172

you inconvenience. But I do beseech you, Mr Jones, to permit me to be present. It would mean so much to me. So very much. I have bought a helmet,' he added eagerly, holding it out for me to see. I was irritated, but he looked so pathetic that I said that I'd see if he couldn't come into the slate quarry with us. He would probably cope with that.

Paeony arrived soon afterwards, and then a motley assortment of vehicles began to turn up and disgorge a motley assortment of people. I liked the WMEG members; one of the attractions of mine exploration is that it brings you into contact with quite a cross-section of society. Not all of them are the tough, outdoor type; there are ex-miners and engineers who provide expertise, along with academics, bus drivers, dentists, bricklayers and OAP's, all welded together by genuine enthusiasm. Most are male, though there's a leaven of ladies who help to keep things civilised. But today, for all my liking of them, I felt vaguely resentful that Paeony and I weren't doing this on our own.

I introduced her to Val and Derek. Val's eyebrows went up. 'We don't normally....'

'I'm twenty-four.'

'Whoops! Sorry love.'

Greene was hovering in the background. 'And this is Dr Angevin Greene,' I said, 'He'd like to come too.'

Val's eyebrows went up even further. 'They're not members. They'll have to sign a disclaimer.'

'That's fine. They'll come as my guests, if that's all right.'

People whose vehicles were sufficiently rugged drove up the track to the slate quarry, giving a lift to the others. Val and Derek had a battered Volvo that obviously thought it had four wheel drive. I took Greene in the Justy, and Paeony sat in the back with Huw Griffiths, a tall, fresh-faced medical student home from Cardiff University, who was going to do the placing of the bolts. They were soon deep in technicalities.

We all spilled out at the quarry and surveyed the entrance. 'No sign of lead mine spoil', Derek said, pointing to the heaps around us, 'This is all slate'.

'They didn't bring any material out here. The lead mine entrance is further down the valley.'

Angevin Greene was trying on his helmet. He didn't have a lamp, but he was carrying a torch. Val was squeezing into a boiler suit that made her look like Michelin Woman. She was deep in conversation with an irritating Royal Mail employee from Wrexham known in the Group as Postman Prat.

I showed them the way down the steep slope into the first and second chambers. The helmet lamps bobbed about as they slithered on the loose slate, and the beams danced over the walls on either side. Our voices and the clattering of the rocks echoed from the roof. Angevin Greene was finding it heavy going, and needed a hand over the steeper bits. Paeony was talking animatedly to Huw Griffiths, who was carrying a large toolbox as well as more obvious items of gear. When we reached the third chamber I led them down to the bottom and pointed to the two little openings high above us. 'That's the lead mine.'

'Strewth!' said Val, 'However did you get up there?'

'We didn't. We came down.'

'So which way did you get in?' Derek asked.

'Through the lead workings. But we can't get in that way any more. The way's blocked now.'

'Is it?' said Derek thoughtfully.

Huw Griffiths and Paeony were sorting out ropes. They had clearly sized each other up and decided they were both competent. 'That's the passage we came through,' I said, pointing, 'There's our rope. But I think there's something interesting in the other one. Could you start there?'

'These bolts are expensive, you know,' Huw said, 'And we can't get them out again.'

'I think it could be worth it.'

Derek was fixing up a couple of powerful lamps to illuminate the face. Huw and Paeony were working enthusiastically and efficiently together, chattering away. I felt a twinge of jealousy, but the feeling was quickly overcome by impatience to see what they were going to find.

When they were ready Huw started to climb. He had a big rechargeable drill hanging from his belt, and every now and then the cavern was filled with an echoing screech as it tore into the rock. When he'd screwed in a bolt he would suspend a sort of platform from it and stand on it while he reached up to fix the next. He looked as comfortable as if he were cleaning windows. It was slow work but he moved smoothly up the face, his dark shadow climbing ahead of him.

Paeony was adjusting ropes and occasionally sending up extra bits of ironmongery on the end of a line. 'A lot of climbers think it's cheating,' she said defensively. But I can't see any other way of getting up there. Anyway, it's supposed to be all right to put bolts in slate. And he does it very well.'

Doing it very well, Huw managed to find a few cracks which speeded things up a bit. Even so the climb took him over an hour, and most of the party went off to explore other parts of the slate workings. I wasn't going to stir from the bottom of the face. Greene was standing nearby, watching tensely.

At last Huw neared the edge of the opening. He fixed one last bolt, clipped himself on to it and pulled himself upright to look inside. For a moment he didn't say anything, and I was in a fever of impatience. 'What's there?' I shouted up, 'What can you see?'

'It doesn't go very far.' He was shielding his eyes against the glare from the lights below. 'Only a few feet. But you were right. There is something here.'

'What is it?'

'It's a wooden box.'

'I knew it!' I grabbed Paeony and tried to dance. Then I calmed down a bit and called, 'Can you lower it down?'

The process was complicated, and involved Paeony tying an extra rope to the bottom of Huw's safety line which he then pulled up. It took him a long time to knot the rope securely round the box. 'It's quite heavy,' he called, 'You'd better stand clear.' At last the box appeared over the edge and begin its slow descent.

When it was almost down Paeony guided it gently to the ground and untied the knot. I grabbed a screwdriver from the toolbox and advanced towards it. 'Wait for Huw,' she said. I ground my teeth, and waited.

The box was smaller then expected, and more rectangular than square. It was made of some dark wood, thickly coated with dust that had congealed into mud. The lid was curved like an old-fashioned chest, and the whole thing was bound with metal straps that had rusted badly. There was a key-hole in the front. I couldn't see an inscription of any kind. Its age was indeterminate, but it looked old enough to date from Owain's time.

Our shouts had attracted more of the members from the caverns, and Huw was working his way systematically down the face. Soon there was a circle around the box. Derek was holding a lamp.

'Right,' Paeony said, 'Everybody's here. Let's see what's inside.'

I eased the end of the screwdriver between the lid and the box and

175

twisted. At first it wouldn't give. I tried a different spot and a new angle, trying to get a purchase. At last there was a cracking sound. The lock must have been rusted through, because it gave way without a struggle. All around, necks craned expectantly. There was a breathless silence. Angevin Greene was breathing down my neck. Slowly, I lifted the lid.

Beneath it there was a layer of dark red cloth that looked like velvet. I pulled it gently away, and it revealed a row of blackened silver coins, resting on another piece of velvet. I lifted it gently with the coins still in place, and laid it to one side. Below was a bundle of papers. I lifted them out. Beneath was a round disc, a foot or so in diameter, dark in colour. I took hold of it and removed it from the box. It was surprisingly thick and heavy. As it came into the light I saw that it was engraved with a head, wearing a crown.

Around the edge of the disc was lettering. I couldn't make it out at first. Then I recognised it was in Welsh. The disc seemed to be made of slate.

'Who speaks Welsh?' Val asked. 'Huw, tell us what it says.'

I passed the object to Huw. He squinted at it, revolving it slowly in his hands.

'Well, would you believe it?' he said. 'It says: "In commemoration of the Diamond Jubilee of Her Gracious Majesty Queen Victoria, in the year of Our Lord 1897. God Save the Queen."'

There was a babble of excitement. Val slapped me on the back. 'Well done, John. That was a real find!'

Derek was leafing eagerly through the papers. 'Look! The Montgomeryshire Gazette and Times for June 1897. And here's a copy of an illuminated address from the quarrymen, and a list of their names. How extraordinary! I've heard of boxes like this being walled up in buildings, or buried under foundation stones, but it's the first time I've heard of one being placed in a mine.'

'There's patriotism for you,' said Postman Prat.

The slate plaque was being passed from hand to hand with expressions of enthusiasm. I slipped away to where Paeony was standing. 'Never mind,' she said, 'At least we found something. It is quite interesting really.'

'Fascinating.'

The excitement gradually died down, and Huw Griffiths began to scale the opposite wall, having satisfied himself that Paeony's rope was secure. Soon other ropes were rigged, and one or two of the more experienced members began to hoist themselves up to the tunnel from we had descended. It was a long way for SRT, and the less athletic stayed down below or carried on investigating the slate workings which were clearly extensive.

Paeony and I declined the opportunity of revisiting Owain's Mine. Eventually the people who had been up there returned, plastered with mud but impressed by what they'd seen. 'It's definitely an early mine,' Derek said, 'We got as far as a sump. Did you come through there? I wouldn't have fancied that myself.'

By mid-afternoon the Group were feeling in need of liquid refreshment, and we packed up and climbed back to the surface. Angevin Greene was sitting there out in the open, looking glum; I'd forgotten all about him. Everyone else seemed to have enjoyed the day, and none of the Group regretted their change of plan. Finding the box had been the highlight, and Val and Derek offered to look after it and take it to the Welsh Slate Museum. We were happy to let it go.

Paeony and I opted not to go to the pub. We went back to Cadwaladr's, and when everyone else had driven off we sat on his wall and had a rather dejected picnic. Angevin Greene was hanging about, waiting for his taxi. He wandered over to us. 'I fear Prince Francis will be most disappointed,' he said accusingly, 'I had taken the liberty of informing him that there might be - ah - developments.'

Greene had taken too many liberties. 'It's none of his business,' I snapped at him, and he shuffled off offended to the other side of the road.

'Maybe we're on the wrong track completely,' Paeony said. 'We don't know that Owain hid the Crown, if that's what it was, in Cwm Llwyd Mine. We don't know that it's in a mine at all. What were the actual words Owain used? Of course, Mr Lord's box with the journal disappeared, didn't it? We haven't got the exact wording.'

'We have, actually. I'd almost forgotten. Bob gave me a photocopy of that particular page. I think it's still in my wallet.' I fished it out and unfolded the sheet.

Paeony peered at it, fascinated. 'So that's Owain's writing.'

The florid script was disconcerting at first, but when you got used to it the letters were perfectly recognisable. I pointed to the crucial line. 'This is the bit that made us think of the mine. "Gorchuddiwyd â charreg, mewn uchelfan."' My pronunciation left a lot to be desired.

'It means: "Hidden under the rock, in a high place". The journal was found at Bryn Teg, which is in the next valley to Cwm Llwyd. There were other papers with it relating to mining, and accounts listing sales of silver and lead. We don't know that the Morgans had any other mines.'

'Morgans lived at Bryn Teg before Berwyn was built,' Paeony said, 'And the family kept it on. Owain was actually born there, you know. He might have hidden the papers there for some reason; maybe he was afraid of a search. But why should he have hidden the lead accounts?'

'Bob thought he might have been supplying silver to the King. What does he mean by "under the rock"? We need a Welsh speaker, ideally someone with a knowledge of seventeenth century Welsh.'

'Why don't we start by asking Cadwaladr? He's not quite as old as that, but I know he recites Welsh poetry - he goes to all the Eisteddfodau.'

'Why didn't I think of him?'

We went and knocked on Cadwaladr's door, and he asked us in for a cup of tea. It was the first time Paeony had been into his farmhouse. Though it was a bachelor establishment it was immaculately tidy. There was a massive dresser built against one wall, and a big range with an overmantel painted with flowers and inscribed: 'Cartref melys Gartref.'

'Home, sweet home,' I said.

'So you know some Welsh then,' said Cadwaladr. He moved a big brown kettle onto the hob and produced a tin of biscuits.

'Not enough. We were wondering if you could help us with this.' I passed him the paper, and he got out his reading glasses and studied it.

'"A treasure of great price." Now what could that be, I wonder?'

There was an awkward silence. 'Now then. I was reading something in the 'World' the other day. There was a photograph in it, just like that funny little chap who went down the mine with you today. Looking for a crown, he was. Now could there be a connection?'

There was no point in trying to hide things from Cadwaladr. I'd been surprised that no-one in the Group had seemed to recognise Greene; maybe they didn't read the "World". 'Yes, there could be a connection. This was written by Owain Morgan. After Charles I was executed, we think he may have stolen the crown and hidden it.'

'That would be just like old Owain. He was an old rogue, but a good poet. Did you know he wrote poetry in Welsh? Now let's see what he's put here.' Cadwaladr looked at the paper again.

'We weren't sure about "gorchuddiwyd â charreg". Bob Lord

thought it meant "buried under the rock" or "under the mountain". That's what made us think of the mine.'

'Well,' said Cadwaladr, 'It might do, or it might not. It would be an odd way of putting it. Of course, the way Welsh people speak depends on where they live. The language varies more with place than it does with time, if you follow me. Now to me "gorchuddiwyd" doesn't exactly mean "underneath". It means "under the stone" in the same way as that biscuit's under the chocolate, or the door's under the paint. I suppose it could mean that he'd buried it, though I wouldn't say it that way myself.'

Paeony had picked up the chocolate biscuit and was studying it. 'This is coated with chocolate. But you can't coat something with stone.'

'That's true. It doesn't make much sense to me.'

Something was stirring just beneath the surface of my consciousness. 'Paeony,' I said, 'In the one of the boxes - there was a plan of the park. You said there'd once been a hermitage, and a grotto. Wasn't there a well?'

'There was a petrifying well', she said slowly, 'I'm not sure how it worked. It was supposed to turn things to stone.'

'When I was a little boy in Batley, we used to go to Knaresborough sometimes, on a Sunday afternoon. You could get there from Leeds on the train. There was Mother Shipton's Cave, down by the river. And just a bit further along there was a petrifying well. It wasn't really a well at all: there was an overhanging cliff, with water running down the rock and dripping off it like a curtain. People used to hang up bowler hats, and teapots, and old boots, where the water could run over them, about twenty feet up. They weren't actually turned to stone, but they were covered with a mineral deposit that was hard and made them look as if they were. It only took a year or two. They had a museum there with a weird collection of petrified objects.'

'Our well isn't there any more', Paeony said, 'It dried up years ago, I think. I don't even know where it was. What do you think, Mr Pugh? Could that be what Owain meant?'

'Well now. It could. I can't be sure. It seems an odd thing to do with a crown. But if there were lots of funny things hanging up there, I don't suppose people would pay much attention. They wouldn't think it was real, would they? And it would be in a high place, like it says here.'

The kettle lid was starting to rattle, and steam was gushing from the

179

spout. Cadwaladr picked up a big brown teapot, found it was still full of tealeaves and went off to empty them outside. He hadn't closed the door when we came in. On the doorstep he stopped and said sharply: 'What do you think you're doing?'

I followed him to the door. Charles Angevin Greene was standing a yard or so along from the doorway, looking uncomfortable.

'Ah - I had come to ask whether you would be kind enough to - ah - let me have a drink of water,' he quavered unconvincingly.

'Were you listening?'

'Ah - as it happened I did catch a few words. Quite unintentionally, I assure you. Did I understand you to say that you have a new - ah - hypothesis? This is really most exciting. Prince Francis will be fascinated to learn that the Crown may have been - ah - metamorphosed in this way. Perhaps you would like to meet His Royal Highness? I am quite certain that, once the Crown is restored to him, he will reassert his rightful claim...'

I exploded. 'Will you please stop sticking your nose in?' You've no right to eavesdrop on private conversations. And you can stuff Prince Francis, he can take a running jump.'

Greene went bright red and looked as if he was going to bust a gut. Then he turned and stalked off across the farmyard. At this opportune moment his taxi arrived, and he got into it and was whisked away.

Paeony was laughing. 'Poor man. You were a bit hard on him.'

'No more than he deserved. The man's a menace.'

We drank our tea, and told Cadwaladr more about the crown and the research that Bob had done.

'Well, I wish you luck,' he said, 'I think you'll need it, after all this time. And you're quite right to keep it dark. A lot of other people might be interested, and they might not have the same motives as you.'

We thanked Cadwaladr and went back out to the road. 'That idea of yours, about the petrifying well,' Paeony said, 'Could it really be right?'

'I don't know. But how else could something be covered in stone? And I suppose you could describe that cliff at Knaresborough as a high place. But even if the well's still there I don't see how the Crown could be, after all this time.'

'I think you ought to talk to Daddy,' she said decisively. 'We'd better tell him what we're looking for, especially if it could be somewhere at Berwyn. I think he's wondering where I keep disappearing to.'

'Yes, it's time we did. Why don't we do it now?'

CHAPTER 15

So we set off, and drove to Berwyn. We seemed to spend a lot of time driving the same way in separate cars. On the way I was mulling over my latest theory, and how I was going to explain it to Lord Berwyn. It was starting to seem a bit far-fetched.

The house's fantastic skyline was silhouetted against a dramatic evening sky: it wouldn't have been surprising to see a black figure in a pointed hat flying over it on a broomstick. Paeony took me in the back way, along the corridor with the row of bells.

'They're usually in the Library in the evenings.'

Inside it was already dark and the lighting dim, no doubt to save expense. She led me up a broad, heavily carved staircase, lit by a single bulb on one of the newel posts and lined with shadowy Morgans who peered down disapprovingly on their latest visitor. An electric chair lift had been installed along one wall.

On a broad landing part way up the stairs was a heavily carved wooden stand. Perched on it, a little incongruously, was a small wooden cask, its staves black with age, bound round with brass hoops. 'That's Owain's firkin,' Paeony said. I stared at it, impressed. As barrels went it wasn't very big, but for a drinking vessel it was something else. Full of ale it would have been hard enough to lift it, let alone drain it at one draught.

'I wonder what his cubic capacity was.'

At the head of the stairs was a tall pair of doors with heavy brass handles: she turned one of them, and we went in.

The Library at Berwyn was a noble but sombre room, galleried so that the books extended almost unbroken to the high ceiling. All was in shadow save for one pool of light in an alcove at the far end, where a fire was burning quietly. On either side was a tall armchair, each with its shaded lamp. Leather bindings softly reflected the glow. Lord and

Lady Berwyn were sitting reading; a wheelchair was parked a few feet away.

Lady Berwyn got up. 'How nice', she said. 'It's Mr Jones, isn't it? Do come and sit down. Paeony, bring a chair. Would you like a cup of coffee? Or would you prefer tea?'

'Something stronger?' Lord Berwyn said, 'Speak up. Don't be afraid to ask.'

'I'd like coffee, please.' I'd been apprehensive about arriving uninvited: it was good to be made so welcome.

Paeony's mother walked to one of the bookcases and reached towards it. It opened with a click, and she slipped out through the hidden door. It was covered with the gold-tooled spines of old, calf-bound books.

'I hear the two of you have been going down mines,' Lord Berwyn said.

'We were exploring in Cwm Llwyd. We've found the original mines that your ancestors worked in the seventeenth century.'

He looked interested. 'Have you indeed? We did very well out of them, you know, at the time. Always thought it was a pity the mountain land was sold. Bound to be more under there, if we could find it. Ever tried dowsing?'

It took me a moment to work out the connection. 'Er - no. It's supposed to be possible to find minerals that way, but I've never tried.'

'I tried it once. It worked. Dug up a gas main. Nearly blew the place up. So you found what you were looking for.'

'Not altogether. We weren't just looking for the mine. We were hoping to find something there.'

'Wait till Mother comes back,' Paeony said, 'And we'll tell you the story.'

And when Lady Berwyn came back with a tray, we told them, between us, about Owain Morgan's journal, about Bob Lord's theory and our attempts to prove it, and about our search for the mine and for the Crown. Neither of us mentioned our encounters with Quinn's associates, or the collapse in the stope. Lord and Lady Berwyn heard us out, asking the occasional question but making no comment. When we had come to the end they sat for a while looking pensive.

'Owain Morgan's journal,' Lord Berwyn said at last, 'The pages that Mr Lord found. They were burned presumably, in the fire?'

'They could have been. But I believe they may have been stolen by the people who started it. I only have a copy of one page.' I took out the crumpled, folded sheet and gave it to him.

Lord Berwyn peered at the writing, with its twirls and flourishes. Then he picked up his stick, hooked it round the frame of his wheelchair and yanked it towards him. Grasping the arms of his chair he pulled himself upright, moved slowly to the wheelchair and lowered himself into it. It was an ordinary, hand-powered chair and he propelled it vigorously to the far end of the room, switched on a lamp and selected a book from a lower shelf. Then he came back with the book on his knee, and held it out.

It was a small volume, rather crudely bound in vellum that was wrinkled and discoloured with age. There was no title. I opened it. It was loosely sewn, written in manuscript, in a familiar, florid hand. The language was Welsh. Towards the middle a number of pages seemed to have been removed.

'Always wondered what had happened to those pages', Lord Berwyn said. 'It would be nice to have them back.'

I was holding in my hand the book in which Owain had recorded his thoughts three hundred and fifty years ago, and from which he had cut the sheets Bob Lord had found.

'My father had a translation made, back in '48'. Lord Berwyn passed me a thin bundle of yellowed typescript. 'Afraid we've lost our Welsh, don't you know, over the years.'

I looked at the first page. Owain had written: 'In this book I write my thoughts in the worst of times. Through the fondness of a Prince and the greed and jealousy of his subjects this land is despoiled and its sacred institutions exposed to ridicule and destruction. Now I will keep my house and my counsel, and I will remember those things that other men forget. For the day will come when they are prized again.'

'It's all a bit of a diatribe', Lord Berwyn said. 'He used it to let off steam, I suppose. Pretty rude about the roundheads. Wouldn't have been popular if they'd read it.'

The translator had indicated the absence of a number of pages, and several sheets of the typescript had been left blank. I turned to the pages immediately before them. There was a scathing reference to the trial of Charles I which must then have been in progress, but nothing that could be construed as referring to the Crown. The same applied to the section that followed: Owain had clearly excised anything directly incriminating. What threat had arisen during the Commonwealth years to make him remove the evidence and conceal it at Bryn Teg? Perhaps the fear that some kind of raid was imminent?

I turned to the final page of the translation and read the last few sentences. Then I read them out aloud. '"The Protector burns in Hell: his son is deposed, the people clamour for their King. Today Thomas has come from London with joyful news. The Convention has called upon our noble King, Charles the Second, to take his martyred father's throne. Now that which is his by right shall be restored to him. God Save the King".'

'It was Thomas Davies who took the Crown from the Abbey,' Paeony said, 'They were going to give it to Charles when he came back from France. But Thomas brought the plague from London, and they both died before they had the chance.'

'So you think the thing's still buried somewhere,' Lord Berwyn said.

'John has a theory.'

Hesitantly I told them what Cadwaladr had said about the words Owain had used, and my interpretation of them. 'It's just an idea. There isn't really any evidence. But I remembered the petrifying well, and I thought it could have worked.'

Lord Berwyn tugged at his moustache. 'The well certainly existed. I've no idea if it was there in Owain's time, but it probably was. The Georgians made quite a fuss about it. Watkyn Morgan built a grotto near it. Installed a hermit, too. Fellow used to pop out and recite poetry to impress the visitors. But that sort of thing went out of fashion, and the well dried up. Molly, get the 1780 map.'

Paeony went to a tall, narrow cupboard in the wall and took out a metal tube about six feet long. From it she slid a rolled map which she spread out on the big library table, flicking on a lamp nearby. Lord Berwyn spun his chair round and propelled it across. 'Here it is,' she said, 'This was just after they made the lake. The well and the grotto are over here, where the hill comes down nearly to the water.'

The map showed the whole of the park: it was beautifully drawn and tinted, with the family arms and their dragons prominent in one corner. Paeony pointed to where a little cliff had been sketched in not far from the water: there was even a robed and bearded figure sitting in front of it.

'Afraid you won't find much now,' her father said, 'Whole area's been planted with conifers. William Morgan started it. Then it was felled and replanted thirty years ago. Fifteen thousand European larch. Should have been thinned, but we didn't have the staff. You might find a few rocks in there, that's all. Not much chance you'd find a crown.'

Lady Berwyn had quietly left the room while we were looking at the map. Now she returned, and held out a small object for us to see. It was an old-fashioned child's shoe, like a tiny boot, only about three inches long. When she put it down on the table, there was a little clatter.

'This has been in a drawer as long as I've been here. It's supposed to have come from the well. It's the only thing we have.'

The shoe was coated with a hard, shiny deposit rather like stalagmite, greyish-yellow in colour. The layer was quite thin, and in places it had cracked and flaked away to reveal the soft leather below.

'It's just like the things they used to have at Knaresborough,' I said. My idea suddenly seemed less fanciful.

Lord Berwyn was still shaking his head, not so much about the probability of my hypothesis as about the likelihood of our finding any trace of the well, let alone the Crown. We agreed I'd come back next morning, and that Paeony and I would undertake a thorough search of the area shown on the map. But I had a feeling we'd be hunting for the proverbial needle.

The next day was hot and sticky. We set out armed with brush hooks and dressed in what we hoped was suitable clothing. In fact a suit of armour would have been more appropriate. The hillside beyond the lake rose steeply and was clothed in an almost impenetrable jungle. The repeated planting and felling had disturbed the ground and obscured any original features: some of the trees were windblown, and their roots added to the general tangle. The larches were close-planted and hadn't been brashed, so that the dead lower branches formed a dense thicket and the only way to get between them was to crawl. We were soon scratched and grazed, and the needles pricked our hands and worked their way into our socks. You couldn't see more than a few yards in any direction, and it was impossible to cover the ground systematically. We did find a sort of rocky shelf at one point, but there was no sign of a proper cliff, or a cave, or a spring.

'This isn't funny,' I said at last. 'We're getting nowhere. Let's get out.' We scrambled downhill, and emerged, perspiring, dirty and dishevelled, beside the lake.

'Everything's changed. There hasn't been a well here for a hundred years, maybe more. The rock has probably collapsed.' Paeony flopped down on the shore. The fruitless search had taken several hours, and both of us were feeling thoroughly dispirited.

'Maybe it was here once. But you'd have to fell the plantation to get a sight of the ground, and even then I doubt if there'd be anything to see.'

'Let's have some lunch.'

We plodded back to the house and confessed that we'd drawn a blank. I was feeling foolish. We had a rather despondent meal, and afterwards neither of us felt like continuing the search. Paeony suggested a ride in the park, but I opted out. I could remember the look in her eye after she'd fallen off the quad bike, when she said she had just the mount for me. I asked her if I could spend a bit of time in the Library.

I watched her lead the horse out of the stable, its muscles rippling under the dark, gleaming coat. Feelings of inadequacy suddenly returned. 'Paeony,' I said, 'Why me? I mean, I'm not exactly Schwarzenegger. Why me?'

She paused for a little longer than was really tactful. 'I don't know,' she said eventually. 'I suppose it's because you're just you. I mean, most people are someone else.'

'Thank you. I'll try to go on being me, if that's really what you want. As long as you promise to go on being you.'

'If you're sure you can stand it.' She gave me a grin and Arnie a nudge with her heel. He ambled off obediently. I followed them under the arch and watched her riding at a comfortable trot along the drive, then easing the horse onto a broad strip of grass and breaking into a delicate canter. I kept walking, and turning the corner saw them in the distance, floating across the sunlit turf of the park between the arching trees.

I walked on through the gardens. Gnarled bushes of lavender were in full flower, the scent hanging heavy on the warm air. I passed through an arch cut in a yew hedge and came across Lord Berwyn, sitting in his chair in shirt sleeves and a battered straw hat, snipping the faded blooms from a border of tea roses. He had a pair of secateurs with a long handle, and was using another gadget to pick up the trimmings and drop them carefully into a bulging bin bag tied to an arm of the chair. He seemed totally engrossed, but he spoke as I came up behind him.

'Molly says you're a gardener.'

'Yes. Vegetables mostly. Where I live it seems a bit wild for garden flowers. Vegetables fit in. I think they've always been grown at Tan-y-Coed. Nothing exotic, just potatoes and onions and cabbages. I like growing things from seed.'

'You need continuity in a garden.' He snipped another head from the bush. 'Plants need time. Too many people in a hurry. Throwing their money around in garden centres. Can't be bothered to watch things grow. But you don't have to be shy of colour y'know, in moderation.'

'I suppose it is a bit austere,' I said, 'But there are bulbs in spring.'

'Put some shrubs in. Trees too. Something for your children. Try the double gean. It's native, and it'll flower after your daffodils.' He dropped a twig into the bag.

'I think I will,' I said. There was a pause. He'd stopped his pruning.

'Are you fond of her?' Lord Berwyn asked.

'Very.'

'So am I. She seems to like you.'

'Yes. I don't know why.'

'She's a sensible girl. Makes her own decisions now. I won't push her either way. It's up to the two of you.'

'Thank you,' I said.

He unclipped the bin bag from the chair. 'If you're going that way, take this if you would. You'll see the heap.'

I took the bag.

'Would you mind very much if I had a look at the Library?'

'You know the way up. Look at what you like.'

I said thank you again. As I was going he said, 'If you want cuttings, help yourself.'

I emptied the bag onto a pile of prunings and hedge trimmings and walked on round the house, head spinning and a glow inside.

I came to the entrance court, and walked across the gravel and up the steps. Turning the handle on the boot cleaner I held my shoes against the revolving bristles, carefully brushing off the mud before I went in.

For years I'd yearned to have the run of a real country house library, to be free to take the ancient books from the shelves and browse through them at leisure. In the houses you pay to go round there are eagle-eyed guardians, ready to pounce. I felt a little thrill of pleasure when I entered the great room and found I had it to myself. But even with permission it was a guilty pleasure, as if someone might come at any minute to frogmarch me off the premises.

I ran my finger along the finely tooled spines, inspecting the titles before choosing which to take down. There were calf-bound editions of the classics, many volumes of history and a big collection of Welsh and border country topography, some beautifully illustrated with engravings and maps. Then there were the usual collections of sermons and religious tracts, treatises on agricultural improvement and bound volumes of long forgotten periodicals. Besides the older books there were many hundreds from the last century and this one: on military history, field sports, gardening and wildlife. Most had the Morgan bookplate gummed onto the endpaper, with the inevitable dragon. There was some poetry but not much fiction: maybe the Berwyns had more books elsewhere in the house.

I'd been regaling myself for an hour or so when a title caught my eye. It was on the spine of a massive tome, more recent than most of the books I'd looked at. The book was called 'A History of the Crown Jewels of Europe'. The author was Lord Twining; the date of publication 1960. The blurb on the dust jacket described it as 'A truly monumental work', and so it was: the format was imposing, and there were over 700 pages and hundreds of mouth-watering illustrations. Paeony came in to find me admiring it. 'Borrow it. You can read it in bed.'

'I don't think my arms are strong enough. But I'd love to take it, if you don't mind.'

I left early that evening, thinking I'd better not impose too much on the family, and took the book with me. At tea Lord Berwyn had mentioned the name of the old Head Forester, now retired, who'd planted the larches years before. He suggested we could ask him whether he had any recollection of the site where the well had been, and Paeony said she might go to see him at his cottage that evening. She would ring me if there was anything to report. On the way back to Tan-y-Coed I reflected that, realistically, there wasn't much chance.

Back home I did some much needed washing and clearing up. It was dark by the time I'd finished, and I remembered the book I'd borrowed was still on the back seat of the car. I switched on the outside lights and went out to get it. There were two exterior lights at Tan-y-Coed: one over the door which lit the terrace at the front, and one on the back corner of the building which cast a certain amount of light on the path up to the place where I parked the car. Both were controlled by a single switch by the door, just above the switch for the light in the living room. I went up the path, collected the book and made my way back down to the cottage. For some reason I didn't switch off the lights when I came in.

I like reading in bed, but as I'd told Paeony Lord Twining's magnum opus didn't exactly lend itself to that. So I laid the book out on the dining table, and turned to the introduction, which described the early development of crowns from the days of the Byzantine Emperors. But I was soon leafing through the text, gazing at the photographs of glittering regalia from the great museums of Europe. They were in black and white, but they still managed to convey a vivid impression of the romance and splendour of the objects they portrayed. In the chapter on England I read something I didn't know: that the Kings and Queens of England are the only sovereigns who are still actually crowned at a coronation ceremony, and wear their crowns on state occasions. The other crowns of Europe languish permanently in glass cases, and never adorn a royal head. The chapter had a lengthy section on St Edward's Crown, but I caught myself yawning and decided on an early night.

I marked the page and went upstairs to my one and only bedroom. The room was in darkness, and as I opened the door the little square of light that was the tiny back window revealed a view of the path still illuminated by the light on the corner of the house. I was about to turn on the bedroom light when a movement outside caught my eye. I froze, and then moved closer to the window. Three men were coming down the path. Two of them had a familiar look.

I tumbled down the stairs in a panic, but they'd be on the terrace in seconds, and if I tried to escape through the door I'd run straight into them. To unscrew the lock on the back window would have taken time I didn't have. For an instant I stood paralysed in the kitchen: then I grabbed the phone and at the same moment someone passed the front window.

There was no time to dial: they'd be in the house before the operator said: 'Which service?' I punched the record button on the answerphone and said 'Help, quick. Get the police.' I banged the receiver down at the precise moment that someone kicked open the door.

The three of them seemed to fill the room. One was a hulking figure with dark skin, who looked like a boxer gone to seed. The second was a small, rat-faced man, going thin on top. The third had smooth, regular features, and wore a well-cut suit and an air of authority. He stood calmly by the door as the other two seized me by the arms and forced me into a chair. His eyes appraised me for a moment, as if I'd been an object offered to him for sale. His lip twisted fractionally; he evidently wasn't impressed. Then he said: 'You are John Jones.' It was a statement, not a question.

'Who are you?' But I knew the answer.

'My name is Quinn.'

Last night I'd bolted the door and put on the chain as soon as I'd got in. It wouldn't have kept them out, but it might have given me a few more seconds. Tonight I hadn't bothered. Stupid.

The dark-skinned man had gone upstairs and was banging about. He was soon down again. 'Nobody,' he said.

Quinn nodded. The smaller man was going round the ground floor, such as it was; then he went outside briefly and came back again. He shook his head at Quinn. Quinn himself was glancing round the room; he eyed the dresser in the same way he looked at me. 'Denbighshire, around 1800. Crude, and full of worm.'

Then his eyes lit on the book, still lying on the table. The title was boldly emblazoned on the dust jacket. He walked over to look at it. 'A History of the Crown Jewels of Europe', he read, and opened it at the point I'd marked with a circular from Reader's Digest. 'St Edward's Crown. Fancy that.'

I was watching him from the chair, mesmerised. No-one was holding me down, but I was quite incapable of getting up. I was cursing my idiocy in staying at Tan-y-Coed, on my own, with Carl Quinn at large. It was inevitable he would come looking for me. He hadn't wasted much time.

Quinn stood for a while at the table, turning the pages, fascinated by the book. Then he seated himself comfortably on the sofa, whilst his two henchmen leant against the wall. Everything about him was stylish, from his discreetly tinted hair to his gold cuff links and Italian shoes. He looked as if he'd come to sell expensive life insurance. His voice was well modulated, his manner cool and detached, not hinting at villainy. The one disconcerting thing about him was that he never blinked, and never took his eyes off my face. The irises were so dark that they fused with the pupils into little black holes.

'I think we should talk,' he said, reasonably. 'You and I are looking for the same thing. We can either compete, or cooperate. In your case, competition would have a number of disadvantages. I think you're intelligent enough to appreciate what they are. You're a historian, like me. Why don't we work together?'

'What do you want?'

'St Edward's Crown. I think you can help me to find it.'

Answers like 'I don't know what you mean' went through my mind. They wouldn't cut much ice with Quinn.

'I don't know where it is.'

'But you've been looking. And you knew where to look.'

'Bob Lord told me where to look. He told you what he told me.'

'Bob Lord told me a lot of things,' said Quinn, 'I gather you've been continuing his research. It's a pity he was unable to complete it himself. Terrorism is wasteful and unproductive, Mr Jones. Civilised people should be able to resolve their differences by sitting down and talking, like we are doing now.'

I felt revolted. 'Do you really expect me to believe that Bob Lord was killed by terrorists?'

Quinn went very still. 'It is very much in your interest to believe it,' he said softly.

I clenched my teeth and tried to think. I was in enough danger, without making things worse for myself. My only hope would be to offer co-operation, and try to play for time.

The telephone by the window gave a little click, followed by a hum. Someone had dialled my number, and the answering machine had been activated. Quinn heard the sound, and jerked his head. The big man strode over and jerked the wire out of the wall. The hum stopped.

Paeony had been going to telephone if the forester had come up with anything useful. I had no way of knowing whether she, or whoever else was on the line, would have had time to hear the message I'd recorded. I could only hope they had.

'Most scholars nowadays are professionals,' Quinn said. 'Lord was an amateur in the old sense of the word, a lover of learning. I looked forward to our conversations. I learned a great deal from him. We talked about philosophy as well as history, though he was a better historian than a philosopher. And he was quite useless as a psychologist. Odd that such an able man could be so stupid.'

'Why do you call him stupid?'

'He was naive.' Quinn spoke with clinical detachment. 'He was convinced that every man and woman in the world really wanted to be good. He even believed that of me. Or at least, he made himself believe it. If he'd believed otherwise, he would have had to rethink his philosophy. That was stupid. He had very little understanding of human nature, and none at all of mine. I played him like a fish. Do you know my secret, Jones?'

'What is it?'

'I don't care,' Quinn said. 'I found that out as a child. When people said 'Oh dear, poor so-and-so', I didn't give a damn. I never have. It's a very useful attribute. Or if I do care it's for things, not for people.'

'What sort of things?'

'Beautiful things.' There was animation in Quinn's face now. 'I like beautiful things. Not just gold and jewels, but artistry, craftsmanship. And old things too, things that made history. Not modern trash. I got a degree, you know, at Walton. In History of Art. You and I have things in common. What was it for you, that made you want to find the Crown?'

'Bob wanted to find it.' I couldn't believe I was sitting there, making conversation with this man. 'Both of us thought it was worth finding.'

'I'll tell you something,' said Quinn, 'When I was eight I saw the film of the Coronation. In fact there were two films, and I saw them both. I made my parents take me to see them again and again. It was the colour I liked, and the gold and the glitter. I had a little model of the State Coach, all gold with a crown on top and eight white horses. I played with it till it broke, and then I made them buy me another one, bigger.'

The little, rat-faced man was picking his teeth; the other was rubbing his back against the wall and staring into space. Quinn ignored them. 'Have you ever seen the Crown Jewels, in the Tower of London?'

'Yes. I went when I was little.'

'My parents wouldn't take me. We lived in Liverpool, and they said it was too far. I made them sorry. They took me in the end, when I was older. But I was disappointed. They're crude, vulgar, modern. That crown that they call St Edward's, a great lumpish thing, not even a decent reproduction of the original. And the rest, all glitzy diamonds from the 1920's, art deco. No taste, no history. But when I had money, when I was able to travel, I saw the real thing. In Munich, in Vienna, in Budapest. Wonderful things, delicate, intricate, studded with rubies, all glowing colour. The Empress's Crown in the Treasury of Palermo. The Hungarian Crown of St Stephen. The Crown of Otto the First in the Schatzkammer, over a thousand years old. I saw them all. I carried out my first robbery in Vienna. Mugged an American woman in an alleyway to buy my ticket home.'

'You talk about beautiful things. But things are made by people. You can't have art without artists. You can't have craftsmanship without craftsmen.'

Quinn laughed. 'Do you know who made the Crown we're looking for? He was a monk called Spearhavoc. The King gave him gold and jewels to make the crown, and made him Bishop of London. And do you know what he did? He used some of the gold, and ran off with the rest. He took the cathedral kitty too. They never saw him again. It's all in that book you've been reading. The man who made the Crown was a rogue, and for that matter so were most of the men who wore it. But he made a wonderful thing.' His voice hardened. 'And the thing he made still exists. I want to see it. I want to hold it. I want to own it. So you see, I need to know where it is. And you're going to tell me.'

'All right,' I said, 'I'll tell you what I've found.' And I started describing my researches in as much detail as I could, concentrating on what I'd found in the WMEG library. My only chance of survival was to gain time, to hope that my message had been heard, for it was hardly likely that Quinn would let me join him in his search for the Crown. He would dispose of me as soon he was sure he knew everything I knew.

Quinn listened, though he must have known much that I told him already. There was no interruption until I began to describe the exploration of the Cwm Llwyd mine. Then the little, rat-faced man suddenly said, 'Ask him what happened to Frank.'

Quinn's lips tightened in irritation. 'A friend of my friend went into the mine and didn't come out. Do you know what happened to him?'

'He sat down in the wrong place. A few hundred tons of rock fell on his head.'

'The bastard nearly killed us too,' the rat-faced man said, 'He led us into that hole.'

'I wasn't leading you anywhere. I was trying to get away.'

'Both of you are wasting my time,' Quinn said flatly. Rat-face slumped sulkily against the wall.

'Frank was careless,' Quinn said. 'I'm a careful man. I don't take unnecessary risks. Now I understand you went back to the mine yesterday, with a group of people. You expected to find the Crown. Apparently you found a souvenir of Queen Victoria.'

'How do you know that?'

'I have sources. Now the question is: have you exhausted the possibilities of the Cwm Llwyd mine?'

'I don't know. We crawled through all the old passages. There could be something we missed in the later stages, when we were trying to get out, but several of the WMEG members went in to survey them. Of course, some of the passages were blasted away during quarrying. If the Crown ever was there, it's probably been destroyed.'

'But you have another idea, don't you Mr Jones?' Quinn said. 'A new idea. An idea that has nothing to do with mines. Would you like to tell me what it is?'

I tried to look blank. 'What new idea?'

Quinn leaned forward, the black eyes boring into mine. 'I'll ask you again. But only once. Let me prompt you. You were talking about a well.'

I was trying to think how Quinn knew of yesterday's events. There was only one explanation: Charles Angevin Greene. Quinn was unlikely to have missed the publicity about Greene and the Crown: he'd probably got in touch with him and pumped him for what he knew. Greene had heard me at Cadwaladr's talking about the petrifying well.

'Bob Lord interpreted the Welsh wording of Owain's journal as meaning that the Crown was underground,' I said, 'That might have been a mistranslation. The Crown may have been covered with stone in a different sense. I thought it might have been petrified. But that was just a wild idea.'

'If the Crown was petrified,' Quinn said. 'That presupposes the existence of a petrifying well. You see, I know about these things. You apparently know of a well. Where is it?' I said nothing.

'Another question. While you were looking for the Crown you had a girl with you. A red-head. Attractive, so my friend here tells me. Who is she? Where does she live?'

I swallowed. 'She knows nothing about it.'

'Don't insult my intelligence. You were talking to her about the well. She called it 'our well'. Where is it?'

'We looked for it. We couldn't find it.'

'Where did you look?'

This had to be my bottom line. I wasn't going to mention Berwyn, or Paeony's name. 'That's my business,' I said. 'I'm afraid I can't tell you.'

Quinn turned impatiently to the other two. 'Tie him up.'

The two of them went into action. This was the moment they'd been waiting for, and it had been a long wait. The big man produced a roll of flex, and Rat-Face pinned my wrist to the arm of my chair. It was an old-fashioned chair with an upholstered back and seat and flat wooden arms; you could adjust it to recline at a comfortable angle, and the arms came in handy for balancing a mug or a glass. They lashed each wrist to a chair arm and my ankles to the legs; then with a nasty smile Rat-Face took a turn round my neck and hitched it tightly to the frame of the chair back.

'Now,' Quinn said, 'Do you have any tools in the house?'

'What's wrong with yours?'

'Hit him.'

Rat-Face lashed me across the side of the face. The flex bit into my neck as my head rocked with the blow.

'They're under the sink.' Quinn's sudden transformation from urbane conversationalist to violent criminal was as shocking as the violence itself.

My head was ringing, and one of my teeth had gashed the inside of my cheek. The big man was rummaging about in my tool box. 'Start with a hammer on his fingers.'

They flattened the palm of my hand against the wooden chair arm. I looked away. I was aware of Rat-Face raising the hammer and bringing it down on the top joint of one of my fingers, and a stab of agony shot through my hand and up my arm.

'Again,' Quinn said. There was another thud, and more blinding pain.

I'd hit my own finger with a hammer when aiming for a nail, and once as a child I'd had two fingers badly trapped in a car door. I'd never forgotten how excruciating it had been. But I couldn't believe that this pain was being imposed deliberately, and that it could be quite so sustained and severe. The hammer came crashing down again. I looked at my fingers, and saw they were already swollen and discoloured, with blood oozing from around the nails.

Quinn motioned to Rat-Face to stop for a moment. My hand was throbbing unbearably. No other part of me existed, all my consciousness was focused on my fingers. 'Who is the girl?' asked Quinn. 'Where is the well? Where is the Crown?' I bit my lip.

He nodded. Rat-Face brought the hammer down again, concentrating on the same few fingers, and the searing pain was redoubled. I was drenched with sweat, and the noose around my neck seemed to tighten at every blow.

I heard Quinn say, 'What else is in the toolbox?' There was a rattle.

'There's a pair of pliers,' the big man said, 'Or a hacksaw.'

'Use the saw. He doesn't need all those fingers.'

Rat-Face let me have a look at the hacksaw. 'It's a bit blunt,' he said, 'But it'll get through bone, no problem.'

'Start with the little one, and work along,' Quinn said. I felt the hacksaw blade scrape the skin, and then begin to bite.

The door opposite my chair swung open. In the doorway stood Paeony. She was holding a double-barrelled twelve-bore shotgun. She levelled it at the three men standing round me. 'Don't move,' she said.

They were frozen into immobility. I thought nothing would end the silence.

Quinn broke it in the end. 'Well, well. The lady in question. How dramatic. The heroine comes to the rescue.'

'Let him go.'

Rat-Face and the big man had begun to move away from the chair in opposite directions; they were sidling around the walls of the room. 'Stand still!' she shouted at them, swinging the barrel of the gun from one to the other. They halted for a moment.

Quinn hadn't moved. He was standing close behind my chair. I felt something stroking the side of my neck.

'This is a knife. It's very sharp. Feel it.' There was a sharp prick, and I felt the blood trickling down.

'Don't make my hand slip.'

Paeony was looking desperate. 'I'll shoot.'

'I doubt it. You'd kill your boy friend, even if I didn't kill him first.'

The two men were moving again, executing a pincer movement, each one stopping when the gun swung towards him, starting again when it swung away.

'Tell her to put the gun down.' Quinn dug the knife a little further in. I saw her eyes widen, her mouth open.

She was still pointing the gun at Quinn, and at me, when the big man took her from one side. I braced myself for the explosion, but it didn't come. She let go of the gun without a struggle, and the man broke it and ejected the cartridges.

'That's better,' Quinn said. 'Tie her up.'

Rat-Face advanced, licking his lips. 'Let me get to work on her. She'll tell me everything she ever knew.'

'Shut up.' Quinn was working it out. 'She came here with a gun. Why? How did she know? Who else knows?'

'How did you know?' Rat-Face repeated. Paeony said nothing.

I couldn't understand why she'd come on her own. I'd said, 'Get the police'. Had the message been cut off before she'd heard the end? How long had it been since she'd heard it? The drive from Berwyn was a long one, in the dark: in daylight it took a good hour. How long had I been talking to Quinn?

'Thanks for coming,' I said.

Quinn seemed to come to a decision. 'Five minutes. And then we go. If necessary we'll take them with us - what's left of them.' He turned to Paeony. 'He talked about a well. A petrifying well. Where is it?'

She glared at him defiantly.

'Lou,' Quinn said, and passed him the knife.

'Tell him,' I said to Paeony.

'Why the hell should I?'

'For God's sake tell him!'

And then a deep, commanding, amplified voice came echoing from the darkness outside the house.

'This is the police. This is the police. Put down your weapons and come outside with your hands raised.'

Quinn's face twisted. The other two stood with their mouths open. Nobody moved. The voice came again: 'This is the police. I repeat, come outside with your hands raised. Lay down all weapons. Do not attempt to resist.'

'No,' Quinn said suddenly. He looked across at Paeony, and I knew what was going through his mind.

'She wouldn't go. She wouldn't co-operate. You'd never get her away, in the dark.'

I don't think he was listening; he was weighing the options of taking a hostage or making a break for it alone. Rat-Face was jabbering at him, and Quinn said 'Shut up' and moved towards the door. He stood there for a second until the voice rang out again; then he snapped off the light switches, inside and outside. The room and the land around the house were suddenly in darkness. He jerked open the door, and revealed the faint grey of the night sky framed in the doorway. The next second Quinn's figure was outlined against it: with one step he was through the door and onto the terrace wall, with another he had leaped down into the steeply sloping garden below the house and vanished.

I expected another shout, a rush of feet or a hail of gunfire, but there was nothing, just silence. The voice came again: 'This is the police. Come out with your hands raised.' The other two were still somewhere in the darkened room. I heard Paeony say: 'You'd better get away while you can.' A second later the two of them made a simultaneous dash for the door. A chair went clattering across the floor, and for a moment they were ludicrously jammed together in the doorway: then following Quinn they jumped over the wall, and I heard them land heavily and go crashing down the hillside towards the stream.

The voice from the loudspeaker was booming. But there were no shots, and the noises faded away.

'What the hell is happening?'

She had groped her way over to my chair, and was feeling for the knots in the flex. I asked if she could free my neck. The pressure quickly relaxed, and the relief was inexpressible. Soon she was untying my wrists and ankles.

'Is it safe to put the lights on?'

'I should think so. But keep out of the line of the door.'

The lights came on. I was sitting holding my damaged fingers under my other arm, feeling too sick and dizzy to get up. Paeony picked up her shotgun, found the two rounds, pushed them back and shut up the gun with a click. 'Bastards,' she said, 'I should have shot them all.'

Then the reaction got to her, and she sat down suddenly on the sofa. A moment later she gasped in fear, and levelled the gun at the door.

A huge figure had appeared in the doorway, dressed from head to foot in black leathers and a massive shining black crash helmet. It entered, ducking its head beneath the lintel. 'Where's Quinn?' it said.

'Don't shoot. It's Joseph.'

Joseph removed the helmet to reveal a head almost as large and just as black. 'Where did he go?'

'Over the wall. And his two sidekicks went after him.'

'I heard them go. But I didn't hear Quinn.'

'How did you know they were here?'

'I had a call,' Joseph said, 'From this young lady, I believe. My bike travels fast. I left Birmingham eighty minutes ago.'

'Why didn't you ring the police?' I asked her.

'I did. I rang them first, and then I had the idea of ringing Joseph. You gave me his number.'

'Just as well.' My head was clearing a bit, but my hand still hurt like hell.

'But if you're not the police,' Paeony said to Joseph, 'What about the loudspeaker?'

Joseph turned to the door and picked something up off the terrace wall. It was a loudhailer; one of the shiny plastic ones powered by batteries. 'The Club bought this for me. We use it at fights and athletics meetings. It was strapped to the back of the bike. On the way up I thought of a use for it. I don't carry weapons, not now.'

'I thought I knew the voice,' I said. 'How long had you been out there?'

'Only a few minutes.' He turned to Paeony. 'I saw you go in. I was just behind you, though you didn't see me. I followed you and looked through the window. I thought you might be grateful for a diversion. What did Quinn want?' He was asking me.

'Information.' I showed them my hand.

Paeony winced at the sight of the blackened, swollen fingers. 'We'd better get those X-rayed.'

'You're lucky they are still attached,' Joseph remarked. People were still telling me how lucky I was.

'I don't understand what's happened to the police,' Paeony said, 'They told me they were coming.'

She went to the door, and Joseph followed her. I managed to get to my feet, thought I was going to be sick and staggered over to the sink. The nausea came and went. I held my fingers under the tap for a moment; the water turned pink, but it seemed to help. They'd left the hammer on the draining board with my blood still on it, and I rinsed it in the stream from the tap. Then I got the dishcloth and wiped the bloodstains off the chair arm. I wanted the place to look normal again.

Paeony and Joseph came back inside. 'Won't the police want to see that?' she asked.

'I suppose they would. I wasn't thinking straight.'

She bandaged my fingers. A few minutes later we heard a vehicle approaching, and went out to see headlights through the trees. We went up cautiously towards the track, keeping in the shadow of the wall, and found a uniformed constable getting out of a panda car. 'Now then,' he said. 'Would you be the young lady who telephoned us? Miss Paeony Morgan?'

'Yes, I am. Where have you been?'

'Your place takes a bit of finding,' the policeman said, 'I've been right up to the top of the valley. Got the farmer out of bed. And we're short staffed you know, Sunday night. There was a bit of trouble last night in Newtown, when the pubs came out, you know how it is. Sunday's a bit quieter, like. They sent me from Llanidloes. So what's it all about?'

We took him down to the cottage, and tried to explain what had happened. Joseph had quietly vanished, taking the loudhailer with him. I told the officer about Carl Quinn, and he wrote the name carefully down in his notebook. I showed him my bandaged hand, and he looked concerned. 'Nasty. You'd better get that looked at. A hammer, you said. Where is it now? We might want it, for evidence.'

I got the hammer out of the sink.

'It looks as if somebody's washed it up,' he said. 'Pity, that.'

We had the lengths of flex, for what they were worth. When Paeony showed him the shotgun he frowned. 'Have you got a licence for that, Miss?'

'Of course I have.' He made her take the cartridges out and gave her a lecture on the dangers of keeping a loaded gun in the house, which left her seething.

'Now, this Mr Joseph.'

'I think Joseph is his first name,' I said, 'I don't know his surname.'

'Joseph. You say he was impersonating a police officer, and speaking through a loudhailer.'

'Yes. He frightened Quinn away.'

'And where would he be now, sir?'

'He seems to have gone. I suppose he's gone back to Birmingham. I don't know his address. But I can give you his phone number.'

'Well, I suppose we can always ring him up.'

'Look,' I said, 'Detective-Inspector Humphreys, at Llangollen, knows something about this. Can you let him know what's happened?'

'Llangollen, now that'd be Clwyd-Gwynedd Police,' the policeman observed, 'We're Mid-Wales Constabulary you know. You're in Powys, up here. But I expect our superintendent will have a word with him if he thinks it's necessary.' And he made another note.

Eventually the policeman left. He had listened politely to what we had to say, but I didn't have the impression that he was going to put the country on red alert when he got back to the station. We'd agreed we would go into Newtown and make a statement. 'Damn it!' said Paeony in frustration, 'He didn't seem to take us seriously.'

'I expect it all sounded a bit weird. Especially the bit about Joseph, when he'd disappeared. I'd better ring Humphreys myself tomorrow. We should have got in touch before. This is all getting a bit beyond me.'

Paeony insisted on driving me straight to the Orthopaedic. In the car I started shaking, and couldn't stop.

In casualty they X-rayed my fingers and found, much to my surprise, that only two small bones were cracked. 'Hallo there, Mr Jones,' the plump nurse said brightly as she passed through the waiting area. 'It's your finger this time, is it? You have been in the wars!'

Everyone was very solicitous. 'It's really nasty, isn't it?' the casualty nurse said sympathetically as she applied the plaster, 'Did you get it caught in a machine? Do you know, we had to amputate a man's fingers last week, he was trying to get a stone out of a mower and hadn't turned it off. You were lucky, weren't you?'

CHAPTER 16

Paeony drove me to Berwyn for what remained of the night. They'd given me some fairly powerful pain-killers, but I didn't get much sleep. In the morning I rang Llangollen police and asked to speak to Detective-Inspector Humphreys. 'I'm afraid Mr Humphreys isn't here at the moment,' a voice told me, 'Would you like to speak to Detective-Sergeant Pritchard?'

This was tiresome, and it had happened before. I asked when Humphreys would be back, and they didn't know. I said I'd try later. Humphreys had been sceptical to say the least, yet he'd struck me as reasonably shrewd and basically fair. I was still determined I wasn't going to speak to Pritchard. Anyway, we were going to Newtown.

I stayed in the flat for a day or two to convalesce and enjoy some tender loving care. The pain gradually began to subside, though I still got the shakes at times. But the stoicism that had been inculcated as a child soon took over: it didn't do to make a fuss. And Paeony was a born nurse, treating her patient with sympathetic firmness when his conscience started to hint it was time to be up and about. 'I like having you in bed,' she said.

Paeony drove me to Newtown, and we made a statement which was taken down with studious detachment by a detective-sergeant. He said they'd be in touch, and we ought to be careful with shotguns.

Irritated we went back to Berwyn. There we spent an hour or two in a desultory sort of way looking through estate maps and records in the hope of finding out more about the petrifying well, but they didn't add a great deal to the little we knew. On the night of Quinn's visit Paeony had gone to see the forester, who had told her that he'd known there used to be a well, but had never found any trace of it; he thought the site might have been obliterated when the previous crop of trees had been planted. She'd wondered if it was worth ringing me at Tan-y-Coed to tell me, and had fortunately decided that it was. But somehow the quest for the Crown had become increasingly unreal; there now seemed little chance of our ever finding it, and Carl Quinn's intervention had killed the romance.

Lord and Lady Berwyn had gone to London. 'Daddy's gone to a meeting at the Royal Horticultural Society. Then he's going to the House of Lords. He says it's the best club in London, and it gives him the chance to air his prejudices. It means Mother can do some shopping.'

'Are you really all alone here? Doesn't it give you the creeps?'

'It's home. I grew up here, I'm used to it. Anyway, the main part of the house is shut up when they're gone. I use my flat. It's no more remote than Tan-y-Coed, and a lot easier to get to.'

I rang Llangollen again, and this time was told that Inspector Humphreys had been on sick leave. 'We're expecting him back tomorrow or the day after,' a friendly policewoman said, so it seemed worth waiting. I again declined the offer to speak to Pritchard.

Eventually I ran out of socks and got Paeony to run me back to Tan-y-Coed. On the way I called at a cash point and took the opportunity to get a balance on my account. Funds were beginning to run low, and the Justy was due for a service. I was going to have to treat my job hunting with more urgency.

There was quite a wad of letters in the box at the end of the track. One was from the fertiliser company to say their current vacancy had been filled, but they were keeping my name on file. Some of the life insurance firms I'd written to seemed to be falling over themselves to offer me a job. Working for them didn't appeal, but I couldn't afford to be too choosy.

I persuaded Paeony that I would survive on my own for a day or so. I needed to pursue my job search, and to be at home when people rang me back. It was hardly likely that Quinn would come back after his recent experience. Somebody had to look after Arnie, which meant she couldn't move into Tan-y-Coed. So we agreed she would go back to Berwyn that evening, and that we'd keep phoning each other. I promised to keep trying to get hold of Humphreys. She assumed I'd be more or less immobilised, but I was pretty sure that I could drive the Justy if I had to.

The next day I filled in more forms and did some ringing round. I'd postponed a decision about the life insurance in the hope of finding something a little more attractive. Towards lunchtime I took a break, and went to sit out on the terrace in the sunshine with a mug of coffee and 'A History of the Crown Jewels of Europe'. I had no serious intent when I laid it on the wall; I was just intending to pass an idle half hour. This time I turned to the Introduction, and started to read Lord Twining's account of how crowns first evolved.

Twining drew a distinction between the open crown, like a circlet around the head, and the closed or imperial crown which has arches that meet in the centre. Charles Angevin Greene had traced the design back to the Emperor Constantine and Twining seemed to confirm this, though he also mentioned an alternative theory that it might have derived from the military head-dress worn by Teutonic rulers in the early middle ages. His introduction referred to illustrations in later chapters and I leafed through the book to look at them. I was taking care to keep my coffee mug well away: a spill would have been sacrilege.

I was holding a leaf half turned when something clicked. I turned back to the illustration I'd been looking at, and looked again. There was something there that I'd seen before. Something familiar. I nipped back into the house for pencil and paper and started jotting down sentences, sketching drawings. In the process my hunch gradually became a certainty. A picture came together in my mind. Suddenly, I knew just what Owain had done. I knew what he and Thomas had plotted, and how the Treasure they had rescued had been concealed. I knew precisely where Owain had hidden it, three and a half centuries ago. I knew where I would find the Crown.

I left the book on the wall and rushed inside to phone Paeony. The Berwyn number was switched through to her flat when the house was empty, and she answered in seconds. 'Paeony,' I said, 'I know where it is. The Crown. I think it was at Berwyn all the time.'

'How can it have been here? Where was it? Where is it now?'

'It's where Owain put it. I'll tell you when I get there. Tell your father to put the champagne on ice. We're going to have something to celebrate.'

'I'm still on my own. They don't get back from London till tomorrow.'

'We'll save them some. I'm coming over.'

'Have you rung that inspector?'

'I keep trying. I haven't got through to him yet.'

'Can you drive? How's the hand?'

'Mending nicely.'

I got half way up to the car, remembered the book, and bolted back to get it. The notes went into my pocket. Then I was bumping down the track without too much regard for the springs.

I'd just crossed the bridge when I had to jam on the brakes. A white car was coming down the other way, with 'Heddlu' in mirror writing across the bonnet. It wasn't a panda car this time, but a proper white patrol car with stripes along the sides. Sitting next to the driver was Detective-Sergeant Pritchard. He got out and came forward.

'Back up.'

'You back up.'

'Do as you're bloody well told.'

I backed up, parked the car in its place by the wall and got out. Pritchard and the driver got out too, along with a third man who'd been sitting in the back. It was Fenshaw.

'Aren't you going to invite us in?' Pritchard asked.

'You're off your patch. This is Powys.'

'We're not in Ireland, you know. You can't hide across the border.' He gave Fenshaw a knowing look.

I shrugged and motioned the way down the path. When we got inside he jabbed his finger into my chest and said: 'On the day Lord was killed you were in Llangollen.'

'Of course I was. I went to see Bob. I was with him all evening. You already know that.'

'You were in the town.'

I thought for a moment. 'I may have been. I think I did some shopping.'

'Buying bedsocks for granny, were you?'

Fenshaw intervened. 'You spoke to two men, did you not, on the Bridge?'

I looked at him blankly; then it came back to me. 'I talked to Glyn Lewis. He's my neighbour, up at Blaen-y-Cwm. He was talking to somebody else. A fellow with a beard, I think.'

'A fellow with a beard,' Pritchard repeated, 'Who was he?'

'I haven't a clue. We weren't introduced. Why are you asking after all this time?'

'We had the town under surveillance,' Fenshaw said, 'You have been identified. We have a record.' He looked gratified by his own efficiency.

'You mean you had video cameras filming in the centre of Llangollen?' Fenshaw didn't answer. 'I suppose somebody's been going through the tapes and just recognised me. I was buying groceries, before I went to Bob's. I was a bit early.'

'We know the man you were talking to,' Fenshaw said. 'We know him very well. He was charged three years ago with arson. He was acquitted on a technicality. We've been keeping a close eye on him ever since. He was in the town that day along with certain other people with extreme views. Lewis has nationalist connections. You were speaking to them that afternoon. You were behaving secretively. You were at Mr Lord's house that evening. The house was destroyed by fire during the night.'

'Glyn Lewis has nothing to do with terrorists,' I said angrily, 'And neither have I. This is a complete waste of time. Where's Humphreys? I've been trying to get hold of him for days. There's something he ought to know.'

'Humphreys is off sick,' Pritchard said.

'Mr Humphreys has a duodenal ulcer,' the driver suddenly put in, helpfully. He looked young and keen, with yellow hair and cheeks like a baby's bottom.

Pritchard glared at him. 'Speak when you're spoken to.' The young man looked crestfallen.

'I'm in charge of this case for the time being,' Pritchard said.

Fenshaw motioned to Pritchard and took him over to the door. There was a whispered conversation. Then Pritchard came back. 'I'm taking you in. You're under arrest.'

'I've not done anything to be arrested for,' I said furiously, 'What am I being charged with?'

'You're not being charged. I'm detaining you under the Prevention of Terrorism Act. We have the right to detain you for five days. That'll give us plenty of time to find out what you're up to.'

I felt my jaw drop. 'That's fatuous. I'm not up to anything. You're out of your tiny mind.'

'Sit down,' Pritchard said, 'We're going to take a look around.'

For the second time in a week I was sitting in my own living room while three men took over the house. Or rather, in this case, took it apart. Fenshaw disappeared upstairs, presumably to go through my underwear and look under the bed. Pritchard started emptying the kitchen drawers, and then transferred his attention to my books, taking each one down, riffling through it and then dumping it on the floor. The young man produced a neat little set of tools and started unscrewing bits off the calor gas cooker. 'You'd better turn the gas off first,' I told him, and he found the connection and screwed the valve shut. Then he got out a screwdriver and began looking for electrical appliances. There weren't many of them, so he started work on the telephone.

Fenshaw came down the stairs looking peeved. He obviously hadn't found anything incriminating. He went out to investigate the Ty Bach. Pritchard had a thrill when he looked under the sink and found a big can of paraffin, three packets of firelighters and half a dozen boxes of matches. I pointed out that I still used oil lamps for lighting and a coal fire for heat. They'd practically finished when the young man suddenly said, 'There's something on his phone.'

'That's it, tell the world,' Pritchard snapped. 'Didn't they teach you anything at that bloody university?' He went over to look at the disembowelled instrument. 'Put it in your bag. Has Mr Fenshaw finished? Right, let's go.'

They frogmarched me up to the car, and I was made to sit sandwiched between Pritchard and Fenshaw in the back.

'Are we going to Llangollen?'

'You'll find out,' Pritchard said. The driver was taking the long way round by the main road, but it soon became obvious that was where we were heading.

'Listen. I told you before about Carl Quinn. They've let him out of Walton. He was at Tan-y-Coed on Sunday night. He tortured me.' I showed them my fingers with the now rather grubby plaster. 'He was trying to get information out of me. I have a witness. Lord Berwyn's daughter, to be precise.'

'Going up in the world, aren't we?'

'We made a statement at Newtown,' I said through my teeth, 'You'll have it on file.'

'They're Mid-Wales Constabulary at Newtown. We're Clwyd-Gwynedd.'

'Give me strength.'

These characters just weren't real, I thought. You read about stupid policemen, but I'd been brought up to think that most of them did a decent job. I'd been catapulted into a comic strip world. I was like the Bob Hoskins character in 'Who framed Roger Rabbit?': a real live person beset by crazy toons.

I turned to Fenshaw. 'He said there was something on my phone. Was it a bug?'

He didn't answer.

'You have to have permission to tap phones. Did you get it?

'I am not required to answer that.' Fenshaw was dabbing his moustache. 'But I'm quite prepared to tell you that we did not install a listening device on your telephone. If we have reason to listen to people's conversations, we use less obvious methods.'

I couldn't believe him. 'If you didn't bug my phone, who did?'

'Carl Quinn maybe,' said Pritchard and tittered. He was picking his teeth with a bit of matchstick.

I started to think. Joseph had told me to ring him from a phone box, and not from the house. He obviously knew how Quinn worked. How many calls had I made? Paeony and I had been speaking on the phone when we'd arranged our visit to Cwm Llwyd on the day Inman had tried to ambush us in the stope. That call could have been intercepted. And the bug could have been planted when Tan-y-Coed was searched, several weeks before. Then I thought of the call I'd made to Paeony that morning, and my skin began to crawl.

'Listen,' I said with all the urgency I could muster, 'I telephoned somebody this morning. Paeony Morgan, Lord Berwyn's daughter, the one who was here on Sunday. She's on her own at Berwyn: the house is empty. She said so on the phone. I told her I know the Crown is there. Quinn's looking for it. His people must have heard the call. Quinn will be on his way.'

There was a disbelieving silence. Pritchard flicked the matchstick out of the car window. 'He's still on about the crown jewels,' he remarked to Fenshaw, 'We'd better ring the Queen.'

'Perhaps we should remind you that wasting police time is a criminal offence,' Fenshaw said.

'For God's sake, will you listen?' I shouted at them. 'How incompetent can you get? No wonder Humphreys has an ulcer.'

'Being offensive won't help you at all,' Fenshaw said primly.

I was fuming, trying to think of some way of alerting Paeony to the danger. We were entering the outskirts of Llangollen now, and the car slowed down. Traffic seemed unusually heavy, and we passed under a banner advertising the International Musical Eisteddfod. It must be under way. There were posters everywhere, and the road was criss-crossed with flags of the nations. All the lamp-posts were decorated, and there were people hurrying along the pavements towards the town centre. The vehicles were nose to tail, stopping and starting, and we came to a halt behind a battered bus with lettering on the back in some Slavonic language. The driver drummed with his fingers on the wheel.

'What's the matter?' asked Fenshaw, speaking across me.

'It's the bloody Eisteddfod,' said Pritchard, 'We're full of foreigners. Folk dancers and choirs and weirdoes. You can't move for them. The whole place grinds to a bloody halt.'

A police constable appeared from behind the bus; our driver wound his window down and the officer said something to him in Welsh. 'What are they talking about?' Fenshaw asked irritably.

'It's the parade. They're just forming up. They all march through the town to the Pavilion, in their fancy dress. It goes on for hours. The nick's right in the middle of it. Either we sit here for the rest of the afternoon or we get out and walk.'

'We'll walk.'

Fenshaw got out, and Pritchard gave me a shove. He shuffled across the seat after me and got out of the same door. They took an arm each. 'Bring the car through when you can,' Pritchard told the driver. Then they began to march me along the road, much to the interest of the crowds who were starting to line the route.

We got to the end of the main street leading down to the bridge, where there's a set of traffic lights. There were cars still trying to get out of the town, and another policeman was gesticulating and waving them through. Further down the street was a sea of flags and bunting. The roadway down towards the bridge was packed with a multi-coloured throng wearing every conceivable kind of national costume, their head-dresses waving above the crowd. A gaggle of girls in brilliantly embroidered dresses and lacy aprons was standing on the pavement, laughing and chattering in an unknown tongue. Bagpipes skirled in the distance. A party of ferocious looking warriors was advancing down a side street, attired in animal skins and brandishing shields and musical instruments.

'Bloody wogs,' said Pritchard.

We had got some way down the main street, and progress through the crowd was getting slower. We were the only ones not in holiday mood. Pritchard and Fenshaw were using their elbows, shoving their way through past a pub from which came a raucous version of 'The Foggy, Foggy Dew'. The combination of fortissimo and rallentando suggested the final chorus was reaching its climax. If the singers were planning to compete, they were unlikely to be among the medals.

Seconds later there was a burst of cheering. I looked back to see the double doors of the pub burst open, and out poured a posse of bearded morris dancers, bedecked in bells and garlands of flowers and led by a fantastic figure with a horse's head. Totally unable to see where he was going he capered straight for us, letting out piercing neighs. The others galloped roaring and whooping in pursuit.

The three of us in line abreast didn't stand a chance. As we were swept away I heard Fenshaw cursing and Pritchard bawling, and suddenly found I was free.

I turned and belted back up the street towards the traffic lights. Instantly I was enmeshed in a phalanx of imposing matrons in long dresses and purple sashes: some sort of gospel choir. 'Excuse me,' I said desperately, struggling to extricate myself from a massive, all-embracing bosom. Shouts were coming from somewhere behind, and there was an indignant squawk. A space opened in front of me and I dived through it.

I was face to face with the Maoris. They were performing some sort of chaka. I had a glimpse of their leader towering over me, dressed in wrinkled dark brown skin hung about with assorted vegetables. His eyes glared down on me from a face as old as time, with grizzled hair and a great flat nose with something sharp thrust through it. He was barring my way with a huge, knobbly object that could have been an instrument or a weapon.

'Excuse me.'

'My pleasure, man.'

He stepped aside and I bolted through the gap.

The shouts behind grew louder, and seemed now to be mingled with cries of pain. I hadn't a clue where I was running to. I reached the traffic still stuck at the top of the street, remembered the policeman directing it and tried to dodge behind the cars. The onlookers seemed to have followed the procession down the street, and the pavement was suddenly clear. I heard Pritchard shout, 'There he is.' The pavement was narrow, and I found myself between a shop front and a car with a caravan in tow. It was a large caravan, with a door on my side. I tugged at the door and it opened. I fell through it, slammed it behind me and crouched down as low as I could.

There were running footsteps outside. Somebody shouted, 'Look in the shop.' At that moment the caravan set off with a jerk. I lay on the floor as it rounded the corner and gathered speed.

I hadn't planned to escape, it had just happened. Now I was trying to think what to do. The caravan had turned right, so it might be heading for the hills of Snowdonia. On the other hand it was probably bound for one of the Eisteddfod camp sites, in which case it wouldn't be going very far at all. I looked round it. On one of the seats that doubled as a bed was a pile of colourful costumes. The caravan was almost certainly stopping somewhere in Llangollen.

Seeing the costumes gave me an idea. If I was now an escaped detainee under the Prevention of Terrorism Act, a lot of people were going to be looking for me very quickly. The priority had to be to get word to Paeony, to warn her, if it wasn't already too late, that Quinn would be on his way. The best way to be inconspicuous in Llangollen in Eisteddfod Week was to dress up as outrageously as everybody else. Still sitting on the floor I quickly started sorting through the costumes, trying to work out whether they were male or female. The situation was quite farcical enough, and I had no wish to be chased around North Wales in drag.

The costumes were all identical: baggy white trousers embellished with garish embroidery and ribbons, and a long white shirt or tunic with flowers on it. There was also a sort of kilt or broad apron in bright red, striped with white, presumably worn over the trousers. There were three or four sets in various sizes, and I picked the biggest and pulled on a shirt and a pair of trousers over my own, trying to keep down below the level of the windows. The kilt tied round my waist with ribbons. There was a straw hat with flowers on it, and shoes with wooden soles which I ignored. The outfit looked vaguely Greek.

The caravan was slowing down, and had almost stopped. Outside the window was a blue triangular sign with a tent on it. I grabbed the hat, opened the door of the caravan and stepped out. Somebody was standing near the entrance to the camp site, looking at me curiously. I gave him a friendly nod and nipped round the back of the caravan. After a moment it set off again.

I was still on the outskirts of the town. The first priority was to find a telephone, so I jammed the hat on my head and set off walking back towards the centre. The main Eisteddfod site was signposted and I wondered whether to make for it, but there was too much risk of running into other kilted folk-dancers. There'd only been a handful of costumes in the caravan, and somewhere in Llangollen there might be other people wearing the rest. I didn't even know what language I was supposed to speak.

Closer to the centre the pavements were crowded with visitors. People were grinning at me cheerfully: there was a festive atmosphere of good will and hospitality. I heard a child ask, 'Where's he from, Dad?', and wished I'd been able to hear the reply. In the distance, a police siren was wailing on the main road. My hand was starting to throb.

The first phone box I came to had a queue outside, so I kept walking and soon heard a hubbub of sound and activity ahead. There was the squeal of pipes and a clash of percussion: I rounded a corner and found myself back at the parade. Over the heads of the onlookers I saw an elongated figure striding by on stilts, and behind it a policeman's helmet.

I stepped back quickly; no doubt the police waveband was already buzzing with news of my escape. I found a parallel road leading down towards the river, and dodged down it. The sound of the music was muffled here and there were fewer people about, but there weren't any phone boxes. The kilt kept descending to my knees and threatening to trip me up; I hitched it back to my waist and kept going.

At the bottom was a sort of walkway leading along the river bank towards the bridge. Standing by the wall I could see a red call box on the far side, surrounded by a crowd of onlookers watching the procession as it sang and danced its way over the bridge and on towards the festival site. A band of fiddles and accordions was playing a jig at demented speed, and above it I could hear the fanfare of another police siren. The phone box looked to be empty. I decided to risk crossing the bridge to get to it before reinforcements arrived.

Shrill giggles came from behind me: a bevy of Japanese girls were focusing their cameras. I forced a grin, and they twittered with delight. One of the bolder ones made a swoop and pushed her arm through mine, posing for the others. She ran back to join the crowd and was immediately replaced by another. Shutters clicked and flashes flashed. Now I had a girl on each side, clutching my elbows as I tried to get away. The crowd parted to reveal an enormous lens, and behind it a toothy individual in a scruffy anorak. 'Ta, boyo,' he said, clicking away, 'Mercy bocoo. County Times, Friday. Have a look'.

I wriggled free at last, and hurried along towards the bridge. As I approached it there was a twanging of balalaikas and cheers rang out. I

212

was forcing my way through the throng and without the costume there would have been objections; as it was people made way smiling and I ended up at the front. A group of Cossacks in fur hats and bright blue tunics were swinging by, leaping in the air and whirling sabres round their heads. Behind them was a line of girls carrying little arches draped with flowers. I stepped out and joined in between, and marched across the bridge between the lines of spectators to the accompaniment of loud applause.

Once on the other side I dropped out and edged my way through the crowd to the phone box. It was still empty, and I shoved a coin in the slot and keyed in Paeony's number. The ringing tone went on and on. I let it ring for ever. There was no reply.

I slammed down the phone and emerged from the phone box to see a new party crossing the bridge, clad in red and white. Their costume may or may not have been the same as mine, but some of them were waving in my direction and I had visions of being hauled off to join the dance. Behind me was a small shop, and I opened the door and stepped quickly inside. The red and whites went dancing by: their dress was actually quite different. At the same moment two policemen went hurrying past in the other direction.

I was aware of a pungent aroma of pot-pourri, and turned round to see a plump lady edging out from behind a counter loaded with little bottles and advancing with a beaming smile. 'How nice!' she said, speaking slowly and distinctly, 'Welcome! Welcome to Llangollen! Where do you come from?'

I thought desperately. What language could I be sure she wouldn't speak? Basque? Estonian?

'Albania,' I said with a treacly accent and a sickly smile.

'Goodness me!' said the lady sympathetically, 'That is a long way, isn't it? Do they have aromatherapy in Albania?'

'Naw Eengleesh. Senk you. Goot day.' I opened the door again and backed nervously out of the shop, bowing obsequiously.

I hadn't a clue what to do now. Looking back towards the bridge I saw that the two officers who had passed the shop had stationed themselves on it and were scrutinising the passers-by. There was no going back that way. Hanging on to my kilt with one hand, I started walking along the road that led alongside the river, away from the centre of the town and the procession. If I couldn't telephone Paeony, I had somehow to get to Berwyn. But I had no transport, and no way of getting there. I thought of hiring a taxi: I still had my wallet and fortunately I'd been to the bank the day before. Walking along without any particular objective I passed a car park by the river and then saw a blue light flashing some way ahead. A patrol car was drawn up across the road, partially blocking it. Police were stopping everybody going out of the town. In the distance, more sirens were wailing.

I turned round and started walking back again. Waves of despair were washing over me. Here I was, trapped in Llangollen in this ridiculous costume: it was only a small place, and I was bound to be recognised soon. Back at the bridge the police were still there. The procession seemed to have passed, and people were moving away: I was conspicuous now. Not knowing where to go, I turned off up a narrow road that led away from the river, and steeply uphill.

The road led onto another bridge, humped and perched curiously above the town, and below it were the quiet waters of a canal. There was an old warehouse, and a painted sign that said 'Horse drawn boat trips. See the Aqueduct.' A long narrow boat was moored below the bridge, with a canopy over it; it was full of people. A man was ringing a handbell. 'Leaving now,' he called, 'Room for a few more. Don't miss the aqueduct!'

Someone was already untying the rope. I ran down onto the towpath and stepped aboard. My costume produced smiles of welcome all round. People made room for me, and as I sat down the boatman pushed off and we were gliding through the water.

Ahead a grey horse was plodding along, swishing its tail, and a long towline trailed between its harness and the boat. We moved at a steady two miles an hour, with no sound except the clopping of the horse and the eager chatter of the passengers. It was odd to be travelling by water high above the town. The canal ran parallel to the road, and looking down I saw we were passing the police car, its light still flashing. There was a queue of traffic, and the police were peering into each car and scanning the faces of the passengers. I thought I recognised Sergeant Pritchard, and pulled my straw hat down over my eyes.

I was arousing a certain amount of interest in the boat. None of the other passengers were wearing national costume; they were ordinary holidaymakers on a day out. Those who had been well brought up were trying not to stare, or were giving me encouraging little nods if I looked in their direction. Others were goggling, or grinning at each other. Sitting opposite me was an earnest looking lady in a long dress and sandals, accompanied by a little girl dripping Laura Ashley. She leaned forward, smiled at me graciously and said, 'Good afternoon.'

'Goot day,' I said stiffly.

'Welcome - to - Wales,' the lady said, pronouncing each word individually.

'Senk you.' I was sweating. The last thing I wanted was a conversation.

'Where - are - you - from?' the lady enunciated.

I might as well stick to my adopted nationality. 'Al - bania,' I said carefully and then, 'Ti - rana'. It was the only town I'd heard of in Albania.

'How - fascinating. We - go - to - Greece - every - year. Greece - is - near - Albania. It - is - very - beautiful. I'm - sure - Albania - is - very - beautiful - too.'

Thank God I hadn't claimed to be Greek. 'Naw Eengleesh,' I said and shook my head vigorously.

The lady was undeterred. She pointed to herself and said, 'Wendy'. Then she pointed to the little girl. 'Tululah.' Finally she pointed to me. 'You? Your - name?'

I racked my brains for an Albanian name.

'Zog.'

The lady looked impressed.

'Say something in Albanian,' said the little girl brightly.

'Naw Eengleesh.' I was getting desperate.

'What did you do to your hand?'

'Naw Eengleesh.'

We proceeded at our stately pace, and I was now in a fever of impatience. As a getaway vehicle the boat left much to be desired. Any other time I might have enjoyed drifting down the Dee Valley at walking pace, but not today. I sat there, tying my toes and my intestines in invisible knots. After half an hour or so we were clear of Llangollen, but I was still trapped: the bank was only a couple of yards away, but I could hardly jump overboard.

The boat was being steered by a young man attired in a waistcoat, with a red spotted handkerchief knotted round his neck and a flat cap at a jaunty angle. He was entertaining the passengers with a lively patter about the canal, the boat and the horse. He had a Black Country accent which he'd obviously been practising hard. I did my best to ignore him and work out a plan of escape.

Bushes glided by on either side, branches swished overhead, fishes plopped, dragonflies hung on the air. The Act of Parliament for the Ellesmere Canal was passed in 1793. The boat was built like an old ice breaker, but there wasn't much ice to break today, was there? The horse was called Polly and she liked a good roll in the clover, ha ha. Right on cue, Polly defecated copiously onto the towpath. Tululah squealed ecstatically.

Our speed was so slow that we were presently overtaken by two ducks, swimming purposefully. Wendy pointed to them and said, 'Duck.'

'Duck,' Tululah repeated. They looked at me expectantly.

'Tack,' I said through gritted teeth.

The voyage had already lasted an eternity. Why was everyone was sitting there so patiently? Somehow I had to get off. Suddenly the boat was in the shadow of a bridge, and the towpath was only a foot behind me. But as I whipped round we were through, and the canal widened again. We were turning sharply to the right, passing between moored boats which were just too far to jump onto. Then the channel abruptly narrowed until it was barely wider than the boat. I twisted in my seat, thinking to hop onto the bank, and found I was looking straight down a hundred foot drop.

'And this is what you've all been waiting for,' the young man was saying, 'Here we are, crossing the great Pont-Cysyllte Aqueduct. Designed by the famous engineer Thomas Telford and opened on 26th November, 1805. It has 19 arches, it's 121 feet high and no less than 1,007 feet long. It's known as one of the Seven Wonders of the Waterways. Would you like to know the other six? Of course you would....' The boat was crawling along, rubbing against the side, but there was no way I could have escaped without a parachute.

We reached the far end at last, and the horse stopped. The red spotted handkerchief stepped nonchalantly ashore, hooked on a rope and began to turn the boat round for its return trip. It swung slowly through 180 degrees, and my side came into the bank. The time had come for a pierhead jump. Standing up, I said: 'I - walk - now,' put one foot on the seat and stepped out onto the towpath.

The boatman opened his mouth to object: I hadn't paid. I fumbled for my wallet, handed him a note, bowed politely and gave the passengers a friendly wave. They all waved back. The man shrugged, clicked to his horse, and set off back towards Llangollen.

There was a thick growth of bushes round the canal, and I pushed my way into them and divested myself of my kilt and the rest of my costume. Wearing my own clothes there was a risk of being recognised, but I could hardly travel further afield accoutred as I was. Pulling off the trousers I noticed a label sewn inside. It said: 'Property of the Britannia Mill Clog Dancers, Ramsbottom, Lancs.'

I folded the garments carefully and laid them on the bank. Then I looked round for a road. The roar of traffic came through the trees, and the main A5 proved to be barely a hundred yards from the end of the aqueduct. There was a pub opposite, and I walked into the bar and found a payphone. I dialled the Berwyn number and waited at least two minutes. Then I jiggled the hook and tried again. Still no reply.

Back on the road I sat on a wall with my head in my hands, trying to work out my next move. How long was it since I'd spoken to Paeony on the phone? Four hours? Five? If Quinn had been listening in he would have been at Berwyn long ago. On the other hand, they might have been using some kind of recording device, and might not yet have replayed the tape. The absence of a reply from Paeony might be sinister, but it might not. Maybe she was out on Arnie. Somehow I had to get to Berwyn and quickly, but it was a long, roundabout way from Llangollen and I could hardly get there on the bus. The Justy was back at Tan-y-Coed, and that wasn't much closer. The police would probably have been onto the taxi firms, and stealing cars wasn't really in my line.

From down the road came a snarl of exhausts. There was a petrol station a hundred yards away, and a small flotilla of motor cycles was pulling into it, the riders twisting their throttles to give a suitably intimidating roar. I remembered Joseph and his motor bike: Birmingham to Tan-y-Coed in eighty minutes. Maybe I could persuade someone to give me a ride.

I stood up and walked down the road to the garage. The bikers were tanking up. They weren't the kind with flashy leathers; this lot seemed to prefer grease. I approached one of them, bent over his bike, at random and said, 'Excuse me. I need to get to Berwyn House, urgently. It's about thirty miles. I'm willing to pay.'

There was a silence. The rider straightened up and looked me up and down. He was about seven feet tall. His face and beard were caked with oil and grime, and matted curls trailed from under his helmet. He wore a filthy black zipper jacket adorned with occult devices, and his bike had handlebars five feet high from which little pennants fluttered in the breeze. It glittered with chrome plate; he obviously used his beard to polish it. His friends started to cluster round. 'He thinks you're a fucking minicab driver,' said one of them, leering.

'How much, man?' the big rider asked.

'Two pounds a mile?'

'Five.'

'Three. It's all I've got.'

'Ninety quid. Let's see it.'

I got the money out of my wallet and gave him three twenties. 'The rest when we get there.'

A girl with lank, dirty hair emerged from the loos behind the garage, doing up the belt of her grease-encrusted jeans.

'Give him your helmet.'

'What for?'

'Fucking give it him.' He handed her a note. 'Buy yourself some chips. I'll see you later.' He turned to me. 'Get on.'

I put on the helmet and got astride the bike. 'Hold tight, man,' he said. There was a whiff of scorched rubber, and we were thundering down the A5.

The ride was the most hair-raising experience of my life. The bike seat had a high back: if it hadn't I'd have been left sitting on the garage forecourt. I hung on like grim death as the world and my life flashed by. Most of the A5 is a broad single carriageway. We simply swerved onto the white line in the middle and tore along between the two lines of traffic. As a child I'd once seen a television film called 'London to Brighton in Five Minutes', and this was how it was. We flashed past the vehicles on the left; the ones on the right were just a blur. At the roundabouts I half expected we would fly straight over the top, but he laid the bike over first one way and then the other so that the foot rests raised sparks from the carriageway. His rank hair and greasy scarf battered my face in the slipstream. My shirt fluttered wildly on my back. The exhaust blared out deafeningly below. I clung to his waist, closed my eyes and waited for death.

Nearer Berwyn on the twisting country roads the ride was like a theme park in hell. We stopped briefly once for me to stammer directions; otherwise I swear we never slowed down at all. At some point I noticed that the broad back of the rider was emblazoned with an apocalyptic image of the grim reaper, complete with scythe. I heard demoniacal laughter as we missed a tractor by millimetres.

The devil's angels must have been watching over us that day.

Suddenly we were leaping over the potholes of the Berwyn drive. The bike skidded into the forecourt of the house and stopped with a mighty scrunch. At first I couldn't get off; my joints and muscles seemed to have set solid around the frame of the bike. Finally I prised them free.

The biker held out a grimy gauntlet. I pressed the notes into it with trembling fingers. 'That's a Harley for you, man,' he said. Then he whirled the bike round, whipped the front wheel off the ground and tore away, ploughing a deep furrow in the gravel. I sank down in a quaking heap.

CHAPTER 17

I pulled myself together and went round to the back of the house looking for Paeony. The door at the bottom of the steps up to the flat was closed. There was no response to the bell, so I tried the door and found it was unlocked. I ran up the stairs and into the flat. There were clothes on the floor and the rug was askew, but tidying up had never been one of her priorities. The place was empty. I went back down to the yard, fearing the worst. Then noises came from the direction of the stable. I walked quickly across and there she was, washing the remains of whitewash out of a couple of buckets.

'Hello,' she said, 'Where have you been? You said you were coming over.'

'Where have you been? I've been trying to ring.'

'I've been whitewashing the stable. When you didn't turn up I thought I might as well do something useful. What was that about the Crown?'

I sat heavily down on a bale of straw. 'Are you all right?' she asked. 'You shouldn't have been driving with that hand.'

'I didn't drive. Listen - when I rang you to tell you the Crown was here, there's a good chance Carl Quinn was listening in. I think my phone was bugged. He could be on his way. I thought he might be here already. But then I got arrested - that prat Fenshaw and Sergeant Pritchard still think I'm some sort of terrorist. I had a bit of trouble getting here.'

'But how can the Crown be here at Berwyn? We would have found it.'

'Come with me, and I'll show you.'

I started walking through the archway, out of the stable yard and round towards the front of the house. As we went I pulled out the notes I'd made from Lord Twining's History.

'We've been blind. It's an arched crown we're looking for, an imperial crown. That means there was a circlet round the head, and two intersecting arches mounted on it. The original purpose of the arches was to protect the head from sword blows. The openings in between were filled with leather, or with light metal plates. Much later, when they'd forgotten the arches ever had a protective function, they made them higher, and filled them in with velvet, and added a big finial on the top, with an orb and a cross. But we're not looking for a seventeenth century crown: the real St Edward's Crown is six hundred years earlier. It's going to be a lot flatter. More like this. I've copied it from Twining's book.'

As I showed her the rough drawing I'd done we were turning into the forecourt. Above us Owain Morgan's great porch rose towards the sky. Paeony was still holding the drawing. 'But - that doesn't really look like a crown at all,' she was saying, 'It looks like a helmet. It looks like...'

'Yes,' I said, 'That's what it is. The first arched crown was the state helmet that Constantine wore, back in 350 A.D. The basic shape never changed for centuries. It was used for the Confessor's crown, as a matter of course. And there it is. Up there, over the Royal Arms, between the lions. It looks like a helmet. But it's not. And it's not carved, it's petrified, it's coated with stone. That's St. Edward's Crown.'

We stood looking up at the carvings high above us. 'I always thought the helmet was a bit small,' Paeony said. 'Everything else is over life size, and it looked a bit insignificant, out of scale.'

'Owain was making a point. He was baring his bum again at the parliamentarians. He didn't hide the Crown away: he put it on display, where everyone could see it. But that was just where nobody would ever think of looking for it. In a high place, under stone.'

'How are we going to get to it?' The question wasn't aimed at me: she was posing herself a climbing problem. 'We could climb up, but it would be simpler to abseil down. Safer too; some of the stone's perished.' She had already set off, walking briskly back towards the courtyard. I hurried in pursuit.

Paeony collected rope and karabiners and a harness from the flat, and unlocked the back door of the main house. We were walking along the passage with its row of bells when I said: 'What about Quinn?'

She stopped. 'The gun room's in here.' We entered a small room where dusty trophies hung on the walls. Framed sepia photographs told of slaughter on a grand scale. Paeony unlocked one of a row of tall cupboards. She took out her shotgun, and selected some cartridges from a drawer. 'Can you use a gun?'

'I've done some clay shooting.'

She handed me a Purdey that must have been worth several thousand pounds. 'This time I'm going to shoot first. Just don't get between me and Quinn.'

She led me on through the silent house as far as the great staircase. We climbed past Owain Morgan's barrel, past the door to the library, up a further flight to the second floor. There we crossed a landing to where a narrower, darker stair led up to what must have been the servants' quarters under the roof. 'I used to love to play up here,' Paeony said, 'There are dozens of rooms. When I was hiding they could never find me.'

We went up one more flight where the treads were thick with dust, till a door blocked our way. A key hung on a nail beside it, and she poked it into the keyhole. It squealed as it turned, and the evening light streamed in.

We were standing on the rooftop of Berwyn. I'd expected it to be more or less flat, but the parapet and mock battlements were taller than they looked from below and concealed a jumble of low pitched roofs, some slated, some covered with lead. The valleys between intersected at right angles, forming a maze. Above them the great arched chimneys marched across the whole width of the building, rising far above our heads. On every side the strange array of obelisks, balls and pinnacles that made up the skyline of the house stood sentinel, like some weird topiary of stone; the roof was patterned by their shadows.

'The front is this way.' I followed her down a ramp, and along one of the valleys between two parallel slopes of slate. We turned sharply, and ahead of us was a section of vertical walling, maybe eight or ten feet high. A short wooden ladder led up to the higher section of the roof, and we climbed it.

We were on a broad, flat expanse of lead, broken only by three of the tall, square chimneys. Around the edge were battlements, lower here and pierced with geometrical shapes below the heavy crenellations. In the centre of one side, perched on the parapet, was the stone dragon that dominated the entrance front of the house; as big as a calf. The lead roof under our feet was littered with twigs, pine cones and small branches. 'The jackdaws bring them up here,' Paeony said.

We left the shotguns by the ladder and walked over to the parapet beside the dragon. The forecourt was far below. I could see the furrow the Harley Davidson had left in the gravel. From up here the three-storeyed porch that projected into it seemed tiny in relation to the area beneath. Like the rest of the house it had looked from below to have a flat roof, but in fact there was a small hipped roof of slate to throw off the rain, with miniature battlements around it and obelisks at the corners. It was about twenty feet below us, and perhaps sixty feet above the ground. The two pot-bellied lions weren't perched on the battlements but on a ledge a few feet lower down, and from our angle you could only see their upper half. They looked as if they were sitting up and begging. The helmet, or the crown, was between their paws.

'The thing looks solid,' she said doubtfully, staring down.

'It's much less weathered.' The lions were eroded and misshapen: the blackened outer layer of stone had flaked away in places to reveal a yellowish powdery surface beneath. The crown or helmet was a uniform, greyish colour.

'With a lifeline I could climb straight down. We used to do building climbs at university. At night mostly, and on tougher buildings than this. With all that carving it ought to be a doddle. Some of the ledges are a foot wide. But the stone's a bit dodgy. This dragon's loose for a start. We'll stick to abseiling. We need a belay.'

She looked around the roof. The stonework of the parapet, like that of the porch below, was flaking and deeply pitted: a number of the carvings were missing or reduced to lumpish, unrecognisable shapes. The stone dragon in the centre lacked part of a wing and one foot, and another foot was almost eroded away. 'I'm trying to persuade Daddy to put in for a grant. We could get these restored. He's so pig-headed. It runs in the family.'

She set off with a rope across the roof to one of the chimneys, walked round it and made the end secure. 'That won't shift. I hope it's long enough.' She buckled on her harness and peered over the edge. 'Just about.'

'How are you going to get it off?'

'I'll see how it's fixed. We'll probably need some tools. But I've got a pocket knife, I'll try scraping at it a bit first. We should be able to tell if there really is gold under the stone.'

We were standing side by side, leaning over and looking down. Paeony straightened up, and at that moment there was a crack.

Something sharp hit me on the cheek. A fresh chip had appeared in the stone of the dragon. I turned round.

Carl Quinn was standing at the head of the ladder that led up from the lower part of the roof. He cast a long, dark shadow towards us. He was holding a gun, and he was smiling.

Quinn advanced across the roof. 'Walk that way.' He motioned to the right. We walked slowly along behind the parapet until we were about thirty feet away. 'Sit down.' We did as we were told.

Quinn stepped up to the parapet and looked over. 'So that's what we were looking for,' he said softly.

Paeony prodded me with an elbow. Appearing at the top of the ladder was a high, domed forehead and a bespectacled face. 'Angevin Greene,' I said incredulously.

Greene stepped unsteadily onto the lead surface of the roof and made his way towards Quinn.

'There it is, Doctor,' Quinn said, pointing down. 'Between the lions. Could it be the Crown?'

I heard Greene's sharp intake of breath, and then his high-pitched voice, a-tremble with excitement. 'It is! I do believe.... It is indeed! The shape.... Like a helmet, of course... The Byzantine influence... You see the flattened form, the outline... Directly reminiscent of the Empress's Crown at Palermo... It can be nothing else. Mr Quinn, this is a great day. We have the Crown, the true Crown, the Crown of England.' He was clinging onto Quinn, doing a little dance.

I found my breath. 'You bloody fool,' I shouted at Greene, 'Don't you realise this man's a criminal? He's just shot at us.'

'Just a warning shot,' said Quinn, 'It was necessary. They were going to damage the Crown.'

Greene nodded vigorously; he had recovered his composure. 'Unlike you, Mr Jones,' he said scathingly, 'Mr Quinn has the interests of this nation at heart. He is a scholar, and a philanthropist, and a true upholder of the Stuart cause. He was good enough to telephone me as soon as he had read the article that I had - ah - inspired. I am proud to have been of assistance to him. He has given me his word that the Crown will be returned to the family which is entitled to bear it.'

'No chance,' I said, 'He doesn't give a toss for the Stuarts. He wants it for himself.'

'These people are blatant treasure hunters, Dr Greene,' Quinn said, 'They will stop at nothing. There is no slander to which they will not stoop.' Even then, I marvelled at his ability to model his language on Greene's. He picked up the second rope that Paeony had brought as a lifeline and handed it to Greene, then walked in our direction. 'Lie down on your faces.'

'Drop dead,' said Paeony.

Quinn's gun jerked, and there was a thud from the lead beside her.

'Another warning shot. The last one. I suggest you do as you're told.' We rolled onto our stomachs, and I suddenly felt desperately vulnerable, expecting a bullet in the back of the neck. 'Please tie their hands together, Doctor.' I felt Greene fumbling away.

'Where are your other friends?' I asked Quinn.

'Their contracts expired.'

Greene had botched the job, but when he'd finished Quinn came and did it again himself, brutally and efficiently. Then he made us drag ourselves to the parapet, passed the rope through the pierced stonework and lashed us to it.

'Thank you, Doctor. They'll be quite safe now.'

Quinn went back towards the part of the roof that overlooked the porch; he was planning his approach. He looked back at us, and at Greene, and examined the abseil rope that Paeony had left knotted around the chimney. Then he seemed to reach a decision.

'Doctor, would you be kind enough to fetch something from my car? I'm afraid I forgot to bring it up with me. It's a can of solvent; I think it may be helpful in removing the Crown from its mounting. There are two cans actually, if you don't mind, and a small bag of tools. You'll find them in the boot. I do apologise for asking you.'

'Not at all, Mr Quinn,' Greene said. 'I am glad that you have given thought to - ah - detaching the Crown. It is vital that we should do no damage at this juncture. It is likely to be extremely fragile. But I am sure you are aware of that. I shall return as soon as I can.' He started to shuffle off towards the ladder.

'Dr Greene!' I shouted desperately. 'Listen to me! He's a killer! He'll kill us all.'

Greene reached the top of the ladder, turned round carefully and stepped onto it. Then he looked across at me, disapprovingly. 'I regret to say you have clearly been watching too many programmes on the television, Mr Jones. I am disappointed in you. A man of your education should make better use of his time.' He slowly disappeared from view.

'I don't believe it,' I said to Paeony. 'Is he mad, or am I?'

Quinn picked up the two shotguns from where we'd left them at the top of the ladder. 'After pheasants, I suppose.' He came over and sat on the parapet, just far enough away, and looked over the edge.

'So there it is,' he said. '"Under the stone". The Crown of St Edward. The ultimate artefact. A supreme work of craftsmanship. Perhaps the noblest object we will ever see. The find of the century.'

'We found it.'

'So you did. What a shame no-one will ever know.'

'Just take the thing and go. Haven't you harmed enough people?'

'People shouldn't get in my way.' Quinn was still looking down.

I was trying to explore the ropes behind me with my fingers, but with two of them in plaster I couldn't get a grip.

'What do you mean to do with us?' Paeony asked. He didn't answer.

'What are you going to do about Greene?' I said.

'A dedicated man, our Dr Greene. A scholar, like us. An idealist, in his way. Idealists are tiresome if you try to oppose them, but useful if they think you're on their side. Bob Lord was useful, for a while. But people are expendable. There are sixty million of them in Britain, give or take a few. I take a few, what does it matter? They won't be missed. The Crown is unique.'

He said it so casually; it took a moment for the chill to set in.

'How do you think you're going to get the Crown?' Paeony said.

'In the same way as you intended to get it. I see you've provided a rope. I may not have quite your expertise, but I do have a head for heights. That business about a solvent was nonsense of course; a hammer will do. But the petrol will come in useful to destroy the evidence. This place should burn nicely. If Jones's body is still recognisable, they'll probably think he started the fire.'

'But you can't burn the house down!' Paeony said in horror. She seemed more distressed about the possible destruction of Berwyn than about the prospect that we might share its fate.

Quinn shrugged. 'In some ways it's a pity. But the house is half Victorian, and aesthetically it's a shambles. In France they were building Versailles when were designing crude monstrosities like this. And the contents of these places are mostly lumber. All bad pictures and stags' heads. The Crown is the only object of importance.'

'If you kill us,' I said, 'They'll treat it as double murder. The police will throw in everything they've got. You won't have a chance.'

'On the contrary, I'll have no chance if I leave you alive. But I'd rather avoid shooting you if possible; handgun wounds can attract attention, even on charred corpses. Ideally I'd prefer it if you burned to death; I imagine the fire will destroy the ropes. But it might be safer to find another way to kill you first.'

Angevin Greene's quavering voice interrupted him. 'Ah - Mr Quinn - I have brought the cans. They are here, at the foot of the ladder. I'm afraid I find it a little difficult to climb the ladder whilst carrying a load. They are rather heavy.'

'Never mind, Doctor,' Quinn said reassuringly, 'Just leave them there, and come on up.' He had stood up, and walked a few paces away from us. Greene's head appeared at the top of the ladder, and he started to pull himself further up.

Too late, I realised Quinn was holding one of the shotguns. 'Look out!' I shouted. There was an explosion. Greene's face was pouring blood. He swayed, his hands briefly pawed at the air, and then he toppled backwards: I heard his body strike the roof a few feet below. Paeony screamed.

Quinn placed the gun on the roof. 'That will confuse the police. In the unlikely event of their finding anything to piece together. The eminent monarchist Dr Charles Angevin Greene, killed by one of Lord Berwyn's shotguns. A wonderful piece, too. A pre-war Purdey. You don't find that sort of craftsmanship today.'

The two of us sat a few yards apart, tied by the same rope. Quinn had made sure we weren't close enough to touch each other, or interfere with each other's bonds. She couldn't see me without twisting her head round painfully. I could see her hands pulling and twisting at the line that tied them; her fingers couldn't reach the knots. 'He's totally inhuman,' she said.

'And he's proud of it. He says it's his strength, that he doesn't care for anyone. I suppose he's a psychopath. People mean nothing to him, whether they're alive or dead.'

Quinn ignored us. He disappeared down the ladder, and didn't immediately return. I was jerking and tugging on the line around my wrists, but it was top quality climbing rope with a breaking strain approaching a ton, and I only managed to tighten the knots even more. I tried alternately pulling and shoving at the stonework behind me, but there was nothing to sprag my feet against and this bit of the parapet looked newer than the rest; the stone was smooth and hard.

'Paeony, try to pull when I do. See if we can get the stones to shift.'

We tried to work together to put strain on the parapet, but nothing happened. 'All this part was redone when I was little.' She was gasping with the effort. 'It came down in a gale. I don't think we'll shift it.'

'For God's sake,' I said desperately. 'What the hell are we doing here? Who cares about the bloody Crown? It's you I care about. I'm as bad as he is. You've been in danger time and time again, because of me.'

'Don't talk rubbish! We're in it together. We love each other, don't we? I wanted it just as much as you did. Just keep pulling.'

Quinn reappeared, and as he came up the ladder I was aware of the sweet, sickly smell of petrol. 'The attics should burn well, and the stairs,' he said briskly. 'And I've saved a bit for you.'

He tipped up the can he was carrying and swept it round in an arc. The liquid gushed out and came trickling across the lead to the gutter where we were tied. My head was full of the smell of it. Utter horror came over me.

'Death by misadventure,' he said, 'When there's a fire, people get burned.'

'You shit,' Paeony said.

He set to work briskly now. He crossed to the parapet and stood for a few moments beside the stone dragon, working out his route. Then he picked up the end of the rope that Paeony had fastened round the chimney and knotted it round his waist. 'Very thoughtful of you. There's no point in taking unnecessary risks.'

Paeony was trying to rub the rope against a sharp-edged moulding along the base of the parapet. There was blood on her wrist. It was a modern rope designed to resist fraying; I couldn't think it would work, but I started doing the same.

'He doesn't know how to abseil,' she whispered, 'He's using it as a lifeline. He hasn't got a harness. I think he's tied a slip knot. If he falls off it'll cut him in two.'

'I hope to God it does.'

Quinn might have lacked technical knowledge, but he was agile and fearless. He avoided the length of battlements immediately above the porch, where the stone was most perished and eroded, and stepped over a few yards further along. We could catch glimpses of him through the piercing of the stonework we were tied to, but with our backs to it we had to roll our heads backwards and sideways and squint painfully. We were still rubbing the rope furiously against the stone.

Paeony could see more than I could. 'He's traversing across. The stone seems to be holding. He's nearly half way down already. He's a natural climber. But the rope's getting in his way, he doesn't know how to handle it.'

I caught sight of Quinn through one of the trefoil-shaped holes in the battlements: as he edged across I could see a little more. 'If anybody came to the house now he's in full view.'

'Daddy doesn't encourage callers. Anyone with business usually goes round the back.'

Rub, rub, rub. My wrists were aching, and my fingers were on fire. Paeony had worn her way through the woven outer casing of the rope, but she'd made virtually no impression on the inner core.

Quinn now seemed to be about level with the side wall of the porch, and only a few feet above it. 'His rope's too short,' Paeony said suddenly, 'I thought it might be when I had to tie it round the chimney. He's used a bit more tying it round his waist. He's stopped on a window sill. I think he's taking it off.'

I could see Quinn wriggling out of the loop he'd made in the rope. He must be standing on a ledge under one of the long windows. He left the rope hanging and edged his way along until he was directly above the middle of the porch roof. Then he jumped lightly down onto it, straddling the ridge.

It was easier to see Quinn as he moved away from the wall. He made his way crabwise down the sloping roof and then slid himself along until he reached the stone lions; I could see their heads sticking up above the top of the porch. Then he lay down on his stomach and reached over the edge. From our angle we couldn't see the Crown, but I guessed it was just about within reach. There was the sharp tap of a hammer.

The smell of the petrol was in our nostrils. We were still squirming desperately against the stone.

Quinn chipped away for several minutes: then came the rasp of a hacksaw. There must have been a metal clamp of some kind. The sawing was followed by more tapping.

Evening was setting in now, and it was getting harder to see. The sky had turned an angry red. My neck and shoulders were aching, and I eased myself round to try to relieve the strain. A movement caught my eye. 'My God!' I said, 'Look.'

The head of Charles Angevin Greene was visible above the edge of the roof. He was pulling himself up the ladder from the lower level. As we watched the head rose higher, and we could see his chest. It was a mass of blood and shredded clothing; above it his face was flayed, shining wetly; part of one cheek seemed to be torn away. His fingers scrabbled at the smooth cladding of the roof; he forced himself up another rung of the ladder, then slumped forward, his legs still trailing over the edge. He lay for a moment, and then began to drag himself, a few inches at a time, across the sheets of lead. As he crawled, he left a thin trail of blood.

There was a cracking sound from below. A moment later Quinn was wriggling backwards onto the roof of the porch. As he straightened up I could see he was holding something.

'He's got the Crown,' Paeony said.

Quinn was examining the stone helmet carefully, turning it over. Then, grasping it in one hand, he started to edge his way back along the side of the porch roof towards the main facade of the house.

A few yards away from us, Greene's progress was agonisingly slow. He couldn't see where he was going, and was using one hand to wipe the blood out of his eyes. It was amazing he could move at all. He was making little gasping noises. He was working his way towards the stone dragon on the parapet.

'Dr Greene,' I hissed at him, 'This way. You can untie us. This way. Over here.'

Greene ignored me: perhaps he couldn't hear. He kept crawling until he finally reached the edge: then his fingers groped upwards until they found the carved moulding of the battlements, and he began to pull himself upright.

Quinn was climbing the sloping roof of the porch, holding onto the wall of the house with one hand to stop himself from sliding back. He was having difficulty bracing himself with the other against the slates and holding on to the crown at the same time. It seemed to be heavy. As I watched he heaved himself onto the ridge and reached up for the ledge below the window.

Greene was standing immediately above him now, peering over the edge. He caught sight of Quinn, and let out a little scream of rage. Quinn looked up and saw him. His face twisted.

Greene was babbling incoherently. He turned and groped around on the roof, picking up twigs and bits of stick. Then he pulled himself back to his feet and started to throw them. It was pathetic, like the actions of a little child: the twigs went spinning down, missing Quinn by yards. Even if they'd hit him, they would have simply bounced off.

Quinn hauled himself up onto the ledge. Greene was still hurling bits of rubbish. Now he started clutching at the stonework, whimpering, trying to break bits away, looking for something to throw. He was clawing at the dragon's wing, attempting to twist it free. The stone was smeared with blood.

Quinn sneered at him. The wall and the lintel of the window gave him some shelter, not that he needed it.

I'd stopped rubbing on the rope and was frantically trying to attract Greene's attention. Paeony was calling to him too. He gave no sign he knew that we were there; all his attention was on the man below, and the object he was holding.

The carving was so perished that a small piece of the wing came off in Greene's hand. He threw it wildly, and it clattered harmlessly across the roof of the porch. He twisted at the tail and managed to break off a sizeable lump. He flung it, and it bounced off the wall not far from Quinn and hurtled to the ground.

Quinn snarled. He started to move along the ledge.

There was a pool of blood at Greene's feet, but he seemed to have found new strength. He was tugging at the dragon's head, heaving it this way and that, trying to twist it free. Suddenly something seemed to give. With a squeal of triumph Greene put his shoulder to the carved beast, his feet slipping and sliding on the lead roof.

The figure wobbled and lurched; one end dropped, and then the last leg cracked and the whole massive creature went crashing down.

Quinn was still on the ledge below. Had he still been directly beneath, the dragon would have crushed him or swept him away. As it was, he'd edged a few feet along, and it missed by inches. It smashed into the roof of the porch, then slid down the slope amongst an avalanche of splintered slate, crashed through the battlements where the Crown had been, and went hurtling down to the forecourt below.

I think both of us had forgotten our escape attempts; we were looking on appalled.

Quinn glared up at Greene, who had collapsed across the parapet where the dragon had been. Then he began to move again, making for the route he had taken on the descent and for the rope, which was still dangling by the wall. Greene saw him, and yelped. He pulled himself along, keeping level with Quinn and bleating. He kept scrabbling on the roof and clawing at the parapet, looking for further missiles. Quinn ignored him, moving as quickly as he could but encumbered by the Crown, until he got to the rope. He had left the loop in the end, and reached up for it.

Greene was draped over the parapet, blood dripping from his face. He saw the rope hanging below him, and groped for it. Quinn had the other end, tugged viciously and easily pulled it through Greene's fingers. The upper end was still secured safely round the chimney, and Greene had no chance of untying it. There was nothing left for him to throw.

Quinn had the Crown wedged by his shoulder against a dripstone. I couldn't see how he was going to climb carrying it. It was just a helmet, solid, bowl-shaped, there was nothing to tie it by. But then he simply got hold of it with one hand, ducked down and pushed his head into it. The weight of the thing was evident as he straightened up. He was a monstrous sight, like some Saracen warrior scaling the wall of a Crusader castle.

Greene went beserk. He was screaming incomprehensible abuse, shaking his fist, plucking at the rope.

Quinn ignored him. I thought he might ignore the rope and climb without it, but maybe he thought with Greene above he needed a lifeline. He stuck his right arm through the loop and then his head with its stone helmet; hanging onto the rope higher up with his right hand he started to work the loop down over his other shoulder.

I was watching Quinn; Paeony was watching Greene. It was getting hard to see in the gathering gloom. She says Greene was still hanging over the battlements, keening, frothing, clutching Quinn's rope, reaching out for the Crown. Without any warning a section of stonework crumbled under his weight. Greene tumbled head first straight over the edge. I saw him fall: his body struck Quinn full across the shoulders and knocked him off the wall.

For a second Quinn was dangling with one hand from the rope, trying to free his left arm; then his grip gave way. He fell only a yard or so before the loop brought him up short, snapped over his shoulder and tightened. Quinn swung wildly, one arm sticking grotesquely up in the air, the noose tight about his neck and his right armpit. He was scrabbling at the wall with his left hand. Greene continued to fall, somersaulting, till he hit the ground.

Quinn's body was twitching convulsively, his arm flailing, his legs kicking out, dancing in the air. I could hear him rasping, choking. He was clawing for the rope above his head, but the Crown on his head seemed to hamper him and his fingers couldn't get a grip. He was tiring, weakening as I watched, flapping ineffectually like a hooked fish. I saw him make one wild, despairing lunge: then abruptly he went limp. His head lolled sideways. The Crown slipped from it and went spinning away, falling it seemed in slow motion, till it struck the gravel close to the body of Angevin Greene.

Paeony and I sat huddled by the wall. Both of us were in shock, trembling uncontrollably, unable to speak. It was a long time before I made some further attempt to undo the ropes, and I soon gave up. My strength seemed to have gone, and even Paeony struggled only fitfully. Dusk was upon us, and there was little chance of release before night came.

But we didn't have to spend the night on the roof. Only a few minutes had passed before we heard a scrunch of gravel, and a white car pulled into the forecourt. It bore the insignia of the Mid-Wales Constabulary. It drew up with a flourish, and two police officers jumped out. One of them knelt beside the crumpled body of Charles Angevin Greene. The other picked something up from the gravel, and I thought I saw the gleam of gold.

Barely thirty seconds later another car arrived, with the badge of Clwyd-Gwynedd Police. As the passengers got out I recognised Pritchard, Fenshaw, and Detective-Inspector Humphreys. They looked up open-mouthed to see the figure of Carl Quinn swaying in the wind, hanging like a tangled puppet from the battlements of Berwyn.

After that, recollections become confused. We must have shouted; they must have found us, and cut us free. Just one further event remains clear in my memory. We were down in the courtyard; I remember looking away from the sheeted body lying there. Another car had arrived, its blue light still turning, eerily illumining the scene like a giant strobe. I had my arm round Paeony, she had her arm round me. Someone brought an object to me and asked me if I knew what it was.

It was rough and heavy. It was too dark to see properly, and we took it back into the light of the hall and put it down on a table.

Lumps of the stone coating had been knocked off in the fall, and the gold shone through. The surface looked pristine, untarnished. I could see areas of ornamentation, one dark red stone in a heavy setting. One of the arches must have hit the gravel first; it was bent and twisted, and had sheered off the circlet at the join. But otherwise the thing we were looking at was intact, entire. Not a helmet, but a crown.

I turned it over for a better look. Paeony was leaning across to see.

There was something odd about the metal, where the Crown had broken. The newly exposed surface was rough and jagged. On the outside, it was yellow. But inside, across the break, on both the arch and the circlet, the colour was different. It was a dull, leaden silver-grey.

'It isn't gold at all,' Paeony said. 'It's a fake.'

I started to laugh, and found I couldn't stop.

CHAPTER 18

A couple of weeks had passed. Paeony and I were riding in the park at Berwyn.

Being together had helped us to recover, at least partially, from our ordeal at the hands of Quinn. Inevitably she was more resilient than I was. Following the principle that the best therapy was to do something constructive, she'd spent a lot of the time teaching me to ride.

I'd maligned her by assuming she'd produce some bucking beast that would throw me off the moment I'd scrambled on. Dolly Grey was a gentle fifteen hander that she'd ridden before she'd acquired Arnie, tolerant and biddable. Paeony had begun to teach me the subtle language which enables a rider to communicate his intentions, and it was starting to get through. It was good to be riding at her side, sharing her interest, finding I enjoyed it after all, even if I still surreptitiously clutched the saddle now and then. We'd even managed a canter, and I was flushed with exertion and pride.

'We'd better be heading back,' Paeony said. 'That Dr. Baverstock will be here in half an hour.'

We'd both had a letter from a Dr George Baverstock, on the letterhead of the Victoria and Albert Museum. He'd wanted to come and see us. I couldn't understand why he thought it was worth the bother; we knew the Crown wasn't genuine, and I'd lost interest. In any case, the fact that both of us were still alive was of far greater concern. But it seemed rude to refuse, and Paeony had written back and invited him to meet us at Berwyn.

The police had taken the Crown away with them, leaving us a receipt, and we hadn't demurred. When Paeony's parents returned Lord Berwyn had taken charge; he'd talked to various people on the phone, but I hadn't been much involved.

We rode slowly back beside the lake, where the swallows were skimming. Ahead a heron rose, flapping lazily. A group of cows was standing under a clump of trees, nibbling leaves from the sweeping branches. The peace of centuries lay over the ancient parkland.

Lady Berwyn had served tea in the library. Dr Baverstock was already waiting for us, a stout little man with a neat beard, dressed rather incongruously in a tweed jacket and a bow tie. He'd brought a young acolyte who hovered diffidently in the background. He shook our hands enthusiastically, and waited impatiently while the tea was poured and the pot replenished from a little silver kettle that swivelled on a stand.

'I've been asked by the Palace to undertake the examination of the Crown,' he said briskly. 'In fact I'm chairing a small group of scholars with different areas of expertise. So far we've only been able to make a cursory inspection, of course, but we've reached some interim conclusions. We'd like to know a little more about how the Crown came to be here.'

'But the thing's not genuine,' I said. 'That was obvious as soon as we looked at it. It isn't gold.'

Baverstock nodded vigorously. 'Indeed it's not. As you no doubt saw, the gold is only skin deep. Quite a thick skin actually, it's heavily gilded. The core is part silver, part lead: hence the weight. But you shouldn't jump to conclusions about its authenticity.'

'I don't see how it can be authentic,' Paeony said. 'Kings don't generally wear gold-plated crowns. It must be some sort of replica.'

'That was our assumption too. But once we had removed the stone coating - and it came off remarkably easily - the Crown proved to be extremely interesting. It seems more than just a replica. The style and detailing are absolutely right for the eleventh century. And the workmanship is frankly breathtaking.'

'So you don't think that ancestor of mine got up to any jiggery-pokery,' Lord Berwyn said.

'I think it's inconceivable that that Crown could have been made in the seventeenth century. We're unanimous in believing that it's a genuine medieval piece.'

'If it's genuine,' Paeony objected, 'Why isn't it gold?'

Dr Baverstock eyed her appreciatively. 'An excellent question. Up to now we've come up with three possible answers to it. I'll try to summarise them for you.'

He nodded to the acolyte, who produced a large brown envelope from his briefcase. Baverstock laid it on the library table. 'The first possibility is that a replica was substituted some time after the Crown was removed from the Confessor's tomb, which I believe occurred in the reign of Henry III. As far as we know it remained in the Abbey from that time on. It's not impossible that it could have been tampered with. But we think it's unlikely. For one thing, the Crown was venerated as a holy relic; it was valued precisely because it was the original, worn by the Saint himself. It was one of the Abbey's greatest treasures; it would have been jealously guarded. And in addition, there are features of the Crown's construction that seem to us to rule out such a late date.'

'But a switch could have been made earlier,' I said.

'That was the next possibility we looked at. A number of Kings of England were buried with replica crowns. It's conceivable that this one might have been made as a copy of the Confessor's crown, in 1066, for burial with his body. Stylistically that's certainly possible. But the quality of the workmanship argues against it. The surface decoration is far more elaborate than on any other crown of the period still extant.' He took several large colour photographs from the envelope and spread them across the table. They showed details of the Crown's ornamentation. I felt oddly indifferent as I looked at them.

'You'll observe the fine scrollwork, some incised, some in relief. Metalwork of this period is extremely rare. Most was destroyed at the Reformation. The only parallel we have is in certain jewelled book-bindings, English work of the eleventh century. It's immensely intricate. The process must have taken months to complete. It's hard to believe so much trouble would have been taken over a mere funeral crown, even if the time had been available. And then there's the matter of the lead. It seems to have been incorporated to make the Crown more convincingly heavy, to resemble solid gold. Funeral crowns were usually made of iron.'

He had slid a large transparency from the envelope; some sort of X-ray. He took it over to the window and held it against the pane. We all gathered round. 'The layers of metal have been laminated together. It was a technique the medieval smiths knew well; it was used in weapons. In this section you can see the darker lines of the lead.'

Paeony was looking puzzled. 'That would mean a deliberate deception by somebody.'

'Precisely.' He took us back to the photographs on the table. 'Now the linear character of the ornamentation, and its high quality, strongly indicate a late Saxon provenance. There are details reminiscent of ecclesiastical work of the period, in the illuminated gospels: a fusion of the Celtic and the Germanic. The craftsmanship is outstanding. And yet, as you say, a deception underlies it all. Which brings us to the third possibility.'

'Spearhavoc,' I said.

Baverstock looked disconcerted. 'Yes. Spearhafoc actually. I believe the 'f' is more correct. You know of him, evidently.'

'I know he made a crown, and ran off with some of the gold.'

'Quite. We know that he was a remarkable man: an abbot, later a bishop, and also a great craftsman. We know from documentary evidence that he was commissioned to make the Crown in 1052. We know that he subsequently absconded to France with a quantity of gold, along with the contents of the diocesan treasury, and was never seen again. A medieval craftsman of his calibre would have had the skill to produce a hybrid crown of the kind we have. A late Saxon monastic goldsmith, as he was, could well have created the design. And Spearhafoc had the impudence. We can't know for certain, of course. But I very strongly suspect he was involved.'

'But why did nobody realise?' Paeony asked.

'It was an extraordinarily convincing piece of work. It must have been greatly admired. And of course, it's always possible that one or two people did suspect, but kept quiet for some reason. Cover-ups weren't invented in the twentieth century. The Crown was buried with the Confessor only fourteen years after it was made. After it was disinterred, it was so revered that it's unlikely anyone investigated it closely. And remember, it was always kept at the Abbey, not in the Jewel House where people with greater expertise might have looked at it. It was only taken out for coronations.'

'How sure are you about this?' I asked.

'As I said, we'll never know for certain. One of my colleagues still leans towards the funeral crown theory. But for a group of academics we've achieved a surprising degree of consensus. This crown is a major work of art, and almost certainly dates from the eleventh century. Most of us think that it very probably is the true St Edward's Crown, the Crown made for the Confessor. And we're agreed that it's almost certainly the Crown with which all the sovereigns of England, from Edward I to Charles I, were crowned.'

'And they never knew,' Paeony said. 'Nobody knew.'

'One man knew,' I said, 'Spearhavoc must be laughing in his grave.'

CHAPTER 19

A fortnight later I was back in the garden at Tan-y-Coed, hoeing between the rows of onions and lettuces that were almost ready for harvest. It was good to know that there would be someone to help me eat them now. It was a wonderful August day; the sun was on my back, and the soil was in good heart. The Crown story had broken in the press, and immediate financial problems had been considerably eased following a phone call to Wayne Drew and the negotiation of an exclusive deal with the 'World' which Lord Berwyn had been considerate enough to sanction. I'd sent a modest donation to Joseph's youth club. Now the fertiliser company was recruiting again, and had called me back. In short, things were looking good.

Val Potter had rung the previous evening, to tell me that Huw Griffiths and an WMEG party had successfully completed the job of restoring the box and its contents to their perch in the Cwm Llwyd slate quarry. In the end they'd all decided that it was a pity to remove it to a museum, and that they'd better put it back again. They'd consulted me about it and asked if I'd like to go along, but I was quite happy to leave it to them.

'And do you know?' Val had said, 'There was old Cadwaladr Pugh riding a quad bike round the mountainside, and going like the clappers. I couldn't believe my eyes.'

As I worked there was a quiet cough, and I glanced up to see Inspector Humphreys watching me from the terrace. I downed tools, and he accepted the offer of a cup of tea. I went in to put the kettle on, and we sat on the wall in the sunshine.

'We've had a bit of news,' Humphreys said, 'About that first arson case. Mr Mitchell's cottage, just down the road. I thought you might like to know. The Cheshire force arrested two yobboes last week, out of Birkenhead. They were trying to set fire to a barn near Gresford. They've asked for a number of other cases to be taken into consideration. That was one of them. They'd done one or two in Wales, isolated places.'

'So it wasn't terrorists at all.'

'People jump to conclusions.' Humphreys looked uncomfortable. 'I'm old enough to know better. We hadn't had a political case for quite a time. And that attack on Mr Lord's house had something fishy about it all along. Do you know what Quinn's friends had sprayed on the gate? "Cymru am byth", like they put on bloody ashtrays. It should have stuck out a mile. But certain people were applying a bit of pressure. Maybe they were afraid their operations were going to be wound down.'

'Have you let Bob's family know?'

'We've been in touch.'

I made the tea, and Humphreys asked for two sugars. 'We're questioning those associates of Quinn. We've found some incendiary materials, and they've no alibi. We might be able to make charges stick. We can get them for false imprisonment anyway, and GBH too, if you'll testify.'

'How did Mr Fenshaw take it?' I couldn't resist asking. He'd kept himself well in the background at Berwyn, and hadn't opened his mouth.

'He's been moved on,' Humphreys said shortly, 'And the Chief Constable's talking about improving co-operation with neighbouring forces. Your case threw up a few problems in that department. If I hadn't rung them at Newtown you'd probably still be up on that roof.' He stirred his tea meditatively.

'There's one other thing,' he said after a while, 'You mentioned a deed box was missing from Mr Lord's house, a fireproof one. We found something like that at one of Quinn's hide-outs. Full of old papers. We want it as an exhibit at the moment, but I dare say you might be able to come to an arrangement with the family about it.'

'I think Lord Berwyn would be glad to have the papers back.'

Humphreys finished his tea and stood up to go. He'd come in his own car and left it on the road, and I offered to walk up with him. 'I could retire to a place like this,' he said as we crossed the bridge. The river was gurgling merrily below. 'But I don't think the missus would take to it. It's a bit quiet.'

'It has its moments.'

Humphreys got into his Rover and drove away. I stayed up on the lane for a while, looking at the chimney of Tan-y-Coed through the tree-tops. The valley was drowsy in the afternoon sun. I looked down towards Ty-Newydd, and wondered whether the Mitchells would rebuild now that they knew they hadn't been the victims of a premeditated attack. They probably would.

I heard the clatter of Glyn Lewis's Land Rover coming down from Blaen-y-Cwm, and waited for him to pass. He pulled up beside me. Gwen and Eiluned were with him. 'How are you?' he asked.

'Pretty good. Are you off to Oswestry?'

'Welshpool. To the solicitors. You'll have some more neighbours before long. We're buying the Waen.' He meant the ruined cottage in the forest up above Tan-y-Coed, where Gwen had been born.

'Surely you're not moving?'

'It's for Gareth,' Gwen said, 'He's got engaged to a girl from Bala, a student teacher. She's just got a job at the school in Llanrhaeadr. We're going to do the place up for them.'

'It might get a bit noisier where you are,' Glyn said, 'Welsh speaking they'll be, too.'

'That's wonderful news. And had you heard about the Mitchells' cottage - who did it, I mean?'

'The boys from Birkenhead? Yes, I'd heard. There's the English for you. They're not content with buying up the cottages, they have to come and burn them down.' He let in the clutch, and with a wave he drove away.

I walked back to Tan-y-Coed and hoed another row of onions.

CHAPTER 20

A couple of months had gone by, and I was lying beside Paeony in the bedroom of a sinfully luxurious hotel suite in the West End of London. The early morning sunshine was filtering through elaborate drapes. I was counting freckles. 'There are twenty-three more on the right shoulder than on the left,' I said at last. 'And they go down further too. Look, they go right down to here.'

'That's quite enough,' said Paeony firmly, sitting up. 'We have things to do. We have to meet the Queen.'

'Spoil sport.'

'She's sending a car at half past nine. I can't go like this.'

'You'll be fine as long as you wear your hat.' I told her, and got jabbed in the stomach.

When the invitation to the Palace had come I hadn't wanted to go. Genuine or not, I felt I didn't care if I never saw the Crown again. It was Paeony who persuaded me. 'You can't turn down a royal command,' she said. 'And anyway, I want to dress up. We mightn't get another chance.'

An hour later we were being whisked down the Mall in a vehicle that felt as if it would be more at home behind a pair of horses. It was a golden autumn morning, and the leaves were falling. Paeony was wearing the hat, which had been the occasion of much deliberation and a good deal of banter, and a matching creation in pale blue: she looked superb. I'd invested in a smart new suit. This was an informal invitation to the Palace: there was to be a formal ceremony later at Westminster Abbey, with much pageantry, at which Lord Berwyn, on behalf of his ancestor, would restore St Edward's Crown to its rightful wearer and it would be returned to the Abbey treasury from which it had been taken three hundred years before. Bob Lord's son and daughter would be there, the Unitarian minister from Shrewsbury would read a lesson, and

Cadwaladr would enjoy singing the Welsh hymns that they'd requested. Joseph was coming too, and some Walton inmates, past and present. But first we'd been told that the Queen would like to meet the people who, by accident or design, had been most intimately involved in the Crown's recovery.

We were approaching the Victoria Memorial. 'Can I say something corny?' I asked, 'About finding treasures? Treasures that really matter.'

She squeezed my hand. 'Just think it. I'm thinking it too.'

The sun shone brightly as we swept between the gilded gates and through the mysterious archway with the red-coated sentries on either side. The car stopped under a canopy in the central courtyard, and the door was whipped open. A silver-haired gentleman in a discreetly striped suit was waiting for us. He guided us up the carpeted steps, through tall, windowed doors and on up a broad staircase. Then we were passing through a long, high room hung with crimson silk, beneath a brilliantly gilded ceiling. More double doors, an ante-room, and suddenly we were in a much smaller room with tall windows open to give a view of the gardens and the lake. The scale was private, domestic even. On a small gilt table in the centre of the room was the Crown.

A door at the far side of the room opened, and the Queen stepped through. I hadn't expected her to be so small. They said she couldn't smile, but she was smiling now. She greeted us warmly, sat us down, and I found myself telling the story of the Crown's recovery once again. The Queen was fascinated.

'We owe a great deal to Mr Lord. I'm glad I shall be meeting his children. We must place his work on record.'

'Bob would be glad. But he would want Owain Morgan to be remembered most of all, and Thomas Davies too. They were the ones who saved the Crown.'

'A lot of people seem to have had a hand in it. And put themselves in danger too. I hope you feel that it was all worth it.'

'The Crown's a great treasure,' I said. 'But I'm not sure now, about the risks. In the end, people matter more.'

'Of course they do.' Her eyes went to the framed photograph of the balding ex-sailor on a table by the window.

'You won't have had the chance to have proper look at the Crown,' the Queen said eventually, 'Would you like to?'

'Yes please,' Paeony said. We hadn't seen it since that day at Berwyn.

The Queen led us to the table. The Crown had been placed on a stand. It had been immaculately cleaned and restored, but it still had a slightly battered look, as befitted its great age. There was something strangely primitive about its squat, powerful shape. The circlet and the arches that rose from it were heavy and massive, but overlaid with a shimmering filigree of golden wires, twisting and intersecting with infinite complexity and sparkling with tiny flowers and stylised foliage. The space between the arches had been newly filled in with crimson leather. All around the circlet were big, deep-coloured stones, uncut, in heavy, ornate settings. Where the arches met was a miniature orb, surmounted by a tiny cross with pearls hanging from the arms. And there were two pendants like golden bells, hanging from the sides.

The contrast between the almost barbaric form of the Crown and the exquisite delicacy of its execution took my breath away. And strangely, though I knew what was beneath its surface, there was no hint of deception. Its maker had worked as lovingly upon it as if it had been gold all through.

'I'm confused,' I said. 'I can't decide if it's genuine, or if it's not. I know it isn't gold inside.'

'Not many things are,' the Queen said. 'But it's very old. A lot of famous people wore it. And it's very beautiful, you know.'

The resentment, hatred almost, that I'd come to feel for the Crown was melting away. 'Carl Quinn was right about one thing,' I said, 'It really is a supreme work of craftsmanship.'

'Do touch it if you like.'

I ran my fingers over the gleaming metal that Spearhavoc, artist and rogue, had shaped almost a thousand years ago.

'We had a letter from Prince Franz of Bavaria the other day,' the Queen said. 'Some people think he ought to be King, you know, because he's descended from Charles I, though I'm descended from his father, of course - King Charles's, I mean. He wrote to congratulate me on getting it back. Such a nice letter.'

I couldn't take my eyes, or my fingers, off the Crown. It was working its magic, like that other crown I'd gaped at, behind the glass in the Jewel Chamber, long ago. And I felt the same urge now as I'd felt then, when Auntie Annie had dragged me bawling away.

At last the Queen said, 'We really are very much indebted to you, Mr Jones, and to you too of course, Miss Morgan. Do tell us if there's anything more we can do to thank you.'

I swallowed. Oh, what the hell.

'Er - there is one thing, ma'am,' I said. Paeony looked surprised.
'Yes?'

'I wonder... I know it's taking a liberty, but it's something I've always wanted to do, since I was little.'

'Yes?' the Queen said again, a little apprehensively.

'I wonder if I could possibly - just for a second - put it on?'

There was a moment's silence. Paeony looked appalled. The man in the striped suit looked thunderstruck. The Queen looked non-plussed. Then she smiled. 'Why not? Sit down for a moment. Sir Giles...'

I sat down, and struggling to conceal his displeasure Sir Giles lifted up the Crown, carried it across and placed it none too gently on my head.

With almost five pounds weight of gold, silver and lead, apart from the stones, St Edward's Crown was unexpectedly heavy. Although the circlet had been lined with a thin layer of fur, it was also too big. My head is on the small side. The Crown stayed poised as it was for a second or two; then it sank down over my ears, and the Queen and everybody else disappeared from view. The gold rim ground into the bridge of my nose.

There was a brief struggle as the Queen and Paeony tried to get the Crown off my head. At last I saw daylight once again, and the Crown was restored to its stand. I found myself dabbing at a small graze on my nose, and Sir Giles was despatched for a plaster which was applied in person by the royal fingers.

We took our leave of the Queen, and were ushered out through the Throne Room and down the great staircase. The car stood waiting, its chauffeur holding the open door. Sunlight was pouring into the courtyard, and the air was clear and mild.

'Why don't we walk?' Paeony said suddenly.

'Good idea. It's all right Sir Giles, thank you, we won't need the car.'

Hand in hand, we walked across the courtyard and through the arch. We passed between the motionless guardsmen in their bearskins and scarlet tunics and on across the wide expanse of forecourt to the great gates with their crowds of curious, whispering tourists. We gave them a courteous smile. As we crossed the roadway, the traffic seemed to give way before us.

A gentle breeze was blowing the leaves about our feet. They were every colour between crimson and butter-yellow, but mostly shades of gold: deep gold, pale gold, red-gold, green-gold, old gold. They were spiralling down from the branches overhead, the sun gleaming through them. Great drifts of them lay on the green turf under the trees. We waded through, letting our feet drag, hearing them rustle. Still holding hands, we walked out across the sparkling landscape of St James's Park.